I0745887

SHE CONFESSED, DIDN'T SHE

T. MATT RYAN

**KITSAP
PUBLISHING**

She Confessed, Didn't She?
First edition, published 2017

By T. Matt Ryan
Cover design: Nick Johnson at Cima Creative

Copyright © 2017, T. Matt Ryan

ISBN-13: 978-1-942661-47-4

Published by Kitsap Publishing
Poulsbo, WA 98370
www.KitsapPublishing.com

Printed in the United States of America

TD 20170301

50-10 9 8 7 6 5 4 3 2 1

DEDICATION

To my dear friend, Dick Mace

ACKNOWLEDGEMENTS

My wife, Pat Ryan, for patience, wisdom, listening, and being a helpful critic.

Brian Roberts for bringing his legal knowledge to bear when editing.

Nick Johnson of Cima Creative for creating the book cover.

Bob Schumacher and friends at the Café Noir for teaching me the craft of writing.

Jack Archer and Steve Garfein, critics and supporters.

See page 300 for a List of Characters.

CHAPTER 1

Gloria Caulfels hefted her laptop computer bag onto her right shoulder as she closed the front door of the somewhat run-down apartment building. She hunched her shoulders against the chill of a foggy late summer evening in Oakland. In the distance, beyond the subdued roar of the MacArthur Freeway, lonesome foghorns carried in from San Francisco Bay. She nodded to the private investigator, Winston "Win" Griffith, slouched down in the seat of his van across the street, just before she turned onto the sidewalk and headed toward her car. A tall woman, Gloria still walked with the measured grace of the high-fashion model she had once been. Thanks to the miracles of modern plastic surgery, her face carried more than the vestiges of great beauty, hiding from the stranger that here was a woman who could draw Social Security if she chose. Yet her beige business suit was rumpled and shapeless, at least a size or two too large. Comfortable, dark, low-heeled walking shoes left patterned prints in the dew that dampened the cracked cement.

When she turned the corner, out of Win's view, she saw three large men. The loitering trio stood near her car that was parked half a block away. They began ambling toward her, with the tallest in the curbside position. The shortest moved close to the storefronts, and the midsized man spaced himself between them. If she kept to the right, they would funnel her against the buildings. She quickly looked back over her shoulder, then down the street beyond the ominous trio. The street was deserted both ways.

This could get interesting, Gloria thought. *Should I go back?* She elected a path to the left that was close to the curb after she paused a moment and shifted the weighty bag to her left shoulder. She felt relief when her left index finger found and pressed the panic button on the new cell phone Win had given her. *Thank goodness for that app,* she thought. *Win's phone alarm'll go nuts; GPS pinpoints my location; and he'll come running to back me up.* She reached behind her back under the suit coat and wrapped her right hand around the butt of her holstered nine-millimeter Glock Model 19. *I never have liked to retreat. I'll take it slow to give Win time to cover me.*

Her fingers found the safety and she freed the gun from its holster while still hiding it. The three goons picked up their pace. The tallest drifted slightly from the curb toward the center of the sidewalk as if giving her room to pass. Her gaze shifted from one to the other, and she could see that all three were staring at her. *Things are happening too fast. I should have waited for Win.*

As they closed to within an arm's length, this same tall stranger, without any change of expression, thrust his arm straight out in a stiff-arm maneuver, like a football player fending off a tackle. He struck Gloria in the chest, knocking her backward and off her feet. She twisted in the air and landed hard on the laptop. She felt blinding pain in her side; she didn't know it then, but later she would be diagnosed with three bruised ribs. The second man moved in, grabbed her ankles, and pulled her off the laptop. She struggled, jerking her legs wide apart so that he almost lost his grip.

The third man snapped to the second man, "As planned, drag her into the alley and we'll take care of her there." To the big man he barked, "Grab the laptop bag!" Flat on her back, Gloria watched her laptop bag fly upward as the big man snatched it toward him.

Now her adrenalin kicked in, burying the pain. Gloria felt a sense of calm washing her over as, with a smooth but quick motion, she drew and aimed the gun. She pushed the muzzle of the nine-millimeter into the big man's crotch—which was right over her face--and fired once. Her victim's blood-curdling scream caught her by surprise. He took a step backward, and she looked up to see for a fleeting moment the surprise that registered in his bulging pale blue eyes. In a split second the second man grabbed her attention again, still pulling on her ankles. She aimed at his crotch and fired so quickly that he had just let go of her ankles when the bullet crudely castrated him. He doubled over, screaming in Russian, and fell at the feet of the third man, whose hands made jerking moves toward his jacket just as she pointed the Glock at his crotch. The third man slowly moved his hands out to the sides and upward. Behind Gloria, the big man staggered and dropped the laptop bag. He first bent over as if he were going to pick it up, then hunkered, then flopped onto his back.

Gloria sat up, holding the Glock in both hands, and shifted her aim to the third man's belly. She audibly sucked in a breath before she ordered, "Turn around, down on your knees. Keep your damned arms stretched out."

He looked back over his shoulder as he begged, "Please lady, don't shoot!"

"Don't tempt me. Keep those arms out. Spread your legs! Nose on the sidewalk or you'll be singing soprano."

Meanwhile the Russian rolled on the ground, holding his crotch with both hands and continued to scream. Red bloodstains soaked his light-colored trousers and stained his fingers. The big man lay where he fell. His face was pale and his eyes, uncomprehending, started to glaze over.

With a painful effort, Gloria pulled her cell phone out of her pocket. As she fumbled to pull open the mouthpiece, the third man pleaded again, "Please lady, don't waste me. I have a wife and kids."

As she punched nine-one-one, she said, "Like I said, don't tempt me. Who put you up to this?" Her voice tightened, then trailed off. The nine-one-one operator said "Hello? Hello?" twice before Gloria found her voice again and replied, "I'm Gloria Caulfels Esquire. I'm hurt and I've got the three men at gunpoint. I've drilled two of them … and if the third one moves, I'll blow his balls off too."

"Where are you?"

"Next to the alley and around the corner from the Carlton Arms."

"Please stay on the line …"

The Russian found his voice and whined like a child caught with a hand in the cookie jar. "Marteen, you said she was an old woman. It was to be so easy to take her. Look at my blood! I am dying! Oleg is dying too!"

"Shut up, Yuri!" the third man growled at the Russian under his breath.

Gloria left her phone open on the sidewalk. She squatted between the third man's legs and pushed the muzzle between his butt cheeks while drawing back the corners of her mouth in a painful grimace. "Marteen, is that your name? And Oleg and Yuri are your friends? Who the hell put you guys up to this? Gimme answers now or I'll give you a lead enema." 'Marteen' squirmed and fearfully looked back over his shoulder, then squeezed his eyes shut as he flattened his nose against the damp sidewalk. "Please, please don't do it!"

While Gloria continued to press 'Marteen,' Yuri began to recover. He reached into his waistband for a small automatic, the classic Saturday night special. He pulled the gun clear and rolled onto his back with the gun arm extended. The muzzle was coming down to point at Gloria just as she caught the movement. She was just beginning to lift her gun as a shot rang out. Yuri's gun flew out of his hand and clattered to the ground inches from 'Marteen''s hand. Hardly lifting his head, 'Marteen' stretched his arm and grabbed for the little gun. His fingertips had barely touched the butt when Gloria shot him in the shoulder. His whole body jerked.

"Sangre de Dios!" screamed 'Marteen.'

From up the street came a booming bass voice, "Boss, I heard the shots, so I came running."

Gloria stood up, wincing in pain, and said between gasps, "That was close! You saved my life! Thank you, Win."

"Are you all right?"

"I fell on my laptop. It hurts to breathe. I thought they were muggers, but obviously they're more than that. I've seen the Latino guy in the courthouse."

Win Griffith carried himself with a near-military bearing, like the policeman he once was. Retired on disability in Oregon because of hearing loss, he was Black by race but tan by complexion.

He looked past the moaning Yuri, who had curled into a ball, and Oleg, who was lying on his back with both hands laying on his belly, to the Latino, who was lying on the ground. His arms were stretched above his head, with the uninjured arm cradling the wounded one. Win kicked the gun away and roughly pulled the man's head back. "This here's a narc, Martin Ramirez! What the hell's going on?"

Gloria held her side and spoke in a low, almost husky voice. "That's what I want to know. He was running the show. Could this have been a diversion?"

Win pointed back toward the apartment house. "Roy is on alert. I called him and told him not to open the door for anyone but me. They'll have to have plenty of firepower to match my man's Uzi. I dialed nine-one-one too. I can't believe Tibbie would be this stupid."

"Tibbie doesn't have to get in. All he has to do is scare my witness enough that she won't testify tomorrow. And there goes my case!" Gloria leaned back against the building before asking, "Officer Ramirez, who convinced you to throw away a career? I want to know who put you up to this. Was it Tiburon Fuentes?"

Ramirez pushed his face closer to the cement and his hands shook. Win's voice rang with intimidation, "Talk to this woman now. The only deal you'll be able to make after you go downtown is to spend your time in solitary forever or die in the general population. The brothers love this woman. They'll hunt you down and kill you."

Ramirez raised his head, "Damn, lady, you're crazy!"

"Officer, I have to know. Is my witness in danger?"

Ramirez whined, "He'll have my ass."

Looking him down with cold blue eyes, she said, "I'll have more than your ass. We're talking witness tampering, conspiracy, on top of the whole laundry list of what went down here. You'd better have money for your own attorney because I don't think anyone in my office could render you an adequate defense."

"Tibbie." The word tumbled out of Ramirez's mouth as if it were inadvertent.

Win's deep voice resonated, "Tibbie. For the record, you mean Detective Lieutenant Tiburon Fuentes, don't you?"

Ramirez nodded, "Yes. He was sure that working the old woman over would be enough to scare his wife. Or at least delay the trial enough to make contact with her."

In a moment of silence following that admission, the canned voice of the nine-one-one operator called, "Mrs. Caulfels, Mrs. Caulfels, please answer. What happened? Please, Mrs. Caulfels!" The operator was left hanging as their attention was drawn from the phone to the distant sound of a siren.

Reporter Art Williams had been dozing in the police cruiser's passenger seat when the radio came to life. He was wide awake with adrenalin pumping by the time the canned voice completed her report of multiple calls about a shooting around the corner from the Carlton Arms. The dispatcher's voice was almost drowned out by the siren while she reported more shots and verbal threats on an open line before Gloria's phone went dead.

This was no routine evening for the freshly hired reporter for the *Oakland Tribune*. His editor had arranged for the handsome six-footer to take a couple of night shifts as a way of getting to know his beat. The evening up to this point had been strong bitter coffee, routine traffic stops, and two faulty burglar alarms. Now he was sweating every intersection as the patrol car zipped through red lights. Then he heard a familiar name, "Gloria Caulfels," crackle over the airwaves.

Larry MacBrogan, the middle-aged cop who drove the patrol car, muttered, "Gloria Caulfels, the hotshot public defender. I hope it was one of the slimeballs she got off the hook. That damned old bitch!"

Art raised his voice to be heard over the siren, "Gloria Caulfels… this is a real coincidence. I'm spending my days covering the Symon Dubinski murder trial. She's defending that Russian hood. It's pretty much open and shut. I don't know why he didn't plead guilty."

"They ought to round up the whole bunch of those commie bastards and send them all back to Siberia. I thought it was bad when the Crips and the Bloods were fighting to control the turf. These new guys are into everything. They're all bad news. And that old bitch is out there deepening their beachhead. I have no use for that woman!"

"Why?"

"She goes after people. She destroyed Sandy Dennison just two years short of his retirement. For crying out loud, the guy is human. He made mistakes. Now he's working security at some mall up in Oregon, and those scumbags walked. There she is, sitting against the wall talking on her cell phone."

"Who's the big Black guy with her?"

"Win Griffith, PI. He's a retired cop with a sweet deal. I've heard he's okay. He works for some foundation that pays to help the public defenders. The PI probably saved her butt."

As soon as Officer MacBrogan saw the trio on the sidewalk, he keyed his radio, "Roll the medics. There are three down on the sidewalk and blood all over the place. Notify Homicide."

Gloria flipped the mouthpiece back against her cell phone as she said, "Officer MacBrogan, we meet again. Whatever you do, keep your hands in your pockets. This is one crime scene I don't want you to screw up."

MacBrogan's face turned red while his big hands doubled into fists. He studied the scene for at least two deep breaths before looking up the street at the flashing lights of an aid car. Without bothering to look back, he asked through clenched teeth, "What happened, Mrs. Caulfels?"

The undercover narc raised his head slightly and said, "MacBrogan, it's me, Martin, Martin Ramirez, Narcotics Special Task Force. Watch out for this old woman, she is crazy!"

By now the numbing effects of adrenalin had dissipated, and every move and every breath brought pain to Gloria. She looked from one officer to the other. *Just how rotten is this thin blue line? I should have never given Win my Glock. Wait, there's that cute young reporter.*

She caught Art's attention for a moment, but he remained outside the perimeter of the crime scene tape. She noted his chock-full head of unruly blond hair and that he wore an open-collar dress shirt under a tweed sports coat. *I wouldn't put it past Tibbie to shoot me on the way to the emergency room. I need protection. He'll have to do.*

The first medic laid a hand on MacBrogan's shoulder, "Larry, they're responding with two more aid cars. Another night in the city! We've got our work cut out for ourselves here."

While the medics were working on the three wounded men, Gloria motioned to Art. Moments later he slipped under the tape and squatted next to her. "Hello, Mrs. Caulfels. How are you doing?"

She grabbed his arm as she said, "Call me Gloria. Thank God you're here. Stick with me until we get to the hospital and I'll give you a story."

Art hesitated. Gloria remembered the same look on his face earlier that day when she gave him her cold stare after he asked her for a comment. She braced herself for rejection. Then Art smiled, "Sure, be glad to."

⁘

Before the three men and the woman had been loaded into ambulances, the street was blocked by patrol cars with flashing lights. Win stood just outside the perimeter of yellow crime scene tape with Gloria's laptop bag over his shoulder. MacBrogan, with pen poised over a lined pad on a clipboard, said to him, "I'm surprised you hit that Russian in the balls. Is that what they taught you up in Oregon?"

Win placed his thirty-eight in the officer's hand. "I didn't. I'll trust you with this weapon. I fired once to keep Yuri from shooting Mrs. Caulfels. But by that time she'd already put a round into each of them."

"All three? I'll be damned! She must be one hell of a shot."

"A sharpshooter, if I ever saw one. I've been on the range with her many times." Win pulled out Gloria's Glock from his pocket and laid it in MacBrogan's hand, "I'm sure your ballistics people will want to test this weapon. I checked the clip, it's three rounds short of full. By the way, I'll be contacting your Internal Affairs about the narcs."

CHAPTER 2

Art Williams finished jotting down Gloria's version of the mugging before the medics lifted her stretcher. Even with an oxygen tube in her nose and pain meds dripping into her arm, her voice had lost none of its authority. He was surprised at how easily she convinced the crew that she needed his assurance until they got her to the hospital. The way she gripped his hand and the wide blue eyes with white all around the irises made Art think, *Here is one very frightened woman.*

One of the medics signaled Art to sit in the jump seat at the head of the stretcher, but Gloria tightened her grip on his hand, "No, there's room on the bench. I want eye contact when I talk to him."

Once the doors were closed and the ambulance was on its way, Art expected to hear the siren screaming. But—no siren. He was forming the words in his head to ask why they were running silent when Gloria squeezed his hand to get his attention. "I asked them to leave the siren off to avoid drawing attention. I don't like cases tried in the press. What happened to me tonight is certainly newsworthy in its own right, although it's connected to my case. I must have stepped on some big toes in court this week. I'm scared."

She read my mind. Did I have surprise written all over my face? "Whose toes?"

"I don't know. I turn over stones every day. Maybe someone was pissed off by my cross-examination of the state's forensic guy."

Art mentally went over the testimony from the last two days. *She may have the reputation as being hell on wheels, but all the points I saw her make this week were pretty obscure--something about saliva in a gag, and something about tying Russian knots. What a waste of time, the guy is guilty. So far, her defense hasn't produced anything newsworthy.* Clearing his throat, he commented, "I've got to say that by the time you were done with the forensic guy, I had some doubts about his ability as a criminalist. But," he asked, "What's so important about how much saliva was in the gag?"

"In due time, Mr. Williams. I'm not tipping my hand tonight. Besides, I have subpoenaed the medic who loosened the gag."

"Also, what's so important about Russian knots, or how the pop can was being held?"

"Good questions, good questions. You stayed awake and took good notes. I like the way you write."

After Art acknowledged the compliment, Gloria said nothing until after the ambulance lurched around a corner. "While I was waiting for them to put me in the ambulance, I told myself, this is why I've devoted my life to be a public defender. This case makes it all worthwhile. Peter Godoniski is innocent."

Art rolled his eyes, "You've got to be kidding. His fingerprints were found at the scene. His DNA matched the hair found at the scene. There is a witness who saw him on the street. He lied to the police. And there are witnesses who spiked his first alibi."

"You don't mince words. But," Gloria asked, "If a prosecutor or law officer can look at a defendant and believe he's guilty, why can't I have that kind of faith in a man's innocence? Violence isn't in Peter's character."

Wait a minute, thought Art. *Godoniski's as tall as I am at six feet. He's muscular enough to knock the victim to the floor with one punch, which he admitted.* "Gloria, the closest Godoniski has come to fitting *your* mold was when he sat at the table with tears running down his cheeks while you made the medical examiner describe exactly how Dubinski was shot. There's a phrase for that: crocodile tears. Or he was upset because the description was right on."

"Yes, my work is cut out for me. I must convince the jury that those were all tears of sorrow, not regret. Peter is a very sensitive man who grieves at the loss of his friend. However, I have an uphill battle ahead. Peter's no angel, and he has never been very open or truthful with me. We wasted too much time because he wouldn't tell the truth and concocted a phony alibi. He never came up with the real story until I leaned on him to plead instead of taking a chance on the death penalty. I'm frustrated now because there may be too little I can do to save him."

Art recalled the newsroom stories about Gloria Caulfels as to why she practiced as a public defender. He thought she was way overqualified. He decided to ask.

For a moment she stared up at him from the ambulance cot, eyes clouded with tears. Then she replied, "My husband was falsely convicted of a crime just after we graduated from high school. He spent over a year in prison until his conviction was overturned. I've dedicated my life working to make sure no one else who is innocent would ever suffer what my husband did."

"What happened?"

"It's too long and tragic a story to get into right now. Someday, maybe I'll write a book. Art, your readers will want to know why my opponents pulled such a dumb stunt tonight. I have to figure how to get this into evidence to build Peter's alibi."

"But the prosecution destroyed his alibi."

"That was his first alibi. Now that I got the real story out of him, he has an alibi that will stand up. I interviewed her tonight: Alya Fuentes, wife of Detective Tiburon Fuentes. Peter was busy in Tibbie's bed at the time of the murder. He left around dawn."

"I heard that name back on the street. Who is Tiburon Fuentes?"

"My, you are new. Tibbie is the head of the Narcotics Special Task Force, with a well-earned reputation as a man not to cross."

"Then the kid must be nuts! How could this Russian immigrant get involved with a detective's wife? How old is she?"

"Alya's twenty-four, an astonishingly beautiful woman, a classic trophy wife. They met while Tibbie was vacationing in Russia. She was nineteen with nothing going for her when her brothers told her to marry him. Hers has not been a happy marriage."

"How did Peter meet her?"

"In citizenship class."

"When did her husband find out?"

"I had no idea until tonight. We had one hell of a time even finding Alya. I spent close to four hours with her going over every point, every detail for tomorrow. She opened up. That's why it was so late. She not only corroborated my client's alibi, she will say that her husband knew of their affair before the murder. Tibbie obstructed justice. I keep asking myself, Is it enough? Will her testimony overcome the circumstantial evidence?"

Art made motions with his hands as if he were dealing cards. "What hand did you play?"

"We played a long shot. Win spread the word to his old buddies on the force about their cuckolded boss. Tibbie rose to the bait. His Latino pride was bruised bad enough that Alya now understands why Tibbie's wives one, two, and three walked. He beat her within an inch of her life. That's when she fled to the safe house, and she's afraid he'll finish the job if he can get to her. She told me it's better to be alive and be deported to Russia than to be dead in America."

The medic interrupted, "Mrs. Caulfels, how are you doing? You're sure doing a lot of talking. Can you hold on a while longer? The driver has run into some traffic."

"As long as I don't move, I'm doing fine. Don't turn on that siren."

Art looked up from his scribbled notes. "What's being done to protect Alya's life?"

"The U.S. Marshals will relieve Win and his crew come morning."

"Mrs. Caulfels, surely you have more than this?"

"As soon as she was in the safe house, I asked for a search warrant of the Fuentes house. We took his mattress and bed linen for DNA testing."

"That must have made his day. So Detective Fuentes came home to find both his wife and his bed missing? How long has the kid been in jail?"

Her lips curved into a warm smile, "Eight months, usually long enough for evidence to disappear. However, Alya isn't what you'd call a model housekeeper. She said she never changed the mattress pad, or much else either."

"How many other different DNA samples were collected?"

"None except Tibbie's. Since Peter's arrest, he has kept her isolated, a virtual prisoner. We also have the throw pillow that has Peter's semen on it. Who knows what else the feds will find in the papers we turned over?" commented Gloria.

"Would I be correct if I report that you confirmed that you expect to have supporting evidence that Peter bedded Alya in her husband's bed on the night of the murder?"

"I don't know if we'll be that lucky. Tibbie obviously believes it."

Art had just finished his notes when she said, "Add that I'm hopeful there will be enough to crack the facade of circumstantial coincidences that is at the heart of the prosecution's chimera."

"Is there anything else you have to say about the prosecutor?"

Gloria smiled. "Please don't tempt me."

"Will you tell me when you find out about the DNA and whatever else you have?"

"No promises. I want to see how you handle what I told you so far."

"Fair enough. Earlier, you mentioned something about your husband being wrongfully sent to prison. Would you care to talk about it now?"

Art became aware of the ambulance's idling engine in the silence that followed. The driver said, "Mrs. Caulfels, we're waiting to get close enough to move you safely into the emergency room."

Finally Gloria blinked away a tear, swallowed, and began, "What I have to say is personal. No notes and not for publication. The night of our senior prom, Joe and I were in the back seat together. We were just kids! He had just asked me to marry him. Deputy sheriffs arrested us. They beat him up. While one took him in, the other raped me. Joe pleaded guilty because he didn't want me to testify. I moved heaven and earth to get the case reopened."

"What happened to the deputy who raped you?"

She looked into his eyes and studied his face for a moment, then turned her gaze downward. "He disappeared right after Labor Day that year and was discovered buried in cement the following year."

"Where did this happen?" asked Art.

"In Colorado, where I grew up. I should never have talked about it. I live with the pain of what that fat bastard did. Please don't bring it up again."

"Okay, I understand."

She exhaled a sigh of relief. "Thank you. I haven't felt as threatened since then, until tonight. Compared to what's going on here, that was a Sunday picnic. These Russians have no conscience! Between Fuentes and them, I'm scared. They're thoroughly evil. My only reason for insisting that you ride with me is so that if I don't survive, the world will still know. Young Peter and the others will not be forgotten."

Art remained at Gloria's side while she was processed into the emergency room. He overheard the call to her husband, Joe, who was away on business in Los Angeles. Then he listened to her side of her conversations when she called the judge and her granddaughter, Vera, during the wait to enter the triage area. In contrast to her tears and words of endearment with Joe, she deftly bargained with the judge until he gave her a conditional extension until she could return to court. She extracted a promise from him to formally contact the state attorney general about the Oakland Police.

Vera, her granddaughter, was in bed when she called. Nevertheless Gloria tactfully ordered her to drive to the hospital to take her home, or--if she were to be held overnight--give Art a ride to the *Oakland Tribune*. He felt a bit put upon when Gloria placed her hand on his as she said, "Now don't you leave before Vera comes. I want her to meet you. Trust me when I say that if ever there was an incarnation of the Emperor Butterfly, she is it."

Art soon was guided into the waiting room. The last he saw of Gloria was her confrontation with a triage nurse over the cell phone. He thought, *The old woman is plainly playing matchmaker. Why describe Vera as an Emperor Butterfly? What is an Emperor Butterfly?*

By the time Art finished the transmission of his story to the newsroom, TV news crews and reporters crowded the emergency room entrance. Art found a sparsely populated area where a small group of hospital employees were on smoke break. There he saw one of the news crews set up to go on the air. They supported an upcoming young Black reporter. She stood with her back to the hospital and spoke on cue, "That's right, Lloyd, one of the gunshot victims has just died. The second is listed in serious condition with a single gunshot wound to the groin and a second to the right hand. Officer Martin Ramirez, who was shot twice, is out of danger. All we know about the shooter is that she is an older woman. Her name has not been released. She sustained undisclosed injuries and is being treated as we speak."

The reporter paused long enough to listen to an unheard question from the studio before she continued, "Oakland Police have been very uncommunicative about the circumstances of this shooting except to say that it is under investigation. We do know that Officer Ramirez is assigned to the special narcotics detail. This could be a drug deal gone bad."

Art wanted to shout, *Drug deal? You're spinning rumors. Read the whole story in the Tribune tomorrow morning! I've scooped all of you.* The thought passed, and he mulled over whether to call a cab or wait for Gloria's granddaughter to show up.

Not long after Art went into the waiting room, he watched as a tall young woman with broad, muscular shoulders strode across the room to the desk. Her long, thick, black hair was piled atop her head in a French twist. What he had never seen before was a dark brown knob sticking out of the top that made her look like she was wearing a shako. Around her neck was a worn black leather collar with a silver buckle right under her chin. She had high cheekbones and eyes that had the tilt and slant of an Asian. In spite of her plain knit sweater and an unfashionably long skirt almost down to her ankles, she moved with a fluid, catlike grace.

He bounded to his feet on overhearing her identify herself as Gloria Caulfels' granddaughter, Vera Li. Art thought, *I'm glad I decided to wait for Gloria's Emperor Butterfly. She is one beautiful woman.*

The nurse replied, "Mrs. Caulfels told me you'd be coming. She is being examined."

"When can I see her?" Vera's voice betrayed concern.

"Don't worry, it's not life threatening. Please have a seat. I'll tell the doctor where to find you."

When Vera turned around, Art introduced himself. He was taken by her warm smile. Her black eyes danced. "Well, Mr. Arthur Williams, you must be the best reporter in the Bay Area. My grandmother swore she would never again grant an interview. Yet she insisted that I meet you and take you back to your paper. What's your secret?"

The thought ran through his head, *Hers is the beautiful face that the cameraman stops on when panning across a crowd.* He cleared his throat and answered, "Maybe she took pity on me. I'm brand new at the *Tribune*. Your grandmother is one very tough lady."

"That runs in our family. I heard about the shooting on the radio on the way in. They talked about three people being shot. Was she one of them?"

Art shook his head, "No, after they mugged her, she did the shooting."

"Bagged all three, that's my grandmother for sure! What happened to her?"

He recounted what Gloria had told him. He recited almost word for word his description of Gloria in the article he had submitted, elaborating on the adjectives "heroic," "tough," and "level headed." Vera nodded in agreement when he concluded, "These aren't the words people typically use to describe a woman."

She added, "When I was small, she was so formidable that I was afraid of her. Now that I have stayed with her, I've come to know that beneath her tough exterior is a very tender and caring grandmother."

"Formidable, that's an interesting word. It can be taken two ways. Do you mean she's the kind of person you shouldn't mess with, or that she inspires awe?"

Vera laughed, "Both! Now I see why she likes you so much. You have a probing mind. Grandmother has carried a gun for as long as I can remember. My mother hates guns so much that she made Grandmother promise not to teach me to shoot while I was in high school. I started when I went to college."

Art liked Vera's voice. When she spoke, it had a mellow, smooth quality that reminded him of expensive velvet. In those first minutes together, he realized he was in the company of a woman he could easily fall for. She acted like the adult granddaughter she was, making calls to family members. The one to whom she showed the most affection was her grandfather, Joe Caulfels. Art had tapped into the paper's database on his laptop, and learned that Joe was a recently retired mathematics professor at Cal Berkeley who had become quite wealthy from royalties.

Later she asked questions. Much to his surprise, she bluntly inquired if he was "hooked up" with someone. He noticed a momentary, almost imperceptible upturn of the corners of her mouth when he told her no, he was still getting over the girl he had lived with during his senior year in college. She let him ramble on about growing up on his dad's ranch on the Owyhee River in southeastern Oregon. He chose college in Pullman, Washington, because the family had moved to Richland after his father died. His first job on graduation was with a weekly paper in Drain, Oregon. He won two journalism awards that year; one was for investigative reporting to solve an eight-year-old cold case of the murder of a seven-year-old girl. Those awards, along with some luck, were the reasons he made the cut to get hired at the *Tribune*.

His brief turn to talk about himself was enough for Vera to relax and talk at length about Gloria's family. Vera's mother, Gloria's youngest daughter, had married a Korean Episcopal priest just after graduating from high school, while she was doing missionary work in Seoul. Her father was now serving in a mission called San Elmo in Costa Rica. Vera's name was spelled Li, not Lee. She had two younger brothers.

Vera said she had just finished her junior year at Mills College. While both mother and grandmother saw Vera as an attorney, she envisioned herself going into law enforcement after graduation. She recently qualified as an expert marksman and, earlier, as a black belt in aikido.

The emergency room physician interrupted them to report that Gloria wanted to see them before she went to sleep. He predicted that she would be wheelchair bound for a time due to her hip injuries. During the brief visit to her room, Gloria stalled the nurse from injecting a sedative long enough to hold Vera's and Art's hands. "Vera, Art, I want to see more of the two of you together."

Art thought, *What should I do? This is a first for me. It's plain as anything that the old woman is playing matchmaker for a girl who shouldn't need it.*

He wasn't surprised when Vera drove to an all-night coffee shop, saying she was hungry. While he seated her, Art had a close-up view of the wooden knob that stuck out of the pile of her hair along the back of her head. He had to ask what it was.

"This is what I carry instead of a firearm." She made a sweeping motion up over her head and laid a six-inch rattail file with a sharpened point on the table. "Grandmother gave it to me. She showed me exactly where and how to shove it into a man's stomach to kill him."

"Then I guess I should describe you as formidable, too."

"If you wish. I'm a born again virgin and I promised my grandfather to remain that way until my wedding night. This file and my knowledge of the *budo* arts are a kind of insurance."

He weighed what Vera had just said. Born again or not, he was looking at one of the most beautiful women he'd ever met. Her eyes were inviting, her lips full, and her smile mesmerized him. Art nodded. "In light of what goes on today, we must build trust. That's not formidable, it's admirable."

She blushed ever so slightly. "Th-thank you. I've learned from my mistakes. Grandfather Joe approves."

"Vera, I could tell by the way your grandmother talked about you that she does too. Tell me more about your family."

Vera never did finish her Danish, but went on about the family, mostly about her two uncles and an aunt, Gloria's other children. The only name he recognized was a soap opera star, Carolyn Connolly, whom Vera called "the Auntie Mame of the family."

When he asked how and where Joe and Gloria met, Vera shrugged her shoulders. "It was someplace back east, Colorado or Wyoming. No one ever talks about it. I think it was Wyoming because Grandpa Joe told me he was a member of the Wind River Arapaho." Laughing, she said, "I'm too much Korean to consider being an Indian too."

Then, frowning, she concluded, "Something bad happened, that's all Mother ever said. You really do know how to ask prying questions."

Much later, Art watched the taillights of Vera's red Miata fade into the predawn darkness on the street outside the *Tribune* offices. He was surprised he had lost track of time. It was just past four in the morning. Yet he was pleased that he had spent so much time with her. He leaned on the top of his car, exhausted but at ease. Who would believe he was getting home at this hour without even kissing the girl? He had to admit, Vera Li was very pleasant to be around. He had accomplished his goal for the evening. He had her phone number.

CHAPTER 3

Art flipped open the morning paper with one hand while balancing a full cup of coffee in the other. The jolt of caffeine wasn't enough to compensate for sleeping less than four hours. He had let his mind wander back to Vera. His eyes scanned the front page above the fold at least three times before Art's mental fog thinned enough for his brain to connect the five-column-wide headlines in bold letters with the story below. The banner headline shouted in bold caps, FORMER PLAY-MATE GUNS DOWN THREE WOULD-BE RAPISTS. It wasn't until he read his byline in bold print that he realized, this was his story! What befuddled him, besides fatigue and calling the attackers "would-be rapists," was the big color photograph to the left. The subject was obviously a very young and stunningly beautiful blue-eyed brunette. He studied her for some moments, taking in every detail. Yes, he concluded this was Gloria Caulfels tastefully posed in the buff when she was far, far younger. She was turned away from the camera just enough to hide most of her breasts behind her arm. She was looking over her bare shoulder with an inviting expression. The bottom of the photograph was cropped just below the waist. He read the first paragraph twice before concluding it was just as he had written it except for the phrase inserted in the first sentence, "a 1955 *Playboy* Playmate of the Month," after her name. Art thought, *1955 to 1996, that picture is forty-one years old! Damn, now I understand why she doesn't give interviews. She never said anything to me about Playboy. Well, I can kiss that source goodbye.* He swallowed a gulp of coffee large enough for it to burn all the way to his stomach.

Nothing was going right. A nurse answered the phone in Gloria's room. She wasn't there. One glance at his watch, and he groaned. With no murder trial today, he should have gone to the courthouse to cover the morning arraignments. He decided to cruise over there and see what he could glean.

At the courthouse, Art's blue mood was lifted by lunchtime. There had been two or three compliments from the courthouse regulars. One of the bailiffs joined him at his table and said between bites of his sandwich, "What'd ya do to get a story outta the old bitch?"

"Beats me. She invited me into the ambulance with her."

"Unbelievable! I've been watching her ever since I came back from 'Nam in sixty-nine. Can't name a reporter on this beat who's not been verbally straight-armed or bulldozed. Ask her to clarify anything, or even explain one of her press releases or the meaning of one of her verbal daggers--nada."

"I'm not kidding you. I'm covering the Symon Dubinski murder. She seems to like what I write."

"Like what you write? Don't ever be lulled by her voice. It's sweet and feminine, but look at those eyes, as cold a blue as you'd ever see. I have watched her destroy dozens of inexperienced prosecutors. She knows the law better than the judges. She has her way with them like no other PD. If I ever were facing criminal charges, I'd ask for the old bitch in a heartbeat."

"Why do you call her that?"

"It's the way she is, like shooting those two guys in the balls. You can count on the old bitch to hit where it hurts most. Talk to any cop who has had to withstand her cross-examination. She takes no prisoners."

Vera's words about her rattail file, "... to hit where it hurts most ..." She's cut from the same stock, Art thought.

The bailiff lightly poked Art's arm as he continued, "That took guts to contrast the self-righteous Counselor Caulfels today with the bimbo of yesteryear. Mark my words, she never gets even. She gets ahead."

⟡

Once Art was back at the paper in mid-afternoon, he downloaded email. Somewhere among the first ten messages was one from Vera Li, addressed to the publisher with a copy to him. "I suggest that you check the computer hard drive of the writer of this article on Gloria Caulfels for more and worse pictures. As a woman, I am outraged at the lack of decency on the part of your senior editors, to allow an inexperienced reporter to make a spectacle of my grandmother. Your tasteless insult added to the serious injury caused by her attackers. I was heartbroken to find her crying as she looked at this picture. Your paper owes our family an apology. --- To Art Williams: To think I spent all that time talking with you after you had twisted that story. Throw away my phone number. I don't want to see you, ever!"

She made herself very clear. Had I met with her, she probably would have run me through with her rattail file. Red really screwed me up. How can I turn this around and keep my job?

There were other emails, mostly from others on the paper congratulating him on his first front-page story. A couple of others from the public patted him on the back. One chided the paper for cropping the picture at the waist.

Art gritted his teeth when he heard a voicemail summons from his boss, Red Magen. He pulled the card with Vera's phone number on it from his pocket and was about to flip it into the trash when he paused, then dialed her number. The phone rang until the answering machine droned its litany.

After the beeps, he began, "Hello Vera, this is Art. Please call me. We need to talk. I was with you when they put the paper to bed. Remember ....."

Vera's loud, high-pitched voice interrupted him. "I told you not to call me, ever! Who told you my grandmother posed for Playboy?"

"Nobody, I just...."

"How could you cheapen Grandmother by putting that awful picture right on the front page?"

"Vera, I write the stories. I'm upset with the editor. He chooses the headlines..."

"I'm devastated. It had nothing to do with her defending herself."

"You're right. But I didn't have anything to do with the *Playboy* photo or reference. Is there anything else in the story that's incorrect?"

She spat, "Your story is an insult heaped on injury. I went to comfort her after I found out Grandpa Joe died. I found her lying there looking at the paper and crying. You did that!"

"Wait, when? What happened?" Art sat tall in his chair and pressed the receiver against his ear.

"A heart attack, after he picked up Grandmother's car. They found him only three blocks from the hospital. He was sitting at a stop sign with the car in park..." Her voice trailed off in the second sentence.

"What a shock! I'm terribly sorry." Art wanted to reach through the phone and hold her.

Her voice breaking, she explained, "Grandpa Joe has had a bad heart most of his life. He stayed up all night and then insisted on picking up her car. If I had stayed at the hospital, I would have been there to take him home and this wouldn't have happened." She sobbed, "I loved my grandfather very much!"

"Please tell your grandmother I'm doubly sorry for how badly the story turned out and for her loss. Don't blame yourself for not being with your grandfather. As I recall, you were following her instructions."

"Yes, but I knew he would come straight to the hospital. I could have taken you back much earlier. I'm very angry with you!" She hung up.

Red's first words as Art walked into his office were, "Young man that was a fine piece of journalism! Good initiative, I like that."

"Boss, I didn't know that Gloria Caulfels was a *Playboy* Playmate! You've upset her and I'm afraid I won't be getting any more from her. Isn't 1955 reaching back a bit far?"

The editor grinned as he opened a dog-eared manila folder and lifted out a faded centerfold, "Thank God for the Internet and scanners. The story may be old, but even old sex sells papers. She made it twice. She did it again when she posed in the first mother-daughter photo shoot. Most women her age would be flattered to be remembered for their beauty."

Art studied the centerfold photo. There was no doubt. Gloria had set the standard for "centerfold quality." He noted that the blue eyes weren't cold, but twinkling, and her smile was an invitation. Art carefully folded it, then, waving it over Red's desk, the young reporter said, "You don't understand the damage you've done. This damned picture hit her wrong! Her husband died this morning. He had a heart attack three blocks from the hospital."

Art watched the editor stiffen and his eyes bulge as the words sank in. *By golly, the boss does have a conscience.*

Red asked, "Did you say Joe Caulfels is dead?"

Art nodded.

"Oh my God, I can't believe it." Red took care as he slid the folded cheesecake photo into an envelope and placed it into a file in his desk before continuing, "What a follow-on! He'll be missed, greatly missed. He's done so much good for the Bay Area. He was generous with his money and even more generous with his time. We'll do a page one obit plus a one- or two-page spread on him."

Red's excited gestures grow with every sentence. "I'll alert the Business desk to synopsize his relationships with Silicon Valley; and Education to cover Berkeley and his consulting with the feds. He was involved in some hush-hush stuff at the Livermore Lab in the sixties. Art, you need an education about the Caulfels clan. Hit the archives and write up the historical spread. Coordinate with the other editors."

"Okay, boss." Art thought, *Oh great, I'm back to cub reporting.*

"It's going to be tough because we only have the last six months on the computer. He's been very outspoken on public education and at odds with his fellow professors for years. About five or ten years ago, the *Chronicle* did an in-depth article on a program he started at San Quentin. Find out when and where the funeral or memorial service will be. I want you to cover it. Afterward, stay long enough to mix with the crowd. Pay your respects to Mrs. Caulfels. Be prepared to have your ears pinned back. She can be downright nasty."

⊰•—═♦═—•⊱

The hours Art spent in the dusty and gloomy tomb of the paper, where its past was buried, weren't his idea of fun. The wizened clerk, whom Art thought was perfect for a part in a Dickens tale, said, "It didn't take you long to get sent down here."

"Yeah, I screwed up. I shouldn't have made an issue of my lead posing bare-ass back in the fifties."

"Gloria Caulfels, that was your story? Not to worry, Red's put you on the fast track. Let me walk you through the keywords listings so you can find your way around the index card system that we used before the database program."

Art started with the current year and worked back. By the time he had run through seven years of cataloged subjects, he had a good picture of Professor Joseph Caulfels and why he deserved front-page tribute. Here was a man for all seasons. One professor described his work as the mathematical glue that holds spreadsheets and databases together. He held patents on a number of algorithms that were used in every major software. He was a stockholder and on the boards of three Silicon Valley startups that had grown into billion-dollar companies. He'd been involved in a number of charities and fund-raising activities. Art found a thread of reaction by the education establishment from preschool to university graduate level, responding to the professor's attacks on the direction they were headed. Often cited were the results of his redirection of a private school system in Goodwin, Colorado, and a prison program that he started at San Quentin to teach math to convicts. At his retirement, there were many testimonials from his former students and yes, even fellow professors. There was recognition from the California Department of Corrections that was magnified by praise from the convicts themselves.

As for the widow, Gloria, Art looked for material to assemble into a sidebar. There were many articles, which Art soon concluded were all fluff. However, they were interesting fluff, the stuff that editors love. After all, it isn't just sex that sells papers, but violence and the tribulations of those who commit violence. Gloria's clients were interesting people with violent lives, but it wasn't just whom she represented, it was how. She was regularly described as the attorney who caused a precedent to be set on appeal, or who forced a retrial because of improper procedures. Hung juries seemed to be one of her specialties.

The *Tribune* had a regular category called "Pyrrhic Victories," where they bewailed generous plea bargains that set perps free with a slap on the wrist, who subsequently committed even worse crimes. Gloria's clients were often written up in that column. Prosecutors were only too happy to complain about Gloria to the *Tribune*, so the pages were filled with their side of the story. Gloria usually kept her silence. This left the reporters to describe the verdicts on their own. Her rare quotes were sharp and usually unfriendly, such as, "You've spent eleven irresponsible months turning my innocent client into an ogre. Thank God I found twelve open-minded people who don't read your paper."

Thanks to the cataloging system, he gleaned one item of interest about Gloria from the sports page. Four years before, she had won a shooting trophy in an event sponsored by the National Rifle Association. It was newsworthy because she was the oldest woman ever to win this particular pistol competition. *No wonder she was such a deadeye on the street yesterday.*

He learned about Gloria's oldest son, Major Andy Caulfels, who had served in Operation Desert Storm as a fighter pilot. He had shot down a MiG and later had been among the pilots who attacked the retreating Iraqi army.

Searching more than six years back, Art found few gleanings about Joe. Other than a few short items about Joe's math program at San Quentin, most were photographs of him as the man accompanying Gloria to one event or other.

A 1975 item described a publicist's dream where, as the first mother-daughter Playmates, Gloria posed nude with her daughter Carole, who had adopted the stage name Carolyn Connolly. At age eighteen, Carole was becoming an established actress in the daytime soaps. The centerfold gave her a splash of wanted publicity.

For Gloria, it was a horse of another color. Prosecutors of three Northern California counties threatened Bar Association sanctions. Red Magen, surprisingly, wrote an editorial in her defense. Along with the editorial Red ran a picture of Gloria dressed for court in a demure, loose-fitting suit with the skirt far down her calf. *It could be the same one she wore yesterday,* thought Art. Red praised her skills as a public defender and concluded it with a barb from Gloria, "I never dress to distract these salaried attorneys. They have a hard enough time concentrating long enough to give an effective summation." After all the heat and smoke, there was nothing more. If the Bar Association ever took official notice of the well-airbrushed photos of a forty-five-year-old mother of four, it was not recorded.

While he organized his gleanings for distribution to the various editors, Art thought, *How on earth did this saint of a man put up with this "hell-on-wheels" trial lawyer for fifty years? Yet look at how well all the children turned out. I could be happy in a family like this.*

⊷┅┉▣ ▣┉┅⊶

By the day of the funeral service, Art's head was so full of the life of

Joe Caulfels, going all the way back to 1970, that he felt he could give a creditable eulogy.

Art threaded his way across the Bay to the Episcopal Grace Cathedral on Nob Hill. With Red's instructions fresh in his head, he thought *I'm not going to attend this service because it's a news assignment. It's something I need to do. I hope I'm granted just a moment to express my concern to Gloria and do what Red is unwilling to do--apologize.*

He was impressed that the Episcopal Bishop of San Francisco officiated, accompanied by a flock of priests. He was even more impressed by the turnout. He wondered if anyone was running anything in the Bay Area.

The moment came when the service was over and the program was turned over to the family. Major Andrew Caulfels, resplendent in his medal-bedecked uniform, stepped forward. In a voice that broke, he managed but a few sentences about how his father nurtured his love of flying and was never too busy to help him with his homework. He concluded by saying, "I had a bad temper when I was growing up. Over and over he told me that the only way I could end hate was to love. I'm going to miss him."

Major Caulfels handed the mike down to his mother, who was sitting in an electric wheelchair. Gloria gazed out at the audience for what seemed an eternity and then said in a very soft voice, "They say that people come to funerals more for the living than the dead. However, after spending my life working the criminal defense bar, I know most of you are not here for me."

As the weak, nervous laughter died out, she continued, "You're here for the same reason I am, to say farewell to the most wonderful, most godly man you ever met. Andy's words reminded me that I never went down into Joe's arms that I didn't feel surrounded by love and the gentleness of his spirit. My son's words also reminded me of the first morning of our honeymoon. It was more than six months after we married in the prison at Canon City, Colorado. At the end of that terrible ordeal, on the first day of our life together, he took me by the hand. He guided me to kneel with him at the side of the bed. There he offered a prayer that shaped our lives. He thanked the Lord for giving us that day in freedom with no bars on the windows and no locks to keep us in. He asked for guidance that we might find the way to all the good works that the Lord has prepared for us to walk in."

She lowered the mike and loudly sniffed. Gloria looked over the audience from one side to the other. "He touched all of our lives in marvelous ways. I learned to live without hate in my heart. In those early days, his good works nearly drove me to despair. Whenever one of the ex-cons from Canon City called, we were always at least good for a meal and, too often, a touch--a twenty or a fifty. Sometimes we went hungry the last day or two of the month. While Joe did more for more people than it seems possible, I'm most grateful for how he raised our children. Each day they make me proud. The good that they each do in their lives every day will ease the pain of my loss. Thank you all for coming today. I am overwhelmed by your concern."

An aged, wiry man in a top-of-the-line business suit took the microphone. His dark complexion contrasted with his white hair. He had the beginnings of a smile on his lips as he took the mike in his hand. "I'm Jesse Sollair and I'm one of those ex-cons. I'd been in Canon City almost two years already on a twelve-year ticket when I met Joe. I'd hijacked a truckload of tires from just outside the Gates plant in Denver back in forty-three. My brother had beaten the tar out of the driver. I deserved every one of the twelve years I was facing. I was mad at the world and felt sorry for myself. Then I met Joe, two years younger than me. He was at peace inside. At first I thought it was because he was in shock. But here he was, facing eighty years to life on what we soon found out was a trumped-up charge. They'd almost killed him in the county jail, leaving him with a bad ticker. They were trying to drive his family out of town and send his old man back to prison."

Jesse's eyes filled with tears and his voice wavered, "He was the angel sent to save me. He told me that the one place they couldn't control was the heart. And he had made the decision that there was only room in his heart for love. I saw him walk that walk that summer, when two of the three deputies that arrested him were sent to Canon City to do hard time. He was decent to them. By the time Joe's conviction was thrown out, he taught me enough to take the exam to get a high school diploma."

The old man took a deep breath and looked down at Gloria, "Yeah, I know I'm taking too long, but this is the good part. They let me out in fifty-five. All that time, Joe had written me enough to keep in touch. I had found the Lord and wanted to start a new life away from my family. Joe arranged a bus ticket out here to San Francisco. They sent the money even though they knew Gloria was about to be blackballed after being fired from her job at a big law firm. There would be tuition due for him. They expected that the Lord would provide. The Lord did provide: Gloria went back to modeling. Mr. Hugh Hefner asked her to pose."

"What I have to show for having known Joe Caulfels is a lifetime of friendship; the same wonderful wife for thirty-six years; two children, both college graduates; three grandchildren; my own home, and my own business. I contrast that to my brother, who never had the opportunity to meet Joe. He died in a fight in Joliet in seventy-one. Thank you, Joe. Thank you, Gloria, for the life you have given me."

Art filled his notepad with Jesse's testimony. He was pleased to have the recorder to catch all those who came after Jesse. These included Joe's fellow professors at Berkeley, scientists from Livermore, friends, and more ex-cons from San Quentin where he had headed the high school math program for years. Each painted a unique picture of a brilliant man who had the rare gift of touching other lives in a positive way. He was generous with his time, his talents, and his wealth. Art was grateful that none took as long as Jesse. None came close to matching his story.

Later, Art waited his turn in a long line to greet Gloria and meet her children and grandchildren. He planned to greet each by name and ask questions based on his search through the newspaper morgue. The two tall sons, handsome like their father, and Carole, still a ravishing beauty, stood closest to their mother. At the end and slightly separated from the others was Gloria's youngest daughter Jenny, plain and careworn, with mousey brown hair. Vera stood at her side.

As soon as Art spotted Vera, all the data he had memorized got scrambled. He couldn't take his eyes off her. Her luxuriant hair was down, framing her face. She was wearing a dark blue dress that, while modest, complimented her lithe figure and color. *Could there be a way to turn this around? She is so beautiful.*

When he found himself in front of Vera, he stood frozen, pausing much too long for a moving reception line. All he could do was look into her face.

She waited for him to speak, then her eyes flashed. In a low voice, through clenched teeth, Vera spat, "Why are you here? I told you I didn't want to see you again, ever!"

Art blinked as if a trance was broken. "Vera, I didn't come to see you. I came to pay my respects and to apologize to your grandmother for the picture they ran with the article. I understand why you're upset. I wish we had met under different conditions. I really enjoyed our time together."

Vera's eyes widened slightly and she touched his arm, "I did too. That's why it hurt so much. Goodbye." She then turned to the next person in the receiving line and left him to introduce himself to her mother, Jenny.

Art's composure was so shaken that he mistakenly called Jenny Carole as he shook hands with her. Each handshake brought him closer to Gloria, who was every bit the good hostess, talking amiably with everyone who came along. Again and again he recited to himself the apology. When at last he was standing in front of her, he braced himself for the worst. Instead and to his surprise, she extended a warm hand and firmly took his. She smiled in response to his greeting. "Art, this is a pleasant surprise. Thank you for coming today. I'm sorry you never had the opportunity to meet my husband."

"Mrs. Caulfels, I came here today primarily because I want to apologize for the picture that was printed with the article I wrote. Vera told me how upset you were. Please accept my apologies."

Gloria looked down the line toward her granddaughter and back at Art with a puzzled look on her face, then said, "Apologize? It's a tonic for an old woman's ego to have the world remember she was once a beautiful young woman who could command a premium to pose, dressed or undressed. I don't dwell on it at age sixty-seven, but I never forget those times either."

Art looked back down the line toward Vera and back at Gloria. He exhaled a chestful of air, "Then you weren't offended by the picture?"

"Of course not. Is that why she's upset with you?"

"That's what she says. It was the editor who chose it, not me."

Gloria sat back in the wheelchair and laughed. "Well, old Red never has taken his mind off naked women. Tell him I told you so. Art, I was hurting at that moment. The tears Vera saw were because I remembered who I was looking at when the shutter snapped. Joe was standing behind the photographer. Being desired and loved like that can only be a memory now."

She pressed a card into his hand. "Give me a call in a couple of weeks. My hip ought to be healed enough to be out of this wheelchair by then. You have no reason to apologize. Your work is very professional. Thank you for coming to my rescue."

"And thank you for giving me the opportunity."

"Please thank Red for me and tell him I'm overwhelmed by the *Tribune*'s in-depth treatment of Joe's passing. See you in court."

While Art walked away, he glanced at the card. Her number was the same as Vera's. Still looking at the card, he almost bumped into a balding older man who was just a little taller than he was. The stranger said, "My name is Andrew Foyle from Goodwin, Colorado, and you?"

"I'm Art Williams."

"How did you come to know my friend, Joe Caulfels?"

"I never did, but I wish I had. He was a wonderful man."

"Yes, he was."

"Are you family too?"

"No, Joe was my first friend, my best friend."

"Then you grew up together in Colorado?"

"Yes. What brought you here today?"

Art looked back at Vera, then said, "I'm a reporter for the *Oakland Tribune*. I met Mrs. Caulfels at court. I came to apologize for the gross way my editor handled my story and to express my condolences."

Foyle followed his gaze, then, turning to walk away, remarked, "I'd say you had more on your mind than apologizing to the widow." That made Art realize that Vera had so completely captured his attention that he'd forgotten his data and missed the opportunity to talk to the head of the educational foundation that sponsored Joe Caulfels' work.

Art thought, *Caught again. How do I convince Vera I'm not the villain she thinks I am?*

At Oakland Police headquarters, the sign on the glassed-in office read DET LT T FUENTES. Art tapped on the glass.

A big man with a swarthy complexion looked up from his papers. He looked even burlier as he stood and swaggered toward the door.

Quite an impressive figure, thought Art. *If John Wayne were a Latino, this is what he'd look like.*

"Mr. Williams of the *Tribune*? Come in and rest your haunches. I can spare you a few minutes, which gives me a break from my paperwork. I hate paperwork. It's the bane of a cop's existence."

"Thanks. You said over the phone that there wasn't much you could say about the Ramirez matter."

"Right. The Internal Affairs investigators have put a lid on it. Also, much of what I do tell you has to be off the record. Not only because of Officer Ramirez, but because I don't want the dope dealers to know my strategy for my unit."

Art looked up at the wall behind Fuentes, which was papered with clippings about him and the work of his narcotics unit. *This guy is full of himself,* he thought. *Once I get him going, he may tell me more than he intended.* "I did some research on you in the newspaper files, and you have quite an impressive arrest record. Lately, though, there have been criticisms that you seem to be 'soft on' or 'cozy with' the Russian Mafia because you haven't arrested any of them."

The big man bristled. "Those critics can stick their crap right back where it came from, up where the sun don't shine. They ignore the fact that the Russians haven't been in this trade for long. Most of them are, like, fresh off the boat. But they're clever. They use Black and Latino hustlers to do their street dealing, so they don't get any dirt on themselves. Off the record, the only way to get at them is to go undercover. That takes time."

"Undercover? Would that be like Officer Ramirez?"

"Yeah, that would be Ramirez. Now, dammit, his cover's blown and we have to start all over."

"But can you? They'll be vigilant now. And are you concerned that they might go for some retribution against you? They can be pretty violent."

The swarthy face went noticeably pale. Fuentes gulped and paused.

"Yeah, I know about their reputation … but if you did your research, you know it's been tried before." He pointed to a framed clipping on the wall. "Like old Chen-Lui Chang there. Called himself the Drug Lord of Oakland's Chinatown and boasted he would off me. Now he's 'lord' of a single cell in San Quentin." He shook a finger. "When you go messing with the shark, you're gonna get bitten."

"The shark … yes, that brings up a question that's been bugging me since I found out *tiburon* is Spanish for 'shark.' Is that your real name, or did you assume it?"

"Oh, it's real, thanks to my father's wicked sense of humor. Tiburon, California, is an upscale village on the North Bay that's nearly a hundred percent rich Anglos. Poor Latino families like mine are not found or welcomed there—but I was born there, by accident, you might say. My mother was a maid in one of those big houses, and she went into premature labor in her employer's kitchen. So my father had me baptized José Tiburon Fuentes. José, because the priests say every Catholic baby has to have a saint's name."

"So what did they call you? José or Tibbie?"

"It was Tibbie at home and, at first, José at school. I got them to change it at school when I saw the impression my middle name made on the Latino kids. I liked it. I still like it. I think it strikes some fear into the Latino dealers. Even the Russians translate it as *Akyna*, and the Anglo dealers call me Shark the Narc."

What an ego, though Art. *He knows what the Russians might do, but he seems to think he's bulletproof.* "Back to the main subject, why do you think Officer Ramirez was part of the attack on Gloria Caulfels?"

"Anything I say about him is off the record. But I don't agree he was 'part of' that incident. Yeah, he was there. But when you're undercover, sometimes you have to stand by while a caper goes down that you would stop if you were in uniform. Ramirez never touched a hair on Mrs. Caulfels."

"He drew a gun on her. How about that?"

"I call that self-defense. Or else he was trying to arrest her. The way I hear it, she had already shot two *hombres* and was waving a gun around wildly. She was a danger to the public."

That's not how I wrote it, thought Art. *He's putting his own spin on it.* "Is it pure coincidence, Lieutenant, that the tape the Russians wanted was made by your wife?"

"My wife? That bitch! That *puta*!" Fuentes raged. "I wish I'd never laid eyes on her!" He continued in a calmer voice, "Don't print that. My personal involvement with a Russian woman has complicated my life to where I'm under suspicion. They're making me go on administrative leave. I should have stuck to Latina women, but my three Latina marriages didn't work out either. Four times at bat, four times struck out."

The detective stared at Art before he continued, "Yeah, they knew she was my wife, but that's not why they wanted the tapes. They wanted to know if she had any good alibi for Godoniski, because they want him put away in the worst way. Officer Ramirez just happened to be in the wrong place at the wrong time."

After a few more questions and self-serving answers, Art saw he would not get any more meaty information and got up to leave.

Fuentes said in parting, "You understand that most of what I said has to be off the record because of the investigation? But I want to leave you with one thing—and you can print this for your readers—that I have the best damn crew of narcs in California, and I'm behind them one hundred percent. If any of my guys comes up on charges—and Ramirez isn't the first—I have his back all the way to the verdict."

"I'll be sure the public knows that," replied Art. He left thinking the Narcotics Special Task Force might be in real trouble this time.

CHAPTER 4

Four men in business suits sat at the far table on the deck outside the posh Sausalito restaurant well after the lunch crowd had returned to work. The two without neckties were young and burly, with fair complexions, and carried themselves erect as if they had military training. They didn't pay much attention to what was going on at the table, but never missed what moved outside and inside the building. The other two were each entirely focused on what the other was saying.

Gregory Rojas, one of the older men, considered himself the consummate politician. He looked the part with an athletic build, silver airbrushed hair, and a straight prominent nose over a well-trimmed salt and pepper mustache. His suit was from the best racks at Nordstrom.

Give Greg an opening, after your introduction to him, and he'd tell you his family had been Spanish immigrants who arrived just in time for the Gold Rush and followed that with exploits that made them people to be reckoned with. Like his father, he was a lawyer. Instead of practicing law, however, Greg had spent most of his life in government and Democratic politics, including being elected and reelected to the Alameda County Board of Supervisors. Of late, he touted his abilities at raising big money for Democratic presidential and gubernatorial campaigns. This skill guaranteed him access to the highest places in both federal and state governments.

Yet, if one were a careful observer, one could not help but notice that this powerful man wasn't sitting too comfortably at the table. He was squirming and his back was stiff.

Greg's full attention was on the man sitting across from him with his back to the water. Alexander Tsamonicoff's every sentence was punctuated with gestures by his fleshy, powerful hands. Greg thought, *I've never seen Alex on edge like this. The body armor makes him look like a fat caterpillar draped in Italian silk. Now that I'm out here, I owe it to him to break the news, good and bad, in a careful manner. I just don't want the news to be so bad that it disrupts our relationship. In any event, I want this over as quickly as possible. There'll be other days when I can talk with Alex about candidates' needs.*

Greg feared he was going to get his first glimpse of what lay beneath the veneer of the "Russian Mafia." The supervisor reminded himself that there were files and dossiers open on the Russian, from the CIA and FBI on down to the state's organized crime task force. Greg had heard Alex refer to the forces of law and order as a "pack of wolves lurking just beyond the tree line." He recalled Howard Newton's admonition, "Tact is the art of making a point without making an enemy," while he kept his mouth shut and listened.

Alex pulled a cardboard file folder from his briefcase. He gripped it so hard that he was creasing it. "I have copy autopsy and medical examiner's reports. This woman, she fired into his crotch! How can one bullet do so much harm?"

Greg steepled his fingers close to his mouth, then said in an oily voice, "I'm sorry. What a burden for you to take back to Russia to his family that Oleg was killed by an old woman."

"Old woman! Old woman! What old woman shoots men in groin with bullets that crumble into pieces?" Alex punctuated each phrase or sentence by shoving his index finger onto a page of the report. "Bladder exploded, sliced open aorta, severed artery to his left kidney. There were bullet fragments in his liver. Poor Oleg bled to death before ambulance arrived."

Greg thought, *The bastard got what was coming to him. Yes, they were legal nine-millimeter hollow points*, but he said, "My friend, I've heard the nine-one-one tape. No cop would keep his badge if he did things to a suspect that she did to Officer Ramirez. Dale Bleasman told me she shoved the gun against his balls."

"But no one is going to do a thing about it! My nephew Yuri had his manhood shot away by this feminist witch! My brother, he blames me!" Alex's lip trembled as he said, "Why you think I sweat in this bulletproof vest? We meet here in Sausalito because I don't want confrontation with my own family. What can be done to this old woman?"

No sooner had Greg said, "I'll ask my deputy to make a complaint to the Bar Association, but it's highly unlikely they'll do anything. She is the *grand dame* of the PD bar," than he realized he'd said the wrong thing. For the first time, both bodyguards were staring at him. Alex's bloodshot eyes were bulging.

Greg looked on the arrival of the waitress with another round of drinks much the way a wayfaring homesteader would the cavalry. *What have I gotten myself into? They could drag me onto that big boat tied up over there and toss me overboard beyond the Farallons.*

Yet he didn't get up and leave with her. Greg sat there as if paralyzed while she returned to the bar. Only then did Alex break the silence. "Who the hell is this Gloria Caulfels? Tell me what you know about her."

"She's always been a loose cannon. When I was growing up, she was hired into my father's law firm, Sharkley, Wattersen, and Rojas. They usually didn't hire women lawyers in those days, but she stood first in her class at Hastings and aced the bar exam. I remember her. She was not only smart, she was beautiful; always dressed to the nines, a former New York fashion model. I was a teenager and I had a crush on her for a time… but then it happened."

"What happened?"

"Things went on in those days that aren't allowed today. The women who worked in the firm, except for one savvy legal stenographer, were young, single, and available. If they got married, they either quit or were fired."

"What does this have to do with this evil woman?"

"There were expectations about their availability. As an attorney, Gloria Caulfels must have felt she was different from the other women in the firm. Leon Wattersen didn't. I think she had been there about a year at the time. They were in Sacramento arguing a case before the California State Appeals Court. After spending too long in the hotel bar, he went into her room in the middle of the night. While he was trying to get into her bed, she drove a four- or five-inch-long rattail file in between his ribs, puncturing his lung. Then she filed charges against him for attempted rape."

"My God, did he go to jail?"

"No, he died of pneumonia about ninety days later. The morning after the incident, she appeared in court with a black eye and argued the case by herself, using Wattersen's notes. My dad got there before noon. He was surprised because she was doing a good job, so he let her continue. It was the last big win for the firm."

"Last win? What happened to the firm?"

"The partnership fell apart. I don't know if it was because of the fall-out from the scandal, or because Leon carried the firm."

"They arrested her, no?"

Greg shook his head, "No, self-defense. But of course she was kicked out of the firm—the first associate they let go. She went back to modeling and landed in the centerfold of *Playboy* magazine. I think they would have disbarred her for that if she hadn't been pregnant at the time of the hearing. Eventually she surfaced again, working as a public defender."

The silver-haired politician waited for the busboy to clear a nearby table that was within earshot. He dreaded passing on the message from his friend, Prosecutor Dale Bleasman. When the boy left, Greg leaned across the table to get his mouth close to Alex's ear. He lowered his voice to a near-whisper. "There's another matter, Alex. Dale says that Ramirez spilled the beans to Internal Affairs and fully implicated Tibbie Fuentes in the incident. They'll be interviewing Tibbie very soon. They know nothing about you, or us for that matter. Dale felt you ought to know."

"Yes, thank you. I am relieved. Please tell your ambitious prosecutor that I appreciate his concern. I understand why he could not come today. Too bad about wife. If Tibbie had told me of his needs, I would have found him good Russian wife."

Greg said, "He really blew it when he kept her in that cabin."

"Yes, Tibbie misled us badly. We must decide how to deal with him. It troubles me when I find treachery in my organization. Symon Dubinski couldn't follow orders. Peter Godoniski reneged on his promise. Now I learn he double-crossed us and was screwing Alya Fuentes at same time."

Greg said, "There's more than enough evidence to convict Tibbie if the witnesses testify."

Alex gripped his spoon with four fingers and placed his thumb against the bowl. He pressed hard against the bowl as if he were going to pop it off. "If I had known Tibbie's reasons, we would have been far more direct in dealing with these worms. Trial start again tomorrow with Peter out of reach in jail. You will tell Mr. Bleasman how important it is that he win. Put Peter away for life. He must stand out as an example. Then I decide how to deal with this Caulfels woman. No one gets away with destruction of a family member's balls."

Art Williams made sure he was in court early to get the front row seat closest to the power outlet to plug in his brand new laptop. Now he had to show appreciation for the confidence Red placed in him. He awoke early and used the extra time to review the notes and articles he'd accumulated before Gloria was attacked. He thought, *Gloria scored big with the jury by catching the state off guard and making the criminalists look incompetent. But she still hasn't managed to raise a reasonable doubt. Unless Gloria can work a miracle with Alya, Peter will be found guilty.*

He turned around when the silence of the empty courtroom was broken by the solid bump on the door followed by the whir of an electric motor. Gloria steered her wheelchair down the aisle closest to Art. She stopped just behind the bar at the gate separating the spectators from the court. "Art, you're here early today. I'm in no shape to plug my cord into the socket under the table. Could you do it, please?"

He opened the gate and she drove through. He hefted her laptop from a tray onto the table. While Art plugged it in, Gloria put on her glasses and opened the laptop.

After he stood up, Gloria said, "Thank you. I think you've made an impression on Vera."

"I know. It wasn't a good one."

"No, no, I suspect she doesn't want to admit her true feelings. Someday I'll explain why. She is a wonderful young woman. After the trial, please accept an invitation to dinner."

"Thank you. This is the first time I've seen you wear glasses."

Putting her index finger on the arch over her nose, she grumbled, "I lost a contact when I was mugged. I had high hopes the forensic people would find it at the scene, but just like the Dubinski murder scene, they obviously didn't do a thorough job."

He had hardly returned to his seat when deputy prosecutor Baylor Gates entered, followed by Dale Bleasman, the Alameda County prosecutor. Gloria looked back over her shoulder and with a smile said, "Oh my, we are honored to have the Grand Dragon, the exalted Poo-Bah himself, today. Dale, I hope you're here to speed up the end to the injustice being done to this young man."

Art saw Gates shake his head while Dale Bleasman bit his lower lip and narrowed his eyes. Art's impression of Bleasman was that he truly looked the part of a prosecutor. He was a handsome man with an athletic build and silver sideburns. He spoke with sonorous authority. Yet Art sensed a discomfiture, a tension like that felt by a quarterback who's been sacked too many times. Bleasman forced a smile before he said, "Gloria, you should have convinced him to take our offer. This is a case the people can ill afford to lose. The evidence is all there and it fits tightly. We will stay the course."

"Mr. Prosecutor, don't ever say I didn't offer you a way out."

"Gloria, *you* offer *me* a way out? Is this charade the best you can do? I'm sorry about your injuries and especially about your loss. We all miss your husband and the wonderful work he did for this community."

"Thank you, Dale."

Art thought, *I'd hate to play poker with her. Gloria hides her emotions very well.*

The rest of the players and spectators in the courtroom drama took their places. Peter Godoniski was brought in wearing a dark blue business suit and a yellow necktie. In a thickly accented voice whose timbre and pitch filled the chamber, he asked Gloria, "This is the day you prove I am innocent, yes? I am innocent. I don't want to die." By the time she had finished softly comforting him, the judge arrived and gaveled the court into session.

Art sensed more tension in the prosecutors than in the defendant, who had responded well to Gloria's motherly assurances. Gates threw out a handful of procedural technicalities to thwart recalling the criminalist for additional cross-examination. He was overruled on all of them, and the judge firmly lectured him on the inadequacy of his final objection.

The bespectacled criminalist, Shane Joyce, had been run through the wringer by Gloria in the last session. Today he took the stand with as much relish as a new volunteer on a cold day mounts the dunking seat in a carnival game. Gloria took up where she had left off, with the can of pop, a Jolt Cola. Joyce reiterated that the can had had two identifiable fingerprints plus six smeared or partial prints. He blamed the smears on someone wearing oily rubber gloves.

Gloria asked, "Who handed Peter the can of Jolt?"

"I dunno."

She produced a pop can of the same size appropriately marked with similar prints. "Does the pop can you allege my client drank from after murdering Mr. Dubinski match this pop can, both in size and location of fingerprints and other markings?"

After Joyce affirmed that the cans matched, Gloria set her can in front of him and asked him to pick it up and drink from it, using the same finger and thumb as marked. He complied. Had she not caught the can, it would have fallen on the floor. As it was, close to a quarter of the can sloshed onto Joyce's lap. He stood up in a vain attempt to avoid getting wet. The criminalist blurted out, "Dammit, the defendant couldn't have drunk from that can. He was handing it to somebody."

"Wouldn't you say that the odds are against Symon being the one who took the can?" asked Gloria.

"Yes. He was tied up."

Dale Bleasman bounced to his feet. "I object to this line of questioning. It has nothing to do with matters under examination."

Gloria said, "I beg your pardon, Mr. Prosecutor. I refer you to the opening statement in which your Mr. Gates painted a picture of my client standing over a murdered Symon Dubinski downing a Jolt."

Gotcha, thought Art. The judge sounded as if he were talking to a rambunctious three-year-old as he again overruled the prosecutor, who flopped into his chair. Like every other pair of eyes that were awake, Art's followed Gloria while she maneuvered her wheelchair back to the defense table. She studied her laptop for a moment, then asked, "Wouldn't you agree, if Peter didn't down a Jolt with his mitt, you must acquit?

"I guess so," Joyce nodded.

"Your witness, Mr. Bleasman."

Up until this last exchange, she only seemed to be reinforcing the state's evidence about the fingerprints, Art thought. *Now she's turned it back on them. That was a neat touch, to adapt "If the glove doesn't fit, you must acquit," from the O.J. Simpson trial. Thank you, Gloria, you gave me the lead for today's article.*

Gloria rolled the chair to place herself where the next witness on cross, another criminalist, Mitch Brown, had to look toward the jury if he was to look at her. Her voice was soft, almost velvety. "Sir, in my review of your testimony, I am unclear as to why there is so little trace evidence at the murder scene. And as for what little there is, beyond the blond hair of the defendant and the pop can, I am at a loss to understand why you failed to identify its origins."

The tone of the criminalist was patronizing. "We are positive on the matches with the defendant. As for what didn't match, there were some of the usual rug and clothing fibers that had been tracked in over time. Oh, and there were a couple of pubic hairs behind the toilet that we found no match for. And a piece of a broken fingernail that we identified as belonging to the previous tenant."

"And no other fingerprints?"

"Look, this was a vacant apartment. Like I said, it had been cleaned very thoroughly. There were some partials, but nothing other than the defendant's."

"How long have you been doing this work and testifying in court?"

"Fifteen years."

"How many times have you searched a crime scene for fingerprints and had nothing to report?"

"There must have been a few times. I just can't recall."

Gloria held aloft a piece of paper. "Your Honor, I submit the complete listing of cases in which the witness has testified as exhibit 2-34."

Dale was immediately on his feet. "You can't do this. We've never had a chance to examine it. I object, Your Honor."

"Prosecutor Bleasman, aren't you aware of what goes on in your own office?" The judge held up the exhibit. "Read for me the letterhead."

The prosecutor glared at the judge as he read his own letterhead into the record: "Office of the Prosecuting Attorney."

The judge struck his gavel. "Objection overruled. Now sit down and let's continue."

Art thought, *Bleasman has taken the lead and done nothing but anger the judge. I was hoping for something to hang a story on, like Gloria introducing Alya.*

Gloria asked the next question, "And the only clear, unsmudged prints you found in the whole apartment were those on the pop can and nowhere else?"

The witness answered, "That is correct."

"One last question. There were a number of minute tufts of a blue nylon-cotton blend I refer to as items 23, 46, 73, and 132. Did you have any luck identifying them?"

The witness, looked down at the list on his lap before answering, "This is a common fiber, a mixture of cotton and nylon found in work clothes."

"And you found none that matched any clothing ever worn by the defendant. Is that correct?"

"That is correct."

"Thank you. That will be all."

The prosecution rested its case. Gloria moved for an end to the trial with a directed acquittal. Even Art was taken aback when she argued, "In all my years practicing before the bar, never before have I represented a client who has had to overcome evidence fabricated by a cabal of conspirators bent on obstructing justice."

Both Dale Bleasman and Baylor Gates bounced to their feet and interrupted her with shouted rebuttals. After gaveling the court to order, the judge blistered Gloria's ears with a stern lecture to present coherent arguments, not personal attacks on the state. He threatened a mistrial. Gloria asked him to put off that decision until after she presented her evidence. Dale had turned pale during the interchange. Obviously angered by the frontal assaults, the judge ordered an early recess for lunch and called the lawyers into his office.

⊷═◉ ◉═⊶

In the courthouse basement cafeteria, Art was busying himself between writing and eating when the drone of the TV sportscast was interrupted by a grim-faced news reader. "Breaking news! Detective

42

Tiburon Fuentes was gunned down in the parking garage beneath his attorney's office in Oakland. Detective Fuentes was on administrative leave pending investigation of charges related to domestic violence. Now to our reporter at the office building...."

"...So gruesome that pictures of the ambush can't be shown," said the field news reporter. "Persons unknown blew the top off the head of Detective Lieutenant Tiburon Fuentes close by his sedan. Fuentes led the Oakland Special Narcotics Task Force. His body was found by a woman who was returning to her car. Wild-eyed and trembling, she told this TV reporter that there were blood and brains all around him, both on the cars and on the ground."

The segment closed out with a still of Alya, accompanied by a voice-over announcing that Detective Fuentes, days before, had been placed on administrative leave over allegations that he had imprisoned and beaten his wife. Restraining and protective orders had been issued against him.

Before the court reconvened, Art overheard a uniformed officer tell a bailiff that the lenses on the security cameras at the Fuentes murder scene had been covered with tape. No one heard the shots and no one saw anyone suspicious. On coming into the courtroom, Art noted that three armed officers stood by the door as added security. The visitor's gallery was empty, and Bleasman was at the tail end of another argument, this time challenging the propriety of calling Yuri Tsamonicoff for the defense.

The whole court erupted in laughter when Gloria quipped, "Your Honor, I see no reason to worry about Tsamonicoff. He's harmless. The last time he misbehaved, I shot his balls off. Like me, he's still confined to a wheelchair."

After the gaveling had ended, Gloria continued, "He's my witness with every reason to be hostile, but I have the right to give my client a proper defense without micromanagement by Mr. Bleasman."

⋅⊱━⊰⋅

Yuri Tsamonicoff wasn't on his best behavior. He glared at Gloria all the way as he was pushed to the witness stand by a bailiff. He spat in her direction. To the judge, he ranted in Russian about the injustice of nothing being done to punish that woman who destroyed his future. He pointed to his crotch and ignored the judge's words and gavel. After a time he fell silent with both hands pressed against the wounded portion of his anatomy, while the judge lectured him about courtroom behavior and the translator conveyed the message.

Gloria's voice was cold and controlled. "Mr. Tsamonicoff, we have one thing in common. I don't want to see or talk to you, and you don't want to see or talk to me. But we must for this one time. The rest of the life of an innocent man, your friend since childhood, is at stake here."

Yuri rose up from his nearly doubled-over position. "Go ahead, ask question."

Once he was sworn, she asked, "Mr. Tsamonicoff, please tell the court what you were doing at 1472 Yancy Street, Apartment 105, before Symon Dubinski's death."

"I clean four days before Symon die."

"Did you know when you cleaned the apartment that Symon was going to be executed in that apartment?"

Yuri shook his head, giving a silent no. On the judge's instructions, he testified in words, slipping back and forth between Russian and English, often in mid-sentence. He said that he and Oleg had spent a day and a half cleaning the apartment using rented commercial equipment. They had both worn blue jumpsuits, and he thought the color of the tufts of cloth was close to the same color as the samples collected at the scene. They had worn rubber gloves and hot, uncomfortable swimmer's caps the whole time. Tibbie Fuentes had taken those from them once the job was over. He didn't know what had been done with the clothing. Fuentes didn't pay them for their work until after he had inspected the unit using a magnifying glass. He made them do the living room twice. Yuri had not seen the defendant in the three months before the murder because he had stopped working with him.

Gloria's voice throughout was warm and solicitous, completely without an edge. She rolled the wheelchair back and forth from the laptop on her table to a place almost in front of Yuri. The witness's eyes followed Gloria much the way a trapped predator's would. He said that the only one of the Russians who had been in contact with Peter had been the dead man, Symon. Only Gloria's tapping her laptop's keys broke the courtroom's silence until she asked in a low, husky voice, "After

Peter Godoniski's arrest for Symon's murder, was there anyone other than Peter who said or did something that would lead you to believe they were involved in the murder?"

Yuri jerked his arms in a vain attempt to escape his restraints before he looked at Gloria. "I give you Tibbie. That is enough, Fifth Amendment, Fifth Amendment, I not speak."

"I understand. It's been pretty tough in here, hasn't it, Yuri? But you've done okay." He nodded and relaxed. He looked at her out of the corner of his eye. Gloria continued, "I'll bet you could slug down a big can of Jolt about now."

"Not today, too strong, keeps me awake too long."

"Aha, you've tried it. Where was that?"

"Symon used to buy it. He liked it because it helped keep us awake when we were delivering cars to Portland and Seattle."

"Portland, Oregon?"

"Da--yes."

"And earlier you testified that when you finished cleaning the apartment the cupboards were bare; the refrigerator was clean, empty, and unplugged? And there was no food or drink in the apartment?"

"Tibbie would not have paid us if there were."

"About Portland, do you still deliver cars up there very often?"

"Yes."

"When was the last time you and Symon both went up?"

Yuri needed to look at his trip logs, which Gloria produced for him, to give the answer. He pinpointed the run that arrived in Portland two months and two weeks before Symon's murder.

Gloria asked, "Why did you stop working together?"

He looked away and shrugged his shoulders. She pressed, but in a very soft voice, "Did Symon get into some kind of trouble?"

The wounded Russian pressed both hands into his crotch and rocked forward. He stared at the judge but said nothing. After a few minutes, Prosecutor Bleasman sat tall in his seat. "I object. Mr. Tsamonicoff has invoked the Fifth Amendment."

Dale was slow on that one, thought Gloria, *he must have been asleep over there. What's with this prosecutor? He ought to stick to managing his office.*

"Sustained," declared the judge.

Yuri cleared his throat and mumbled, "Is okay. Detective ask about Jolt too. Was some kind trouble. I don't know what it was. Maybe he anger my uncle."

Gloria powered her wheelchair toward the defense table. "Glad you're awake, Dale. Your witness, Mr. Prosecutor.

CHAPTER 5

In the lull between the wounded Russian vacating the witness chair and the call for the next witness, Win Griffith came forward and whispered in Gloria's ear. "I've searched from top to bottom. Alya is missing. Security remembers her clearing the entrance checkpoint."

Visibly disturbed, Gloria turned and scanned the visitor's gallery without making eye contact with Art. She thought, *What the hell is going on? My one witness that will win the day disappears. Dale knows damn well what she\s going to say. He wouldn't stoop that low. Or would he?*

Shaking her head the whole time, she scribbled a note to the judge. By the time she finished, her face was red and her eyes narrowed. The judge's face flashed anger as he directed the bailiff to have the jury leave the room.

The door had no sooner shut than Gloria began, "Your Honor, I am at a loss as to the whereabouts of my next witness. My investigator, Win Griffith, let Alya Fuentes off in front of this building and saw her walk toward the entrance some forty-five minutes ago. She was supposed to wait in the basement cafeteria while he parked."

The judge tapped the handle to his gavel on the brass nameplate on his bench that read, "The Honorable Dolph Rogerson." "Mrs. Caulfels, time in my court is not replaceable."

"Your Honor, I apologize. She simply disappeared in the courthouse. In light of the murder of her husband earlier today, I am very much concerned for her safely. Both had been subpoenaed to testify. Their absence does great harm to the defense's ability to present its case. I would like to ask your indulgence to recess while we search the building."

"You are pushing the limits with your request for delay. I am disappointed that you don't have a better handle on the organization of the defense. Very well, I'll give you half an hour. And only half an hour!"

Twenty minutes later, Gloria was watching the time tick away. She mentally went over what tactics she was going to employ if Win couldn't find Alya in the next ten minutes. Art approached her. "Gloria, I've started a story that reads, 'Alya Fuentes, widow of slain Detective Fuentes, missing.' What can I say beyond that? Is there any connection between Prosecutor Bleasman taking lead chair and her disappearance?"

Gloria replied, "I don't know. He's been at his squirrelly worst today. We'll know soon if somebody got to Alya or she simply ran. Win is reviewing the surveillance footage."

"Why did Win let her out before parking the car?"

"She didn't want to walk from the lot because it's sprinkling this afternoon ... Excuse me, I've got a call on my cell."

Art watched Gloria's face transform into a broad smile. She winked at him while giving him a thumbs-up, "You're sure she's in there?" ... "Stay right there, don't let them out of your sight."... "No, don't go in. I want a bailiff to rescue her." She snapped the cell's cover closed. "Win just found Alya Fuentes in one of the holding rooms. She's there with police detectives. I'm going to have their collective asses."

Art held open the door to the judge's chambers to permit Gloria to drive her wheelchair at top speed all the way to his desk. "Judge Rogerson, we found her! In the strongest terms, I object to this gross overreaching by the state. I respectfully seek your intercession to retrieve Alya Fuentes from the clutches of what is obviously an out-of-control police department. She was taken into custody inside the courthouse."

"What the devil for?" asked the judge.

"Homicide swept her up. My best guess is that they are attempting to question her about Tiburon Fuentes's murder. The only reason I found out was that she asked for a lawyer, and the police notified one of my colleagues in the Public Defender's Office. May I question my witness?"

⊶≻═◉ ◉═≺⊷

The tearful Alya Fuentes, who entered chambers on Win Griffith's arm, looked thoroughly frightened. The streaks of mascara down her cheeks took away something from her natural beauty and helped deflect the impression that she was way overdressed for a widow. The only thing about her dress that was appropriate for mourning was the color. The very-high-fashion black sheath was cut low in front, with a finely woven black net that allowed a teasing view of the inner sides of high, firm breasts. Her hair had been blown and teased into a frame of golden perfection around an oval face with a firm chin. Her red lips were full and sensuous.

There were two aspects of Alya that didn't go with the sexy image: she wore a neck brace that reminded Art of the ruffs in classic paintings of long-forgotten European royalty; and under her arm she carried a red inflatable donut-shaped cushion.

As Alya was escorted into the judge's chambers, Art snapped several pictures with his digital camera. Flipping through them and admiring his work, he thought, *If sex sells papers, this ought to sell a truckload.*

Much to his surprise, a few minutes later, Deputy Prosecutor Gates appeared, headed for the same door. Art sidled over, fell in alongside him, and asked, "What's going on?"

Gates pursed his lips before saying, "That damned woman. She could have called the Public Defender's Office and they would have sent her up."

"Are you talking about the narc's widow, Alya Fuentes?"

"No, Gloria Caulfels. She knows more ways to grandstand, but this time it's gonna backfire. That dizzy blonde should have been standing by here in the court when we convened."

"What prompted the police to shortstop her?"

"What, that's not obvious to you? The coldblooded execution of Detective Lieutenant Tiburon Fuentes, an active-duty member of this city's police force."

"How was she involved?"

Gates drew his fingers in front of his neck. "If you first don't succeed, so the saying goes. If they hadn't found Tibbie in time, that beer and oxycodone cocktail she fed him would have been fatal."

Art recalled his interview of Tibbie and all that preceded it. "Wasn't it lucky the process server who delivered the restraining and no-contact orders happened to be a paramedic?"

"Theirs isn't an amicable agreement to disagree."

Gates closed the door to the chambers behind him, leaving Art standing in the hall, looking for a place to sit so he could use his laptop. Minutes later Alya Fuentes came out, escorted by the bailiff and Win Griffith. Art thought, *I wonder if they'll hang an attempted murder charge on her?*

The young reporter chose to remain nearby until the attorneys exited chambers. The two lawyers burst through the door, with Gloria in the lead. Once the door was closed behind him, Gates growled, "Gloria, you've pissed off my boss, and now you've pissed off the judge. You don't score points by saying things like, 'There may be more corruption than two Rambo narcs.'"

Gloria responded, "Don't take it personally, Baylor, I'm not blaming you or Dale—I'm asking you to open your eyes. Act One: Tibbie sets up a mugging, leaving me driving this wheelchair. Act Two: Tibbie gets wasted. Act Three: enroute to court to testify, Alya is shortstopped by his fellow officers."

"Not blaming me? Tell that to the judge. I'm the one he unloaded on." The young prosecutor's Adam's apple bobbled. "The whole department is shook up over Tibbie's murder."

"You saw the woman. Alya Fuentes is near hysteria."

"Counselor, I don 't know how you do it, but you got what you wanted--a delay until tomorrow morning, and no questions about her husband's murder until after she testifies."

Art took a place alongside the deputy prosecutor. "Why the wait?"

Gates made a waving gesture with his arm and pointed at Gloria. "Because she sold the judge on her fantastic theories. She convinced him to let her trot out all her conspiracy arguments and hash those out before any attempt is made to include Alya Fuentes as a person of interest in Tibbie's murder."

"Come off it, Baylor," said Gloria, "Alya had every reason to keep Tibbie alive until she gets her citizenship." She turned to the reporter. "Art, I'm going to need a hand loading the wheelchair into the back of the van. Could you follow me out to the parking lot after adjournment?"

Art thought the request was strange, but agreed. *Great, maybe she has a story for me.*

He returned to his seat moments before the judge gaveled the court into session. Looking down at Alya, who was seated in the first row behind Gloria, the judge said, "Mrs. Fuentes, I'm terribly sorry about your loss today. Your late husband appeared before this court many times. I've been given assurances by both law enforcement and the prosecutor that there will be no repeats of the way you were treated on your way into this court today."

Alya rose to her feet by the time he finished talking. "Thank you, Your Honor, for sending man to bring me here. I afraid."

Now there was a delay while they shackled Peter to return to the jail, but even so, Art had to hustle to pack up his laptop in time to fall in at the rear of the short procession leaving the courtroom for the elevator. Win Griffith took the lead and acted as blocker, making a hole through the media swarm just beyond the courtroom doors. Art closed the distance with Alya, who was just behind Gloria. Gloria aimed her battery-powered wheelchair so as to flatten a TV cameraman against the wall. She caught him off guard, devoting his full attention to getting the curvaceous Alya on tape, and he almost dropped his camera. Next she brushed away a reporter's microphone. "Sorry, no publicity today."

In her wake, the cameraman growled at her retreating backside, "Damn you, you old bitch!"

From the back corner of the elevator, Art watched Gloria back the chair so as to leave just enough space for Alya to stand behind her. The media people crowded and jostled in front, shouting questions, and the small elevator's interior was painted brilliantly with the flashes of the camera lights. In that pause between her backing in and the elevator doors closing, Gloria sang out, "Think about this. My client and Alya Fuentes fled a country where they snatched millions of innocent people off the street. What sort of police department do we have?"

Art thought, *A movie director couldn't have posed them better. This clip, with Gloria's comment and a pale wide-eyed Alya standing behind her, will surely be the teaser for the evening news on all the local TV stations.*

Once outside the courthouse, Art was surprised by the number of people crowded around the large Ford Explorer with tinted windows parked in the closest disabled parking space. Art noted the federal license plates and U.S. Marshal's markings. The first face he recognized was Vera Li's. She was wearing the same outfit she wore the night they met, right down to the rattail file in its usual place. Much to his surprise, she beamed him a smile. As for the others, he recognized two of them as city detectives whose names he hadn't learned. The third, he greeted, "Detective Hackelby, did Gloria ask for the marshal's SUV?"

"No, strictly witness protection. Let's say we're protecting one of our own. After all, Mrs. Fuentes is an officer's widow."

"You wouldn't know that from the way they treated her inside the courthouse."

The detective steepled his hands and stared at Art. "That started out as a miscommunication. I didn't know she was here to testify. She could have told me. Instead she acted real strange. She almost started to run."

"Run? In those stiletto heels? Wearing a neck brace?"

"We'll see if I overreacted. In any event, I'm sure we'll have it all sorted out right after she testifies tomorrow."

Just before Win lifted Gloria into the seat next to Alya's, she said, "Art, would you be a dear and help Vera load my chair?"

Again to Art's surprise, Vera winked at him as she sat herself in the wheelchair. He followed her while she drove it around to the rear doors and backed it until it was almost against the bumper. Before dismounting she said, "Art, seeing you here today is an answered prayer. I thought I'd never have the chance to apologize. Grandmother told me why she was crying that day. She remembered she was looking at Grandpa Joe when the *Playboy* picture was taken. I'm sorry. Nobody ever told me my very straight-laced grandmother used to pose naked."

"Nor me. Apology accepted. I remember how poorly I handled things when my father died, so I understand. It takes time to work through the grieving process." *Damn, so this is why Gloria wanted me,* thought Art. *I don't know if I want to get burned again,* he told himself. "Thank you," he said. "Now take good care of your grandmother."

⋅⊶⋅⊷⋅

The next morning, Prosecutor Bleasman introduced a series of motions before the jury was brought in. Then as Art watched, Bleasman, Gates, and four police officers took broadside after broadside delivered by a very angry Judge Rogerson. Art realized he needed a law degree to understand the technical reasons for the prosecutor's flurry of motions. Bleasman lost on most of them, but he did win an order barring the defense from introducing evidence of the fact that Tibbie had worked Alya over with a cane, because that incident occurred after Peter was arrested. Art thought that was reasonable, and concluded that Gloria's opposition was more to needle the other side than to mount an offensive. By the time the judge had turned back just about every other one of Bleasman's motions, Art concluded that the prosecutor's discomfiture wasn't so much because Gloria was winning as it was because he had irritated the bench.

Every head in the courtroom turned to follow Ayla Fuentes as she came up to the witness stand—except for Bleasman's. Grinding his teeth, he was still glaring at Gloria out of the corner of his eye. Alya wore the neck brace and same black dress she had poured herself into the day before. While being sworn in, she smiled, answering in clear but accented English.

She placed the red donut cushion on the witness chair and grimaced as she eased herself onto it.

Gloria asked her to describe how she came to marry Detective Lieutenant Tiburon Fuentes. Alya replied, "He tell me he is looking for young fertile wife to bear him many sons. I think him a very rich and powerful operative like KGB officer. He very happy when I promise to bear him many sons."

"How old were you when you met the forty-two-year-old detective?"

"Nineteen."

"Why didn't you keep that promise?"

"Impossible, Tibbie had no sperm." Alya shrugged her shoulders and turned her hands over with palms up.

"What was his reaction?"

"He hit me. He swore at me. He call me bad names. Then when I find out Alya wife number four, he cry. He beg forgiveness. I forgive and he buy me many good things, like this dress. Then he keep punching me, so I forgive some more and he take me shopping some more."

"Why didn't you divorce him?"

"If I go back Russia, men just as bad. I want to be citizen of United

States of America." She held her arm out in the direction of Peter, the defendant. "Here, I found a good gentle man. I tell myself I can put up with Tibbie long enough to become citizen, so I compromise."

"What do you mean, 'you compromised'?"

"Internal Affairs man tell me to go back to Russia after he ask me about black eye and bruises. If I go back, I never see Peter again. So we talk to lady. She talk about developing alternatives. I compromise. I agree to spankings by Tibbie whenever he feel I deserve it."

"You agreed to being spanked? Why?"

"If I can't stop him from hitting me, at least he will do it where it doesn't show."

Gloria then proceeded through a series of questions that established that Alya had met Peter Godoniski at an English-as-a-second-language class. She had been intimate with the defendant off and on until he was arrested.

Gloria asked, "If you wanted to be a citizen, why did you have an affair with the defendant?"

"At first, I want to give Tibbie a son, so he will stop hurting me."

"Did you ever conceive?"

"No, when Tibbie found out about Peter... I should have gone back to Russia."

"What was his reaction?"

"Anger. He build spanking bench and strap me on it at his cabin out in woods."

At this point Gloria brought out graphics to show the jury exactly what Alya was talking about. The projection screen filled with the photos of a rather crudely constructed contrivance that looked like a modified sawhorse with shelves extending beyond the legs and straps hanging loose. Art thought, *Oh great, the tabloids will be all over this. This Tibbie was one sick dude.*

Alya had been in nearly constant motion, shifting from one side of the witness chair to the other with pain showing on her face. Now she pushed up with her forearms, arching her back as if bracing herself. As she looked away from the screen, tears streamed down her cheeks. She rose from the witness chair saying, "Please, Mr. Judge, may I stand? My bottom hurts too much." The judge nodded.

Alya grimaced while she shifted weight from one foot to the other. "He give me many, many swats."

Dale was on his feet. "I object, Your Honor. It was agreed that nothing about the spanking would be brought up because it happened after the arrest. That woman is up to her usual tricks to end-run your rulings," he said while pointing at Gloria.

"Please, Mr. Judge, let me give answers standing. I hurt," begged Alya.

"If you are comfortable standing, remain on your feet, Mrs. Fuentes. Counselor, you are overruled. This testimony is not about the spanking. I don't care how many times you've been reelected, Mr. Bleasman, but in this court, you will treat opposing counsel with probity. 'That woman' is an officer of the court. Proceed, Mrs. Caulfels."

"Thank you, Your Honor." Gloria pulled on the lapels of her baggy suit coat and asked, "Mrs. Fuentes, after your husband discovered your affair with Peter for the first time, did he make any threats or place any limitations on you? What were they?"

"While I am tied to that thing, I watch him go into my purse. He take everything: all my identification; my passport, my green card, my checkbook, my cash, and my car keys. He leave me key to our apartment and a single debit card. He tell me I belong to him. He will never let me go. He control everything, who I see, where I go, everything. If I have another affair, he promise he will beat my ass until it bleeds. Those were his words."

"Did you tell the defendant, Peter Godoniski, about all of the incidents, from the spanking bench through the threats?"

"Yes, everything."

"Why did you continue sleeping with Peter?"

"I love good gentle Peter." Alya again pointed toward the defendant and smiled.

Gloria maneuvered her wheelchair back to the defense table where she picked up another sheet of paper. "On the night Symon Dubiniski was murdered, tell the court who you were with and what you did."

Alya remained standing in front of the witness chair. She leaned forward and placed her hands on the railing, "Tibbie call me in late afternoon. He say he working with police from other cities and not to expect him until morning. I call Peter on disposable cell phone. He arrive just after eight. We go to bed. Peter wanted me to leave with him. We talked too long. I thought it was all over when Tibbie parked right next to Peter's Mercedes. I hid Peter in my closet."

Art, like all others in the courtroom, watched Alya stand tall and look at her lover. He thought, *Lady, lady, don't leave us hanging. What happened next?*

The judged asked, "Are you finished, Mrs. Fuentes?"

Alya took a sip of water. "Tibbie was good lover for one time and then Tibbie always pass out. After he started snoring, I guided Peter to patio door. I wish I had left with him."

After Gloria signaled completion and the judge called for a thirty-minute recess, Art mentally reviewed Alya's testimony. *There's no doubt Gloria made some powerful points, but it's no slam dunk. That guard is correct. Bleasman could still win this round.*

◆◆◆

During the recess, Art was surprised to find Alya standing alone, looking out the window at the end of a corridor. He believed this would be his one opportunity to get the rest of the story, so he introduced himself and asked for an interview.

Alya said, "Yes, if you write truth that Peter was with me."

Art said, "I will quote you. Now let me ask some questions that will flesh out your story. How did your husband find out you were with Peter the night of the murder?"

"He found cell phone I used to call Peter. Maybe he remembered Peter's car."

"In the papers you filed to get the restraining order, you swore that your neck was injured at the apartment, yet you escaped from the cabin in the mountains. How did you get there from the apartment?"

"How? Tibbie attacked me when I was in bed asleep. By time I was awake, he handcuffed me and taped my mouth shut. I never see him so drunk and angry. I try to escape. He rip off my teddy. He throw me against wall and hit me in stomach." Alya pointed to the neck brace. "By time Tibbie drive me to cabin, I hurt all over. Doctor say I bruise spinal cord."

"After seeing your visceral reaction to pictures of the spanking bench, I can well understand that you would rather not delve into those details."

Alya said, "I was lucky. I thought he meant to kill me. He left me in cold cellar for three days. Always before, when Tibbie treat me bad, he act shocked afterward, beg forgiveness, and act very tender, what Mrs. Caulfels calls lovey-dovey. This time, he doesn't touch me until we return to apartment. He tell me I am going where it is safe. He say he arrange for someone to fly me out of Truckee airport for Mexico."

"How did you get away and contact Gloria Caulfels?"

Alya inhaled a deep breath, then exhaled. "I mixed three oxycodone pain pills with his beer. He passed out. I took his car and cell phone. I called Mrs. Caulfels. She sent Win Griffith to pick me up."

"And you filed charges against him?"

"Yes, with Win's help. Win has kept me safe."

"Do you have any idea who murdered Tibbie?"

She shrugged her shoulders, "I don't know. That's what I told those detectives yesterday."

⋅►▌◾◉ ◉◾▌◄⋅

After Art thanked Alya for the interview, he returned to a nearly empty courtroom to find the defendant escorted by a guard. Peter smiled at Art, then returned to talking with the guard. "Today my dearest love spoke. I am innocent."

The guard replied, "Look, Godoniski, don't count on it. Prosecutor Bleasman still has his cross. The narc's widow has every reason to lie to bail you out."

Art looked up to see Bleasman take his place at the prosecution table. *There's my story. What a scowl,* Art thought. *From the look on his face, you'd think he was being found guilty. Who is this Godoniski that he warrants this full court press, with the prosecutor taking the lead mid-trial? Tibbie tampered with a witness, and some capo offs him after he screws up?*

On cue from the judge, Prosecutor Bleasman rose from his chair, with the grace of a boa constrictor under the spell of a snake charmer, to take his place in front of Alya. "Mrs. Fuentes, how much did you pay to get posted on the web site to solicit sex?"

Art watched Alya's face grow pale and her eyes widen. Gloria objected but was overruled. *The prosecutor just showed his hole card,* thought Art.

Alya looked at the judge, who said, "Please answer the question."

The blonde witness asked, "What is 'solicit sex'? Are you saying I am whore?"

Now it was the prosecution's turn for show and tell. Gates punched a button on his laptop that brought up the image of a naked teenage Alya, taken from an angle that left nothing to the imagination. Bleasman pressed the button again. "There're more, Mrs. Fuentes. Can you translate the tag line across the bottom?"

She studied the image on the screen. "I am so ashamed. I must tell truth."

"Please, Mrs. Fuentes."

"It says, 'You can't go wrong with Sexy Alya.'

Art thought, *I'd better be careful about making comparisons in ink between young Gloria and her client, or old Red will be off to the races with some side-by-sides. I'll be back to square one with Vera.*

Bleasman held up a folio of computer disks and repeated, "'You can't go wrong with Sexy Alya.' Your Honor, I submit her folio plus instructions and a translation in English."

Alya screamed, "Why you do this, Mr. Prosecutor? I never became prostitute! These pictures were my brothers' idea … to convince Tibbie to marry me."

Gloria stood and waved her yellow legal pad. "Your Honor, I object to this line of questioning. It's character assassination. We'll stipulate that Mrs. Fuentes's brothers subjected her to involuntary sexual trafficking."

Art mused, *That's it, Gloria. You got 'em coming and going.*

The judge ruled in favor of Gloria. Bleasman retreated to the prosecution's table and asked the witness, "When you married Tiburon Fuentes, did you promise to be faithful to him?"

"Yes."

"Later, did you tell him you would stop seeing your lover, Peter Godoniski?"

"Yes."

"And you lied to him both times?"

"Yes, and he lied to me."

"Mrs. Fuentes, what freedom did your late husband allow you?"

"None really."

"Did he monitor the phone bills for your calls?"

"Yes"

"After hearing your words that you fell in love with the defendant, it seems impossible that you ever had the ability to even call Peter Godoniski. Your husband would have discovered the relationship when he saw the bills. Didn't you also lie under oath when you said you spent the night with Peter?"

Alya stood tall by the witness chair. She inhaled deeply, puffing out her ample chest, "No, Mr. Persecutor, more than anything in the world, I want to become citizen of United States of America. If I lie here under oath, I can never be citizen."

"The proper title is Prosecutor. And you feel that they let liars become citizens?"

"If people of this country can reelect man like President Clinton, who tells many big lies, surely there is room for me, who tells little lies to keep my husband from beating me more."

The room burst into laughter. Bleasman turned red and mumbled, "No more questions."

He leaned over with both hands on the defense's tabletop. "Damn you, Gloria Caulfels, you set me up! You fed her that Clinton story to embarrass me."

The judge pounded his gavel. "Mr. Bleasman! Mr. Bleasman, cease this disruption or I will hold you in contempt. And from you, Mrs. Caulfels, not a word." Gloria said nothing, but grinned like a Cheshire cat behind Bleasman's back.

Art thought, *What's going on with this prosecutor? He's playing straight man to Alya. As for Gloria Caulfels, she's acting like a female Perry Mason.*

The rest of the day was filled with expert testimony, beginning with an internist who had a long list of credentials related to spousal abuse. Then Gloria called a professor from Mills College who had a doctorate in twentieth-century Russian and Eastern European history. Art found his testimony educational if you want to learn about corruption, pathos, and uncertainty of life in the crumbled Soviet Empire. Art was intrigued by pictures of unearthed bodies with their hands tied behind their backs with the same quick-binding knot that was used on Symon Dubinski. Other photographs were of the backs of the heads of executed men and women. Each had been shot almost in the same place Symon had been shot.

There was testimony from a pathologist from Northern Illinois who had gained considerable experience in the Gacy murders. Using diagrams, she demonstrated how the strong, thin cord could easily injure the victim, making every move painful; and how the longer the victim was tied, the deeper the cord cut. Using blown-up photographs of the hands and forearms, she showed how she arrived at the conclusion that Symon had been bound for as many as four to six hours before execution. Noting the amount of blood on the back of Symon's trousers, she declared that the rope, fully saturated with blood, was further confirmation of her estimate.

When the prosecutor challenged her estimate, she cited the testimony about the thoroughly saturated gag in the victim's mouth as further confirmation. When Bleasman scoffed at her rebuttal, she suggested that he volunteer to be gagged and they would measure how long it took for the cloth to be saturated. That brought laughter, followed by a sharp reprimand from the judge. Bleasman made a few verbal feints before retreating to his table, ending the cross-examination.

The prosecutor didn't challenge the medic who was first on the scene when he described finding the cords buried in bloodied cuts in Symon's wrists. Nor did he challenge the medic's description of the bloodied pants that were in evidence.

Gloria called the operations manager of the Portland bottling plant that made Jolt. By the time he was done, the sale of the pop can in evidence had been pinpointed to truck stops in the ports along the Columbia River and along Interstate 5. The date of sale was in the same time frame when Symon's trip log showed he had driven a truckload of used luxury cars to Portland for shipment to the Russian Far East. Symon's return to the Bay Area coincided with Peter's visit to him.

Gloria spent a day and a half using two experts from the University of Washington to overcome the strong testimony of the one witness,

Louis Duparre, who placed Peter near the scene of the murder. They testified about the fallibility of eyewitness identifications. Here, however, Art felt that Bleasman scored well. His cross-examination brought out that neither of them had spoken with the witness and they were presenting information based on tests they had performed elsewhere.

Bleasman stopped by the defense table. "Mrs. Caulfels, I'm making one last offer. Involuntary manslaughter, five years."

"Dale, admit you made a mistake. Peter is innocent."

"You'll be lucky if you get a hung jury." Bleasman turned and walked away.

CHAPTER 6

Jostling by members of the press and spectators taking their seats generated a discordant noise as background to the lawyers, who were arguing legal technicalities before the jury was seated for the day. On the level of courtroom drama, it was dry and boring, but to the protagonists in this trial, it was the verbal equivalent of hand-to-hand combat. The prosecution had challenged everything, it seemed. Art had been through these sideshows long enough to understand that Gloria had chosen her battles wisely, aiming penetrating broadsides of legal precedent and dicta that well protected her course of attack. She countered the prosecutor's continual frontal assaults, just giving a little here and there. Although Bleasman gloated with each minor victory, it was plain to Art that he had met his match. His little victories each carried a high price. Everyone in the courtroom, save Dale Bleasman, could see the judge's annoyance with his tactics.

Today's main issue was the admissibility of the testimony of one of Peter's cellmates, Clyde Lacwurth, whom Gloria had called to testify about Peter's unfamiliarity with guns. The prosecutor began, "Your Honor, whatever this convicted felon has to say is hearsay. There were no firearms in the cell."

Gloria pointed at him."Mr. Bleasman, Lacwurth was your own snitch! You are abetting a conspiracy to withhold exculpatory evidence. Your Honor, using this kind of logic, the prosecutor is asking you to set the precedent that *any* conversation with a cellmate is hearsay and inadmissible. I ask you to follow the well-established precedents I have outlined for you and end this stalling."

Bleasman pointed a shaking finger at Gloria. "Your Honor, it should be clear that the defense counsel is using Fabian tactics to mount a rearguard action. She is doing her best to confuse and delay."

Judge Rogerson took off his glasses, rubbed his eyes, and paused a moment with a wry yet slightly amused expression. "'Fabian tactics' by Caulfels? Gads, I haven't heard that classical expression since law school. You have your nerve, sir, after all the time this court has used in your behalf. As for this latest motion, I'm doing you a favor by denying it. I caution you, Mr. Prosecutor, to be careful about what you pray for lest you find it used against you in the next case."

Fifteen minutes later, with the jury present, Clyde Lacwurth was sworn in and answered the preliminary questions. "...And what do you do for a living, sir?" asked Gloria. The jury all took note when he calmly answered, "Professional defendant." At thirty-nine years of age, Lacwurth had been in San Quentin prison for twelve years and was four years short of being eligible for parole. Three weeks after Peter Godoniski's arrest, Lacwurth had shared a cell with him for five days in the Oakland jail, where Lacwurth had been transferred to testify at another trial. He identified Homicide Detective James Hackelby as the individual who told him he was sharing a cell with a professional killer who was awaiting trial. No, he said, neither Hackleby nor any of the other cops made any promises to him. But it was clear when he went into the cell, said Clyde, that he could do himself some good by having good ears and a retentive memory.

Gloria asked, "Mr. Lacwurth, after you gave your testimony in that court case, did you meet again with any law officers or prosecutors?"

Clyde nodded his head toward the other table in front of the bench. "Yeah, Detective Hackelby and the young guy sitting over there... Assistant Prosecutor Baylor Gates."

"And what did you tell them?"

"Told them they had the wrong guy. He ain't no killer."

"And by the wrong guy, you mean the defendant sitting here before you?"

Clyde pointed toward the defendant. "Yes, the Russky, Peter Godoniski."

"What caused you to think that?"

Looking over at Peter, Clyde answered, "He's a pussycat. He's a scared kid who's afraid of his own shadow. Look, I want out bad, and I know how to get people to say things. I asked him about guns. Turns out he ain't touched a gun in his life!"

"What made you believe that?"

"I asked him. He didn't know what a safety is or what to do with it. He didn't know about clips or firing pins. Or the difference between a BB gun and a shooter. He knows now, but only because I taught him."

"And what was the reaction of the police when you told them that?"

"They just laughed and told me they had an airtight case. They said you hear people all the time who say they didn't do the crime. I know that, and usually I just roll my eyes when some con says that. But with this Russky, I knew, I just knew, there was something wrong. Peter's an auto mechanic. He ain't a hit man."

"And what did you do once you were back in San Quentin?"

"I placed a call to your husband because I'm one of the algebra teachers in his math program."

"Did you talk to him?"

Smiling, Clyde answered, "No, I talked to you."

"And what did you tell me?"

"What I just said here."

"Thank you, Mr. Lacwurth. Your witness, Mr. Bleasman."

The prosecutor rose from his seat and scanned his yellow legal pad before ambling over to the witness box. He cleared his throat and smiled at the witness. "Mr. Lacwurth, what is this program that involved you with Dr. Caulfels, a University of California professor?"

"Long before my time, Dr. Caulfels—Joe to us--started coming over and teaching people enough algebra and mathematics that they could teach somebody else. There's some foundation that puts money in to support his work. Thanks to Joe, years ago I had no trouble getting my GED.

"And you are so smart that you can listen to what a man says and know without a doubt that he is or is not experienced with firearms?"

Clyde rubbed his chin, then nodded slightly. "No, I'm not smart, but I ain't so dumb that I'd pull a heist with some scared kid who never laid his hands on a shooter and doesn't want to either. I told both Gates and the detective that I wouldn't want Peter as my backup. He may know cars, but he don't know squat about guns."

Gloria called Winston Griffith. After establishing his bona fides and the fact that he had Alya's written permission to search her apartment, Gloria asked him about the fruits of his search. A throw pillow and bedclothes were introduced, along with lab reports that matched Peter's DNA to the samples. Phone records confirmed that Alya made a call to Peter's workplace on the day of the murder.

On cross, under close questioning from Bleasman, Winston was forced to admit that he didn't know when the sperm samples were deposited. Bleasman rubbed his hands in triumph. *Another small victory for him*, thought Art, *but it's not over till it's over.*

Finally Peter took the stand. His hand trembled as he was sworn in. Gloria began her examination in her gentlest voice, drawing out details about his background. He told of a childhood living in Tver, a city on the main road between St. Petersburg and Moscow. He'd always had a fascination with cars and, by the time he was fifteen, he was working in what would be called a "chop shop" in this country. By the time he was seventeen, he had moved to a shop that took cars stolen from Western Europe and made them roadworthy enough to sell in Russia for a good price.

Like his other friends, Yuri and Symon, he didn't report in when he was supposed to for his duty in the Russian Army. Gloria drew out of him his feelings about war, violence, and guns. Peter had never touched a gun, and he was against all violence. Instead he went to Germany, where he went through a mechanic's course at the Mercedes plant. When he returned to Russia, he worked exclusively on Mercedes. Then about six years ago, he was asked if he would like to come to America and work for the same company. He jumped at the opportunity.

After he had been in the United States two and a half years, he discovered that what was taken for granted as a necessary evil in Russia was a felony here. He found out that if he were caught, he would be deported and would never be able to return. The chance of that happening worried him very much, so he looked around for a way out of the dark side of the car business.

He was surprised at how easy it was to find another job. He started work at a small garage specializing in luxury cars, and soon met Alya in school. He then found a better job at a Mercedes dealer. They quickly promoted him to journeyman status. His bosses were very good to him, but all during this time, he was hounded by his Russian friends to come back to work with them. There were veiled threats, but he ignored them.

Just before Peter took his citizenship test, Symon invited him to his apartment to celebrate Peter's latest promotion. They drank vodka; Symon mixed his with Jolt, and Peter took his straight, then shifted to Sprite. All through the evening Symon urged him to take off early on Friday and drive a car to Tacoma, Washington, where it was to be loaded on a ship for Russia. It was easy money--a thousand dollars for a one-way trip. They would even pay his fare back on Sunday evening on a shuttle flight.

Peter testified that at first he refused, then, to change the subject, told Symon he would think about it. Money or no money, he said, he wanted no part of driving what he suspected was a hot car. Besides, it took no talent to drive a car. It was beneath his position as a mechanic, where he was earning just over thirty-five dollars an hour. Besides, what he was doing was legal.

Late in the evening, Peter testified, Symon again returned to the subject and Peter again said, "No." By then his friend was drunk and tried to wrestle him to the floor, but Peter broke free and punched him in the eye. He left Symon on the floor.

"That was last time I see him alive," Peter testified. "Last words I hear from Symon, he is still begging me to please drive car up north."

"What car were you driving that night?" asked Gloria.

"A cream-colored 1995 Mercedes. Bottom of the line. It survived a freeway crash."

"Is that your own car?"

"No, boss encourages me to drive trade-ins. That way I can spot if anything is wrong and make the car perfect before they put it on the lot."

"Were you driving any white Mercedes in the recent past?"

"Yes, about a week earlier I drove a ninety-two 320 sedan for a couple of days. Also, the day after Symon died, I drove an eighty-four 190 SE."

"Where were you at 11:30 PM on the night Symon was murdered?"

Peter flashed a quick smile. "I was with Alya Fuentes in her bedroom. We were having an affair. I was with her the whole night until maybe two or three in the morning, I think. I am innocent!"

"Did you shoot Symon Dubinski?"

"No, he was my friend! I have never even held a gun in my life. I am innocent!"

"You have never held a gun. Weren't you involved with what we'd call organized crime in Russia?"

Peter shrugged his shoulders. "More like disorganized crime. Everything is crooked in Russia. All I have ever done is fix cars. If car is stolen, I do not ask questions. I only know about wrenches and screwdrivers and sockets. I am a peaceful man."

"Peter, were you ever in the apartment where Symon was murdered?"

"No, I am innocent!"

"Thank you, Peter, I believe you. Your witness, Mr. Bleasman."

Bleasman leaned back in his chair as he began, "If you're such a peaceful man, why did you hit Symon Dubinski so hard his eye was swollen shut the next day?"

"He was drunk and attacked me. I only hit him once. Maybe I hit him too hard, maybe not."

"You just left him on the floor. Is that correct?"

"Yes, I didn't want to fight or argue. I left."

"Did I understand you to say that you drive a different car almost every day?"

"Yes."

The prosecutor pushed his chair back from the table. He studied his yellow legal pad before asking, "Then how do you remember just exactly what car you were driving on any particular day?"

"I can't. They keep a log at the agency. They give me copy. But I remember the little Mercedes because it needed too much work to make it fit to sell. It was a cream car."

"And at night, isn't it reasonable for someone to mistake a cream-colored car for a white car? Perhaps it was a little dirty?"

"A Mercedes white stands out. We don't let cars on the street with a dealer's tag that are dirty," Symon replied.

"But you told the detectives that you were attending a movie, isn't that so?"

"I feared for Alya because Tibbie was very bad. She wouldn't leave him until she became an American citizen. What I say here is true. I did not kill my friend."

"Mr. Godoniski, you failed to answer my question. Yes or no."

"Yes, I lied to protect dear Alya." Peter wiped a tear from his cheek and loudly sniffed.

Bleasman stood up and strode across the court to stop right in front of the witness stand. "But you did lie?" He stood facing the witness in a courtroom so silent you could have heard a rodent scramble across the floor.

Art noticed that the longer the wait, the more the prosecutor's hands shook, while Peter had gained control of his hands. Unfortunately his voice croaked out a reply, "Yes. Now I know I shouldn't have. I didn't know they have security cameras all over."

"And we are to believe that you've spent most of your life working on hot cars and never used a gun?"

"Why should I? I am what you call golden goose. Car is worth far less without my skills."

Bleasman picked up the plastic bag with the Jolt can inside. "We have heard testimony that your fingerprints are on this can." He picked up the bag with the threads of blond hair inside. "Your DNA matches the DNA in these hairs. If you never were in that apartment, how did your fingerprints and hair get into the apartment?"

"I am innocent! I do not know! Why can't you look at the rest of apartment, walls, doors, windows? My fingerprints weren't there. I was never in the apartment! I am innocent!"

Bleasman stood facing the jury while wagging his fingers at the defendant, "Correction, Mr. Godoniski, you are presumed innocent until proved guilty--and you are guilty. That will be all."

Gloria's last witness was the service manager from the Mercedes agency. He sang Peter's praises. He described Peter as a very quiet, even-tempered man who treated customers with deference. He produced a log, with supporting invoices, that identified each car Peter had driven from a month before the murder until his arrest. He confirmed that the cream-colored Mercedes was the same car the police detectives had impounded. He produced a Polaroid photo that was taken by an insurance claims adjuster. The prosecution didn't cross-examine.

At the end of the third day, the jury retired to their hotel without reaching a verdict. Gloria was greeted at the door of her house by her housekeeper Eudora, "Mrs. Caulfels, Vera called me from the court-house saying that Arthur would have dinner with you and Vera."

"Wonderful, let's use the small table in the formal dining room. Set it as you did last night."

After a sumptuous steak dinner, finished off with apple pie, Gloria thought, *This is the third evening in a row that Art has joined us for dinner. I had to get it started. Vera asked him for the next two times. Thank goodness, I can look across the table and see chemistry coming to life between the two of them. Twice this evening, she touched Art's hand to gain his attention. Why, look, the girl is actually flirting with him. For the first time since Vera came to live here, she has come out of her shell. She is taking an interest in a boy. Thank the Lord for answered prayers. Vera came to us full of anger and frustration after that bastard stole her innocence and childhood.*

These happy moments were taking her mind off the waiting. She had to give Bleasman credit. In spite of his outbursts and his open hostility toward her throughout the trial, he had scored points in summation, even though he was relying on confused logic. She regretted identifying the quick-binding knot as a Russian knot because Bleasman picked up on it. In his summation he rhetorically asked, "Who other than a Russian knows how to tie a Russian knot? Peter Godoniski is a Russian."

Then there was the matter of those hairs. She recalled that one of the jurors nodded ever so slightly each time the prosecutor repeated his litany that the defense had made no attempt to give a rational reason why Peter's hair, with the perfect match, was at the murder scene.

Then there was that eyewitness, Duparre, who placed Peter near the scene of the murder. He was convincing enough that she almost believed him herself. Bleasman had used her own expert's testimony on the fallibility of eyewitness accounts to explain away his calling out the wrong color for the Mercedes. Bleasman was at the top of his game when he pointed out that Peter had become Alya's last chance for a ticket to citizenship now that her husband was dead. She should have seen that coming.

Art interrupted her musing. "Gloria, you've been sitting over there quietly staring into the bottom of that coffee cup. It must be hard to endure the waiting after every trial."

"Yes, one of the things in the back of my mind is the many times I've sat here or in some restaurant with Joe. Win or lose, he lifted me up. Oh, how I miss him. If this is my last case, it is ironic that it has so many parallels to my introduction to law--when Joe was railroaded."

"Yes, Grandmother, you brought that up in your summation. I know so little about where and when you grew up. Was that Goodwin, Colorado?" asked Vera.

"Correct, the incident happened the night of my senior prom in May, 1946. I was deeply in love, an ingénue who ignored the depths of prejudice in both my family and the community. My father, in cahoots with Deputy John Diamond, used his power over a corrupt county to railroad Joe into a conviction for rape." Gloria's eyes overflowed with tears and she shook her head. "There's pain in my heart. I can't go on about this. It's way too soon after Joe's passing."

"Oh Grandmother, I didn't mean to hurt you. I'm sorry." Vera reached across the table to hold Gloria's hand.

Gloria thought, *The last thing I need to think about is the summer of forty-six. The risk is too high.*

Art said, "I need to ask this, Gloria… When I was researching the article on your husband's life, I saw a common thread woven through your lives, defense of the helpless. Too few have thanked you for giving your all. What I want to know is, how do you stay so calm with the jury out?"

"Art, you certainly know what to say. Thank you, I've spent my time in the courts keeping judges and prosecutors honest. As for the Godoniski case, I must admit that when it was handed to me, a plea bargain looked like the only course. Pieces of the circumstantial mosaic fit snugly, and my client had a blown alibi. But Peter never wavered from his declaration, 'I am innocent,' and the prosecution is more desperate than ever. Almost too late, Peter opened up about Alya."

"What about the prosecutor?"

"You've seen Dale at his worst. There have only been a handful of people that I've represented where I was so completely convinced of their innocence. Now that it's over, I pray that I gave enough to convince this jury to set him free."

Art said, "I don't know what more you could have done. How did you find out that Detective Fuentes hired Yuri Tsamonicoff to clean the murder scene?"

"Win Griffith convinced Yuri he had been written off, and then Yuri told the whole story about his role. At this juncture, though, I don't know if the jury got their arms around it. As for me, I lay awake last night recalling the tender words, the love of my wonderful husband. I miss him so."

⋆►═◉ ◉═◄⋆

Gloria rode with Vera to the courthouse at the tail end of the morning rush hour. All the way she tried to figure out why the judge had called a meeting in chambers while the jury was still deliberating. Could this be a hung jury? Was there juror misconduct? By the time she wheeled into the elevator, she was thinking of how to break the news to Peter.

In chambers, Gloria saw that Bleasman was there and, to her surprise, Detective James Hackelby. To her greater surprise, he shook her hand warmly. Bleasman shook it too, but his hand was like a dead fish.

She was surprised again when Judge Rogerson shook her hand and asked when she was going to be able to get out of the wheelchair. She replied, "I'll ramp up my physical therapy as soon as the verdict is in. What's the reason for the conference?"

She thought, *What the hell is going on here? Hackelby hates my guts but greets me like I'm family. Dale stands there acting like he was caught with his hand in the cookie jar. Come on, asshole, look me in the eye when we shake hands. Too bad, the best I can hope for is a retrial. I'll plead him murder two and spare us both the indignity of Dale's attacks.*

Judge Rogerson held up a hand and smiled. "Mrs. Caulfels, for once, please humor me. The rules are not being followed, but the spirit and outcome are the same." He nodded at Detective Hackelby, "It's your show, sir."

The detective said, "Let me make this clear. Mrs. Caulfels, you are among my least favorite people. There is no dose of antacid strong enough that any peace officer can take prior to submitting to one of your inquisitions. I decided that you had gone too far when you fired those broadsides about a conspiracy to obstruct justice. And I don't like to be called incompetent."

Gloria drew in a breath. "Wait a minute ..." She thought, *What's going on? Is he after my ass? She looked toward the judge, seeking an answer.*

The judge's voice was calming. "Let him go on, Gloria."

Hackelby continued, "Like you surmised in your summation, when we notified the prosecutor, I was convinced this Peter fellow was one damn fine actor and guilty as sin. But Lacwurth's call surprised me. The closer the case came to trial, the more I was convinced it was too marginal to prosecute. But Mr. Bleasman was intent on going forward. Then you were mugged and Tibbie was murdered. I apologize for shortstopping Mrs. Fuentes. We acted on an anonymous tip that she was about to flee the county."

Gloria nodded. "Thank you, Detective, but I'm still at a loss as to why we're here."

"On the heels of a chewing out by the judge, I had a meeting with Internal Affairs about Detective Fuentes. There was one thing that stuck in my mind about him. He had this fancy cell phone. It's one of these high-tech digital jobs that encode your voice. I thought it was one of the toys that come with working on a drug task force. It wasn't. We got the records of his calls on that phone. Along with some papers we found in his office, we've been able to confirm some of the information from Art Williams's article, where he reported what Alya Fuentes said. Now we believe that if she hadn't escaped when she did, she'd be dead today."

"What information?" Gloria asked while studying the judge's face. The judge's sole response was to extend an open hand toward the detective.

Hackelby continued, "Williams filed a story about somebody flying Alya to Mexico. Well, we found out from the phone records that calls were placed from within the bounds of the Truckee airport to Tibbie's cell. We concluded these calls were from a private jet just after it landed at Truckee. The pilot left messages: he wanted to know where Tibbie and his package were. The time of the last call coincided with Tibbie and the pilot re-filing his flight plan to fly directly to Mexico City."

Gloria was puzzled. "You're losing me. So they flew back to Mexico City."

"The original flight plan was to Cabo San Lucas, at the tip of Baja California. This would take them out over the Pacific about three hundred miles. The plane is on the DEA watch list because it is owned by members of Los Zetas, one of the Mexican drug cartels By the way, I have something more for your client's case."

Hackelby took a gulp from his coffee cup. "Tibbie passed a tip to the DEA in Washington and Oregon to be on the lookout for a blue Ford Explorer on the weekend that Peter was supposed to be driving the car to Tacoma. The Ford was hot and had about two kilos of Mexican heroin stashed inside the door panels. That car was exported from Tacoma after being delivered for shipment from an eighteen-wheeler. Thanks to our friends in the DEA, Russian authorities found the heroin when it was offloaded at Vladivostok. Tibbie's involvement at the murder scene made me awfully uneasy. Coupled with this earlier attempt to frame his romantic rival, I felt compelled to bring this to the attention of both the prosecutor and the court."

Gloria pointed at the prosecutor. "Did you give this information to Mr. Bleasman before talking to the judge?"

Bleasman snapped, "Just a damn minute, you old bitch! Hell no, he didn't!"

Gloria smiled and slowly waved her index finger. "Probity, please, Mr. Bleasman, probity. Try to control your emotions. We all know what you want him to say, but I want to hear him say it."

Hackelby shook his head. "I kept hoping there would be a decision. The jury won't budge. Yesterday afternoon, I asked the judge to be present at this meeting. I'm convinced Peter Godoniski didn't shoot Symon Dubinski."

Gloria watched Bleasman's face get so red that it looked like his necktie was choking him. The prosecutor growled, "Detective Hackelby, you've done the unpardonable. Come to me, not the judge."

"I believe I did come to you while Mrs. Caulfels was recuperating, sir. I have egg all over my face too," said the detective. "At first the evidence fit together too neatly. Had they not iced Tibbie, we wouldn't have had access to his cell and paper records. This accelerated our determination that he was a dirty cop. The frame he almost pulled off on Dubinski makes us all look bad. Mrs. Caulfels, you are one hell of a lawyer. Please apologize to your client. I'm truly sorry we put him through this hell."

"Thank you, Detective," said Gloria. "Dale do you have a request for a motion to dismiss? Judge …?"

Judge Rogerson cleared his throat and handed a folder to the prosecutor. "We still have two holdouts for conviction. With the information you just heard, plus the contents of this folder, it is clear that there are solid grounds for a mistrial and dismissal with prejudice. Internal Affairs delivered this folder to me, which was found in Fuentes' safe. It contains an inch-thick stack of invoices for large quantities of chemicals commonly used to manufacture amphetamines. The individual authorizing the sales was the sole witness who identified Peter-Louis Duparre. Duparre, has admitted to investigators from the Oakland PD that Lt. Fuentes intimidated him into perjuring himself. Mr. Bleasman, I would look favorably on a motion by the prosecution to dismiss."

Bleasman wrung his hands and looked down at the floor until the judge cleared his throat again. He replied in a small voice, "Yes, Your Honor. I'll do it."

CHAPTER 7

Art Williams looked over Red Magen's shoulder at the *San Francisco Chronicle*'s front-page picture. In the center was a broadly smiling Peter Godoniski on bended knee. He held the hand of a radiant and beautiful Alya Fuentes below the bold headline, FOUND INNOCENT, ASKS TO MARRY NARC'S WIDOW. What caught the reporter's attention wasn't the couple. Nor was it Gloria looking grandmotherly in her wheelchair or the fact that she was clearly brushing away a tear as she looked at the couple. It was the picture of himself in the background holding his open laptop at an awkward angle and obviously staring at Vera Li.

Red tapped the paper and chuckled, "Art, you look like a deer caught in the headlights. How did you get something going with the old witch's niece?"

"For starters, I've never called Gloria a witch or a bitch," Art retorted scornfully. "Unlike *some* people, I feel she deserves a lot of respect. If you can see through the grandstanding, you can see she's usually on the right side of the law."

He continued, "Vera has been in and out of the courthouse chauffeuring her grandmother, and Gloria introduced us when she was in the hospital. Of late, I've been having lunch with them. Either Gloria or Vera has asked me to dinner at their house every evening since the day the jury started deliberating. I've never met anyone like Vera. I thought at first she was very religious because her parents are missionaries. She is quiet and reserved, a good listener. Like her grandmother, she is very sharp."

"And loaded with those Playmate of the Month genes," said Red.

"Well, yes, as a matter of fact, she is quite pretty."

Art thought, *This is crazy. There is far more to Vera than just looks.*

Here I am, whenever we're together, feeling like I've known her for years. Yet we've never yet been out on a date together.

"So she's got you hooked already," said his boss with another low chuckle. Red took a cigar out of its humidor and passed it under his nose while inhaling. He cut off the tip and placed the cigar atop his ear.

"Let's say … she's turned my head. Frankly, Red, I don't know. There is something mysterious about her."

Red held the stogie up. "In moments like these, I fall back on Kipling's wisdom: 'A woman is only a woman, but a good cigar is a smoke.'"

"You can't smoke that thing here in the office."

"Regrettably, I know. First we lost the ambience of the old fashioned typesetter, the Linotype, and now progress takes away the sweet aroma of well-cured tobacco. Tell me, Art, about that palace Gloria lives in, up at the top of the hills behind Berkeley. What's it like inside?"

"It's actually pretty old, built back in the fifties, but it has a spectacular view and big rooms. Gloria has a gym with all sorts of equipment and an elaborate gun range in the basement. Vera practices some kind of martial arts."

"A gun range! No wonder she popped those three yahoos," Red marveled. "It must have taken quite a piece of change to buy and build those digs, even back in the fifties."

"Gloria told me they built there because it was windy and cool. Her husband had a heat stroke in prison and almost died. That's why they came to California."

"Interesting."

Art said, "Until the night before the judge declared the mistrial, I thought Gloria Caulfels had ice water in her veins. She took the pressure of this trial on the heels of her husband's death without an outward sign of emotion or any loss of focus. Inside, it's another matter. It wasn't until Peter proposed to Alya that she let her emotions show. Over dinner last night, just about all she did was reminisce about her husband, Joe. After dessert, she read us some of the letters he wrote her when he was in prison back in 1947. When I left, she was still weeping and staring off into space. I wouldn't be surprised if she retires now."

"Retires? That old barracuda will be taking bites out of prosecutors' backsides and finding ways to get criminals back on the street until she can't draw a breath. Oh, by the way, Art, the *Chronicle* may have the photographer, but we have the reporter. You did one hell of a job on this trial. That was a prize-winning close when you quoted Peter, 'Yes, this is America. I am innocent! I am free!'"

"Thanks, boss." Art thought, *Everybody is missing one critical element: she's working her way through the grieving process. As I think back on last night, I see Gloria as a woman with a long way to go.*

Red held up a typed sheet. "I have approval from the publisher to spend some dollars on travel to do a feature on the Caulfels family. Joe's death and Gloria's victory have made this very timely. I can pull you off the crime beat if you'd like to do it."

Art blinked his eyes and drew in a breath. "Why, of course." He thought, *Grab the ring. This is the kind of opportunity that doesn't come around every day.*

"Good, Art Williams, good. You've more than earned it. If you're thinking of getting serious, this will be a good chance to find out if you can live with the skeletons in their closets."

Art looked at him sideways. *What skeletons?* "What should I be looking for?" he replied.

Red handed him a note. "On second thought, Art …," he hesitated. "Since you've developed a relationship with the granddaughter, I'm not sure you're the one to do this. What do you say?"

"I've yet to take her out on a date. I'm sure I can handle it."

Art sensed his boss relaxing as he handed him a sheet from a phone message pad. "Good. You've caught the attention of the man upstairs, and he wants to see how you do on the investigative side. Here, take this phone number. This is the number for a Daphne Kazor up in Napa County."

"Kazor. What kind of a name is Kazor?"

"Eastern European, I think. Some time ago, she came to me saying Dale Bleasman gave her my name."

Dale Bleasman? thought Art. *After the way he carried on during the Godoniski trial, is he asking the newspaper to go after Gloria?* "What's this Daphne's connection to Joe and Gloria?"

"Oh, I wouldn't want to interfere in your quest by telling you what you're going to find out. I'll only say this: she said she was born in

Goodwin, Colorado, which was Gloria's home town, and her father was a deputy sheriff named John Diamond.

"Diamond … That rings a bell. Come on, Red, have you ever met her?" asked Art.

"I met her a couple of times about three or four years ago when the teacher's union was raising hell about salaries. Fat and in her fifties, bitter, divorced, and a very militant member of the California Education Association. The boss thinks she can give you some good background information."

⋯⫸▣ ◉▣◁⋯

What a dump, thought Art as he stepped into the small, crowded living room of Daphne Kazor's old stucco house. At first he could see almost nothing because the dark wood paneling of the room plunged it into deep shadows. *I heard her say "Come in." There's nobody here. Where is she?*

The drawn shades, almost gossamer-thin from age and wear, admitted only little diamonds of the bright California sunshine, slicing abstract patterns out of the shadows onto the wall and floors. Art's eyes adjusted sufficiently to find an overstuffed chair. He called out, "Mrs. Kazor, where are you?"

'Make yourself comfortable in the easy chair. I'll be right in with coffee and some snacks."

As he sought a comfortable place to sit, all he found were springs which had long ago surrendered their last bit of fight to the weighty bodies that had lounged on them. Beyond the kitchen door, he heard heavy footfalls and the creaking of the floor amid the rattle of dishes.

Daphne Kazor came from the kitchen with a tray. She was a middle-aged woman just under five foot five, but with over two hundred fifty pounds spread over a big-boned frame. She offered her guest a cup of coffee from the tray and rotated it to offer slices of donut from a plate on the other end. Art took the cup, refusing cream, sugar, and a slice. She put the tray down on the end table next to her chair and popped two slices into her mouth. Daphne poured rich cream into her coffee from a small ornate pitcher, followed by two large scoops of sugar. "When I was a girl, Mother always used real cream, not some ersatz dry creamer. It's refreshing to know, people are finally coming back to the good old-fashioned ways with their lattes. Are you sure you don't want a donut? It's a long way to dinnertime."

"I'm not hungry, thank you, Mrs. Kazor. The reason I drove all the way out here is that my editor told me that I should query you about the Caulfels family and their Colorado roots."

The fat woman pressed her fingers against her lips while she munched her way through the donut and swallowed it before beginning. "When I read in the paper how that woman got away with killing that man and even wounding a law officer, I just knew I had to speak up. She has gone through her life getting away with murder."

"Mrs. Kazor, I covered that incident. Those men attacked Mrs. Caulfels, and there is no doubt in my mind that she acted in self-defense."

"Well, it wasn't that way with my father. She singlehandedly destroyed my parents' marriage. I was just a little girl and I didn't understand what was going on." She paused; her chin quivered, and a tear swelled in the corner of her eye. "I remember it just like it happened yesterday. On the Sunday just before Labor Day, 1946, Gloria came to our church and told Mother right in front of everyone that she had slept with my father. I didn't understand what she was talking about. Mother was devastated. She had a terrible fight with Daddy when he came home at the end of his shift. She told him to get out of the house. Even while he lifted me up and told me that I was his special girl and that he loved me very much, Mother kept screaming at him. My sister and I thought we had done something wrong."

Daphne dabbed at her eye before continuing, "That was the last time I saw my Daddy. He told me he was going away for a while, but he would be back. I felt scared, but I couldn't understand why."

"Are you saying your father was murdered by Gloria?"

"Yes! He went out on his shift on Thursday evening, and nobody ever saw him alive again. It was the next day, early Friday morning, I heard Daddy's car in the alley. It had a bad muffler and made a whole lot of noise"

"Daphne, what year was this?"

"I just told you--nineteen-hundred and forty-six! You're like all the others. You don't care."

This woman is a piece of work, a regular bitch, thought Art. "I'm sorry, I just want to get it right."

"Then listen! Like I said, I heard the car in the alley. This was strange because ordinarily Daddy parked right in front of the house. I heard the engine idling and the door slam. I was so excited, I got out of bed and ran to the window. I saw Gloria drive away in the patrol car. She was wearing my father's trooper hat. I saw her!"

"Did you tell anyone?"

"My mother, but not right away. I was afraid to say anything because she told me she didn't want his name spoken around the house again."

"When did you tell her?"

"Later that day, after I found the money wrapped up in the paper on the floor in our garage. There was blood on it."

Blood, indeed, how melodramatic, he thought before he asked, "What was her reaction?"

"All Mother did was cry and hold the money against her chest. She thought he'd run away with Gloria. It was only after they found my father's body that she started to take me seriously."

"When was that?"

"Just before Thanksgiving of the next year. They found poor Daddy buried in cement out on a ranch outside Goodwin. It was premeditated murder."

Art thought, *Oh great, now I'm supposed to believe some high school girl plans and executes the perfect crime.*

"She ambushed him, and she also murdered poor old Mae Blackmon and her baby!" Daphne said.

"Who was Mae Blackmon?"

"A dirty old whore, who owned the ranch. Both bodies were found in Mae's cabin. They killed her off so she couldn't talk."

Why would the killer go to all the effort to entomb Diamond in cement, Art mused, *and leave the woman and her baby's bodies to be found?* Out loud he asked, "You say 'they,' who are 'they'?"

"You're not fooling me. I hear it in your voice. You think I'm making all this up. Listen, there were many people who wanted to get my father. He had the goods on Gloria's father and that old sheriff."

Daphne opened a worn accordion folder. She carefully pulled out tri-folded pieces of paper as she continued, "Look, I still have the subpoenas they issued. If he had testified, it would have been the end for her father. Gloria and her friends were in cahoots with Ray Tudbury, the sleazy Communist lawyer that won the election for county prosecutor."

Art took time to peruse each subpoena. He tried to concentrate on the documents, but he wasn't familiar with the names, places, or issues. He thought, *This simply doesn't make sense. I don't see any connection to Gloria.* He made notes while Daphne watched. He thanked her and handed the subpoenas back.

"Mr. Williams, I've gone to newspapers. I've written the FBI. They thought they could shut me up by getting my ex-husband and me fired from our jobs, but I'm still here. I know she was involved! It's been too long a time for my father's killer not to have been brought to justice. Please help me."

"I need to know more. What specific reason did she have for killing your father?"

"Revenge for getting her boyfriend, Joe Caulfels, thrown in prison. Protecting the Knight family fortune. Look, everybody in town knew she was a slut. Daddy found them out drinking and screwing. There's real evidence! I know she was the one! "

Drinking? Not likely. Gloria describes herself as a life-long dry, he thought before saying, "Mrs. Kazor, what is this real evidence?"

Daphne twisted a tissue into a rope, then took a deep breath, "I went back to Colorado in 1979, just after the old Democrat sheriff left office, and talked to the new man. When he found out I was the daughter of a murdered law officer, he listened. He put me in the hands of his chief detective, who reviewed all the evidence with me. It was right there in the notes of the old sheriff, Larry Shyflinski. There were a number of long dark hairs found in the cement and the dirt that was piled into the big tank they buried him in. The old sheriff suspected her, but he didn't do anything. He could have demanded that she give them samples."

"How did the sheriff find hairs in the cement?"

"It was all crumbled. I saw it. They obviously didn't know much about mixing cement, or Daddy would have stayed buried. There was a layer of dirt in the middle that had some blood in it. My father's blood! One of the hairs was found in the dirt. Even if my father did all the things some people say he did, he didn't deserve to die like that."

"Did the new sheriff do anything?" Art asked. He watched her open her mouth wide and pop in a mouthful of donut slices. While she was chewing and swallowing, he thought, *This woman has a real fixation on Gloria. Surely in all this time somebody could have gotten one of Gloria's hairs.*

Daphne said, "I know he made an effort because he told me that if ever she sets foot in Colorado, he'll have her in for questioning. There isn't enough to convince California to extradite her. She used her father's money to ruin my life."

"Ruin your life? What did she do?"

"After her mother died, they set up a fancy foundation. The Knights owned everything--the bank, the TV station, oil wells, commercial real estate, farmland--you name it, it was theirs. Obviously with that kind of riches, the IRS should have gotten some, but they didn't get a nickel! They put it all into this fancy trust. Andrew Foyle runs the damned thing and draws down a six-figure salary. He was a high school friend of Gloria's and was another suspect in Daddy's murder. Well, the first thing they did was create a private school system for Goodwin County that nobody had to pay to go to. Then they hired all the public school teachers to staff it—except eight. My ex and I were public school teachers. We were among the eight who didn't get hired. That was their plan to make us leave! I was so mad! They did it because I wouldn't give up."

Daphne devoured half a donut in two bites and washed it down with more coffee. Art thought, *Wow, what an appetite. I've downed enough gallons of lemonade at the Caulfels' to know drinking is not among Gloria's vices. But could she be a reformed drunk?*

Daphne sat her man-sized coffee cup down and wiped the corners of mouth with her sleeves. "I followed her out here to California in seventy-three. I know exactly where she lives, in that big fancy house on top of the hills behind Berkeley. I've kept a scrapbook of all the newspaper articles. She is thoroughly rotten, evil! She gets brutal murderers and drug dealers off so they can go back and prey on decent people. I've talked to the law officers and prosecutors. They hate her guts!"

"Mrs. Kazor, you've described a side of Mrs. Caulfels of which I wasn't aware. Oh, I'm certainly aware of how the local cops feel about her, but this is entirely new. I'll be going on assignment to Goodwin in the near future. I'll take the notes from our meeting today and use them as background. If I unearth anything, I'll let you know."

Some hours later, as Art walked past Red's office, Red asked him how the meeting with Daphne went. Art replied, "The woman is a nut case. Going up to Napa was a waste of time, except for the bottle of wine I bought on the way back."

Red nodded in agreement, "Well, you're probably right, but it's the kind of lead-in that sells papers."

Or gets you sued for libel, thought Art.

Art studied the hills covered with scrub pine and juniper as the commuter plane made its descent to land at the Goodwin airport. He thought, *I envisioned Goodwin to be more like back home in eastern Oregon. Why, look, almost every piece of land that's not nearly a vertical hillside is developed. The acreage under the approach to the airport is filled with light industrial tilt-up buildings. Look at their traffic-clogged roads. It reminds me more of the Bay Area than eastern Oregon.*

He easily found the sheriff's office in a new brick and glass building along the side of a lush park where huge cottonwood trees raised leafy umbrellas. On the far side of the park was the county courthouse, built of weathered granite with huge columns flanking the entrance.

Art was guided through a door with a keypad security lock to a Spartan office whose walls were decorated with autographed pictures of the uniformed sheriff in the company of, or shaking hands with, men and women Art didn't know, except for one. That was President Ronald Reagan.

The tall sheriff, Philip Sydney, rose and took Art's hand with a firm grip. He looked the part of a western law officer. Dressed in tan gabardine shirt and trousers, both with sharply pressed creases, he carried his revolver in a black leather holster attached to a polished black utility belt. After exchanging greetings, he motioned Art to a solid tan leather chair.

The loquacious law officer told Art far more about his background than the reporter expected. The sheriff disclosed that he had been a trooper for the State Patrol and was elected when the last sheriff retired. "I chose to run because my children became eligible for Knight Foundation Schools. There are no better schools anywhere. Where else could all your children go to college on a full ride scholarship? It's a fantastic system, something they ought to adopt all across the county. The teachers are the absolute best."

Art was taken aback; this didn't jibe with what he'd been hearing. "You paint a far different picture from what Mrs. Kazor told me. I take it your children didn't go to public school." Again and again over the next few days, he heard other Goodwinites say pretty much the same thing about the Knight schools and how their kids had benefited.

The sheriff confirmed what Art surmised. "No, the kids have to go to the Caulfels School to qualify for the scholarships. The only ones who send their kids to the public schools are the people who won't give the full one percent of their income to the foundation. It's an okay system. It works for us. But I don't think you came all this way to hear about the Knight Foundation. So you, too, have met the persistent Daphne Kazor?"

"Yes, and I got an earful of her charges because my editor told me to look into them. He wants me to put together an in-depth story about Joe Caulfels and his family. I'm far more interested, though, in how the schools and scholarships work. I have an appointment with Andrew Foyle of the Foundation."

"If anybody can tell you about the Caulfels and the Knights, it's Mr. Foyle. The truth of the matter is that without his genius, the windfall given this community by the Knight family would not have made the tremendous impact on Goodwin that it has."

"How are Joe and Gloria regarded here?"

"There's hardly a family with children in this county that doesn't revere the man. His ideas about education have made their children successful. I'd say this whole community grieves his loss. As to his wife, I doubt there's more than a handful of people alive outside of law enforcement who know she exists. After all, she left here in 1946 and never came back. Maybe more people ought to know about her. After all, had she not been such a black sheep, her father wouldn't have dis-inherited her and set up the Knight Foundation to begin with."

"Why call Gloria a black sheep?"

"I wasn't even born back then, but I've dug through it all: from when she ran away to Denver with a soldier during the war, on through the whole sordid mess after she left."

"What prompted you to dig through it all?"

"I took office with a cloud of scandal hanging in the background from the cold case of Deputy John Diamond, Mrs. Kazor's father, who was murdered on the job and sealed in a tank full of cement. Gloria's father's bank was robbed of an unheard-of sum for the time, and the robbers were never caught. I'm sure it was an inside job."

"What causes you to come to that conclusion?" asked Art.

"It was the perfect bank robbery, down to using aircraft to get away. Gloria refused to cooperate in the investigation. She hid behind a Mafia-grade mouthpiece of a lawyer. And she's used all the resources she could to block any investigation ever since."

Art thought, *Boy, there's a lot of meat on the Caulfels history, but all I've heard him talk about is supposition. Who can I ask to get some hard details?* Art asked, "Who was in position to block for her?"

"The county prosecutor, Ray Tudbury, was in that position for a long time. Gloria worked her buns off to get him elected prosecutor. He didn't do squat and kept sitting on the case until the trail went cold. Tudbury was a very ambitious liberal Democrat who went on to enjoy a long career in Congress."

"Wasn't this Deputy Diamond the one who raped Gloria?"

"Never charged or convicted. She moved up her departure day to noon of the day after the deputy was last seen alive. She never came back to Goodwin. In fact, she's taken great pains to avoid setting foot in Colorado. For example, she has traveled all over by plane; but she always avoids using flights that pass through Denver. I've heard all about her from my friends in law enforcement in California."

"How did you learn about her avoiding Colorado?"

"It was before my time. Back in the fifties, the Sheriff's Department knew she flew back to New York for modeling jobs. They watched for her at Stapleton Field, but never once did she land in Denver. That takes some doing since Denver is an air hub for the whole Southwest. She's nobody's fool. They tell me she is one of the most vicious and unscrupulous criminal law attorneys in California."

Being a competent defense counsel shouldn't be reason to be a murder suspect, Art mused. He said, "I know nothing of her past here in Colorado. I just finished covering a trial where she thwarted an attempt to frame an innocent man. She is a very skilled trial lawyer."

"Innocent, eh? Well, just about all of them that get to trial are guilty of something, I guess. While I was running for office, I promised Daphne Kazor I would reopen her father's murder from back in 1946. That was 1981. It was a mistake. I opened Pandora's box. I don't know who wasted Diamond. There were more people in this county who had motive than who didn't."

"How's that?"

"Goodwin County was rotten from the top to the bottom, and John Diamond was in the thick of it. You could say he was the axle around which all the wheels of corruption, brutality, and predation turned. After he disappeared, the feds nailed a whole bunch of little fish, including the prosecutor and the sheriff, for tax evasion, but without him to spill what he knew, the big fish got away. My phone was ringing off the hook about raising skeletons from forgotten closets."

Art thought, *This guy sounds like the sheriff back in Oregon when I started asking questions around town.* He asked, "What sort of skeletons?"

"This county could have been sued into insolvency for the abuses that went on in the jail. John Diamond was in the middle of it. He was a bagman for the sheriff. The worst of it was, he was a sadist who meted out private punishments to mostly teenage girls instead of a year in Juvie. He was in cahoots with the old town doctor, who should have been charged with child rape. But by 1981, when Sheriff Shyflinski retired, these were middle-aged women who didn't want the past dredged up. There is a presumption by some that if you lived here in 1946, you were in on it."

"Hmm. So I guess the prime suspects for Diamond's murder would be not only victims looking for revenge, but also fellow perverts who were afraid he'd rat on them?"

"Absolutely. Talk about victims, the county was run by corrupt Republicans, and Democratic candidates mysteriously kept failing to survive until election day. Their relatives had plenty of motive. Add to that list the potential helpers and facilitators of this cabal that Diamond could have exposed, which would include especially Gloria's father. The list gets mind boggling. Unless there is a deathbed confession, no one will ever know for sure who murdered Diamond and who cheered them on."

"Democratic candidates? Gloria is a Democrat." Art regretted saying that because it sent the sheriff off on a tangent, telling more about the sordid political history of Goodwin County. That had been ended, said the sheriff, by the 1946 elections when the people fired both the incumbent sheriff and the prosecutor. When he stopped for breath, Art quickly shifted the conversation back to Diamond's unsolved murder by asking about the long dark hairs found at the murder scene.

The sheriff offered to let him read a copy of the dog-eared forensic report and excused himself. Art opened to a state crime lab's sketch of the trajectory of the bullets, which put the shooter less than two yards in front of Diamond and down low. Art recalled watching Gloria practice on her indoor shooting range with its moving targets. The easy way she handled her Glock and the self-confidence she showed around the range gave him pause when he thought about her using a weapon to kill. He studied the medical examiner's sketch of the wounds and concluded that she could have easily planted four rounds into the body of a handcuffed deputy.

It wasn't until he read the section on "The Gunk Tank" and the evidence that Diamond had been shot outside the tank and his body dumped in the tank that Art dismissed Gloria as a suspect. The difference in weight between Diamond's 280 pounds and Gloria's 100 pounds was too great. He spent the rest of the afternoon working his way into a long list of names of "persons of interest" who were interviewed, and the write-ups of what they said. It looked as if Diamond's daughter might well be sincere in her belief, but there was no credible evidence to back her up. Nor did it help to add in the unsolved murders of Mae Blackmon and her baby son on the same day. *Yet*, he asked himself, *why would a little girl lie?*

He failed to place Gloria in the cast of characters who had reasons to even the score with Deputy Diamond. His search included a group of people with Spanish surnames whose daughters had been abused, Gloria's banker father, and a bevy of elected officials and businessmen who had ample motive but no opportunity.

At day's end Art returned the Diamond file to the sheriff. "I find this unbelievable, that a law enforcement officer could be so completely corrupted. I didn't ever think that things like this could go on in the United States."

"This was a small, isolated mountain town," answered the sheriff, "and the people in power did what they wanted. Look, I hope you downplay this whole subject. They're all dead and buried now. Every time somebody dredges up the past, we have to go through the process all over again of living it down. Goodwin has a booming economy with too many people wanting to live here. We don't need any more tourists coming to town to relive the past."

"I came to do a positive story," said Art. "I looked into Daphne Kazor's accusations because my editor asked me to. I've come to know and yes, respect Mrs. Caulfels while covering the crime beat. She is a skilled marksman today, but was she as a high school girl? She certainly had the motive, but I don't see any evidence in your file to place her at the scene when Diamond was shot. I'll continue to inquire, but my main mission is to focus on the positive aspects of Joe and Gloria's lifework."

"Okay," drawled the sheriff. "When you asked for that file, I was worried we were about to get another dose of negative notoriety, like when CBS devoted a two-hour slot to Goodwin County. I run a clean operation. We treat people fairly and humanely, even when they are the scum of the earth."

"Thank you, Sheriff, for the time you've spent with me and especially your forthright opinions. By the way, you mentioned a Prosecutor Tudbury who became a Congressman. After he retired from Congress, did he return to Goodwin?

"Yes."

"Good, he's high on my list of people to see."

Returning to the motel, Art called Vera. He gave her a five-minute description of Goodwin County and his impression of the sheriff, concluding with his opinion of the unsolved murder of Deputy John Diamond. Her news was about her concern that her grandmother was falling into depression. Vera said she would keep quiet about John Diamond because Grandmother Gloria had taken her aside and asked her not to ask about Goodwin County. It was a painful chapter in her life, she said, and she didn't like to talk about it.

89

CHAPTER 8

Art Williams sat at a table near a large window in the nearly empty restaurant of the Valley View Best Western Motel. He checked his cassette recorder twice, and again counted the number of tiny empty cassettes in his pocket. He was nervous. This was his first interview of a Congressman. He reviewed the notes and questions he planned to ask. He was still digesting the interview he had with the sheriff as well as Vera's reaction when he told her about his search through the file on Diamond's death. The top question on his list was: How did the murdered deputy find his way into that gunk tank?

He wondered, *Was Vera's concern about upsetting Gloria more of the same emotion that precipitated the blowout over the* Playboy *photo? Or were there other reasons why Gloria wouldn't discuss anything about John Diamond?*

He looked out through the huge glass windows of the motel. Immediately below him was a swimming pool supplied by a hot spring, with wisps of steam rising above the warm greenish waters. A few heads were bobbing about, but no one was on his side of the pool. Beyond and below lay the shapes of the buildings melting into the shadows of dusk. Lights were coming on like diamonds falling onto dark blue velvet. Art was taken by the beautiful vista as he contrasted the urbanized valley with the raw beauty of the late afternoon sky. The sun painted light pink hues on the very tops of tall clouds hiding the distant white peaks beneath their dark underbellies.

A strong male voice startled him. "Every time I look out at this spectacular country, I thank God I'm still alive and here to enjoy it. What a sight to behold! You're that reporter fella Williams from California, aren't you?"

Art turned to face an old man, lean and wrinkled, wearing a freshly pressed tan gabardine suit. His shoulders were squared but beginning to stoop. His dark eyes were full of life. Art took the extended hand and felt a firm grip as he replied, "Yes sir, I'm Art Williams from the *Oakland Tribune*."

"I'm Ray Tudbury. I used to be a Congressman, but gave that up. They wanted me back in Washington too damned much. It interfered with my fly-fishing. Andrew Foyle asked me to come on over and meet you. I understand you're here to write about the Caulfels family and the Knight Foundation."

"Yes, sir, I'm writing a feature on Joe and Gloria, with an emphasis on Joe. How long have you known them?"

"I knew you'd ask that. I'll never forget that night. What happened set the course for my life and for this county. I was escorting an old flame to the graduation ball. We were chaperones. It was at the end of May, 1946. Joe and Gloria stepped out of his dad's old Cadillac roadster. He was handsome and she was a feast for the eyes, a real hot number. The way that girl moved sent the message to him and everybody in the room that she was in heat. Later we saw them sneak out of the dance early. Her father came to the hall and made a terrible scene. The next day I read in the paper that the boy had been arrested for rape. It didn't sound right. She was putting the moves on him."

Art asked, "What did you do about it?"

Holding his open hands upward, Tudbury shrugged his shoulders. "Nothing. Not when I should have done something, anyway. I was intent on running for prosecutor, and I didn't have the time or resources to win in court and win the election. Joe languished a long time in that jail, in abusive conditions, because not I nor any other local lawyer stepped up to defend him. He could have died there. No thanks to any of us except Gloria, he survived. He barely survived his time in Canon City too. It was a terrible injustice that was done him, and it weighed on not just my conscience, but this whole county. Gloria told all who would listen that Deputy Diamond raped her, but her pleas were ignored. What happened to that innocent boy after that finally shocked people into seeing the evil and corruption they had chosen not to see. Then I was elected in November along with Sheriff Larry Shyflinski, and together we changed Goodwin into a place people can be proud to call home."

That explains why Gloria mentioned at the memorial service at which she married Joe in prison. "How could people have ignored her?"

"Hate, bigotry, anger, and corruption. Joe was part Indian, and the lily-white Knight family couldn't abide that. Both sets of parents were angry because the kids went behind their backs to tie the knot. The sheriff held Joe in isolation, not that it mattered because his folks turned their backs on him at first.

"Why did Joe let this happen?"

"He was an innocent thrown to the wolves. He was broken down, too, by the isolation and horrible treatment by a crooked deputy, so he confessed to sex with a minor. He couldn't stand to have Gloria testify. He was vulnerable to the charge because she was six months short of eighteen and he was a trifle over. With that confession, they pulled off one of the grossest miscarriages of justice recorded in this county. Evidence was switched. Charging papers were doctored. His defense attorney was no help. And so at trial he was convicted of sexual assault."

"How could his defense attorney allow that?"

"Utterly incompetent. Later, I successfully brought him up for disbarment. There were others who were involved--the sheriff and his wife, maybe the judge too. The town doctor perjured himself. It was the deputy who pulled it all together."

"Who was the deputy?"

"John Diamond. Without using four-letter words to describe him, let's say he was a rascal of the worst sort."

"The same John Diamond who was murdered?"

Tudbury paused. Art kept his eyes on him, but Tudbury couldn't maintain eye contact. The reporter thought, *Now we're getting somewhere.* Tudbury continued to look down as his first measured words were spoken, "Yes, the same one. That crime was never solved."

"I've spoken with his daughter, Daphne Kazor," said Art. "She feels it was a whitewash. She said there wasn't a thorough investigation. Do you believe a man killed him?"

Tudbury stiffened his posture and grimaced in reaction to Art's words. Contemptuous tones were obvious as Tudbury asked, "Oh, you heard from Daffy Daphne? Where the hell did you meet her?"

"She contacted my editor. She lives up in the wine country in the

Napa Valley. What do you know about her?" asked Art.

Tudbury paused as if carefully framing his answer. "Mrs. Kazor had a hard childhood, which she never got over. I was running for a second term in the House when she claimed that I gave Gloria a pass, a "get out of jail free" card, to pay her back for getting me elected prosecutor. Daphne hounded me and my campaign, telling over and over her story about seeing Gloria drive her father's patrol car the morning after he disappeared."

Art wrote himself a note, *When did Gloria learn to drive?*, then said, "I heard about this from Daphne. Why didn't you believe her?"

"It didn't seem possible. Gloria didn't have a driver's license. Her father held her on a short leash after her escapade with the soldier. He wouldn't let her behind the wheel. Besides, she wasn't big enough to lift his body. We convinced the voters that Daffy Daphne was one of those people who tell themselves something so many times that fiction becomes fact. President Kennedy was correct when he said, 'The great enemy of the truth is very often not the lie--deliberate, contrived and dishonest, but the myth, persistent, persuasive, and unrealistic.' What saved me was that Daphne overplayed her hand by making all sorts of harebrained accusations.

"Such as ...?" Art asked. Now the retired Congressman was again looking him in the eye.

Tudbury said, "Such as going after Andrew Foyle for paying for her college education. Poor Andrew had no choice because Lyle Knight left the money in his will for that specific purpose. Somehow she tried to connect Lyle's political contributions in past elections to buying my silence. I was the only Democrat he ever gave money to."

"Did anyone approach Gloria?"

"I did once, when I was in San Francisco for Congressional hearings. We met in the restaurant at the Top of the Mark. She refused to answer. Joe made it clear that they would leave if the subject of John Diamond was broached again. Back to the campaign, my opponent dredged up the confrontation at the Lutheran Church, intimating that I had encouraged her."

"What confrontation?"

"John's wife, Chloe, kicked him out right after Gloria announced publicly that she would testify he had sex with her. She did it right after church in front of everybody, using very graphic language. Daphne was a little girl, too young to understand. She blamed her mother for destroying evidence."

Art asked, "What evidence?"

"Daphne claimed she found a stack of bills in the garage. Chloe claimed she desperately needed money. By the time the body was found, she had either spent or deposited all the bills. Neither mother nor daughter struck me as being credible."

"Who looked into her story?"

Tudbury replied, "Sheriff Shyflinski, of course. He got no cooperation from Gloria."

"Didn't that raise a red flag?"

"Not especially. Gloria and Joe were put through hell by this county. Not just the rape, but also her father accused her of being the brains behind the big bank robbery just over a year after she left Goodwin. There wasn't anything substantive to tie her to it, no sign of windfalls or unearned wealth. She refused to cooperate and claimed that her father had engineered the robbery to cover his own losses."

"Did they ever catch the bank robbers?"

"No, but the FBI believed the ringleader was a former Canon City inmate who had contact with Joe as a medical orderly. Gloria had a solid alibi."

⋅>══◉ ◉══<⋅

After Andrew Foyle shook hands all around, he settled into a seat at the end of the table. "Ray, Art, I apologize for being late. It sounds like you're talking about old Deputy 'Four Eff' Diamond."

Ray said, "We were earlier. Just now, we've been talking about the robbery of Lyle Knight's bank. Our young reporter has been talking to Daffy Daphne."

"And of course, Daphne still believes her father was a saint. Well, he wasn't and he got what he deserved," said Andrew.

"Wait a minute, explain the name 'Deputy Four Eff,' please," requested Art.

Andrew looked up from the menu. "Classified 4F, Diamond was turned down for the draft in World War II. Sheriff hired him as a deputy. He did his dirty work, so the sheriff couldn't fire him. In the course of one night that SOB destroyed the Gloria I knew before the prom. She was just like my daughters at that age, full of raging hormones, radiant in her youthful beauty. She was madly in love with her high school sweetheart."

"It sounds like you knew Gloria well."

"Yes, we grew up as next-door neighbors. She came over to our house early the next morning after the dance. I saw her bleeding wounds. She'd been put through hell. There is no doubt in my mind that John Diamond brutally raped her. Her parents chose to ignore her."

Art asked, "How could any parent ignore her pleas?"

"I don't think either of them could handle her," Andrew explained. "She was willful with a fast reputation, which infuriated her straitlaced parents."

"Nothing has changed there." Art smiled.

"Before I developed an interest in girls, she was bragging about getting laid. When she was fifteen, she thought she was in love. She slipped away with a nineteen-year-old soldier when he went off to the war. Her father had to go to Denver to get her out of Juvie. Then, in addition to making her nearly a prisoner, Lyle paid the soldier to send his friends obscene postcards bragging about his exploits. Talk about humiliation. There's more. Ever hear the word, miscegenation?" recalled Andrew.

Art knew the word meant interracial marriage, but he feigned ignorance, expecting to hear white supremacist talk. Instead he found Andrew to be quite liberal. He revered his late friend, Joe Caulfels. It clearly didn't bother him that Joe's mother was a half-blood Arapaho. But as for Gloria's father, Lyle Knight, Andrew called him a bigot.

Art looked puzzled. "If these two families hated each other so much and her parents kept her on a short leash, how did they manage to get together?"

Andrew continued, "After my father died in the war, Joe used to come by our house after school to help me with chores. He'd take a hot bath at our place because they didn't have running water at home. Gloria was my sister's friend. I don't know when Joe and Gloria noticed one another, but I believe it was sometime during junior year. Then in senior year they were together on the school's debate team. The graduation dance was the first dance she attended in high school. As far as her folks knew, I had asked her. But when we got to the dance, we switched partners."

Tudbury took a freshly baked cookie off the waitress's tray. "As I mentioned, my date and I saw them drive off. She called the parents."

Andrew continued, "Looking back on it, what turned her against her father was the realization she wasn't Daddy's little girl. She set about to destroy her father. I'll never forget my mother's words. She described Gloria as the first known metamorphosis of a butterfly into a scorpion."

"How?" said Art.

"She made it her cause to undermine her father through the job Lyle gave her at the bank. I'll never understand how a man who was such an astute businessman could have been so blind, so unaware of the effects of his own actions. He had never had anybody learn so much so fast. He bragged about her future at the bank. But she had him completely snowed, totally ignorant of her plan to destroy him."

"Give me an example."

"While he was out of town, she copied a bunch of the bank records and slipped them to the IRS. With help from Ray's friend, she enlisted us to dig up dirt in the courthouse. They fed it all to a political reporter for one of the Denver papers."

This doesn't sound like what would spontaneously come out of the heads of a bunch of high school kids, Art thought. He turned to the former prosecutor. "Mr. Tudbury, wasn't it taking a huge gamble to use high school kids fresh out of school to do your dirty work?"

"Art, you are good. Yes, I gave general guidance. None of us had a clue, including yours truly, as to what forces John Diamond had unleashed in Gloria. What I would have given to have had just one OSS agent with the intellect and drive this girl has. She's gifted with a photographic memory. She was ruthless in the ways she laid waste the lives and fortunes of Goodwin's movers and shakers."

Art was getting hungry, but he felt he was on a roll. He had eaten the last of the munchies and gave a hand signal to the waitress for more as he asked, "What happened to her father?"

Tudbury said, "Lyle knew he'd been in a fight. He was bloodied, but landed on his feet in a safe harbor with the help of some high-priced lawyers. Bill Clinton could have taken lessons from Lyle."

"No wonder he disinherited her."

"Correction," said Andrew. "She disinherited her parents, essentially declaring herself an orphan. He railed against Gloria regularly until the day he died. Too bad, because there were no other children."

"So that explains why his estate went to the foundation."

"Yes, sort of. It wasn't that straightforward. Lyle did set up a charitable trust with a modest income provision for Gloria, but only in the event that she and Joe divorced. He left almost everything else to his wife. Later on, she put just about all of it into charitable trusts. He gave me a minority interest in the bank holding company."

"It sounds like you have worked for the Knights either at the bank or at the foundation all your life."

"I didn't plan it that way. I went into the Army right out of college and served two years in combat in Korea. I was planning to make a career of the Army. That ended when my ex sent a process server to greet me when I got to Philly."

Andrew paused for a moment and looked out at the night scene below. His voice broke as he began, "There my wife was, with this rich bastard feeling her up. While I was holding my little Josie for the first time, I heard her say she didn't want 'the brat.' I saw Josie was dirty and there were some bruises. I left with my twenty-one month-old baby girl. If I hadn't, I would have killed the SOB."

"Wow, that's one hell of a story! Did she change her mind?"

"She made the motions, but not until after I brought Josie to my mother's here in Goodwin. There's something to be said for living in a small town. Between the lawyers Lyle hired and my friend here, the prosecutor, we did what was right. I gave up my plans to go Regular Army and got a hardship discharge. Lyle offered me a job."

Late that afternoon, Art suggested they both join him for dinner. Over the next hour and a half, he mostly listened. He sensed a warm bond between these two men, who both cared very much about this community and the good being done through the Knight Foundation. Both were veterans, and each told more tales about the other's service than about his own exploits. In Andrew, Art realized he was talking to the foundation's final decision maker, the man under whose leadership

Joe Caulfels' system had come to pass. He was pleased when Andrew not only agreed to an hours-long one-on-one interview, but also promised to give him introductions to key staffers and board members in the private school system.

About the time the waiter took orders for coffee and dessert, Art put a fresh cassette in his recorder. "Mr. Foyle," he said into the recorder, "to expand on what you said earlier, could you tell me about the day Gloria left Goodwin for good?" He turned the recorder toward Andrew.

The waiter poured more coffee into a half-empty cup. Andrew paused some more while he stirred it and looked the reporter in the eye. "There was a send-off dinner at Gloria's folks' house planned for a Friday evening. She was supposed to leave Saturday noon. Instead she woke me up early Friday to tell me she had changed her reservations to the eleven fifty-five that day. She was afraid they would kill her on the train, so she wanted to leave a day early."

"Kill her? Who?"

"This wasn't paranoia," interjected Tudbury. "After Gloria created a scene at the church with Chloe Diamond, we warned her to stay at home. The FBI had intercepted a phone conversation between the sheriff's wife and Deputy Diamond that made them feel she was in danger. Leaving a day early was prudent."

"This sounds like the sort of thing that would happen in Chicago," interjected Art.

"In Chicago, the organized criminals were outside the law. In Goodwin, they *were* the law. That's why I ran for prosecutor," said Tudbury.

Art thought, *Looks like 'Catch 22' to me. If Gloria had iced Diamond and fessed up, she certainly had self-defense as justification, but if she did it and hid it, they could go after her.*

Andrew continued, "Gloria was pretty frazzled the day she left. My last impression of her was that she looked pretty much like what the cat dragged in. She looked so bad that I was really surprised later when she made it big as a model."

"Frazzled? How do you mean?" Art asked.

"She was dressed in the same shapeless suit and opaque stockings she wore to work. Her hair was piled on her head with that rattail file sticking up. After the rape Gloria stopped taking pride in her appearance, but on that day, the combination of those sunglasses and so much of her hair hanging down loose made her look like she was trying to hide her face. She had applied makeup on her cheeks so thick she looked like a much older woman. Without any inflection or emotion, the last words to her mother were, 'I still love you, mother.'"

Andrew took a sip from his coffee. He paused to savor the taste, then continued, "All the way to the car, she moved like she'd been beaten--slow, with her mouth set against pain. It was a warm day but she was wearing long sleeves and gloves. She had trouble lifting her suitcases, so I helped her get her bags to her compartment. She took off her sunglasses. Before or since, I have never seen Gloria look worse. Her eyes had deep circles around them and they were terribly bloodshot. Just as I was about to leave, she asked for a hug, something she'd never done before. For that moment, she clung to me like a scared little girl. She thanked me for everything I had done for her. She repeated what she told me in the car: that if she were lucky, she would never see Goodwin again. From the parting comments her mother made, I knew she and her father had words the night before. I didn't take her seriously. After all, this is where she was born."

"So she never came back?"

"Nope, it's been over forty years ago, but it's a memory I've never forgotten. What a weight she had on her heart. All the bridges behind her were burning. She was heading off into the world alone."

"How about Joe? Did he ever come back?"

"Yes, after he got out of prison; and again when his father died. Later he was in and out of here regularly while they set up the new school system, but Gloria never accompanied him."

Tudbury said, "About Joe, I'll never forget the day he left for Philly. Diamond's body had been discovered early that same morning."

"When was this?" asked Art.

"Monday before Thanksgiving, November 1947. We were all standing around Calvin Bohl's barn looking at the broken cement cast that had been around the dead deputy's body. Everybody was speculating as to who the killer was. Cal had just bought the spread out of foreclosure from the bank. He ragged Lyle Knight about not telling him the body was there."

Andrew interrupted, "According to Lyle, the sheriff showed up with a bunch of FBI agents, who gave him the third degree about just how much was stolen."

"Yes, they arrived on the same train Joe caught east," Ray said. "It was a regular circus. Inside the barn, Sheriff Shyflinski stood on top of Cal's tractor and made one of those impassioned speeches that any law officer would make about how 'every resource of his department would be focused on unmasking the murderer of this Goodwin County deputy.' Just outside the door, Lyle Knight was screaming at the FBI agents because they told him they couldn't find a shred of evidence that Gloria was involved in the robbery."

"Why Gloria?" Art asked.

"Motive and knowledge. The bank robbery was perfectly executed. The agents who tried to question her didn't like her body language, or her attorney either. The sheriff's list of murder suspects was just about as long as the county voters' registry."

While the two bantered back and forth about what had happened fifty years ago, the waitress filled coffee cups. Art was surprised when the waitress championed her prime suspect, the sheriff's wife, who had left town on election date with all of her husband's money before the ballots were counted. Like a whirlwind, between the old waitress and Andrew, the tales flew, filled with lurid details of bribe taking and sadistic mistreatment of prisoners.

Tudbury, who was becoming more uncomfortable as memories and imaginations went wild, took advantage of a break in the action to say, "There you have it, Art, the skeletons that have been rattling in Goodwin County's closet since 1946."

Taking the signal from Tudbury, Art turned off his recorder. He thought, *Talk about stuff fit for the tabloids! I'll bet I could sell this to one of the network crime shows.*

⟶●⟵

The next morning Art visited the *Goodwin Globe* to search the paper's microfilm library. Tedious as it was, making him wish the computer had been invented fifty years earlier, he felt he hit pay dirt when he came across the article reporting dedication of the state-of-the-art high school that was built with Knight Foundation money. Next to the story was a photograph of a smiling Theo Knight, Gloria's mother, next to a grinning Vera Caulfels. They presented a large cast bronze sign, "Sunny Caulfels High School." Theo had named the school after Joe's big brother, the war hero. What better proof that the enmity went to the grave with Lyle Knight?

Art noted that the editor wrote a scorching editorial about the foundation's first act of charity, the establishment of a fund in Alameda County, California, to underwrite private investigators for public defenders. That explained where the funding came from for Win Griffith's employment. The foundation also funded the mathematics program at San Quentin, which Jesse Sollair had talked about at Joe's funeral. Art surmised that this was as close to an inheritance as Gloria would come.

Art's last interview in Goodwin was with Jenny Vaughn, Andrew Foyle's ex-wife. He anticipated picking up some interesting tidbits because she had been Gloria's roommate at Bryn Mawr and later was her neighbor in San Francisco while Andrew fought in Korea. By necessity, she lived with her daughter and son-in-law; as Art was surprised to discover, Jenny was blind. She was a wiry woman whose white hair was fashioned into a pageboy cut. Her daughter Josie put a half-full glass of water into her mother's hand, then fluffed the pillow in her chair. The older woman eased herself down and felt for the top of the side table before placing the glass on a coaster. She sat tall to face toward the reporter, who sat on a nearby straight-backed chair. Her voice was so soft that Art had to lean over to hear her speak. "So you're here to find out what I remember about Joe and Gloria Caulfels?"

Over the next hour, she reminisced about living with a college roommate who was incredibly beautiful but dressed like a middle-aged spinster. She did nothing but study. She didn't smoke. She didn't drink. She had no interest in boys. They labeled her "Mrs. Grundy" and the name stuck.

To his question, "What did she tell you about Deputy John Diamond?" Jenny replied, "He was the one who did it, the one who raped her. Looking back on it, she suffered from PTSD before it had a name. It took time for her to open up and tie her terrible nightmares to Diamond. Sometimes in her sleep, she screamed or begged him to stop. I have no doubt it really happened the way she said."

Mentally Art was outlining his first draft as he weighed the emotional Daphne's version of events against the impression Gloria made on others. He factored in their descriptions of her injuries and her apparent coping with symptoms of post-traumatic stress disorder.

Art was surprised to learn it was Jenny's father, a marketing executive for Wanamaker's, who gave Gloria her entree into modeling. About Joe, Jenny said, "My first impression was that he was absolutely the most handsome man I had ever seen. His eyes were dark and warm. I've always loved the sound of his voice. He was among the nicest people in the world. There was always a goodness you could feel. The only woman in the world who could catch his eye was Gloria. To my regret, I've spent a lifetime measuring other men against him, and few have come close."

This was good stuff, the information about Gloria's modeling. Art had drawn blanks about it in the other interviews, and it was a subject he knew his editor wanted included. He was greatly relieved when Jenny gave him insights into the risque side of Gloria that brought her to Hugh Hefner's attention. Jenny's father had commissioned the coffee table book that Art saw earlier, what Gloria called her "cheesecake book." Art recalled it as a high-quality hardcover mixture of high-fashion photos mixed with nude figure studies. The motivation for it was that Gloria and Jenny needed the money to move to California.

"For that era," commented Jenny, "that book was soft porn. You talk about scandal. A Bryn Mawr girl photographed in the nude! There was all this tatting about how no one would ever offer her another high-fashion shoot. It hit the streets just after she graduated at the end of the fall term. It was being called a kiss of death to a high-fashion career, but it became just the opposite.

"If that wasn't enough, the second edition added pictures of her popping out of a cake at Joe's birthday party at Penn wearing nothing but a G-string and no pasties. I've often wondered if Hefner didn't get his inspiration for *Playboy* from that book."

"How could she go from being a Mrs. Grundy to this?"

Jenny felt about the tabletop for the plate of munchies. "Well, she still didn't drink or smoke. I think it was her way of letting off steam and thumbing her nose at all the people who didn't accept her. Joe obviously understood, because he always went with her on the photo shoots. They had something from the start that most people never enjoy, a very deep and committed love."

Art's commuter flight bounced from updraft to downdraft across the Rockies toward Denver while he busied himself composing on his laptop. Instead of flying directly back to California, he puddle jumped to Walla Walla, Washington, to visit his mother in a nursing home.

During the long layover in Denver, Art filed the remaining segments. He felt satisfied that he had achieved the balance necessary to fit together the chapters of Joe's and Gloria's divergent lives in the way to best eulogize the accomplishments of Joe while spicing the story with the unique contributions of Gloria and their children. The one member of the family he knew the least about was Vera Li's mother, Jenny. Maybe he'd have other reasons, personal reasons, to visit them at their mission in Central America.

He mentally shifted to another gear when he opened Gloria's book to a page showing her reclining in the nude, looking away and holding a greeting card over her beaver. This was one photo, he decided, that not even his salacious editor would chance to print. *If ever Red moves on,* thought Art, *he'll be on the short list for some supermarket tabloid like* National Enquirer.

Later he reviewed the material he hadn't written about. As far as his readers would know, John Diamond's alleged villainy was extreme and his murder unsolved. Yet Art had questions in the back of his head about Gloria. Maybe sometime down the road, he'd take a fresh look at the evidence.

CHAPTER 9

As Art waited and contemplated, he studied the hand-carved front door of the Caulfels residence. *I didn't realize I could miss Vera so much after such a short time apart. What can I say that would make her laugh, or maybe remember years from now?* No sooner had he pushed the doorbell button than she opened the door. He stood mesmerized, staring at her in a slinky blue dress that hugged her figure starting at the swell of her high breasts. It ended far enough above the knee to showcase her long, straight legs. For a moment, her long dark hair was caught in the afternoon breeze. Gently she brushed back it back in a smooth, fluid motion. Her dark eyes lighted as she focused on Art's. Vera's hand touched his arm and ran down to his hand. Her voice had a breathless quality. "I'm so glad that you accepted Grandmother's invitation to dinner. I missed you."

Then she kissed him. It wasn't one of those "I'm in heat" burners, but it wasn't a cold fish either. He knew he should say something. Instead he held her in his arms in the doorway where the surge of the late afternoon sea breeze rushed by. Art remained frozen for a long moment, not sure whether the goose bumps were from the cooling breeze or her touch. "Darling Vera, I missed you too. Say, is this a new dress today?"

She blushed and nodded. "Thank you. Grandmother took me shopping. I think the skirt is way too short."

"Relax, you do it justice." Art took an extra minute to gently spin her in a circle. His light kiss on her neck brought a giggle.

After Vera closed the front door, she said, "I was surprised to get your call from Walla Walla, Washington. Were you investigating someone else?"

"No, I should have told you. My mother is living in a nursing home there. She has Alzheimer's. It's tough leaving her alone, but there's nothing I can do. She doesn't recognize me. She's on Medicaid, so I can't be all that choosy."

"There I was, blaming you for Grandpa Joe's death when you have to deal with your mother's sickness. I'm sorry. Please accept my apologies. Grandmother was right. With his bad heart, we were lucky to have him as long as we did."

"Vera, I understand. You were doing a healthy thing, letting the pain out. I just wish I could have helped you in some way."

"You already have. I'm saving the articles you wrote for the *Tribune*. You made me proud to be in this family. You gave me insights about them that I never knew. And Grandmother liked what you wrote about Grandpa too."

"I'm glad of that. It wouldn't be much fun coming to dinner if she didn't," said Art. He thought about all that he didn't write regarding the unsolved murder of Deputy John Diamond.

Vera smiled warmly and took his hand. "Silly, come on into the living room. We'll be having dinner soon."

As Art entered the living room, his hostess rose. Gloria grimaced slightly as she found her feet, then smiled. Art greeted her with a hug. "I'm so glad to see you getting around okay. How do you feel?"

"I've had to give up my jogging and exercises," answered Gloria. "The jury is still out as to whether my hip will heal or I will have to have a replacement. Don't get me wrong, I'm not about to start complaining. You timed your arrival perfectly. Eudora just finished chilling a fresh pitcher of lemonade."

He thought, *You can't get a ticket for DUI for drinking lemonade*, as Vera approached him with a tall glass whose sides were frosted with dew. "Thank you very much for inviting me to dinner. I always enjoy the view of the city and the Golden Gate. With the fog starting to roll in, you have a spectacular view."

Gloria joined him looking out the window. "It's a little late in the fall to see fog like this. Yes, we were very lucky to buy this parcel."

Art loosened the string tie on the thick envelope he was carrying as he said, "Gloria, I am deeply in your debt for the help you and especially the foundation people back in Goodwin have given me."

"Thank Andrew Foyle. I severed that umbilical long, long ago."

"I can understand why you did. As I mentioned on the phone, the series was picked up by the *Rocky Mountain News* in Denver and the *Philadelphia Enquirer.* My boss has given me a green light to write a condensed book version for *Reader's Digest.*"

Gloria laughed lightly. "My daughter Carole tells me that you may hear from ABC about making a TV movie on the Peter Godoniski trial. She wants to play me in the film. As for the newspapers and book offers, I'm sorry they had to wait until after Joe was dead to honor him."

"I'm deeply in your debt. They gave me a raise six months early. What scares me is not knowing where I'm going to find the next big story."

Vera said, "Don't worry, I'm sure the Lord will lead you to it."

'Thank you, Vera." *I have to rely on more than faith,* Art thought as he handed the large open envelope to her grandmother. He continued, "Gloria, these are copies of the many letters I received. You have every reason to be proud of his memory. Joe Caulfels was a giant, no doubt about that. I believe the best among them was from Jesse Sollair. I put it on top."

Looking down into the envelope, the widow Caulfels chuckled. "Old Jesse, yes, he and Joe go way back. Unfortunately, he still gets into trouble. Say, since you're looking for that next big story, I'll be representing him on a felony case that starts five weeks from Wednesday."

"Where?"

"Where else, right here in Superior Court, Alameda County. It's a case that I would have probably struck a deal on as a public defender, but Jesse is a proud, stubborn man. No matter which way it goes, it ought to give you something interesting to fill a column or two."

"What did he do?"

"From the rhetoric coming out of the Prosecutor's Office, you would be led to believe he planted a bomb under City Hall. It seems that someone dropped a headache ball on the roof of the City of Covington's planning department, and Jesse stands accused. But let's not talk shop."

Gloria placed the big envelope on a small table. "It was very thoughtful to bring me these letters. I'll save them for later. I'm afraid that if I start reading them, I'll stop being a good hostess and start crying again." Her voice broke. "I miss my Joe terribly. But enough about me, did I hear you say something about your mother being in a nursing home?"

Art recapped what he had told Vera earlier, then felt relieved when Gloria changed the subject. "Art, seeing you and Vera together tonight gives me great pleasure." He watched Vera's blush turn into a come-hither smile. She winked while running her tongue around her lips. He thought, *That's not very born again virginal.*

Hours after the last red had faded from the sky and most of the lights of San Francisco lay hidden behind an encroaching fog bank, Art thanked his hostess and said good night. Vera walked him to his car. Holding her hands as she stood in front of him, he inquired, "Vera, I really enjoyed this evening. I got the distinct feeling that your grandmother is still playing matchmaker. How do you feel? Shall I call you for a date?"

She slipped into his arms, languorously wet her lips with her tongue, and tilted her head back. He kissed her. She put a hand on his neck and pressed against him through the second kiss. Still holding her in his arms, Art whispered, "I take that for a yes."

Vera released him, but remained against him. "I'd be very, very disappointed if you didn't call."

⊹━❧ ❧━⊹

Art called, and Vera accepted, dates on weekends as her senior year schedule at Mills College permitted. He always picked her up at her grandmother's house. They enjoyed movies and dinners together as well as trips to San Francisco and into the Delta between the Bay and Sacramento. Twice he spent all weekend watching her participate in martial arts exhibitions, one in tae kwon do and the other in aikido. He had little understanding of the moves, but in aikido at least, he came away much impressed that this was one woman not to get violent with. In an aikido event called a *rundori* she was attacked by four men, all of them much bigger than she. With a minimum of effort, she eluded them all with smooth, flowing, almost dance-like motions.

He found that Vera had a temper that could flash quickly complete with narrowed black eyes and thinned lips--and would be followed by a girlish pout and an apology after he reacted. One of the flare-ups happened during dinner with Gloria. The older woman later drew him aside and said, "I hope you don't let her scare you off. I don't think she'd act this way if she didn't care about you very deeply. She's still working through some serious pain."

"I don't understand. All I did was ask about her father's family."

"Sung should have gone to prison for what he did. That is why she came to live with us."

"You mean her father abused her?"

"I won't go into details. Let me just say it was more than that."

"Why didn't you do something?"

"It happened in Texas. Jenny wanted to save her marriage."

"Wow, I still don't understand."

Gloria looked away for a time and then into Art's eyes. "I could give you all sorts of excuses for how devout Jenny is, but I think Samuel Johnson summed it up nicely when he wrote that marriage has too many pains but celibacy has no pleasures. There are two small boys who need their father. In spite of it all, Jenny loves the man. I hope that what I just shared with you won't drive a wedge between you and my granddaughter. Vera is very deeply in love with you."

"I'm in love too, Mrs. Caulfels. Wouldn't it be better if I let her know that I know and understand?"

"Give her some time. Joe's death has hit her very hard. It has been a big setback."

Art was beginning to better understand his born again virgin, who was a tease when there was no opportunity but wooden when there was. From then on, he was careful to avoid even the most innocent queries about her parents or her past. There were far too many other things they enjoyed or had in common. He was far more concerned about Gloria, whose blue eyes were often red from crying and circled with dark rings from sleeplessness. Once or twice she openly spoke of looking forward to the day she would be with her Joe again. Other than her work, she had no interests or friends beyond Vera. She was aging years before his eyes.

Twice Gloria invited them to join her in shooting on their indoor range. Art found himself at practice on the type of range used to train police officers with pop-up targets. After the first evening, he understood why this old woman had wreaked so much havoc against her three muggers. She was cautious, yet deadly accurate. As for Vera, he knew that the safest place to be when she was firing was behind her, because Vera often shot at the "friendly" pop-ups too. She could best Gloria only when she was shooting at a fixed target.

Art's own shooting was, compared to Gloria's and Vera's, abysmal. Gloria described his shot spreads as "charts of undiscovered solar systems." He was relieved that neither Gloria nor Vera cared that he missed the targets.

⊷⊶

Art Williams stood inside the door to the Caulfels formal dining room with Vera at his side. He saw that the oak table had been moved closer to the windows to accommodate a row of easels. Most held whiteboards. A ruby red ergonomic office chair replaced the elegant oak chair at the head of the table. A telephone sound station rested in the center of the table with its wires stretched out over and around stacks of dishes. It gave it the look of some kind of squid.

Art thought, *Holy smoke, what did I set myself up for when I pitched Red that Gloria was offering me the opportunity to roam freely behind the scenes during trial preparations? Now that I'm here, I don't know. I feel like a bit player in a TV crime drama while the days fly by. How is she going to get anything organized while she's remodeling and moving from her office? Look at this room, it's not fit to be either a formal dining room or a conference room.*

Vera said, "After you left yesterday, we worked down here until almost nine-thirty."

"Too much bickering between the office consultant and Eudora?"

"Yes, I hope that's over. That man surely took away the lesson never to argue with Grandmother, or with Eudora speaking for Grandmother." Vera pointed to a closed door on the far side of the room. "Grandpa Joe's study will become Grandmother's office as soon as the workmen are finished and all that stuff piled in the garage is moved up here."

"Where are you going to entertain guests after this is all done?"

"It'll be family only, in the breakfast nook out by the kitchen. When he was alive, it was Grandpa Joe's friends we entertained in here, but Grandmother's friends are books. There are so many other things on her mind, like last night. Now that I'm into my senior year, she keeps talking about law school."

"I get the distinct impression she's got other plans for you and me. What do you want?"

She reached out to his hand. "Art, Grandmother knows my heart. More than anything, I love you and will use any excuse to be with you. I suggested she invite you to sit through preparations for trial. I was surprised when she agreed. She trusts you won't write anything that violates the disclosure laws or the attorney-client privilege."

"I won't. Were I the defendant, the last thing I'd want is some snoop like me gathering fodder for tomorrow's edition."

"That's the reason for the non-disclosure agreement. Mr. Sollair has agreed to let you sit in on the preparations, provided you sign it."

"Is that Jesse Sollair, the old guy who spoke at the funeral?" queried Art.

"Yes, he'll be tried for dropping a wrecking ball through the roof of the Covington Planning Department after they turned down a project."

Wow, thought Art *that was in the news. This is the case Gloria mentioned. Carefully written, a story about the trial could be fodder for some prize.* He rubbed his hands together. "What do you know about the case?"

Vera drew an X through "Jesse" on one of the whiteboards. "Jesse says he didn't do it. It all started at Linguini's, where they were celebrating final approval of Jesse's project. Leonard Demartino, head of the Planning Department, arrived after six. He and Jesse had some kind of run-in years ago, and there's been 'bad blood' between them ever since.

"Anyway, on this night Demartino hand carried a letter from Federal Fish and Wildlife that halted future development at the last minute. Seems he had told the feds that the project site might be a habitat for Nicole's voles, and they froze all plans until they're satisfied that none of these voles were present. Demartino made a big thing of it in front of everybody Jesse had invited to the party to celebrate the green light. Jesse went ballistic and threatened him."

Art pointed to the plat map. "So this is 'Covington Re-built,' one-hundred-four acres of residential, commercial, and light industrial?"

"Yes, after Jesse's spent six and a half years and about every cent he owned. Everybody there saw and heard it all. They watched Jesse leave and walk toward the city's offices. He even got a ticket for overtime parking close by the offices." Vera pointed to a list taped to the frame. "See, this is the prosecutor's list of the witnesses who saw and heard his threats. Next to it is the folder of the stills of the destroyed house. When Grandmother looked at them, she told me the odds are poor that she can move all of the jurors' minds past the drama of Jesse's confrontation at Linguini's followed by those pictures. It doesn't matter how understandable was Jesse's reaction to the gloating by his old nemesis. Nor the theatric way Demartino used the imperiled Nicole's vole to upend this project."

"Remember I'm a newbie, so I have to ask: Where's Linguini's? And what's a Nicole's vole?"

"Linguini's is an upscale Italian restaurant a few blocks from the Covington city offices. Nicole's vole is a little rodent that may or may not be an imperiled species. Because Cal Berkeley Professor Nicole Sheen discovered this ugly varmint, unique to the East Bay, they named it after her."

"So they found a nest of varmints?"

"No, they've never even been seen in Covington. But an activist conservation group found scat within the boundaries of Covington Re-built, that *might* be from Nicole's vole. They notified the city, and Demartino petitioned Federal Fish and Wildlife to extend its range to include Covington. Oh, Good morning, Grandmother."

Gloria took the seat at the head of the table. "Good morning, Vera, Art. Thank you for coming in early. I like this arrangement better already. Please be seated. I can make productive use of the time that otherwise is wasted while stuck in traffic. I received notice yesterday that Dale Bleasman replaced Millie Hunter as the prosecution's lead chair. I haven't the foggiest idea what drove him to don his armor other than his belief this is an open and shut case. He's looking for something big to provide cover for his last screw-up. He has the ethics of an underfed shark. He treats this like a terrorist operation in the charging papers, so I want to be prepared."

"Grandmother," Vera said, "you asked what I could commit to this case. I can give you an hour before classes mornings and from four o'clock until dinner, except starting at noon on Wednesdays, Fridays, and all day Saturday."

"Good, we'll honor your Grandpa's memory with church on Sundays."

Thus began their daily routine with Gloria at the head of the table and Art in the chair next to her and opposite Vera. Win Griffith, when he was there, took the seat next to Art. He had taken a liking to the former law officer, who gave him enough to do that he felt he was a contributor, but not so much that he lacked time and opportunity to be with Vera. Other chairs filled and emptied with consultants and clerical help. Eudora moved among them filling coffee cups and dispensing baked goods.

Art felt at home in the comfortable dining room chair across from the girl he was coming around to believe was a "keeper." She was a distraction, a pleasant distraction, the reason he was there. As was her habit, she flirted quite openly even when her grandmother was in the room. He thought she acted like a teenager who had just discovered a boy likes her. During the down time, usually after dinner, she liked to show affection by cuddling, but continued to make it clear that she was a "born again virgin." He enjoyed working with her. She was quick, efficient, and had a good sense of humor. There was something about the way she looked at him out of the corner of her eye, then smiled.

On that first morning, Art pushed a stack of photographs across the table toward Vera. Gloria shortstopped the effort. "I don't know which was more spectacular, the aerial shots showing the huge crane towering over that little house with the hole smashed in the roof, or the inside view with the Covington Community and Development Department sign in the foreground and that huge wrecking ball suspended over a totally destroyed office."

"Grandmother, didn't you say that if it weren't Jesse, you would be talking plea bargain?" asked Vera while she gathered up the photos.

Gloria nodded and smiled. "Win is out there trying to find something I can present to give the jurors reason to have doubt. Jesse's claim of the vendetta with Demartino won't buy a get-out-of-jail ticket."

"But Jesse said he's innocent." said Vera.

"Jesse Sollair is always innocent. That's the problem. I'm afraid his string is about to run out. After Dale's last drubbing, the odds are strong that he will come prepared. It's difficult to fail to cover all the elements of these California Code sections. Oh, here's Win. You're shaking your head and trying to hide a Cheshire cat grin. Whatcha got?"

Gloria's private investigator swallowed the last bite of his sweet roll. "Boss, Jesse's got something going his way. I confirmed that he and Demartino went at it before, when Demartino was working as a planner for the City of El Cerrito. The circumstances aren't that much different than what Demartino is attempting today. Jesse sued for damages and won. Demartino resigned after Jesse collected a $75,000 judgment for his overt trampling of his rights."

"Deja vu! Yes, I remember that case." Gloria glanced into the folder handed to her. "Back then, I referred him to the California Land Use Association for counsel."

Win continued, "In our present case, Demartino claims he was pressured by Councilwoman Elizabeth Holtzmann and a Bay area environmental group, POZUD, Protectors of Zoological Underdogs. That may be because both Professor Sheen and the councilwoman are members."

⊷⊶

Art didn't take long to realize Win had much to do with Gloria's success. While she and the temps, electricians, and computer/office machine people were setting up the new office to her liking, he and Art uncovered vital evidence. They interviewed everyone on the prosecutor's list, plus employees who witnessed Jesse at Linguini's. Three from the prosecutor's list saw Demartino wait inside for at most five minutes before he left and walked toward his office in the Planning Department building. Win released this information to Art to make public, and Art wrote it up along with his own question as to why, if Jesse was guilty, Demartino didn't hear the crane start and drop the wrecking ball.

Their visit to the Covington personnel director produced a copy of Demartino's job application with a listing of his employers and his education. They learned that the crew called out by Fire and Rescue removed the wrecking ball as soon as they got there. They also learned that CSI didn't bother to investigate the scene because, they said, crushed rock and gravel underfoot rendered footprints useless.

Five days before the trial, Gloria looked at revised charging papers. "Ah, the Bleasman touch. Understandably, none of the statutes spell out wrecking balls specifically. They are all written for explosive-caused incidents with clauses added in for those caused by nonexplosive means. The way this is written makes me question Dale's competence. Some of the phrases sound like a civil case. Yes, I'll press him to submit evidence for every element."

She's no dummy, Art thought.

Vera reported on another developer, the unfortunate Van Boh Tranh, who'd run afoul of the City of Covington. The building that was demolished was a converted residence house that had belonged to Tranh. He bought it for fifty dollars and then negotiated with the city for a permit to move it to a lot on which he had an option to buy. Tranh agreed to lease the house to the city to be used by Community Development until the department's permanent offices were ready. If he didn't move the house when the department vacated it, it was to be razed at his expense. Issuance of the permit was conditioned on the results of an environmental impact study to determine if endangered species were present—especially Nicole's vole, which had never been seen in the area.

Vera produced correspondence and leases from Tranh's wife that told of a relationship gone south. In a letter written by Tranh's attorney late in the first year's lease, he had protested cancellation of the permit to move the house. Tranh faced soaring fees and delays while the fruitless search for the vole went on. In the end the city issued a one-hundred-twenty-day time-certain notice to either move the house or have the building razed at Tranh's expense. Art thought, *Van Boh Tranh is being screwed by the city. I'll talk with him.*

Art hung up the phone with his ears ringing after listening to Van Boh Tranh's wife. Forget about paying for tearing down the building. Tranh had left for Aruba with all their money. She wanted to sue the city, but didn't have the money to pay for an attorney. She was mad as hell.

Gloria listened to Art's report, then rubbed her hands. "Dale's pleadings call out the building as owned by the city. I can't believe he is this incompetent. Unless he corrects the charges, I'll win a directed verdict."

"Can you subpoena Tranh from Aruba?" asked Art.

Gloria shook her head. "Splendid work and good thinking, but no. I will make my points without his testimony. Besides, Tranh would deny it. Win, your deductive skills should make the difference when Demartino admits he never saw or heard the crane go into operation."

"You asked about his employment history," said Win. "I have something better than that for a last-minute addition." Win handed her a folder.

Gloria's face lighted up into a broad smile when she opened it. Just then, her cell phone rang. "Jesse, what's up? ... You did what? ... Oh, my! ... The DNA matches a Mediterranean wharf rat? ... I'll keep it in mind, but it has no bearing on your case. I'll see you tomorrow. Bye."

She turned the cell off and returned it to its case. "Jesse had his environmental consultants issue a press release that analysis of the scat matched the DNA to the Mediterranean wharf rat. That ought to draw some media attention to the trial."

⊷⊶

Art ached to get back in harness on the day the trial began. The lead for his story lay in Jesse's environmental advisors' conclusion that the so-called Nicole's vole's droppings actually were those of a Mediterranean wharf rat. In the hallway outside the courtroom, he heard more speculation and rumors about the Nicole's vole that questioned its very existence.

Gloria thanked Art for his contributions and terminated the non-disclosure agreement. He replied, "I ought to be the one doing the thanking. Vera is looking at me
in a different light."

"Nonsense, you gave me the reason why Jesse has to be innocent. You asked why Demartino didn't hear the crane as he walked to his car. If Jesse were guilty, Demartino would have witnessed it because he followed Jesse up the street. That leaves Van Boh Tranh, who conveniently loaded all his cash in a bag and slipped across the border."

"Or Demartino did it himself?"

Art took his place in the first row of spectator seats. He had come to enjoy the verbal fisticuffs between Gloria and Prosecutor Bleasman that preceded every trial. While Bleasman was up to his old self with his Fabian tactics, Gloria conceded points and streamlined her attack. By the time all the motions had been heard and the last juror had been selected, half of the morning had been consumed. Once the trial was under way, Bleasman strutted around the courtroom. It was then that Art realized he was the only press member present in a courtroom devoid of spectators, save for one. *What am I doing here? I know what I'm doing here, I'm taking Vera to lunch without Grandmother in tow.*

The hours of discussions and decisions around Gloria's dining room table were still swimming in the back of his head. Art noted that Bleasman's opening statement began as routine as he expected. What caught his attention was when he pronounced, "… did destroy a public building owned by the City of Covington by hoisting up a wrecking ball and dropping it through the roof of the Planning Department …."

Art thought, *Bleasman has one foot on a banana peel and the other in a trap of his own making. Gloria is going to drop the hammer. After all, the mover took all the stuff the day it happened.*

About the time Bleasman read the third sentence or so, Jesse's face lit up with a smug, cat-ate-the-canary grin. *My gosh, what's with Jesse?* thought Art. *Will Bleasman be swift enough to catch the significance of the city's dealings with Tranh?*

Gloria asked to defer her opening statement until after the prosecution's case was presented. Art took notes of the testimony of Detective Felix Marcom, a scholarly looking man in his fifties, and Leonard Demartino. With testimony and visual presentations, Bleasman did a thorough job of proving that a single drop of a wrecking ball totaled what had once been a two-story, single-family, four-bedroom dwelling.

Gloria questioned Detective Marcom after he testified that he had no fingerprint or footprint evidence. "I normally try capital and serious criminal cases. Can you tell me when is it serious enough in Covington to get off your butt and come into court with convincing evidence that would permit your prosecutor to base his case on something more than 'Jesse Sollair was in the neighborhood?'"

Demartino took the witness chair, a fading athlete whose muscular arms were testing the fabric and threads of his Walmart business suit. On cue, he presented the prosecutor with a ten-inch-thick Community Development file on Jesse Sollair. Bleasman's questions to Demartino required him to thumb through it to cite numerous citations for violation of environmental and building codes. Gloria then countered during cross to require him to admit that the citations were for minor workmanship issues, and to identify the laudatory correspondence and memoranda that were in the same file.

Bleasman used Demartino's testimony describing Jesse's threatening reaction to the Federal Fish and Wildlife letter to paint the defendant as a violent man. Fearful of what Jesse could do, said Demartino, he waited and watched until he saw Jesse leave Linguini's and walk toward the Community Development building.

Gloria's first question on cross was, "What is to say you didn't move that crane across the block yourself and smash your own offices?"

"That's preposterous. Those are my offices and besides I've never run a crane."

"Did you not work as a heavy equipment operator for Kweit Heavy Construction between June of 1973 and September of 1974, and didn't you have qualifications to operate cranes?"

"My God, how did you find that out?" exclaimed Demartino.

"Mr. Demartino, I probably know more about you than you can remember. Do you want me to repeat the question?"

By the time she was done with him, Demartino had painted himself into a corner. He hadn't admitted anything, but he looked guilty.

Just short of noon, Prosecutor Bleasman rested his case. The judge said, "Mrs. Caulfels, as we are close to lunchtime, I am willing to adjourn for that purpose. You could start afresh in the afternoon."

"Thank you, Your Honor, but before having to inconvenience the jurors further, I am asking for a directed verdict acquitting Jesse Sollair. The prosecution did not make its case in chief. More directly, the prosecution has not submitted evidence proving at least one element of the charges. Mr. Bleasman did not submit evidence that 1141 Laurel is a city-owned building. There is good reason--because the building in question belongs to one Van Boh Tranh."

The prosecutor jumped to his feet and rushed to the bench. "This is a preposterous waste of time! The entire block was acquired by the city some years ago."

Gloria's voice dripped a soft sweetness, "Oh, but, Your Honor, here is the record in defense exhibit 210. The city purchased the land, but left the house in Tranh's ownership. You will find an agreement between him and the city renting the building to the Planning Department on a temporary basis for no more than a year. Note the condition that if he couldn't move the structure, it would be razed at his expense. At the end of the first year, Tranh refused to accept a lump-sum lease payment for a second year's lease because it would commit him to leasing the building for another full year. A year ago, he applied for the necessary permits to move the house. No permit was issued. Three weeks before the building was destroyed, the lot listed in Tranh's permit application was sold. You will find a letter from the realtor stating that the owner refused to extend the option to Tranh a third time."

The judge began to look at the papers as Gloria continued, "Your Honor, Tranh certainly had motive, given the frustration of having lost the money he had to pay for the options while being stiff-armed by his local government. Given the prior actions of the city, dropping a headache ball through the roof may have been, in his mind, the only option left. This building was being occupied by the City of Covington in a manner not unlike the way the British housed Hessian troopers during the revolution."

Dale Bleasman's color pegged the scale at livid red. "Your Honor, you can't let this woman pull this stunt. The building in question has been a city office for the last six years. Let me remind you, Your Honor, that Mr. Tranh had ample opportunity to adjudicate any disagreements he had with the city. These were the city's offices that were destroyed!"

"We'll adjourn until tomorrow morning, Mr. Bleasman. I'll give you that long to counter the defense's arguments."

⭑►═◉ ◉═◄⭑

Art Williams enjoyed his outing with Vera, followed by dinner with her that evening. He overheard people laughing about a Mediterranean wharf rat being declared endangered. Red called him during dessert and praised his work. Twice Red read Gloria's comment, "The judge has no choice but to throw the case out, given the incompetence of the prosecution in drawing up the indictment. This is a case that should never have come to trial."

⭑►═◉ ◉═◄⭑

By the time the judge gaveled the court into session the next morning, Art was searching for a seat. Seats in the front row were crowded in what was otherwise an empty courtroom except for a few court watchers, including Vera Li. She gave Art a kiss on his lips before he took his place, squeezed between an artist from a TV station and a reporter for the *Chronicle.*

Art was still mulling over a brief exchange he'd had with Dale Bleasman. When he arrived at the courtroom, Bleasman confronted him with the question, "Why is it, when a witness comes forward and accuses that bitch of murder, you extol her like she's a candidate for beatification? Is that the price you pay for screwing her granddaughter?" Bleasman had immediately turned away so Art was denied the opportunity to respond.

Art watched Bleasman glare at Gloria as he rose to his feet when the judge arrived. He thumbed through the papers before him, then shuffled them before handing the stack to the assistant sitting with him. With his head lowered so that he was making eye contact with the judge's hands at best, Bleasman said, "Your Honor, we have been unable to contact Mr. Tranh. His family informed me that he is on a fishing boat that sailed out of Aruba in the Netherlands Antilles. Without his statement, we have no means to refute the defense's argument. I beg of the court a week."

The judge glared at him. "Mr. Bleasman, I expected documentation verifying that the city had indeed purchased the building in question. Instead, you are asking a week to somehow regroup from what I must say is the most incredible judicial farce I have presided over in my career. I hereby grant a directed acquittal noting that the element of a city-owned building was not proved. And further, that the prosecution did not prove that Mr. Jesse Sollair committed the acts alleged. Mrs. Caulfels, I want to take this opportunity to compliment you on your thorough defense. Had the prosecution asked the same questions prior to bringing this matter to trial, Mr. Sollair would have been spared the expense and threat to his liberty."

Outside the courtroom, Art floated in the midst of the media blocking Prosecutor Bleasman. Bleasman knocked away the hand-held microphones until only those on booms that swung above his head remained. With his head down, he moved to the right along the wall, trying to evade the barrage of questions. "When did you find out the city didn't own the building?" "Who is Mr. Tranh?" "Is the Nicole's vole actually related to the Mediterranean wharf rat?" "Do you intend to refile charges against Mr. Sollair?"

The last of the horde of reporters broke off from Bleasman when Gloria and Jesse came through the door. A TV reporter pushed his black foam-covered microphone into her face as he asked, "Mrs. Caulfels, what is your feeling about the significance of this decision?"

Gloria pointed a well-manicured index finger toward Bleasman's retreating back. "Significance, significance? If he fumbles this badly as a county prosecutor, should the people elect him attorney general for the State of California? Report accurately what was said from the bench."

Bleasman spun around, pushing the press aside. "I knew when I saw all the cameras that you were up to no good."

"Don't blame me, "remarked Gloria. "I'm not in the hunt to run for state attorney general."

"You, you amoral old bitch! That was the lowest, shyster flim-flam! The greasy son of bitch is guilty as hell and you know it."

"No, Mr. Bleasman, my client was found innocent and you were again ensnared in your own pettifoggery."

"Mark my words, you will have a dreadful and painful day of reckoning, I promise."

Gloria smiled. "Well, Mr. Bleasman, we all know you can't shoot straight. Whoever you hire had better hit me with the first shot, because I don't miss."

CHAPTER 10

Art parked his car in front of the empty garage stall at the Caulfels house. *This was more than an invitation to dinner. Damn, that old woman can be persuasive. This will be my only opportunity to maintain a good working relationship with such a dynamite news source. Only that isn't what I've spent every minute thinking about.*

All the way up as he walked to the house, Art had his mind on the date with Vera the week before. *Dammit, I've shown her the respect she's demanded of me over the past six months. I don't want to learn the details of what her father did, so I haven't pressed her whenever she announces she is a born again virgin. Looking back on it, I didn't press her enough. I waited too long to ask her if she wanted to take the next step. I should have asked that question with my hands in my own pockets. It's no wonder she ran away from our last date and didn't let me take her home. Why didn't I accept her apology when she called? Instead I accused her of being a tease. It's all over now, and it's all my fault.*

He strolled to the front door with questions on his mind. Should he make a commitment to Vera or should he chalk it off to experience? If the latter, how would he best do it and keep on the right side of Gloria? Then he asked himself questions to which he knew the answers. Would he ever find another woman who was so gorgeous, who wasn't full of herself about her looks, and so caring about others' feelings? Had he ever met someone so cheerful? Such a good listener? Wasn't she a keeper if there ever was one? By the time he rang the front doorbell, he decided to try again. It was time to let Vera know he was serious and not out for a roll in the hay. He could wait if she would have him.

Expecting Vera, he was surprised when a tired-looking Gloria opened the door. Yet the voice she greeted him with was full of vigor. "Well, am I glad to see you! Congratulations, it looks like you've graduated from the courthouse beat."

"Not quite."

"That's an excellent expose you wrote on the gas pump scams. I'm amazed that these big oil companies would install pumps that could be rigged so easily."

Amazed. The word played across his mind; he was amazed that Vera wasn't there to greet him and amazed that Gloria was talking about the scam he'd just written about. "What surprised me the most," he replied, "was the number of complaints to regulators that were simply ignored. By the way, I've just filed my story for tomorrow. It ties the crooked circuit boards at the gas pumps to the Russian Mafia."

"How did you do that?"

"I showed a photocopy of one of the boards to Peter Godoniski. He confirmed that the printing on them was Cyrillic."

"Oh, yes, Peter and Alya Godoniski. How are they doing?"

"They're obviously very happy together. You wouldn't recognize Alya. I'll bet she's gained forty pounds. I think their baby is due in early June."

"I'm so happy for them."

"Back to the circuit boards. The serial numbers, if you can believe it, tie them to an old Soviet missile factory just outside of Tver, Russia, Peter's home town. I talked to the factory manager, who spoke pretty good English. They used to make missile guidance systems. He said they have converted most of their plant to nonmilitary uses and yes, they produce circuit boards. He was real chatty until I asked if he knew Alexander Tsamonicoff."

"Now there's bad news. Is that in the story?"

"No, I'm working on the follow-up. It's only a matter of time because both the oil companies and the feds are playing hardball with the own-ers of those rigged gas stations. British Petroleum has already pulled their name off the stations, and I'm sure the other companies will fol-low suit. The U.S. Attorney has ticked off a laundry list of felonies."

"And I can say from my experience with the feds," said Gloria, "that I'm sure they'll be willing to deal to catch the big fish."

"It looks like you have some potential clients. A majority of the guys involved in this scam are Russian immigrants."

"No, Art, I'm winding down toward retirement. I've been in the trenches all my life, I don't need to work. To change the subject, I'm very happy to see you. Vera has been nearly impossible since that little spat you two had."

Art couldn't pinpoint what had changed about Gloria. She seemed edgy. *Exactly what did Vera say? It couldn't be all that bad because Gloria invited me to dinner. Is Vera going to read him the riot act?* He said to Gloria, "Just when I thought I had learned to read Vera better, she blew her top. I still don't know what I said or did that warranted her stomping out the door like that."

"Just be patient," answered Gloria.

"I've never been in love like this before. Most of the time she's a joy to be around, but I don't understand the wild cards she plays. She called me almost as soon as she got home and told me it wasn't my fault. But she wouldn't open up. If I'd known how miserable I would be without her, I would have accepted her apology right away. I guess I'm a glutton for punishment."

Gloria eased herself onto a recliner. "Art, she cares an awful lot about you. And from what you said just now, I sense your commitment."

Eudora came in carrying a tray. "I have lemonade and cookies for Missus. What can I get for you, Mr. Williams?"

"This lemonade is fine, thank you."

As she poured the drink, the maid smiled and gave a brief high sign. "Vera will be a few minutes late. Don't forget to compliment her."

Art thought, *First Gloria gets me going on the Russian Mafia and now Eudora gives me instructions. I wonder what's next.*

Some ten minutes later, Art rose as Vera Li entered the room preceded by more than a hint of expensive perfume. He couldn't take his eyes off her. *Wow, this is sexiest dress I have ever seen her wear. She is the most beautiful woman I've ever met.*

He soaked into his memory the figure-hugging sheath, which was cut to disclose a hint of her cleavage. Her long hair was down, and bangs were combed over her forehead. With her dark eyes fixed on him, he had no doubt her smile was just for him. She greeted Art with a hand behind his neck and a warm kiss on the lips, "Art, I really missed you over the last week. I had a hard time concentrating on my studies."

"I missed you too. Say, is that a new dress?"

Turning halfway around to the right and back, she said, "Yes, Grandmother picked it out for me yesterday. Do you like it?"

"Yes, indeed, and the perfume too. Vera, you are radiant. Not just radiant, you are beautiful tonight."

Gloria said, "I told Vera that she needs to come out of her shell, like I did. I was once afraid to show myself to my best advantage, but I had the sense to change when Joe returned. It's time Vera did the same; she'll be graduating from college in June."

Through dinner and dessert, Gloria carried the conversation while Vera openly flirted and Art half-pretended not to notice. Afterward he and Vera walked out onto the deck, ostensibly to watch the lights of the city fade in and out of the fog. The tall Eurasian pressed against him as if trying to stay out of the wind that was whistling by them. He spoke in a voice just a little above a whisper, "You're an entirely different girl tonight than when we were together last. Why did you leave?"

"Art, like I said, I'm sorry." She looked out at the distant lights before continuing, "I was frustrated. I wanted to rip off my clothes and make wild, passionate love." Looking at him, she shook her head slightly. "You ignored my every signal."

He recalled where his hands were and the question he had asked that caused her to leave abruptly. He chose not to bring it up again. Instead he took the time to inhale and exhale while he held her close. "I've been following your ground rules," he said, "Aren't you the same born again virgin I've been dating all these months?"

Vera stuck out her lower lip. "I know I promised Grandpa Joe, but I can't help what I feel. I don't want to be a virgin anymore."

He ran a hand through his blond hair. "Ever since the night we met, I've felt there was something special in you, that you were someone who would be more than a lover."

"How do I show I love you?" Vera continued to look at the night lights.

He turned her so he could look her in the eye. "You do it all the time." He studied her for a time, then swallowed. "Vera, every day since you walked out, I've felt terrible, like I've lost my way. I've been doing a lot of thinking. I don't want to be single anymore. I'll solve your problem after you solve mine."

"Art, Art, what are you saying?"

"I know you are a very old-fashioned girl and I love you for it. Please Vera, will you marry me?"

Her puzzled look brightened into a broad smile "Yes, oh, dear God, thank you! Yes!"

He folded her into his arms for a kiss, and Vera pressed hard against him. Afterward they looked out at the shadow-filled view and the distant lights, then kissed again and again. After about twenty minutes, she began shivering in the chill, breezy night air. Still holding her hand, he led her back into the house.

Her grandmother looked up from her reading. "You two were out on the deck for an awfully long time. Vera, you're shivering."

Art looked at his intended out of the corner of his eye. She was still smiling. He cleared his throat, "Gloria … er … Mrs. Caulfels … would you be the one in the family to ask if I could have Vera's hand in marriage?"

Gloria jumped to her feet faster than Art thought she could move. She embraced the pair. "Yes, yes, yes!" She stepped back to an arm's length and stood tall. "Yes, Mr. Arthur Williams, I highly approve. Have you decided when, or it is too early to ask?"

Looking at his fiancé, Art answered, "No, but I don't believe either of us could live through a long engagement. Vera, darling, why don't you pick a day in the early summer that works for your family?"

As Vera nodded acceptance, Gloria squeezed their arms, tears running down her cheeks. Her voice was breaking. "You don't know how much this means to me to see the two of you so happy and in love. You've just given me something to live for."

"Grandmother, I can't believe you'd say that," said Vera.

"Without Grandpa Joe, my life is empty. He was the rudder that steered me from the shoals. Just today, I got call from the surviving son of the family that Tad Gregory murdered. Remember him? I saved him from the death penalty. The son blames me because Gregory is still alive. What can I say? The man even made my skin crawl, but every criminal deserves a vigorous defense. Yet why does it have to be me, why should I have to live with the aftermath? I've already given notice that I will not seek another contract with the Public Defender's Office."

Art thought, *This isn't good.* After a pause, he said, "Gloria, you will be missed."

"It's Joe who's missed. I'm far too easily distracted by the pain in my heart. Just because the man you love has died, you don't stop loving him."

"I miss Grandpa Joe too," said Vera. "I wanted for him to give me away."

"I would have loved to have seen that," said Gloria.

Vera's voice was almost too low to be heard, "Then maybe I should ask Papa Sung?"

Art had never seen such an instantaneous reaction to another's words. Gloria's blue eyes widened and her eyebrows arched as she spat the word, "What!"

"He is my father. I really don't have anyone else."

The doorbell rang while Vera was talking, but Gloria stood and pointed an accusing finger toward her granddaughter. "No, there's only one reason you'd want him!"

Art thought, *Whatever went on between father and daughter can't be all that bad if she wants him to give her away.* "Gloria, Vera …," he said, "let's talk this out. We don't have to make any decisions tonight."

Gloria glared back at the couple as she walked toward the front door. On opening it, she exclaimed, "Winston, what are you doing up here tonight?"

The big Black man had a hand on Gloria's biceps and was gently pulling her across the threshold. "Boss, you've got a problem. Please step outside."

"Can't this wait?"

Once he had led Gloria to the curb, Win said, "I just happened to be dining with one of my federal friends. They had some complaints about what sounded like casual conversations between three women, Vera, Eudora, and Gloria."

"Where? Who? What are you talking about?"

"You! Your chatter tonight has been screwing up the police frequencies in Sausalito. Congratulations, Gloria, you're a skilled matchmaker."

"What! It can't be. Sausalito's on the other side of the Bay," exclaimed Gloria.

"Your house is bugged."

"Son of a gun! It never dawned on me to make a sweep of my own house while we were moving in. How bad is it?"

"Don't know, it's not an ordinary bugging. They're using state-of-the-art equipment that transmits in coded bursts, which messes up public safety frequencies. This interference has been going on sporadically for quite some time. It would have never been discovered if the bugs didn't transmit on police frequencies."

Gloria shook her fist. "Law enforcement frequencies, those bastards! How stupid! I'm going to make it a federal case."

Win pointed to a step van parked nearby, "I have a team standing by outside. Can I have your permission to call in the bloodhounds and locate these varmints?"

"By all means."

⋆⊱⋆⊰⋆

The arrival of the crew with their equipment ended any semblance of peace in the Caulfels house. Some thirty minutes later, the head technician joined Win, Gloria, Art, and Vera in the living room and placed a playing-card-sized electronic box on the coffee table. "This is the guts of it. Who installed your security system?"

Vera said, "Yun Pei."

"That was some time ago," said Gloria. "Joe told me the security company called and told him our system had failed and they'd replace it at no cost. It was right about the time I was assigned the Godoniski case. That damned Dale Bleasman, I'll have his head!"

Win said, "Wait, don't jump to conclusions. Do you know anything about this Yun Pei?"

Vera glanced at Art for a moment before looking down. "He was very handsome. He was shorter than I am and in his late twenties. He said he was born in North Korea and his family moved to someplace in Russia when he was a teenager."

Gloria said, "And she had quite a crush on him."

"Did you date him?" Win queried.

She shook her head vigorously to emphasize a very definite no. "He lost all interest in me when he found out I'm an American who can't speak any Korean." She reached out for Art's hand. "Then I met my true love."

The technician held up the small box. She used a jeweler's screwdriver as a pointer. "The miniaturization on this encoder-transmitter is state of the art. It perfectly mimics the latest and best used by the FBI. It was extremely difficult to pinpoint and decipher. If they had stayed off the 700-megahertz band, we probably would never have known about them."

Art bent over to study the details. Then he looked at the technician. "I didn't know the FBI imports this stuff from Russia."

"Do they? If they don't, maybe they ought to," said Gloria.

Art fingered his cell phone. "These are the same markings as are on the crooked circuit boards they found at all the gas stations. If you dial the number etched on the edge, you'll get the Feliks Dzerzhinsky Missile Works. It's located outside Tver, Russia. The manager will tell you they're out of the war business."

"Well, it's obvious they're not out of the spy business. Feliks Dzerzhinsky was the first head of the Soviet secret police," said the technician.

Win said, "Alexander Tsamonicoff, our local Russian Mafia godfather, used to work for the KGB. Gloria, do you remember where you called from to set up the time to meet with Alya the night you were mugged?"

"Come to think of it … I'm sure it was from here."

Win said, "I suppose we'll never know for sure, but my best guess is that Tibbie Fuentes was the connection, not Dale Bleasman. Tibbie arranged your ambush by Ramirez and the pair of Russians. Even as incompetent as the prosecutor is, he would have done far better against you if he had your game plan. And in Jesse Sollair's case, you never would have won if he'd been eavesdropping."

"Yes," said Gloria, "but remember how touch-and-go it was until I blew the balls off that pair. There's too much coincidence here. I'm going to call Sacramento tomorrow and give the facts to the state attorney general. So it won't come as a complete surprise, I'll contact that lowlife SOB Bleasman in the morning and tell him what I did. Let him sweat while he watches the chips fall, for a change."

Art again consulted his watch. "Why wait to call him when he can read about it with his morning coffee? I've got time to do a rewrite."

The technician said, "Could I ask you to delay the story until I consult with Washington? I'm sure this is a national security matter."

"Look," said Art, "The Russians know they stole your system. We know they stole your system. Can you give me one reason for not letting on to the American people that it isn't just the Chinese who are robbing us blind of our technology?"

Vera held on to Art's arm. "Darling, you told me you were going to arrange to be off tonight. Why not save it so you can have something to write for tomorrow?"

Art was excited. "And give some bureaucrat who's trying to cover his butt a chance to drop a spike? If Red will give me enough inches, I'll make our engagement part of a front-page story."

Gloria clapped her hands. "Vera, dear, you're going to have to learn to put your man's work first. Besides, all this excitement has taken away most of the evening. Art, I have nothing other than a feeling in my gut to prove that Dale was in on this. However, the connection between the crooked gas pumps and this bugging system isn't a story you should let slip away. Let him sweat."

The technician said, "I suggest you call that alarm company and get another system. With the black box missing, this system can no longer transmit, but I have no idea what else that Korean fellow left tucked away in your house."

They picked the third Saturday in June for the wedding, and time dragged until the countdown to the appointed day was less than a week away. Art was aware of the continuing tension between Gloria and Vera over Papa Sung's role in the wedding. Neither one was willing to discuss reasons or details. In spite of their differences, the grandmother's spirits were lifted. As each part of the celebration fell into place, it became readily apparent that as far as Gloria was concerned, costs were not a factor. Much to Art's surprise, she insisted on buying him a tuxedo, choosing for him the most expensive one in the store. Although the couple both wanted to move into Art's apartment, Gloria continued to insist that they move into an upstairs suite of her house, at least temporarily after the honeymoon.

On the Wednesday before the wedding day, Art and Vera met the plane carrying Sung, Jenny, and their two sons, ages ten and eleven. After the way Gloria described Reverend Sung and his foibles, Art was braced for a stormy welcome. Instead he found the Reverend to be quite charming and urbane. He watched his future father-in-law put his arm around his wife's waist and squeeze her. Jenny glowed and her eyes, which seemed almost ready to tear, sparkled. Vera, however, stiffened and turned her head as Sung hugged her and affectionately kissed her on her cheek.

⊶ ❍ ❍ ⊷

Late in the afternoon, while waiting alone for the wedding rehearsal to begin, Vera was shocked when Papa Sung whispered into her ear, "Darling, you must be the most beautiful woman this Art fellow has ever met. I question if he is the right man for you. He doesn't have the fire and passion to match yours."

"Please, Papa, I love him with all my heart. He is my very best friend. All the fire and passion will come later."

"You love him as a friend, but not as your lover?"

"Papa, I asked you to give me away so you could acknowledge the end of our relationship. I thought you'd be proud of me that I took the vow to be a born again virgin and wait for sex until after we made our commitment before God. I've known this man since last summer, and he honors me and respects me. I love Arthur."

Sung Li stood frozen with his eyes fixed on her as she walked away. At the last moment, he said, "Vera Li, we need to talk."

CHAPTER 11

Art found himself distracted throughout the rehearsal dinner. He was experiencing and enjoying a side of his intended that he never knew existed. Vera was so openly flirtatious, almost risque, that Art was sure she was rehearsing for the wedding night. She rested her hand on the inner side of his thigh. She repeated, at least three or four times, "I love you very much" in a voice he was sure carried down the table. Once during dessert, Vera lightly nipped his ear before whispering, "Tomorrow night, lover, tomorrow night." He felt like he was in paradise.

Midway through dinner, Jenny approached them. "My youngest boy is sick. I've got to take them back to the hotel. He has a terrible case of the runs."

After dinner, as Art walked Vera to her car, Sung approached. "Vera, Jenny took off without me. Would you be a dear and drop me off at the hotel?"

"I'd be happy to do it," Art pointed to his car.

"It's been a very long time since I've had a chance to talk to Vera. Please, grant her father one last opportunity to be with her before her big day. I'd like to have a few moments to chat on the way to my hotel."

Art thought about Gloria's allusions to some sort of improper conduct by Vera's father, but he dismissed the thought when she gave him a long, passionate French kiss. She ended it by exhaling passionately, "Until tomorrow. I love you, Art, very, very much."

He watched the red Miata drive away with its top down until it reached the crest of a hill and disappeared. The Reverend Sung turned halfway around in the passenger seat and looked back at him. Though Sung's face was obscured by the shadows, Art visualized Sung's sour look when he found them necking on the deck the night before.

The bridegroom's trip back to his apartment was a leisurely one. He was happy and just tired enough that his good night's sleep began when his head hit the pillow.

⟶⟩❖⟨⟵

Art awoke with a few butterflies in his stomach, but he buried them under a hearty breakfast. His mind was on the details of the day. He reviewed what he was to wear, checking off what had been packed into the suitcase. He thumbed through the folder where Vera had spelled out the trip logistics for the voyage that would take them to Portland for a week-long sail up the Columbia River. The cruise had been Vera's idea; it would allow them time enough to visit his mother in the nursing home in Walla Walla. He recalled Vera's words and the promises of the nights to come.

He had just taken the plastic bag off the tuxedo when the phone rang. Gloria's voice was loud and angry. "Art, come up to my house immediately. We have a crisis!"

"What's up? I was putting on the handsome tux you gave me."

"Don't bother. I can't tell you over the phone. Hurry!"

He thought, *Don't bother. That does it. There's no way I'm moving into the same house with her. Wait, something big is wrong.* Art struggled to maintain control of his voice. "Gloria, what happened to Vera? Which hospital…?"

"Please, Art, we have a crisis. Get in your car and come up here, now!"

"Tell me, what happened to Vera?"

"I'll explain when you get here." She hung up.

Art was alarmed and at the same time annoyed, *She could have told me something about what's wrong. Is Vera sick? In an accident? Cold feet?*

He weaved through busy Saturday morning traffic on his way up the hill to the Caulfels' substantial residence. He pulled into Gloria's driveway next to the Sungs' rental car. Gloria met him at the door. Art was surprised how old she looked in her bathrobe with her long grey hair hanging loose. Her lips were thin and her eyes were a cold cast of blue. "The damned whore didn't come home last night."

"What? Who?"

"Vera Li, the damned whore, didn't come home last night."

"Whore! You've been the one twisting my arm to marry her. What in blazes are you talking about?"

"We saw her drive off with him."

"So, have you called the hotel or the police?"

Gloria said, "The damned police should have been called seven years ago. Everybody had to be in love with the damned pervert. I told my daughter, but, oh no, she was too much in love with the pervert."

Art was taken aback; he had never seen this side of Gloria. *Vera's no whore. Now I know why they call Gloria a bitch. I let her play match-maker with a reluctant girl. Pervert? What exactly went on between them?* Art rejoined, "Is this what you and Vera have been squabbling about, but haven't the decency to tell me about?"

Gloria slumped and looked at the ground. She said nothing and continued to look away even after he said, "Whore? How dare you! You're the one who coaxed me back and was ecstatic when I proposed."

She scuffed the entryway with her slippered foot, then looked up. "You don't deserve this. Please forgive me. I am so sorry. I should never have reached out to you after she ran away. What I didn't want to see was that she was still in love with him."

"I don't believe it. She never gave me any indication of that, especially last night."

Gloria said, "From the time she came to live with me, I wanted her to play the field and learn to develop healthy relationships. The clever minx sold Joe on that 'born again virgin' crap. That left her free to play the lovesick role, pining over Sung. I should have put my foot down when she insisted on having him give her away. She sold me with the argument that by giving her away, they would both be acknowledging the end of the affair."

"Gloria, you of all people! I can't believe you'd sweep a case of incest under the rug." Art stood nose to nose with Gloria. "I am so damned mad that you kept me in the dark. You can't imagine the hurt I'm feeling. I love Vera. If I'd known, I would never let Sung get into her car. Should I ask when you were going to tell me? After the honeymoon, with an invitation to join one big happy family?"

Gloria said, "Yes, I should have told you. That's cruel. But I had that coming."

Jenny approached them from inside the house, her eyes red from crying. "No, Arthur, we are not that kind of family. I shipped her here to end an affair. Sung isn't her natural father. Something has been wrong for too many years. We should have listened to the people at the orphanage and never adopted the harpy."

"What do you mean? I thought she was your and Sung's daughter. That's what she told me."

"That's what she pretends to be, but the truth of the matter is, she was born the daughter of a drug-dealing Korean whore and some drunken soldier."

"What?"

"Sung and I had been married seven years. I had one miscarriage. That's it. We had given up hope. When we visited the Tangju orphanage, this little six-year-old girl wrapped her arms around my legs and begged to be adopted. She was obviously Eurasian and spoke English without an accent. "She said, 'I am an American! You've got to take me home!'

"We inquired and they said that yes, she was available. She had been born in the United States to a Korean mother and an American father. The mother, a drugged-up prostitute, was serving a long prison term. No one knew where the father was. The director told us she was a poor risk because she was willful and refused to learn Korean. Sung and I prayed. We felt she was our reward from the Almighty for the work we had done."

Gloria all but screamed, "This should never have happened! When she insisted that Sung give her away, I knew she hadn't gotten him out of her heart. She looked me right in the eye and lied. That shifty, lying whore! Art, please forgive me, I should have just let the whole thing drop when she lost interest the first time. It's my fault! That damned whore!"

"This doesn't compute," said Art. "I offered to drive him back to his hotel, but he insisted on going with Vera. How do you know they are together?"

Gloria said, "Stop kidding yourself. This was prearranged. Jenny, did he come to the room at all last night?"

"No! I know damn well what he's doing!"

"Face up to reality, Art!" Gloria yelled at him. "She is a clever, lying minx. I am so ashamed of what I've done to you. If I could only die."

Art thought, *Every memory I have is of the sweetest, most beautiful girl I've ever met. What is it with these people? Can a priest do something so evil? I need to find her and hear her side. I want to hear it from her lips.*

Jenny's voice was almost shrill enough to shatter glass. "Right in front of me, I watched her. She lusted after him, flirting and touching. When I was recovering from giving birth to my youngest, she lured him into her bed. I should never have given him a second chance. Oh, my dear God, what am I going to do? I'm thirty-eight years old and have two young sons. I don't have any education."

Gloria snapped, "Jenny, enough of that. He's going to prison this time."

"Then isn't it time to call the cops?" asked Art.

"There'll be time enough for that," said Gloria. "It's almost noon and the wedding starts at one. Art, stop kidding yourself. She isn't here. She won't be here. And she won't be at the church. As seamy as it sounds, she's rolling in the hay with him as we speak. Go down to the church and tell them the wedding is off. Encourage everyone to go to the reception. Hell, we paid for the food and the caterer. They might as well enjoy it even if we can't."

Jenny said, "All she had to do was look at him or whisper in his ear. She's like a narcotic to Sung."

'I don't believe it. Vera loves me, I know it. I'll drive home and put on my tux and go straight to the church. Call the church and tell them we'll both be a little late." Art spoke the words, but the thoughts piling up in the back of his head were saying the opposite.

"Don't kid yourself," exclaimed Gloria, "once she laid eyes on him, the old chemistry took over. Damn her! Damn her to hell!"

⊷═◉═⊷

Just after Art drove away, Jenny said, "Mother, I told my husband that I needed some time here in the States. Seven years away was too long and I needed to sort things out in my life. He didn't like that and was real upset with me until Vera's letter arrived. They must have had some way to communicate behind our backs. He's flying out late this afternoon so he can preach tomorrow at St. Bede's. It's obvious now. The pair of them will be on the plane to Houston and back to Costa Rica tomorrow night."

"She pined for him out in the open," said Gloria, "until about the time she graduated from high school. Jenny, darling, I just thought of something you must do without delay. Sung committed incest in Texas, and that's where he is going. You lived in Houston, right?"

"No, outside in Harris County."

"Then get on the phone and make a complaint to the Harris County authorities. This is the only window you'll have to nail this pair. If the authorities are smart, they'll hold them both, him for trial and her as a material witness."

"Oh, Mother, I don't know."

Gloria handed Jenny the phone. Her voice was full of motherly authority. "Dammit, you've given them both a second chance. It's time to introduce you to a good divorce lawyer. Let me assure you that we know how to do divorces in California."

"It's been seven years, Mother," said Jenny, who thought there must be some way to save her marriage.

"I know that very well. The definition of incest under Texas law includes sexual relations with an adopted child. After you do that, check out of your hotel and bring the children here. Eudora and I will take care of them."

"Thank you for your offer, Mother, but I already promised Carole to fly down to L.A. tonight. I'll be back in a week or ten days. I've really missed all of you. It's been a long and lonely seven years."

"Why don't you want to stay with me?"

"I'll come back, Mother."

"Well, I don't know if I'll be around. There's no one left who cares for me. Your father was my whole life."

"Please don't make this any more difficult than it already is. Why don't you get into your new dress and come on down to eat some of that feast?"

Gloria reached for the phone. "I'd rather shoot myself. I can't face those people after what this slant-eyed whore did. Here, call the cops down in Texas right now!"

"Yes, Mother."

One-thirty had passed into history and the hour was approaching two when the best man, Major Andy Caulfels, stood in front of the assembled guests. The titter of conversation and movement in the pews dropped off by degrees to silence. He said, "We don't know what happened to the bride. I know she invited many of you, but she's nowhere to be found. We're sorry, but there will be no wedding today. The Caulfels family asks that you all follow them to the hall. We have a huge spread and we know you came here with appetites, so join us. There's more there than we can eat. Please come."

Art and the rest of the wedding party formed an informal reception line. No sooner had the last of the guests passed through the line than the major put a hand on the groom's shoulder. "Art, my friend, I was honored to be chosen as your best man. Let me say this in behalf of my brother and sisters: we, too, were losers today that you couldn't become part of our family. You've got the guts of a Caulfels to stand here and greet these people. I'm disappointed that my mother wouldn't come. I just called the house and Jenny is getting her kids ready to come here."

"Thanks Andy, the feeling is mutual. To let the truth be known, I'm numb. I don't want to believe this has happened. This is not the Vera I asked to marry me. Let's go over and get something to eat."

The crowd ate their fill and commiserated the groom, and most left as quickly as possible, leaving a few hangers-on and the wedding party. Art moved to one side to give bridesmaid Amy Pankery a place to sit. Art knew her as a childhood friend of Vera's whom he met the day before. Amy said, "Does anyone remember way back when Vera came to live with her grandmother?" There was a silence before she continued, "Right after she came here, something happened that made me wonder just who'd be brave enough to marry her."

Art responded, "Brave enough … what do you mean?"

"It all started right here in this hall. She was by far the prettiest girl in the congregation and, much to all the boys' frustrations, she kept them at a distance. There was one boy, Jason Omertsu, who had a terrible crush on her. He was a couple of years older and a very popular football player. He could have had just about any girl. Maybe the fact that she was so aloof was what turned him on. Anyway, much to our surprise, he brought her to a youth group meeting. After the meetings, we used to come down here and neck before our parents came and took us home. The first time Jason laid his hands on her, she literally knocked his feet out from under him, landing him on his butt. He lost his temper and swung at her. She blocked his punch and danced away from him. She started bobbing and weaving like a boxer. Everybody laughed except Jason. Have you ever seen her do that stuff?"

Art thought back to the times he had watched her practice aikido and tae kwon do. She could take care of herself. He had never seen anyone who reacted with the speed she did. He felt she had an advantage because she had trained herself to remain focused and always observe. He reminded Amy that Vera was a black belt.

The bridesmaid said, "Black belt or whatever, no sooner had he started to put up his fists than she leaped almost like a dancer. It was like you see in the Bruce Lee movies. She hit him in the face with her foot and broke his nose. He was lying on the floor with blood gushing. She told him that she really didn't want to date him, it was all her grandmother's idea. Afterward I asked her why and she said, 'Nobody can touch me except the man I love.' I thought she had a crush on somebody else, so I didn't pry. But there was no one. And now I know. Art, you didn't deserve what she did to you any more than Jason deserved a broken nose."

With that, she gave him a sisterly kiss on the cheek and walked across the room, where she cuddled close to her boyfriend.

Art stood up and thrust his fists deep into the pockets of his tux. With shoulders rounded and head down, he kicked imaginary rocks as he headed toward the door. Ahead he saw Jenny with her two boys. She was talking to Major Andy, whose eyes widened as they caught his. He waved to Art to come over. Art heard Jenny say, "Of course I'm sure, Andy. Here is a copy of the schedule: Southwest to Dallas and landing in Houston close to midnight."

Andy's voice was full of urgency. "The Reverend Sung is booked on Southwest Flight 2441 leaving at 5:15. Dammit, Sis, why didn't you tell us this earlier?"

Between sobs, Jenny said, "Mother insisted that I notify the police down there that he's coming. We called, and they promised a Detective Evans would call. I waited as long as I could. The boys were starving."

"What about Mother?" asked Andy.

"She's staying there to make sure the detective gets the word. After all this time away from home, I'm sorry to say I was happy to get out of there. I'd almost forgotten how nasty her moods can be. There's no Ma or our Daddy there to talk sense to her. She was all over my boys. Andy, don't waste your time trying to stop them. I've faxed my written statement. Mother said they'll throw both of them in jail as soon as they land."

I need to get to the bottom of this, here and now. Art grabbed Andy by the arm. "Come on, let's get out to the airport! I want to hear it from Vera's mouth why she is with him."

Andy looked at his watch. "Okay, if I get you there before the plane leaves, you run for the gate. I'll park the car and rendezvous at the gate. Don't try to be a hero or anything like that. Remember, it's over. Just talk to them. Ask her why. Got it?"

Once they were driving south on the Nimitz Freeway, Andy said, "I overheard Amy spinning the tale about Vera. When she first came here, she was full of anger, even got suspended from school because of her temper. She grew out of it. There was one sure thing about our house, no one could long remain angry around my father. That included my mother."

"Your mother's performance today was something out of *1984*, calling Vera a whore and making her the bad guy. If it's true as she describes it, the man seduced a vulnerable teenage girl. And they cast a blind eye on the whole thing."

"Believe me, it's true. When Jenny showed up at Dad and Mom's door with Vera, she made the case that Vera was the seductress. Vera looked and acted like a teenage vamp. Maybe my father was roped in by Sung's preaching. I don't know what swayed them more, fear of Jenny falling back into depression if he was arrested, or the fallout of the scandal on their professional lives. That left Vera as the pawn."

Art thought, *No doubt she felt used again with Gloria conducting a full court press to get us to marry. Had I only known.*

Andy continued, "My father took Vera under his wing. It took time for her heart to heal."

"What I can't get my arms around," said Art, "is pretending there's no family relationship; that somehow Vera faked being their daughter."

"When they came back from Korea, Jenny introduced her as their daughter. Jenny named her after her grandmother Caulfels. Sung called her 'Number One' daughter. My father picked up on it, as 'Granddaughter Number One.' You could tell she was a little girl who wanted to be loved."

"Vera told me about her grandmother. She called her Ma Caulfels. What was she like?"

"Ma was the one who raised us. Mother tucked us into bed and said prayers, but it was Ma who was around and made us toe the line. We all loved her almost as much as Mother. Back in those days, it was tough. Father was a professor and for a long time, he didn't make much money. Or if he did, he gave it away."

Andy cut in and out of traffic on Hegenberger Road. When he wheeled up to the curb at the airport, Art jumped out. He sprinted to the first monitor with flight information and saw that he had six minutes to run to the gate. In his hurry to get through the security checkpoint, Art set off the alarm. A bored, sleepy-looking guard took his time to detect Art's pocket calculator and clear him through. Art sprinted through a crowd of arriving passengers, feinting, pausing, and almost shoving people until he got to the closed jetway door. Outside, a tractor was pushing the jet away from the terminal. He pounded on the wall next to the window. "Damn, damn, damn!"

A ticket agent approached. "I'm sorry, sir, that you missed your flight. Come over to the counter and let me check for a seat on our next flight. Where are you headed, Houston?"

Art worked the tendons in his neck and jaw before finally exhaling a deep breath. "I was hoping to find out if someone was on that flight. Could you tell me if Vera and Sung Li were aboard?"

"The computer out here is closed after departure. I'm sorry."

"Well, do you remember a distinguished-looking Asian, a Korean with silver sideburns?"

The agent nodded. Art took a deep breath. "Was there a tall and quite beautiful Asian woman with long brunette hair with him?"

The agent shrugged his shoulders. "There were some Asian women, but I don't recall any tall ones. Come to think of it, I think the man had a second seat reserved. We had two lines going, so I could have missed her. We seated all the standbys. It was nearly full. I'm sorry I can't help you."

Art felt the bottom fall out of his world. He watched the jet turn and head toward a slot on the departing runway. The urge to call the police and tell them Sung had sex with his daughter was hard to suppress. He asked himself, *What proof did he have?* He answered the question for himself: *None, other than the rantings of an angry family.* This wasn't the first time Vera had blown cold at the wrong time. She could be anywhere.

Fifteen minutes later, Andy caught up with him. The conversation was brief. Art acknowledged that Sung had gotten away and maybe Vera was his seatmate. In response to Art's request to take him back to the church to pick up his car, Andy asked him what he planned to do.

"Tonight I'm swearing off Eudora's lemonade. All that sugar rots your teeth. There's what we newspaper folk call a watering hole down by the *Tribune*. I'm going to go there and see if I can ease this pain in my heart. Maybe there'll be somebody who'll take pity on me. Who knows? Why the hell did Vera lead me on, then dump me like this? This is the second time in my life this has happened. What's wrong with Arthur Williams?"

In the church parking lot, Andy shook his hand and said, "Mother would probably have one of her fits if she heard me say this--but I'd do the same thing if I were in your shoes. I'll follow you down and buy the first round.

CHAPTER 12

What was it that first awakened Vera Li in the dark hotel room: the rush of water through a pipe, the audio of a television when the door of a nearby room opened, or voices of people as they passed the closed door to her room? For some time she lay there in the dark, half awake, listening to these and other sounds, but not comprehending. She drifted back asleep, then awoke with the strong need to go to the bathroom. She ran her fingers through the tangles of her thick, loose hair. *What a mess. Thank God I'm getting my hair done this morning.*

Her limbs were heavy, almost as if they were paralyzed. Blurred red numbers of the room's clock-radio were her only light. By degrees, she felt an unfamiliar mattress until she touched the edge of the bed. Vera found that it took all of her concentration to balance her body over a pair of uneasy legs. Each step brought a burning discomfort between her legs. She bumped into a chair and almost lost her balance. She groped until her fingers felt a lampshade and she found the switch at the bottom. It clicked, but it produced no light. She kept fumbling in the dark until she found a light switch on the wall and turned it on. A single lamp on the far side of the bed swept away the darkness, but the light hurt her eyes at first. Everything she saw was blurred and distorted until slowly her eyes came into semi-focus. Now she realized she was in a hotel room. She didn't recognize anything, but yet there was an uneasy feeling of familiarity about the place.

She had a vague memory of being naked and looking for her clothes, but now she was dressed. She tugged at her bra because it was binding. The sight of the open door to the bathroom spurred her to seek relief. Passing water brought more soreness. Her body had never felt like this before, even after her first time with Papa Sung. What happened?

When she was done, she looked at herself in the mirror. *How am I go-*

ing to get married looking like this? How did my eyes get so bloodshot? What's with these heavy dark rings? Why am I so hungry and thirsty?

She filled a glass with water and gulped it down, followed by another. She had just put the glass under the tap for the third time when she thought she was going to throw up. Compounding her queasy stomach was a touch of light-headedness. *I must be hungry*, she told herself. She stared at her watch until she could finally make out the numbers through the haze. It was 9:05. She thought that this was strange because she had just eaten dinner.

Vera used her fingers to straighten her hair. Puzzled, she wondered where her barrettes were. The memory of Art's kiss came back. With a sense of urgency, she dialed his number and let it ring until the answering machine spoke. By the time Vera realized she was in no condition to match wits with the telephonic robot, the connection had been severed. Disappointed, she hung up without leaving her message.

Through the haze that was clouding her mind, fingers of memory returned. She remembered driving off with Papa Sung. She had reluctantly accepted his invitation to come in for a drink. She had ordered a tall fruit drink, and was annoyed because he teased her for not joining him in a single glass of wine. When he left the table, she thought he was going to bring her mother down from the room. Then everything went haywire. Where was Papa Sung now?

Vera was relieved to find the missing barrettes next to her purse. She gobbled down a couple of hotel-provided energy bars, and that settled her stomach. She found her jacket in the closet, gathered up her purse, and opened the door. She stepped into an empty corridor. *Where am I? This is like a nightmare. Nothing is familiar. What did Papa Sung do to me?*

Vera walked around the whole floor searching for the elevator. Once she was inside, the elevator's closing doors triggered her first significant flashback. There was the sound of breaking glass. Why was she was giggly and unable to keep her balance? Papa Sung helped her to her feet and almost carried her out of the cocktail lounge and across the lobby to the elevator. She wanted to drive home, only her legs had turned to rubber. The flashback ended with the elevator chime after the number indicator blurred and faded into darkness.

How long ago was this? she asked herself. Now the elevator door opened, and she saw a deserted lobby she didn't recognize. She got out and walked around, peering into shops that were now closed. The entry to the cocktail lounge looked familiar. The noise level within told of a full house. The hostess immediately blocked Vera's way, politely asking, "I'm sorry to have to ask this, Miss, but how many drinks did you have today?"

What? I don't drink, Vera thought and shook her head a vigorous no, saying, "... Never ..."

The hostess's eyes widened. "Never drink? I watched you stagger across the lobby. Stop kidding yourself. You were warned not to come in here again."

I don't remember that. Vera stared at the hostess. "I … I … I …?"

"You were falling down drunk. Don't you remember falling onto a table and spilling the drinks last night?

Could that be the sound of broken glass? "Broke glass …?"

"Look at yourself. You're a mess and you smell like a pig."

Vera was shocked at her words. One side of her wanted to punch the woman out. The other side was emotionally washed out and physically exhausted. The sentences that formed in her mind were, *Please help me. I don't know what happened last night. I'm looking for Papa Sung, He's a graying Korean. Have you seen him?* The disjointed words the hostess heard were, "Please .... me .... look .... Papa .... Korean .... you .... seen ....?"

"Papa, you mean the man you were with? No. What's your room number?"

"Don't ... know. ... want .... something .... eat ....," begged Vera.

The hostess fell back a step to block Vera's way into the room. "If you don't leave, I'm calling Security."

She was reaching for her cell phone when Vera said, " Okay .... not .... drinker. ... Won't come here again."

Vera weaved out the hotel's front door. She had no memory of where she had parked her car. It was close to nine forty-five and she wanted to get home. What had begun as a discomfort in her vagina turned into serious pain by the time she had walked twice around the front lot. She felt relieved when a uniformed parking attendant approached. "Miss, have you lost your car?"

"Red Miata."

"A convertible, I know exactly where it is. Please follow me."

Once at the car, Vera thought as she unsnapped and stored the tonneau cover, *Papa Sung making me install the cover should have been a red flag. Why did he do this to me? I loved him!*

She opened her purse. On top was a note and five one-hundred-dollar bills. Puzzled, she tried to read the longhand, but the letters were blurred. She told herself it was because of the poor light. It took a couple of stirrings of the purse's contents to find her keys, and then multiple passes at the steering wheel to find the ignition lock.

Vera's mental fog never lifted all the way to the Caulfels house. Later, she could only recall flashbacks of near misses, screaming brakes, blasting horns, and menacing traffic. Others reacted when she crossed their paths. The first call to nine-one-one came from a hotel security guard, who reported that she almost collided with a row of parked cars and cut off a driver coming into the lot. He delayed his call until the attendant retrieved the license plate number from a spilled stack of papers containing the license numbers of cars to be towed tomorrow. Another driver reported her red Miata weaving across lanes on the MacArthur, but didn't see her exit. There was one last call to nine-one-one at ten-eleven PM when she ran a stop sign some six blocks from home. It was called in on a land line when the driver got home. The red Miata was registered to a Vera Li, with a Mills College address.

Vera made the turn into the driveway. She slammed on the brakes just short of hitting the garage door as it opened. As the door closed behind her, she looked again at the note. With effort, she read aloud, "My darling Vera, I am so very pleased that you feel as I do. After sating our passion, I didn't want to leave you behind. Like I told you, my marriage to Jennifer is dead. Fly to Houston with this $500 and I will divorce her. I'm sorry to have left you as I did. I had to catch this flight as I promised to preach at St. Bede's tomorrow. I will be flying on to San Jose Sunday afternoon. If you don't arrive in time, I'll leave the means and directions so you can join me. My prayers that our love never died have been answered. I love you. Sung"

Sated passion? I couldn't have. What did he do to make me so sore?

I can't remember!

Vera was still shaking her head when the door to the house was thrown open. Gloria, wearing her bathrobe, stormed toward her, gun in hand. "You damned harlot, you have your nerve coming back here tonight!"

"Grandmother, what's wrong?"

"What's wrong, you ask, as if you didn't know! While you and that pervert priest were fucking away the day, you missed your own wedding."

"No, no ... still Friday... don't remember ...."

"It's Saturday night! Let me tell you, I'll never forget today. Your roll in the hay cost thity-five thousand dollars and the most terrible broken heart I've ever seen. Look at you, you're hung over. You know how I feel about alcohol!"

"No ... drinkee? Don't remember .... Terrible ... Grandmother ... listen ... me!"

"No! You listen to me!" Gloria began screaming a nonstop tirade laced with profanity. Vera got out of her car and moved around it with her hands on her ears. As she climbed the stairs, her grandmother followed and screamed at her. Vera mentally blocked out the screeching voice for a moment to remember the last time her grandmother had erupted on her. It was back when she was in high school and broke Jason Omertsu's nose.

As they came into the family room, Vera, who was now crying, thought, *I'm sure if I get something to eat, this headache will go away. I am so screwed up I can hardly talk. Why is she so angry with me? Papa Sung raped me.* "Please, Grandmother, ... have splitting headache. Why you being terrible? Papa Sung ...." She was well aware that what she was saying wasn't what she wanted to say.

"Shut up! You've taken away the last thing I had to live for. I can't bear to face the world. Art Williams was one of the nicest people I've met in years. I'm responsible! I introduced him to you. I did all I could for the two of you. You dropped him cold for that slimy pervert. No, I won't leave you alone. I'll not stop until you're out of my life permanently!"

"Why? Love my Arthur … not Sung. Papa's note … None of this makes sense."

Gloria used the muzzle of her Glock to point at the bills sticking out of the purse. "And you got paid for your favors when you should have been taking marriage vows. You're a slutty whore!"

Vera's face began to color. "No right to keep hammering me! I was the one …."

Gloria leveled the gun at Vera. "Stop whining! You're not spending another night under my roof. Take that suitcase you packed and get the hell out of here. Go back to your Korean lover. Don't ever come back here again."

Vera had never felt so defeated and alone. She faced her grandmother and held her arms out to the sides. "Go ahead, shoot! I'm lost. How can I face anyone after today?"

Gloria lowered the Glock, "That makes two of us. We're both better off dead."

"Grandmother … wait."

"I was screwing up my courage when you got home. I realized none of my children can stand me. Now you've destroyed the last thing I had to live for. I only want to be with Joe. You will do as you are told."

She put the weapon in Vera's hands. "One shot in the back of my head will make it quick and painless. Do it now." She turned, took a few steps, faced the wall, then knelt. As she pulled her hair up, she continued, "Click on the laser and center the red dot at the base of my skull. Squeeze carefully."

Vera dropped the gun on the table as if it was too hot to handle. "Don't want to shoot. Don't want you to die. I love you, Grandmother. Please stand up."

"No one should love me. With my own hands, I've killed three men during my lifetime. I can't count the number of lives ruined or lost because I went that extra mile playing games with prosecutors."

"I love you, Grandmother …."

"Listen to me! You've always done what you're told. Squeeze carefully! This is what I want."

"I can't do this. I don't want you to die," said Vera.

"If you're not up to it, then just shoot me and get the hell out of here.

Think about O.J. Simpson. No gun, no clothes to analyze, and tell them I was alive when you left. Take the tapes from the three surveillance cameras. 'Grandmother was alive when I left.' Say it."

"Grandmother ... alive when I left." Vera's voice was flat and disbelieving. She picked up the gun and clicked on the laser sight, let it flash across the wall, clicked it off, and put the gun down on the table next to Gloria's open laptop. "No ... not going to do this." Vera gritted her teeth and winced with each step while walking through the house toward the front door.

Gloria jumped to her feet and bellowed, "Do what I tell you! Come back here. Vera Li, you can do it. Aim carefully and squeeze the trigger."

Vera felt her way by dragging her hand along the wall until she found the front porch light switch. She was standing in the open door, squinting at the bluish-hued mercury vapor light, by the time her grandmother caught up. Gloria high-stepped past Vera and took a position blocking her path. "Oh, no, you don't. I gave you a job to do, now do it!"

Even as disoriented as she was, Vera knew she shouldn't shoot anybody, especially her grandmother. Yet the most words she could string together were, "Can't ... Feel terrible .... Love you, Grandmother."

"Love me? If you loved me, you would never have insisted on bringing that pious son of a bitch back into this family. I wish I could have killed him like I did the others. He deserves it just as much."

"What others? Why?" Vera asked. Whatever mental disconnect between brain and voice seemed to be past as long as she spoke deliberately.

"All justifiable homicide, thank you. The first was John Diamond, the Goodwin County deputy who framed Joe. It was him or me, and the drunken bum lost. It was a hard night's work burying the fat bastard, but I got it done. I couldn't have pulled it off without the chain fall. Then there was the esteemed Leon Wattersen, Esquire. He made it plain what I had to do if I wanted to keep my job. While he brewed up his libido with alcohol, I waited in bed holding the rattail file. If he hadn't flopped on top of me, I would have punctured his heart too. All the way to the grave, the liar whined that I had consented. And that Russky, that was the shot of a lifetime. Oh, yes, I've tasted blood. It takes courage, but you can do it."

The last sentence echoed in Vera's head. Grandmother wasn't cooling off the way she did before when Grandpa Joe was alive. If that alone wasn't enough for Vera to sense she was in danger, she saw her grandmother's determined look and heard Gloria snap, "If I get my hands on that gun first, they're going to find two bodies here, all right. I'll give you the death you deserve, you fucking whore! I'll blow away both knees and shoot you low in the gut like I did the Russky."

She pushed Vera with both arms on her chest. But now Vera's years of practicing defensive aikido moves paid off. With a reflexive reaction, even before her conscious mind digested Gloria's action, Vera turned and grabbed her grandmother's wrist. A well-placed foot tripped her, and Gloria landed on her stomach. Still holding onto the wrist, Vera applied a twisting pressure that forced the older woman to remain on the floor. Vera said, "Get control of yourself, Grandmother. We need to talk."

Gloria squirmed in silence for close to a minute before she said, "All right, all right, let me up."

No sooner had Gloria regained her feet, with Vera still holding onto her arm, than she snarled, "You deserve to feel some of the pain you've inflicted on the rest of this family, you damned whore. If I get to the Glock first, you're going to feel it, I promise you!"

At this, Vera threw her grandmother back through the open door, where she landed on her knees. Vera used this opportunity to run back to the family room. She grabbed the Glock and held it close to her breast as Gloria followed, carrying three tape cassettes that she put on the table with the laptop. Gloria said, "You'll have to destroy these or they'll nab you for sure."

"Enough of this, please, Grandmother. I love you."

Gloria resumed her position facing the wall. "Good, I knew you wouldn't disappoint me. Don't ever tell anyone, especially not Sung. I've never trusted the bastard, even if he wears a clerical collar! Do as I say, Vera. Aim, squeeze the trigger slowly."

Whenever Vera tried to speak, Gloria continued her tirade--lamenting over and over that everyone wanted her dead, then repeating the aiming instructions with the admonition to never vary from saying that Grandmother was alive when Vera left. She told Vera how to dispose of the gun in parts and to throw out all the clothing she was wearing. Long gone was Gloria's sweet courtroom voice. In its place was a demanding screech that set Vera's teeth on edge.

Two or three times Vera tried to aim the gun. The red dot danced all over in the vicinity of the back of Gloria's head before she again put it on the table. Gloria repeated her threat to kill her granddaughter as painfully as possible. Then she began swearing at her again. She paused and in a tearful, hoarse voice begged Vera to end her misery.

"Please listen to me," begged Vera.

"Do as you were told, dammit," began another barrage of profanity and insults.

Vera aimed the gun. Her finger was on the trigger. For the first time since she had awakened, her vision was clear. She centered the dot on the back of her grandmother's head while Gloria continued repeating her rant again and again.

Vera's thoughts flashed back to that day long ago when she overheard an earlier tirade that Grandpa Joe had endured. Jenny had just left Vera off in California, and the argument was over how to handle the affair Vera had had with Papa Sung. Without a doubt, Gloria would have had Papa Sung arrested, if not shot. Grandpa Joe stopped her rant then with the words, "We're not going to do to another in this family what your father did to us, not with the guilt you carry. We are going to follow the path of forgiveness. What that girl needs is unconditional love. What your daughter seeks is an opportunity to save her marriage."

Vera felt her feelings of anger and fear lifting. *Grandmother has lost it. She won't listen. How can I get her attention?* She pointed the weapon away from Gloria so the laser dot rested on the wall a foot to the right of her head. Vera's mind cleared like a full moon breaking through clouds on an overcast night. She applied a little bit more pressure on the trigger. The sound was sharp and deafening, followed by a roomful of pungent gunsmoke.

"You missed. I should be dead." Gloria pointed to the hole in the wall about two feet above her head.

Vera screamed, "Enough! Grandmother, shut your mouth! Listen! I hate Papa Sung! He raped me! Because of him, I've lost Arthur. I don't know how I lost a whole day. I don't know how it happened! He did it.

I'll kill the son of a bitch."

"Rape? He can't be that foolish."

"I've done it enough times to know when I've been screwed. I don't know what he did. I'm bleeding. It hurts to pee. It hurts to walk. Grandpa Joe said to forgive people. I can't. I'm going after Papa Sung."

"No wait, after you get a good night's sleep, we'll talk this out. First, put the gun down and call Art."

"I tried, but he wasn't there. You called me those names, like whore, around him, didn't you?"

Gloria nodded. Vera watched her grandmother's eyes fill with tears and her whole frame shake as she walked toward the chair in front of her laptop. The bite in Gloria's voice had disappeared. "I've been awful. Forgive me. Please put the gun down and then I'll tell you."

Vera thought, *I've seen enough of her tirades. It's run its course like a tornado. What can't be glazed over is that he's gone, I've lost him. I gave Arthur my heart. There will never be another. It's just as well. I'll go to prison for killing Sung. I'll get some sleep and head for Texas tomorrow.*

⊱⋅☾☽⋅⊰

Gloria eased into the chair and touched the computer's keypad. "What got into my head? It was that evil man, not you. Go to the kitchen and fix yourself something. Give me my Glock."

Vera recalled how other tirades ended when her grandmother snuggled in her grandfather's arms. It was as if a huge switch was flipped inside her head. More than once she had seen Grandmother shake as she had earlier that night. Vera asked, "Are you all right? Can I trust you?"

Gloria's voice took on her usual sweet, feminine tones. "Vera, yes, dear, I'm past the crisis. You saved my life. Please lay the gun down on the counter next to the laptop. While you're in the kitchen, there's some things I have to do on the computer. Then we'll talk about how we're going to deal with that pervert and how to mend fences with Art."

Oh, no, everything is all blurred again. I'll call Art. Vera laid the gun down and took the few steps needed to pick up the phone. While she was dialing, Gloria took her seat in front of the laptop and asked, "Who are you calling?"

"Art."

"I'm terribly sorry. You'll only get his answering machine. He's out. Andy told me that he left him at a bar down by the *Tribune*. He was talking with a girl he met there."

Vera hung up the phone on hearing the first words of the recorded message. *Art is gone, forget about him,* were words that washed though Vera's head again and again.

Gloria was completely absorbed in the computer screen. The Glock lay within an arm's reach of the laptop. "After you fix yourself something to eat," said Gloria, "please clean up the mess I made."

Vera blinked away tears and went into the kitchen. She made herself a sandwich on a grinder roll and poured a glass of milk. Between bites, she put the scattered dishes in the dishwasher and wiped the countertops. She noticed a smell coming from the garbage can. She lifted it and the container of aluminum cans and headed toward the lower level. These were simple tasks she had done many times, but she faltered as her mind raced from Sung to Art and back to the pain between her legs. She lost her balance on the fourth step from the bottom and almost tumbled the rest of the way. Somehow she managed to keep the garbage can upright, but it hit the floor hard and some slopped out. The box of cans tumbled out, spreading across the floor at the foot of the stairs.

Muttering, Vera gathered up the cans with one hand while she pressed the other against her burning private parts. After tossing the cans into the compactor, she started the machine. It ground and munched the metal into a dense cube while she mopped up the spill. She took the garbage out the back door and emptied the can on the compost pile. Her trip upstairs was slow.

Vera caught a strong scent of gunsmoke as soon as she opened the kitchen door. She ignored it until she retraced her steps back to the dining room, where its pungent aroma couldn't be ignored. She expected to see Gloria sitting there at her laptop. She called out, "Grandmother, where are you?"

She saw an irregular fan-shaped pattern of blood and brains that etched the wall. Then she saw Gloria lying on the floor close to where she had been kneeling. Her arms were raised above her head. Through the back of her head was a single bullet hole.

Vera screamed, "Grandmother! Grandmother!" She bent over the body and gasped. A pool of blood was spreading around a face destroyed by the exiting bullet fragments.

Vera backed away, a step at a time. She listened for sounds, but the house was so quiet that the tinkle of the spent cartridge seemed to echo when Vera kicked it along the floor. She picked up the brass cartridge; it was a 9-millimeter. There on the table right beside the laptop was the 9-millimeter Glock.

"How can this be?" she cried out loud. "I don't remember shooting her! All I can remember is the red dot on the back of her head. Yes, I know we talked! She was okay. Why, why is this happening to me?"

Vera walked out onto the deck. She stared at the distant skyline and savored the memory of that recent happy evening when she and Art were here together last. Her own words reverberated in her head, *These are the only hands I will ever allow to touch me*, as she pressed her own hands up to her breasts, remembering when his were beneath hers. Then the reality of her situation sank in. *If I call the police, they'll arrest me for sure. I've heard Grandmother talk about gunshot residue tests enough times. I am so messed up. Forget about ever being Mrs. Arthur Williams. Plan on how to get that bastard Sung before they get me.*

Vera looked out toward the west and the city beyond the bay until the night chill penetrated her senses. She studied the prone body of her grandmother for a long time. She asked herself, *I left the Glock on the table How could I have done this?* She walked back to the table where the gun lay and almost shouted, "Dear God, what have I done? I stood up Art today and now I've murdered my own grandmother! Why! Why?"

Before she stepped into the shower, she left her engagement ring by the bathroom sink. She let the water run over her for a long time. Examining her wounded privates, she muttered, "How did this happen?" She found clean clothes and, while she dressed, told herself that it was all a very realistic nightmare. She would wake up tomorrow and get married. Hesitantly, she went downstairs to see. No, Gloria's body and the gore were still there. It was all real. Vera took a wide berth around the corpse on her way back out onto the deck. There, she looked at the distant San Francisco skyline while she did breathing exercises and martial arts warmups. By the time she was done, the mental fog had dissipated and she could make out each distant light. The admonitions of her grandmother were fresh in her mind. Carefully picking up the Glock, she held the gun with her thumb on the trigger and looked into the barrel.

She held it that way for a few moments, then slowly lowered it. Shaking her head, she muttered, "No, I've got to find Sung. There is no place left to go but to Texas."

Vera checked to be sure the safety was on before she slipped it into her pocket. Then she returned to her room, snapped the black leather collar around her neck, and carefully eased the rattail file into the pouch on the back of her neck. She gathered up the spent cartridge and all the clothes she had worn home, and dropped them on the seat of her car. She packed her other clothes, her passport, and the books of traveler's checks Gloria had given her for the honeymoon.

Before she put the key in the ignition, she reread Sung's note and thought, *Well, Father Sung Li, I may hate your guts for what you've done, but hiding out in Costa Rica with you is my only hope. And yes, Grandmother was alive when I left, but you'll wish you weren't when I'm done with you.*

⋅⊱⊱⊰⊰⋅

Overnight Vera drove east on the Interstate until the first rays of the rising sun reflected off the Miata's windshield. It brought back the same blurred vision she had struggled with the night before. She had hefted item by item out of the car when there was no one behind her, including the Glock, which she had broken down into its components. She took an exit to stop at a roadside restaurant. It wasn't until she took the first sip of orange juice that its taste triggered a momentary sense of dizziness. Closing her eyes, Vera experienced a flashback to the memory of her adopted father coaxing her to drink from the glass in his hand. Now she understood why he grinned with his eyes fixed on the glass. Vera finished her breakfast, leaving the juice nearly untouched.

With vision that was still somewhat blurred and with fresh memories of last night's close calls returning, she stopped at the next motel. She paid cash and immediately went to bed. Sleep was not very restful.

She had the first of many nightmares, actually disjointed flashbacks of what she came to realize was Sung's rape mixed with Gloria's scathing tirades. The wakeful times were filled with conflicting memories that included seeing the red dot on the back of her grandmother's head; the conversation with her; and finding her body.

That afternoon, the sun's rays were casting long shadows across the desert as a rested Vera merged onto Interstate 80 East. She repeated to herself again and again, *Grandmother was alive when I left.*

Remembering Goodwin, Colorado, from Art's articles, she decided to make it her first destination. There was something she felt Art had left untold. Why did the fat woman cause Gloria such angst just by parking in the driveway? Could this have something to do with the deputy Gloria said she had shot? The only person she knew that she could ask was her grandparents' friend, Mr. Andrew Foyle.

During her all-night drive she had stayed tuned to a high-powered San Francisco AM news station. There was no news of Gloria Caulfels' murder. *Good. The longer the time until they found the body, the better my chances of finding Papa Sung before I'm arrested.*

Vera felt somewhat relaxed when she pulled up at the foundation's office building in mid-morning. Andrew Foyle greeted her warmly and had a cup of coffee with her. She broached the subject of her grandmother and Deputy Diamond's death with a "by the way" question just as she was leaving. He looked her directly in the eye, but showed no emotion as he dismissed the notion that it was possible for skinny Gloria Caulfels to move the heavy deputy's body.

Vera asked, "What if she used a chain fall?"

Andrew's eyebrows arched and he stared at her through too long a pause. "That is a good question. I never gave it that much thought."

Vera found a cheap motel, where she slept until well after dark.

CHAPTER 13

The phone rang on Detective Lieutenant Lyndon Evans's desk in his Harris County Sheriff's office. On the fifth ring, he reached out with a hand that moved like a programmed robot to punch the speaker button. His dark eyes never left the scrolling computer screen, even while talking. "Detective Evans speaking."

"This is Coruda Trujillo, Lyndon. The senior warden at St. Bede's just called me. The Father is taking the bait."

A satisfied grin lighted the forty-year-old cop's face as he thought, *Who would have believed we'd get another shot at this slimy bastard after seven years?* He lifted the handset to his oversized ear. "It sounds like your prayers are being answered. When is he coming to town?"

"He's scheduled to give the sermon at the ten-thirty on the third Sunday in June. They'll present the donation afterward. Don't count on him sticking around. I bet he'll be on his way to Costa Rica before sunset. I've done my part. Now it's time to do yours! After all the problems my daughter Frieda has had, you can't let Father Li escape again."

Still scrolling the screen, Evans cradled the phone on his broad shoulder. "Mrs. Trujillo, this has been a long time coming. Since no one ever came after him in Costa Rica, he must think he's home free."

"What a stink you caused by questioning all the other parents at church."

Those people at that church are something else. "I tried to be discreet about it. And as you asked, I kept your identity secret. By the way, how big did you build the purse?"

"Just over five thousand dollars. The Extroms gave just over six hundred. Yes, it's blood money, but no one should complain because, whether he gets it or not, it still goes to do the Lord's work."

"Congratulations. After all this time, Coruda, I had my doubts you'd pull it off."

"We couldn't have done it without Father Li's own charisma. There were many good things about him. That's what people want to remember the charm, his energy, and his dynamite sermons. They like to forget the bad, especially his abandoning us for that Central American mission. The old-timers contrast him to the priests who followed him. In comparison, they're all lackluster. Without the myth, the twisted memory, no one would have ponied up to hear his spellbinding voice again and marvel at his 'good works.' To think I trusted him to be a father figure to my only child."

"We've got plenty of time between now and the third Sunday. Don't you worry, we won't let him slip through our fingers. Is the second girl with whom he had relations still in town?"

"Shelby Extrom, oh, that young woman! She just destroyed a perfectly good marriage by going back to old Perky Handblin."

"Where is she now?"

"I understand Perky's paying her tuition so she can graduate from Tech. She's working part time at Hooters."

"Yes, I remember Shelby now. Yeah, with a build like hers, she's a natural to work at Hooters. Well, we have her statement as well as your daughter's. I need to interview both of them again. Do you know of any others?"

"I'm sure there were others, but this is a taboo subject at St. Bede's. Call any time, Frieda is staying with me until she gets on her feet."

⚓

Late that afternoon Lyndon searched through the dead files and found the seven-year-old Sung Li file. He read where Frieda Trujillo, after threatening to commit suicide because her lover had abandoned her, was given counseling. Only then did her mother, Coruda, find out that the cause of the thirteen-year-old's distress was the recently departed parish priest, Father Sung Li. Lyndon recalled the virginal-looking teenager. Like many Latina girls, she had physically matured early: she was slim and attractive, with dark curly hair, big brown eyes, and full breasts. The detective turned to the transcript of her recorded statement. Papa Sung, she called him. He'd been in her life since she was eleven, playing the role of big brother.

The sexual relationship had begun some nine months before, when she was twelve and went with him as an acolyte to the recording of a television program. He played her well, giving her affection she didn't have at home, yet cautioning her to keep their secret. There was no pregnancy because he arranged for her to have long-term birth control rods implanted. Lyndon recalled his frustration when the prosecutor and his boss both told him that pursuing the case with the priest out of the country was a waste of taxpayer's dollars.

He opened the next folder, with the name SHELBY EXTROM typed on the tab. This was a victim he'd easily remember. Three years ago, Coruda had given him the lead that this girl was another of Li's victims. There was a program on child abuse during a church retreat, and afterward Frieda broke into tears in the discussion circle. Shelby attempted to comfort Frieda and privately learned from her about what Father Li had done to her. Shelby then told Frieda that Sung had been her lover too.

Studying Shelby's photograph, Lyndon remembered this nineteen-year-old blonde as a critical mass of overcharged hormones. She openly flirted with him with her big blue eyes during their interview. She claimed that she initiated the affair with the good Father when she was fifteen, after propositioning him two or three times. During the sermons, she claimed, his voice tingled her G-spot. Then, at the church door on the way out, she whispered her offer as Father Li hugged her. Once the affair began, she liked to talk him into having sex in times and places where there was an element of danger. About three weeks before he left, she had to hide in a closet for an hour, with her skirt and panties in his desk drawer, while the Father counseled a parishioner. Because she was late getting home, he called her parents and told them she had been helping him in the church office. That was their last tryst.

Lyndon was sure that this third-party confirmation would make the case viable.

Detective Evans' first call was to the ex-Lolita, who was now an adult. Shelby came in for an interview, a full-grown vamp with bleached blonde hair, blown and teased to perfection. The designer slacks were tailored to advertise long shapely legs and a firm, flat belly. The blouse was cut to display just enough cleavage to affirm the authenticity of her assets.

He rose as she approached his desk. "Hello, Shelby, thank you for taking the time to drop by. I'm updating the files on outstanding cases. Three years ago, you gave us a statement regarding Father Sung Li." He pushed the papers across to her as he continued, "Please take a moment to go over it. Is there anything you would like to change or add? Have you had contact with any other girls with whom Sung Li had sex?"

Shelby browsed the pages, flipping through to the back with well-manicured fingers. "That's pretty much the way it was. What's the big deal? He wanted it. I wanted it. We did it."

"You were fifteen and he was old enough to be your father. The laws of this state forbid such relationships."

"Pardon me, are you going send the Marines down to Costa Rica and haul him back?"

"No, we're just updating the file. By the way, do you still go to St. Bede's?"

"No, but I always go to church with my parents at Christmas. Mom and Dad still go. I usually don't get home until between three and four a.m. on Sunday. It's my day of rest."

"I understand you're working at Hooters."

"Only until graduation from Tech in December of next year. Perky--that's my man. He promised to line me up some real good interviews. Then I'll have a daytime job without having to stand on my feet."

•>┼══◉ ◉══┼<•

The detective found Frieda sitting on the weather-beaten swing on the porch of the Trujillos' small house. The paint had long ago lost the battle to the sun and weather. It was late enough in the afternoon that the day's heat had dropped down into a pleasant evening. Frieda's back was round and her shoulders forward in the posture of a chronic television viewer. Her belly was that of a woman who had borne children. Her hair was carelessly pulled back, with defiant dark strands twisting down beside her dull dark-brown eyes. Lyndon thought she looked far older than her twenty years. After he sat down next to her, he gave her a gentle hug, then said, "Have you learned how to stay clean this time?"

"I sure hope so, Detective Evans. Thank you for going to bat for me. Rehab is painful medicine, but I needed it after I lost my baby. I don't want to have to go through that again. Mama's all excited about catching the Father. Why does he have to come back now? I just want to put as much distance as I can between me and back then. If I have to go to court, it'll be like living it all over again."

"There is that possibility. Would you be up to reviewing the statement you made way back then?"

"Gee, I don't know."

"Frieda, would you wish to see anyone else treated the way he treated you as a young teenager?"

"Of course not."

"We know that men like him go on from one victim to the next. You can end his reign of terror. I need you to tell only the truth. With that truth, Father Sung will be put in a place where he can't harm other young girls. Here, look through your statement. Can you stand up in court and tell that to the jury?"

Lyndon watched Frieda's eyes and hands while she worked her way through the statement. She read the first page line by line, then skimmed a couple more, then slowed, putting a finger under the words as she read. She closed the folder on finishing. Frieda nodded affirmatively. "It's sort of hazy now, but yeah, that's pretty much the way I remember it," she sighed and leaned back. "There's one thing that's missing."

"And what's that?"

"I was broke in by a stud. Maybe that's what's been wrong with my life. No one after him was anywhere nearly as good as Papa Sung. I haven't found a drug that gave me the kind of high he did. I hate that man. He broke my heart when I was just a little girl. If he'd kept his word, I would have gone to the ends of the earth with him."

⊷▸▮◉ ◉▮◂⊷

Lyndon was pumped up. He met with the prosecutor himself and four senior deputies. While all four deputies agreed they had a case, the prosecutor was reluctant. The man was a priest and had a family. The first words out of the prosecutor's mouth were his usual gripes. Lyndon had endured hearing them enough times that he could recite them: "Cases like this are expensive, time consuming, and too often turn on the testimony of children, who can be easily manipulated." Lyndon needed something to jar the prosecutor loose.

He leaned forward in his chair. "Sir, this isn't just some child care gone bad. Parishioners have dug down into their pockets to create a five-thousand-dollar pot to lure the perp back to Texas. The wheelhorse is Frieda's mother. What are you going to tell them after he flies across the border?"

The prosecutor said, "Okay, Lyndon, I see your point. Yes, it would be better to go ahead with the case than to chance having an over-wrought Coruda Trujillo haunting my campaign next election. Rose, I'll put this case in your capable hands."

Rose Bondurant was one of Lyndon's favorite prosecutors. She had been trying his cases since she was newly hired and he was a newly promoted detective. More important, she was the prosecutor with the highest percentage of convictions in sex-related cases. Rose had brought in a dose of reality therapy with her observation that, given this was Sung's first offense and he had high standing in the community, the prosecution would be open to a plea bargain. Something like eighteen months' probation under some lesser charge--provided he undergo therapy and resign from the clergy.

The warrant for the arrest of Father Sung Li was issued. Now all Lyndon had to do was wait. He didn't look forward to making the arrest at the church if he could help it. His problem was that he couldn't find out just where Li was coming from. He had alerted Customs and Immigration. Would Li come by land or air? Would he ride the bus? Lyndon even had the make and license of Li's car from Costa Rica passed to the officers at the Rio Grande crossings.

On the third Friday in June, Lyndon briefed the sheriff after lunch and then took the rest of the day off, staying up late to watch a rented movie on his VCR. Then there was Saturday, his special day of rest. He spent the morning with his wife. The afternoon was set aside for taking his family and his partner, Detective Sergeant Danielle Dancer, out for a boat ride on Galveston Bay. She had just kicked out her current squeeze after he wouldn't come up with his share of the rent money. It wasn't until they were well out on the bay when Lyndon's day on the water was interrupted by a tornado alert. They rode out a particularly nasty squall on their way to safety in a small marina, and moored there until the all clear was sounded.

When they left the marina, close to last light, they found Danielle's cell phone submerged in water from the storm. If there'd been any calls during the day, they had no hope of getting messages off that phone; so Lyndon called in for voice mail messages using the cell he had left in his car.

The first message was about a call from Oakland, California. The officer who took it described it as a crank call from a "Mrs. Jenny Lee." She was nearly hysterical. Her husband, "Sam Lee," had run off with their twenty-one-year-old daughter, "Vera Lee," on the girl's wedding day. She wanted them arrested as soon as they landed in Houston, which would be close to midnight on Southwest.

The second call, received at 11:28 p.m., was from a woman who identified herself as Gloria Caulfels, Esquire. She wanted to know what action had been taken on the complaint that was faxed in earlier in the day. She swore at the officer when he told her no one had been detailed to meet and arrest the incestuous lovers. She demanded the arrest of one Sung Li for incest that began in Harris County when the daughter was twelve. She said he had tickets for a direct flight to San Jose, Costa Rica, at five-thirty p.m. Sunday on Continental.

Only when the fax was read, showing the proper spelling of Sung and Vera Li's names, was the connection made between the earlier phone call and Sung's arrest warrant. Lyndon and Danielle received the message five minutes after the passengers began disembarking from the Southwest flight. The word to arrest Sung at the airport didn't arrive in time. While they dashed to the airport, Lyndon called the number and spoke with the angriest woman he had dealt with in ages. Gloria swore at him when he misspelled her name. He had never endured such a profanity-laced dressing-down by a supervising officer, let alone a sharp-tongued attorney. Her last words before she slammed down the receiver were, "It's all my fault for letting that whore pull this off. I'd rather shoot myself than show my fucking face."

The detectives arrived at the airport to see the last weary, rumpled passengers pick up their luggage, but the two lovers were not among them. Danielle's cursory review of the surveillance footage confirmed the ticketing information: Father Sung Li had been on the plane, but the second seat he had booked for Vera Li was empty.

Lyndon Evans and his backups were in place at St. Bede's half an hour before the Sunday service. With Li's name posted as the officiating priest for the service, Lyndon decided to wait until after the service to arrest him. He ordered the uniforms to remain out of sight until he called.

Lyndon took an aisle seat in a back pew. He tried his best to be inconspicuous, but all the ushers introduced themselves and welcomed him. Others quietly welcomed him as they passed. He saw Father Li for the first time as the procession was assembling. Lyndon was surprised at how young looking and vigorous the priest was. Just about every one of the late arrivals greeted and hugged him at the door. Everything about the Father exuded spirituality, from the way he led the procession to his deep, sonorous voice that gave a fresh spiritual dignity to the ritual. Unlike his own church, noted Lyndon, there was hardly a person in the congregation who wasn't sitting forward, raptly listening to the sermon. During a break in the service, known as "passing the peace," many of the congregation, including Father Li, greeted the detective warmly. The detective did his best not to answer any questions.

It was late in the service when the visiting priest was presented with the check. He spent almost ten minutes relating how the money would be used, to supply life's needs to the needy recipients and the mission's good works. By the time he was done, many of the women were wiping tears from their eyes. The applause was long and turned into a standing ovation. Following the communion, which the detective took because all baptized persons were invited, he alerted the backups. As Lyndon talked on his radio, Li looked right at him with a blank expression. After the dismissal, the detective waited to be the last in line exiting the sanctuary. He reached his right hand out to the Father, who said, "How long have you been coming to St. Bede's?"

"This is my first day, Father Sung Li. I'd be at my own church with my family if I'd been able to catch you at the airport last night."

"Catch me at the airport? I don't understand. The Clarks picked me up."

Lyndon showed his badge with his free hand. "Father, I am a detective with the Harris County Sheriff's Department. I have a warrant for your arrest for child rape of two girls in this congregation." Lyndon felt the priest's grip tighten as he was pulled forward, almost tipping him off balance, then pushed back and released.

Raising his voice to a booming level, Sung spat, "You have the wrong man. I am a missionary priest from Costa Rica. I came here today to receive a most generous contribution to my ministry."

"No, these charges stem from your conduct seven years ago when you were the priest of this parish."

Li crouched into a semi-squatting position with his arms extended in a martial arts posture. The detective held up a card. "Father Li., *you have the right to remain silent. Anything you say can and will be used against you in a court of law. You have the right to an attorney ....*"

Sung Li shouted, "Don't be ridiculous! You can't arrest me here. I am a priest!"

."*... If you cannot afford an attorney, one will be provided for you. Do you understand the rights I have just read to you? With these rights in mind, do you wish to speak to me?*"

Sung looked out of the corner of his eye at the two uniformed officers blocking his most obvious exit, then shouted, "This is sacrilege! You cannot arrest me now, not here in God's house in my vestments!"

Behind them, wide-eyed parishioners looked on. The largest of the officers said, "I'm sorry, Father, either you surrender peacefully or we are required to use force."

"May I at least remove these vestments in the sacristy? They belong to St. Bede's."

After the vestments were exchanged for handcuffs, one of the uniformed officers carefully left them over the back of the pew closest to the narthex door. Most of the parishioners were nearby to listen as Father Sung Li's rights were re-read to him. Lyndon asked, "Where is your daughter, Vera Li? I need to talk to her."

"This is an outrage! I will not talk without my lawyer."

The detective dialed the California number, but it rang into a message for the answering machine at the Caulfels residence.

At the station, Sung flew into a rage when told that the first arraignment would be on Monday morning. He broke free of one corrections officer's grasp, while the second was barely able to hold onto him. Lyndon punched Sung in the gut with a right followed by a left. Sung didn't calm down until they cuffed his hands behind his back and hobbled him. Even then, the detective thought the tone of his voice reeked of contempt and superiority. "Be advised that I am flying home to Costa Rica this afternoon on a nonrefundable ticket."

Bingham "Bing" Hendersen, a local defense attorney noted for his skill in rape defense, arrived at the jail in mid-afternoon to represent Sung. Within minutes of his arrival, Lyndon was surprised when Bing told him Sung wanted to submit to questioning immediately as he wanted to catch that plane.

"What's with this guy? Doesn't he understand he's inside until the court decides tomorrow?" asked Lyndon.

Bing said, "I advised him to wait and give me a chance to get my feet on the ground. But he insists."

So it was that Lyndon heard the priest give his story, in which he denied any and all wrongdoing. He called Frieda a fragile, neglected child of a neurotic mother. The priest had tried his best, he said, to give the child guidance and fatherly love. Given the disappointing relationship with her mother, however, it was no wonder the girl felt rejected when he left the parish. As for Shelby Extrom, she was an oversexed Lolita whom he tried to counsel into the way of righteousness. Her accusations were pure fantasy. He knew that she had made passes at other men in the congregation. The idea that he would engage in adulterous activity in his office or in the church itself was beyond belief.

Unlike other occasions when Bing represented a client, the defense counsel struggled to sit still through Sung's replies. All the way through, Sung smiled at Lyndon and ignored Bing's requests to confer with him. After the last question, he said calmly, "I'm sure you have found the truth in my answers. That should be all, correct?"

Lyndon thought, *This guy may think he's home free, but he's dug a hole for himself. I'm going to bury him.* The detective knew he wasn't a good poker player because, struggle as he might, he couldn't keep from smiling. He felt the same exhilaration he did the day he saw a huge trout leap out of the water and snag his fly. "Not quite, Father Li, I need to have your explanation about your relationship with your adopted daughter, Vera Li."

Bing looked puzzled for a moment. He began studying the arrest warrant. "Why are you asking about her?"

"She's missing. The Father here was the last person to be seen with her Friday night last."

Lyndon watched the Father's eyes shift back and forth as if he were watching a tennis match before he spoke in a voice barely above a whisper. "We adopted Vera as an orphan when we were in Korea. I came to California to give her away in holy matrimony. It was a time of great happiness and at the same time great turmoil because my wife, Jenny, had tired of me and of the wonderful life we had in our ministry in Costa Rica. We had sent Vera to live with her maternal grandmother so she would have the advantages of a good education. She just graduated with honors from Mills College."

Bing said, "Father Li, I believe I know where you are headed. We need to break to confer."

The priest waved his hand. "Nonsense, just call me Sung. I had expected to have visits from Vera over vacations, but her controlling grandmother would never let her come. In talking to Vera on Friday, I found a young woman who had been pushed into marriage with a young man of marginal talents. My wife's family has great wealth. He was marrying for money and not for love. It all came to a head after the rehearsal dinner. She gave me a ride back to my hotel and on the way confided that she had serious doubts about this tweedy newspaper reporter. She confessed to having bowed to the will of her very tough grandmother. I invited her to come in for a drink. While she sipped from a tall frosted glass, I confided to her that all wasn't well between her stepmother and me. I excused myself to go to the men's room and when I returned, she was falling down drunk. Or maybe she was on some drug. I realized she wasn't fit to drive, so I rented her a room. The condition was temporary. She was hungry for affection. It was only after she resolved not to go through with the marriage that I told her of my strong feelings. Yes, I let my passion get the better of my judgment. She promised to return to Costa Rica with me since Jenny would not."

Lyndon watched the Father's attorney roll his eyes and bite his lower lip. "Having sexual relations with your child by marriage or adoption is the crime of incest in the state of Texas," said Lyndon.

Bing said, "Detective, what he just described occurred in California between consenting adults. Do you know the law there?"

Lyndon tapped his pencil on the table and smiled. "Counselor, what Mrs. Li called me about wasn't a roll in the hay in California last Friday night. It was about the time beginning just about nine years ago, when this man began his seduction of his twelve-year-old adopted daughter. This was an affair that lasted two years until the mother found out. Instead of calling the police, she packed the daughter off to California. And you, the good Father here, conveniently found a new pulpit outside the country."

Bing held both hands out. "Enough, enough, don't say any more."

Sung pounded his fist on the table. "That is a lie. It is not true! My wife went through an extended bout of depression following the birth of our second son. I nurtured and loved her back to health. Unfortunately, she never fully recovered. I chose Costa Rica for *her*. Life there is far less stressful; I can even afford servants. I had hopes that she would never slip back into the pit. I have done my best for her and for my two sons as well. I have chosen to remain at this mission to raise them in a loving home with a father and mother. When Jenny began murmuring about remaining in California, I tried to dissuade her, but it was obvious that her controlling mother had gotten her ear. The old woman never forgave me for not being white. When I realized that this wonderful, vibrant young woman Vera had opened her heart to me, I decided to let Jenny have her way."

"How old are you?"

"Fifty-four."

"How old is Vera?"

"Twenty-one."

Lyndon thought, *I don't believe he understands the law. They're going to drop the hammer on him. Oh, what the hey.* The detective said, "She's young enough to be your granddaughter. And you're going to have me believe that, just like that, she takes one look at you and dumps her fiancé?"

Bing interjected, "Sung, please listen to the detective's reply. Lyndon, where are you going with these questions?"

"To recommend an indictment."

Sung sputtered, "Ridiculous! It was an impulse on both our parts. That's how love is with the young. I'm a realistic man. She will eventually tire of me and seek a companion closer to her own age."

"Father Li, what your wife alleges is that what happened in California is a continuation of an incestuous relationship that began when your daughter was twelve, when you were here in Harris County."

"If she's not suffering from delusions, she is being spoon-fed nonsense by her mother. This is no continuation. I haven't seen Vera for seven years. She was a child when I last saw her, and now has grown into a beautiful, mature woman. I am attracted to the woman, not the child."

Lyndon thought, *If this guy doesn't plead, he'll get the book thrown at him.* He asked, "Why didn't Vera accompany you here?"

"She was in no condition to fly. I left her enough money to fly to Houston if that is her desire. I felt that one of the congregation would direct her on to my home in Costa Rica, should she arrive after my departure."

"What was her problem?"

"In the afternoon, she acted intoxicated and then passed out. I am fearful that, thanks to the old woman's neglect, Vera has slipped into the degenerate California drug culture."

The son of a bitch has all but confessed to drugging her. I think Danielle said she inventoried some pills. Lyndon asked, "What about the second seat out of Oakland? When did you buy it?"

He shrugged his shoulders and looked at his lawyer with an expression Lyndon thought was defiant.

During the silence, the detective smiled. "You don't have to tell me, the airline will."

"It was late Friday evening, I think. I am concerned about missing my flight."

Bing said, "Sung, I cannot help you unless you give me the opportunity. Lyndon, I would like a break to confer with my client."

Lyndon was closing the door to the interrogation room when he heard Bing say, "Sung, keep your mouth shut. Evans is no fool."

This would be the last time Lyndon received any answers from Sung. On stepping out the door into the parking lot, Lyndon found himself surrounded by the media hounds, whom he referred to the sheriff. Every newscast he viewed that night began with a segment on Sung Li. Most began with a video clip of the narthex of St. Bede's and segued into testimony after testimony on the unblemished character of the priest.

By Wednesday's afternoon news, there was footage of Li's Costa Rican mission, with many more testimonials. The paper printed the first of what would become a steady stream of letters criticizing his arrest. This first letter compared the Harris County Sheriff's office to Pilate's centurions. Beside it, the paper ran a photo of Lyndon Evans escorting a handcuffed Sung Li into jail.

Then on Friday came the real news. Rose Bondurant, the assigned prosecutor, dropped into a chair in Lyndon's office. Lyndon liked Rose. He had worked with her since she was a curvaceous blonde. With faded blonde hair and suits that struggled to contain her girth, she had lost all the allure of youth, but in its place was the confident, almost smug air of a successful professional. After some small talk about how the detective's family was doing, she changed the subject. "Lyndon, for once you did the right thing by ignoring me. I never had the faith that Sung would be dumb enough to ever set foot in Texas or run off at the mouth. The evidence is there. This holier-than-thou priest is a pervert. Right now, my greatest fear is that he could slip through our fingers."

"How could he?"

"In spite of our requests to respect the privacy of these young women, the TV stations have a full court press going on out there at St. Bede's. It's no longer a church where you want to admit you sent your daughter to Sunday school. Perky complained to the sheriff that the stringers for the tabloids are in a bidding war. Some awfully attractive offers for Shelby's story are on the table, and he had her quit her job at Hooters because he's afraid of the publicity. I'm worried that she may get cold feet."

"How about putting her in custody as a material witness?"

"It's not that critical yet. The parents of both girls want Li put away, but they don't want their daughters made part of a media circus, nor do they want them in custody. And I heartily agree. The third leg and the strongest leg of our case, I'm convinced, is incest with the adopted daughter. I had a long phone conversation with his wife, Jenny. There is good news and bad news on that front. The good news is that the daughter Vera is en route here to join Sung. They know Vera is somewhere between Colorado and here because she stopped in Goodwin, Colorado, to visit with an old family friend. He saw a mash note Sung Li had written to her."

"What's the bad news?"

"This family has more tragedy than you can believe. The grandmother was murdered, execution style, the evening of the day Sung flew here. He was on the airplane when it happened, so he isn't a suspect. There have been federal phone intercepts of possible solicitations to murder her. Thank the Lord we're in Harris County, Texas, and not California. Among the persons of interest is the Alameda County Prosecuting Attorney."

"What about the daughter?"

"Count on it, they'll want to question her. Jenny said the grandmother and the girl were very close and got along extremely well. When Vera Li shows up, make it your first priority to secure evidence of incest with Sung Li."

"Your wish is my command."

CHAPTER 14

"Holy Mackerel! Art, please come here." Red Magen waved him into the conference room. Here it was, mid-Monday morning of what should have been the first Monday of Art's honeymoon. The only things holding him together were his friends, the crew here at the *Tribune*, and his boss, Red.

Art turned the corner into the conference room and saw the televised image of the aerial shot of the Caulfels' house with words in bold black: DEFENSE ATTORNEY MURDERED. He was stunned. Red spoke in the same compassionate tones he had used on Saturday night after Art had stood in front of the assembled guests to say there would be no wedding. "Art, my friend, this is a terrible way to get this news. Gloria took a shine to you as if you were her own."

Art collapsed into a well-padded office chair as the voice-over commentary announced that the mid-morning programming had been interrupted by "breaking news." The screen filled with the image of the Caulfels house from the street side with a strand of yellow crime scene tape in the foreground. Art's energy drained from his body as the young TV reporter intoned his message, "We are at the home of controversial defense attorney Gloria Caulfels, whose lifeless body was found by her maid when she came to work today. Police have made no statement other than the death was obviously a homicide. We will give you updates as we have them."

As bad as he felt, Art told himself he had something to contribute. He tilted his head back and poured the rest of his coffee down his throat. *I wish my last memories of Gloria were pleasant. To say she was in a bitchy mood is an understatement.*

Red aimed the remote at the set. "I'm sorry for your loss, my friend. What amazes me is that somebody didn't off her years ago."

"That's one hell of thing to say."

On another channel the camera followed Eudora, who threaded her way along the yellow tape. She tried to avoid the flocking media hawks only to have a young male reporter, who could have been a male fashion model, push his microphone under her nose as he asked, "What did you see?"

Her face could have been a Greek tragedy mask; the only sparkle in her eyes was from the light reflecting off her tears. The little Filipino maid answered, "My lady, my employer, was lying on the floor with her arms outstretched above her head, shot in the back of her head. Awful, blood and brains everywhere, just awful. Why do this to a poor widow woman? She was retiring. I am so sad."

"I apologize," said Red. "It was thoughtless of me to make that remark. For more years than I like to admit, whenever the name Gloria Caulfels appears in the copy, the adjective 'controversy' describes it. Review your stories about execution-style MOs. Homicide is going to be checking alibis of a whole range of people, from the prosecuting attorney and half the police force to the Russian Mafia."

"I feel sick inside," said Art. "She took me under her wing, and I deserted her. On Saturday I awakened looking forward to calling her 'grandmother-in-law.' By noon, I saw her with the veneer stripped away, thanks to Vera's perfidy. It wasn't pretty. Her reactions were so extreme that nobody, including yours truly, could stand to be around her."

"Go on out there. Bring me back a story."

Art wanted to tell him to go to hell. Red walked him down to the parking lot and shook his hand. He heard himself say, "Yessir, I'll see what I can do."

Art slipped behind the wheel of his old sedan and turned the key in the ignition. He thought, *Could Vera have done this in reaction to that sharp, darting tongue? No, no, she doted on her grandmother.*

❖

Art slipped into a parking place freshly vacated by one of a caravan of TV vans. Just beyond the yellow crime scene tape stood a familiar figure, Detective Jim Hackelby. He dashed up and shouted, "Jim, what happened? Do you have any leads?"

Art waited at the yellow tape while Hackelby came to him. As he extended his right hand, the detective said, "What a terrible loss, first Joe and now Gloria. Art, weren't you a frequent visitor up here?"

"Yes. I'm devastated. This is the second heavy blow. First her granddaughter Vera abandoned me at the altar, and now this grand old woman has been murdered. Come on, don't me give that look."

"Not so devastated as to leave the notepad at home. No wonder she offered you interviews."

"I know she burned you guys over the years. She was a modern Don Quixote, forever fighting to right the impossible wrong. Oh, she could be crusty and short, but I was looking forward to having my children call her Grandma. Do you have any clues as to who did it?"

Jim said, "It was a very clean, professional hit. One shot in the back of the head. The killer could have entered either by the unlocked front door or the deck. By the way, do you have any idea where her granddaughter is?"

The young reporter shook his head vigorously until his blond hair waved back and forth. The image of Sung sitting next to Vera in the Miata flashed before him for an instant. Art answered, "The devil only knows. The last I saw of her was Friday night. She drove off with her adopted father, the Reverend Sung Li, after the rehearsal dinner. I just missed catching them at the airport late Saturday afternoon. They were going to Texas. By now she's moved in with him in Costa Rica."

"Interesting. How did Vera get along with Mrs. Caulfels?"

"They were very close. Vera loved Gloria, and Gloria was proud of her."

"Were there ever any disagreements?"

"Until she stood me up, nothing I ever noticed. One of the qualities I saw in Vera was how she made an effort to please, to get along, but Gloria was on a rampage on Friday. She exploded when she found out Vera gave a higher priority to pleasing Sung than she did to marrying me."

"She's the loser, my friend. I need your help and cooperation. Before it slips my mind, I need your fingerprints and a DNA swab to help clear the murder scene. Could you drop by the station?"

Art swallowed hard and blinked away a tear. "Thank you, Jim. Sure, I'll do anything to help get this killer."

"Can you think of anyone or anything that would help me find the killer?"

"Yes, it's something I'll never forget. The night I proposed to Vera out on the deck, it was broadcast all over the Bay area, because the house was bugged."

"Bugged?"

"Yes, bugged. Win Griffith and some federal guys swept the place. They showed me some of the stuff. It was very sophisticated and made in Russia."

"Interesting," said the detective. "I just found a journal Gloria kept. I haven't had a chance to go back very far, but that was something she wrote about. Only she didn't blame the Russians. Do you think these bugs were planted back when Joe Caulfels was working for the government?"

"I think you'll have to talk with the experts. My read is that they are very new and state of the art. They're hard to spot and harder to intercept."

"She made some references to the people behind the Symon Dubinski murder."

"Remember, Gloria wasted one Russian capo and blew the balls off another. Maybe this was payback."

"I investigated that case," said Hackelby. If they'd tied her hands behind her back, I'd say it was the exact same MO. It's close enough, though, to give it serious consideration. In that book, she had nothing nice to say about a whole bunch of people, especially Prosecutor Bleasman."

Who does? thought Art. Smiling, Art said, "You had to wait until she was dead to find out you had something in common with her."

The detective wagged his finger. "Don't you go printing anything like that." He continued talking about the journal. "There were some exceptions to her negative comments: she was very positive about you and Vera Li and the wedding. But even there, there was one discordant note having to do with Vera insisting that her father Sung give her away. Gloria described Sung as unchanged, still an immature, leering lecher. She didn't like the way he stared at Vera. If he hadn't caught that plane, he'd be high on my list. Who's Daphne Kazor?"

"A schoolteacher up in Napa. She claimed that Gloria killed her father way back in 1946. She's a nut case."

"She is definitely another person to check out. Thank you, I appreciate the insights you've given me."

⊶⊷

Daphne dropped into the chair in Detective Hackelby's interrogation room with the grace of a working pile driver. She wagged a finger at the end of her fleshy arm. "Detective, I truly resent the open intimidation you used to make me come to Oakland today."

Hackelby smiled. "Mrs. Kazor, like I said during the Miranda warning, you have the right to an attorney. Would you like to call one?"

"Hell, no, just call me Daphne. Like I said on the phone, I'm tickled the wicked witch is dead. I didn't do it. The only reason the government should be spending money to find the killer is to be sure you're giving the reward money to the right person."

"How much money do you think a hit on Mrs. Caulfels is worth?"

"I don't know, thousands upon thousands. I was just speaking rhetorically. Look, as much as I wanted to drive a stake through her black heart, I never even tried to kill her. Look, I teach children in school. I'm not that kind of person."

"Daphne, I'm not accusing you of her murder. I'm trying to sort my way through a lengthy list of suspects. You are an obvious person of interest because of your long-standing feud with Gloria Caulfels."

"My feud is with you dumb law enforcement yahoos, who have let that woman get away with three murders! She murdered my father, and they never dragged her back to Colorado to face charges. She lay in wait and stabbed that poor attorney, Leon Wattersen. He died too. Then she got away with shooting those Russian immigrants."

"Why have you harassed this family so badly and so often that courts have seen fit to issue restraining orders?"

"Look, she's part of the power structure. I'm not. As if murdering my father wasn't enough, they made sure I got sacked from my job in Goodwin. My ex was blackballed until he divorced me. Well, they haven't done away with free speech, and not you or anybody else is shutting me up, no, sir! Gloria Caulfels got what was coming to her."

"Last Saturday night, while the police were searching for a suspected drunken driver, your car was seen within three blocks of the Caulfels residence. We have a rough time of death as early as nine-thirty and as late as half past midnight. This will be refined when forensic tests are complete. The time you were seen was ten thirty-eight. Since you live in Napa, could you tell me why you were in that neighborhood?"

Daphne said, "I knew it. I knew it, as soon as I saw she was shot, I knew you'd come after me and let the killer go. Look, the view from up there at night is spectacular. Why can't I enjoy the view the same as she does? I like to drive by there whenever I can. I don't want her to ever forget about my Daddy. Seeing me helps her remember. Yes, I stopped in front of her big fancy house."

"And you expected her to see you stopping there after ten-thirty at night?"

"You bet. I always stop across the driveway. She has a security camera that automatically trains on me. She got to see me when she reviewed her tape. In fact, I'm sure she saw me then because the front lights went on for a short time and I saw the front door opened a little way, then she shut it just before the light went out."

Jim Hackelby asked, "What time was that?"

"I don't know. Look at the tapes in the security system, they'll tell you. I didn't get out of the car. Now can I go?"

"Did you see Gloria Caulfels at the door?"

"No, but I'm sure she saw me." Daphne leaned toward Hackelby and gestured by pointing her thumb toward her chest.

"Where were you before you went by the Caulfels residence? Were you with someone?"

"Some guy named Roger. I met him at Linguini's in Covington and he bought me a couple glasses of wine. He can't drive, so I gave him a ride to the BART."

"Daphne, the BART doesn't run over the Oakland hills."

"Oh, come off it, I dropped him off before I went up the hill. The guy turned out to be a loser. At my age, that's about all that's left. I didn't take him home to view my etchings. I took him to the BART. I think he lives in the City. That's all I know. Can I go?"

The detective scribbled on a yellow legal pad, then studied Daphne's pudgy face long enough to make her uncomfortable before saying,

"Here's my card. Call me if you get any ideas. And Daphne, don't take any trips out of the area."

She laughed. "On what this state pays me with this hideous cost of living, I can't even afford all the tolls."

⋆⊷⊷◉ ◉⊶⊶⋆

Two days later, Detective Hackelby answered the phone. "Hi, Jim, Felix Marcom with Covington Police. I dropped by Linguini's as you asked. They remember Daphne. She's too large not to be noticed. Apparently she likes their pasta. They recognized her as somewhat of a regular. I talked to the wait staff and they remembered she was with someone, but thought they came in together. They described him as a pretty big guy, sort of overstuffed like she is. He wasn't anybody they recognized. He has a scar below his left eye. I suggest you send your artist over to get a composite before their memories get any dimmer."

"Thanks, buddy, I appreciate the legwork. I'm doubtful she would have the guts or the money to finance a hit, but I'll follow up. By the way, Gloria Caulfels mentioned you in her journal in regard to some case about wrecking a building. Can you think of anything connected with that case that might have given someone a reason to want her dead?"

"Boy, can I! The accused was a contractor named Sollair, who should have been convicted. Our esteemed county prosecutor screwed up the charging papers and she won a directed verdict with prejudice. Dale got his butt chewed by the judge, and she rubbed his nose in it on the courthouse steps. I know he made some threats. There was a new guy with the *Tribune* there, name of Art Williams or something like that. Ask him. I'll bet he taped it."

"You done good. I owe you one. Thanks, Felix."

Hackelby returned to processing the papers from his in-basket. He opened an internal mail envelope and pulled out the sheet. Smiling broadly, he sang out, "Hot dog, Ballistics identified the weapon as a nine-millimeter Glock." The report went on to conclude that the round was too fragmented to allow a firm match, but there were some similarities to the Glock registered to Gloria Caulfels. The hollow points from her Glock broke up when she fired into the Russians. *Now that is a twist,* thought Hackelby. *After coming up dry on fingerprints so far, this is news--except, where is the gun?*

177

The medical examiner's report refined the time of death to Sunday evening, no earlier than ten-thirty and no later than eleven-fifty. Death was instantaneous. Gloria Caulfels was otherwise a very healthy woman. Minor injuries to her knees and shins showed that she had been in some sort of physical confrontation shortly before death. Although there was a pillow she had knelt on earlier, she was kneeling on the floor when shot. Hackelby carefully inserted the report into his file.

He glanced at his sheet of "to-dos" for the Caulfels case. Tops on the list was to interview Vera Li. Next to the name of Winston Griffith was a Post-it note: he was working a case in American Samoa and wouldn't be back for at least another five to seven days. As for both Dale Bleasman and Alexander Tsamonicoff, the local office of the Federal Communications Commission, which had investigated the bugging of Gloria's house, had referred Hackelby to a Washington, DC, phone number. He dialed the number, and that connected him to the FBI. To his frustration, the answering agent blew him off. Hackelby then asked his chief to call the FBI director's office. That wasn't much help: the director's office would only affirm to the chief that they "could be investigating" and that "there might be involvement of certain local elected officials." After this, Hackelby looked at his watch and realized, *It\s time to put the folder away and hit the road if I'm going to be at Gloria's funeral on time.*

⊷►▣ ◉▦◄◅

On Thursday afternoon Art Williams sat in his warming car outside the Caulfels family's church in Berkeley. It was the Fourth of July, but he didn't feel in a holiday mood. Only the strong afternoon sea breeze blowing through the open window kept the car comfortable. He closed his eyes in the vain hope that it would ease the pain in his head and heart. In that moment, that evening with Vera ten days ago all came back. He had noticed that whenever the man he now knew as her adoptive father was present, she was extra affectionate. He remembered touching her breasts and kissing, as well as her words. He recalled Sung Li standing next to Jenny, looking at them out of the corner of his eye, as they turned to go inside. With his eyes narrowed and his jaw set, he had not looked like the very charming father of the bride he had seemed since his arrival. Thinking again about that critical moment when Sung insisted that Vera drive him back to the hotel, he realized he should have given Sung the ultimatum: either ride with him or call a cab.

The jilted and grieving groom wasn't even sure he had to courage to go in when he looked up into the dark eyes of Major Andy Caulfels, who laid a hand on his shoulder. "Come on in, Art, you're family. We want you to join us."

Art followed Major Andy into a chapel where all the other children, the grandchildren, plus Andrew Foyle and his grown children, were gathered holding hands in a circle. After Art joined, Andy said, "Lord, we are gathered here today to ask you to help keep alive our father's wish that we never allow our hearts to be filled with hate, but only your love. You know well our dilemma while we wrestle with the reality that, as in your day, there are men who trade a stack of gold coins for a loved one's life. Lift us up, Lord, so we can feel your healing power. Especially lift up our brother Arthur. Help him to know that only by forgiveness can he heal, truly heal, and go on to find happiness. Amen."

Hearing the words gave Art a warm feeling on the surface, but inside he was alone in his turmoil. This funeral was far different from Joe's: the smaller sanctuary was all but empty. Beyond family, the few guests were mostly lawyers from the criminal defense bar, along with a few deputy prosecutors. Art suspected most of the prosecutors were there to confirm Gloria's death rather than mourn her passing. He nodded to the only others that he recognized, Peter and Alya Godoniski, Jesse Sollair, and his boss Red Magen.

When the microphone was opened for reminiscences by those present, there was a too-long pause before anyone moved. Finally Art rose. He blew his nose because he had been stifling tears. After gaining eye contact with his audience, he said, "Looking around this room, you'd almost think it's the courthouse. And there's my boss, Red Magen. No doubt, without Gloria, he's wondering where I'm going to get my next blockbuster story."

After the laughter quieted, Art continued, "Gloria Caulfels was bigger than life. She was a dragon slayer, who opened the way for women to practice law. That was the side of Gloria Caulfels that most of the world saw. I had the rare privilege of almost becoming a part of this wonderful family. Over the last year, I came to love her in the way a child loves a parent. I'll never know for sure what quality she saw in me that caused her to take me under her wing, giving me interviews that she refused to others. Looking back on it from the hindsight of these past days, I think maybe she was using that access as bait to keep a faltering romance alive. What a tragic coincidence that on that same day she died, my dreams were wiped out. Like me, she was shattered by my fiancé's perfidy."

Art's voice broke. He drew the microphone away from his mouth, then took a deep breath before lifting it back. "This formidable woman let down her guard, giving a professional assassin that clear first shot. Not many people over sixty-five, men or women, have the spunk to brush off a death threat with the retort that whoever they hire 'had better get her with the first bullet, because she doesn't miss.' We know that someone did not miss. What she left for you lawyers is a legend of a pioneering woman attorney, who intimidated generations of prosecutors with a high-quality defense for poor people like Peter Godoniski so they weren't railroaded into prison. What she left for a whole town in Colorado is an inheritance that she could have spent on herself; but instead let it bring prosperity and opportunity to the whole community. And for the family, she leaves the example of a loving wife and grandmother, who had the guts and perseverance to stick by her man in the face of terrible odds. I am honored to have known her. I doubly grieve for her loss as well as for my lost opportunity to be a part of this wonderful family. Even as she lies here in a closed casket, I've heard them speak of forgiveness for that unknown killer. I need to learn from them."

⊷⊶●⊷⊶

After the funeral, Andrew Foyle drew Jenny Li aside. "Your daughter Vera passed through Goodwin about two days after your mother was murdered. She showed me a note in Sung's hand saying he plans to divorce you and marry her. She was en route to Houston to meet him."

Jenny greeted his news with a sarcastic laugh. "Fat chance! My husband was arrested that Sunday after by Harris County police on two counts of child molestation stemming from when he was serving as an Episcopal priest there. I've added incest to the brew. He's being held on $750,000 bail. But I've already tied up everything we own, so he couldn't make bail for a speeding ticket. Let her feel some heartbreak now."

"You should have seen her," said Andrew. She's already had the heartbreak. I don't know what happened the night before the wedding, but she told me she could never come back here and look anyone in the eye after what she did with him. There was much that she said that didn't make much sense. She loves Art, but she can't face him because she slept with her adoptive father. She thought Sung Li drugged her."

"Drugged her! Are you sure?"

"Much of what she said didn't make sense. She was going to Houston to make arrangements to go to Costa Rica to join him. Then she was going to get away from him as quickly as she could. And in the middle of it all, she asked me if I had helped Gloria kill John Diamond."

"Who was John Diamond? I vaguely remember the name."

"He was the deputy who framed Joe back in 1946 and set a whole chain of events in motion. John was found buried in cement over a year after Gloria left Goodwin. It was a crime where just about everybody was a suspect, but it was never solved. Vera said something about a chain fall; that's a block-and-tackle device for lifting heavy loads. She didn't explain herself, but after reflection I see that it could explain how Diamond ended up where he did. Diamond was a heavy guy, too big for Gloria to carry. That's why she was never a serious suspect, but there were those who suspected Gloria anyway and thought maybe somebody else helped her do him in. To her dying day, Gloria never set foot in Colorado after the body was discovered. Nor would she ever even talk about the subject. If she knew anything, she took it to the grave."

As he finished, Art approached. Jenny grabbed his arm and said, "Mother was right. Vera threw you over for my rotten, no-good husband. And he's abandoning me for her.

"How do you know?"

Jenny gestured toward Andrew. "Andrew Foyle saw Vera in Goodwin."

"I thought she went to Houston with him. What is she doing in Colorado?"

"No," said Jenny, "when Sung was arrested, he was alone. She's probably in Houston right now. She showed Mr. Foyle a note from the scumbag saying he's going to divorce me and marry her. Oh, how I'd love to be a little spider up in a corner to watch her give her statement to the Harris County prosecutor about how many times and how many ways the pervert had sex with her. She's burned the bridges behind her … and I've burned the ones in front of her."

⋄⊷◉⊶⋄

Later, Art approached Jim Hackelby. "What have you got to report?"

"We're working on leads. The ME's report is in and a few details from the scene, but it's still a wide-open case. That death threat you mentioned in church--when and who?"

"That was an outburst from Dale Bleasman. He didn't threaten death in so many words, but Gloria seems to have thought he meant it that way. It happened on the courthouse steps."

"Thank you. Was that after the case in which she represented Jesse Sollair?"

"Correct. There was little love lost between those two."

"Thank you for the confirmation. Art, I'm truly sorry for your losses. We aren't going to give up easily on this one, I promise you. By the way, your ex-fiancé didn't go to Houston with Sung Li. He showed up there alone, and he's been arrested for child rape of other girls. I need to interview her. Do you have any idea where she is?"

"Oh, I thought you knew. Jenny told me. She was tipped off by Andrew Foyle, who talked with her on Saturday when she passed through Colorado. She told him she was on her way to Houston. Maybe you ought to put out an APB on her red Miata."

CHAPTER 15

Vera was hungry and exhausted. Here it was Thursday afternoon and she was lost. She asked herself, *Why wasn't I more observant? I drove by way of Austin to take I-10 to St. Bede's. How could I drive all the way into Houston without seeing the exit?*

There was another subject of her self-talk; she kept rehearsing the single-sentence lie, *Grandmother was alive when I left*. She thought she had that much down pat, but was worried about answering any other questions about what went down on Saturday because her recollection was hazy. As for what people at the church thought about her running after Papa Sung, she'd have to take her chances. The sooner she could get to Costa Rica, the better.

Sleep on this journey had not been very restful. Her subconscious mind was assembling and feeding to her conscious mind enough bits and pieces of her father's actions to keep her disturbed. The man had ruined her life. She had spent over two hours on the internet the night before, studying an image of the cutaway of a human torso. Back when Grandmother gave her the rattail file, they discussed where to wield it most effectively. While Gloria spoke mostly of crippling an attacker, she had said that one well-placed hit into the spinal cord with the rattail file would bring either sudden death or paralysis for life. All she had to do was get behind him one time.

At last she saw some familiar landmarks in this monotonously flat land. She drove down the street where she used to pedal her bike past the parsonage that had many happy memories. Ahead stood St. Bede's, looking just about the way she remembered it. Vera parked the red Miata under the shade tree in the otherwise empty parking lot. She walked gracefully toward the church office through air so hot that images were distorted in the superheated rising air.

Just short of the door, she thought, *What if he's here? I'd better be ready.* Vera reached over the top of her head and wrapped her fingers around the handle of the rattail file. Satisfied, she took off her sunglasses with one hand and opened the door with the other.

Vera recognized the secretary in the office, but didn't know her name. Extending a hand, she said, "I'm Vera Li. Did Father Sung Li leave me a note before he left for Costa Rica?"

"Why, you're his daughter! My, how you've grown up. My dear, I've got terrible news for you. Please sit down." The secretary motioned toward the chair beside the desk.

Vera dropped into the chair. "What happened to Papa Sung? Is he sick?"

"It's a terrible scandal and I'm having a hard time believing such a godly man could do such things. He was arrested for incidents they said happened when he was our rector. Coruda Trujillo asked me to call her if you showed up."

"What's this about? Coruda Trujillo … Wasn't she a Sunday school teacher when I was here?"

The secretary nodded while dialing the phone. Vera listened to her tell Coruda that Father Li's daughter was at the office. Even before the secretary could place the receiver in the cradle, Vera asked, "What kind of charges?"

"Since the Father isn't here, I'd rather let Mrs. Trujillo explain. This is not a subject I feel competent to talk about."

"So he never left for Costa Rica?"

"No."

"Did he leave any messages for me?"

"No."

The tendons stood out in her neck as she exhaled. Vera verbalized what she had been thinking, "What am I going to do now? Are you sure?"

"Yes, I am. Could I get you a cup of coffee or a cold soft drink?"

Vera said, "Coffee, please. May I have one of those cookies?"

With the cup in hand and reaching for a second cookie, Vera asked herself, *Should I run? No, that'll arouse suspicion. If he gets out on bail, I'll kill him for what he did to me.*

Vera paced around the office with frequent pauses to look out the window or take another nibble for the fifteen minutes until Coruda drove up. Vera dashed to the door and snapped, "Please tell me, what was he arrested for?"

Coruda's angry voice boomed, "For ruining my daughter's life. For having sex with her and another underage girl." Then her voice softened. "Vera, my heart goes out to you. Having come all this way to be with him, I know this must be terribly painful news. Please come with me. We need to talk in private."

Once in the library, the older woman prayed with Vera for a time. Vera found the prayers somewhat soothing, but not enough to quiet her nerves or her churning insides. When Vera asked for specifics about her father, Coruda quickly spun the saga of Sung Li's downfall, naming her daughter Frieda and Shelby Extrom as his victims.

As Coruda went on, Vera watched her reflection in the mirror on the wall. She didn't like what she saw. In spite of her days on the road with the top down, she looked pale. Her eyes, with dark rings under them, danced back and forth like a trapped animal. *I look awful. How can I fool anybody?*

When Coruda finished, she took Vera's hand in hers and said, "I know what you went through with that fiend. Your mother is pressing charges against him for incest."

"I can't, I just can't believe this is happening to me!"

"So you're still under his spell? Do you love him?"

Her slanted eyes narrowed. "Love him? No, not after what he did to me! I, ah, I just don't think I can go through all the emotional stuff. I need to get out of here."

"What did he do to you?"

Vera felt a flash of anger, then tears gushed amid heart-rending sobs. "That's why I followed him. I don't know. I don't remember much except I was in bed with him. I'm ruined. Can't go back to California. ... Missed my own wedding because of what he did. ... Can't face my family or anybody else. I am so ashamed! My grandmother threw me out and told me to never come back. Now I'm all alone in the world. The jerk is in jail and I can't go back."

"Vera, dear, you're not alone here. We're a big extended family at St.

Bede's. That's it, have a good cry. Get it out of your system. Let me call Detective Lyndon Evans. He wants to talk to you."

Vera stood up. Coruda arose and took a blocking position between her and the door. "Please Vera, we need your testimony to put him away for a good long time."

"Who's Evans? What does he want to know about?"

"Detective Evans wants to learn just exactly what the Father did to you before you went to California."

I'm trapped. What'll I do? Vera thought as she stared at the older woman. After a very long pause she said, "Okay, I'll talk about that."

⇢▬◗ ◖▬⇠

Half an hour later, Detective Evans and his partner, Detective Sergeant Danielle Dancer, joined the two women. Coruda Trujillo made the introductions and excused herself. While Vera sat forward, twisting her wet handkerchief, the detectives sat back. Danielle's voice was relaxed. "How was your trip down?"

Vera shrugged her shoulders. "It was long, hot, and lonely. I almost ran out of money. I've got to get a job."

"What do y'all do?"

"I just graduated from college. Anything, I guess."

Lyndon asked, "What made you drive all the way down South from California?"

"Papa Sung told me he'd pay my way to Costa Rica."

"Is that so you could continue your affair with him?"

Grasping the armrests of the chair so hard her biceps swelled, she drew in a deep breath and spat out the word, "No!"

"I don't understand. Why ..."

Her eyes flashed anger. "You have him in jail and you have to ask that? He has to tell me what he did to me. My life is ruined. I can't show my face in California. My grandmother threw me out of the house. My mother must hate my guts. He had me drugged in a hotel room all through my wedding day. I've lost my chance at happiness. I want to get as far away from California as I far as I can and start over."

Danielle looked at Lyndon as she asked, "Drugged? How? Did he use rophies?"

I want to kill the son of a bitch. Putting her head in her hands, Vera sobbed, "I don't know. I'm all messed up inside. At first I couldn't remember anything. Then I started having terrible flashbacks."

"What kind of flashbacks?" said Danielle.

Vera closed her eyes just long enough to recall memories. She looked at one, then the other, as she blushed. "He was on top of me, pounding, pounding, pounding. I was naked and I couldn't find my clothes. He kept talking to me very sweetly. I couldn't move."

"Where did this happen?" said Lyndon.

"I don't know. The Park Plaza Hotel by the Oakland Airport, I think."

"In California," said Danielle.

She nodded and mouthed yes.

"And you didn't consent?" asked Danielle.

"No! I had done everything I could to show him I loved my Arthur. But after this, I can't face Art."

"Don't you think he'll forgive you?" asked Danielle.

She cupped her breasts. "Why should he? I told him I was a born again virgin. The night before this happened, I told him no other hands would ever touch these. Here I am a black belt … and I did nothing!"

Danielle asked, "A black belt? What kind?"

"Aikido. I could have stopped him if I had been awake."

Lyndon said, "That's impressive. Vera, I believe you have grounds to file charges against him in California. However, we have him in custody here for what he was doing to you and other young girls back when you lived here. We're going to put him away. Your mother provided us with information that he committed incest with you over a two-year period. In order to perfect the charges, we need your statement and eventually your testimony in court. Are you up to it?"

"How long will it take to put him away?"

"If he's smart, he'll negotiate a plea. So far, he's claiming his innocence. He just fired his lawyer, so that's going to slow things down until he gets another one," Lyndon said.

Vera felt like a cornered rat. She looked from one to the other in the ensuing silence. *Negotiate a plea. Somebody like Grandmother will waltz in and they'll give him a soft slap with a wet noodle. If I'm going to spend the rest of my life in prison, I want him to pay.* She wiped away beads of sweat from her forehead. "I want to talk to Papa Sung."

"Why?" asked Lyndon.

"I want to find out what he drugged me with."

"If I were his attorney, I wouldn't let you near him after what you told us," said Danielle. "But he doesn't currently have an attorney, does he? Vera, after you give us a full statement, I'll ask the prosecutor if you can have one no-contact visit." She pointed to the recorder on the table.

Vera nodded, then, with tears running down her cheeks, began, "They adopted me in Korea and brought me here. Mother went into a funk after my youngest brother was born, and it fell to me to do everything but nurse the baby. I cleaned. I cooked. I took care of both my brothers. Papa Sung complained that he was lonely without her companionship, and he sort of … played with me at bedtime. I didn't know what he really wanted until he took me to the doctor and I got a birth control shot of some kind. One night shortly after that, when he was supposed to tuck me in, he climbed in. I'd always done everything he wanted."

"How old were you?"

"Twelve. We became lovers that night."

"Why didn't you say something?"

"I liked it. And I loved him. Then it changed once Mother recovered. She almost caught us, so we had to be far more careful. He bought a used camper bus, and he and I used to go to tae kwon do practice together. Afterward we made love. On my fourteenth birthday, he told me that after I turned eighteen he would marry me. He said that Mother was getting money from a trust fund and could get by without him. Then he told me that he'd answered the call to a pulpit at San Elmo, a mission in Costa Rica. He promised to spend more time with me. This came as a real surprise because everything was going great at St. Bede's. Then one Friday right after that, Mother picked me up at school and told me we were leaving to visit my grandmother in California. I never had a chance to say goodbye."

"Is that when you learned that your mother knew?"

"Not until after we arrived in Oakland. Grandmother Gloria told me that my father had committed a terrible crime by having sex with me. When I told her that I loved him, she told me that if I really loved him, I would never contact him again. If I did, she would make sure he went to prison."

Vera paused, looking from one detective to the other. "I wrote letters to Mother, never to him. I was a silly girl. I swore to myself that I would never love anyone else, and I did everything to discourage boys. I was so nasty that no one asked me out all of my senior year. It wasn't until I was at Mills College that I realized how he had ruined my high school years."

"It sounds like you were very angry," said Lyndon.

"Yes, and I 'm downright furious now. Maybe I won't make a very good witness because of it."

Lyndon smiled. "As long as you tell the truth, you'll be fine. Where are you going to be staying?"

"I don't know … my car, I guess. I'm down to one meal a day so I have enough for gas. I'm going to need some help until I can get a job."

Danielle checked her watch. "Vera, darling, why don't you follow us down to the station? Then you can crash at my place for the night. My live-in and I just split. You'll get real home-style Texas barbecue. What do you say?"

For a time Vera again felt like an animal caught in the headlights. Finally she said, "Thank you, I'll stay one night. I'll find something tomorrow."

⋯⟶◉ ◉⟵⋯

The following morning, Danielle relayed to Vera the message that Ellen and Dale Extrom, the parents of Sung's other victim Shelby, had offered to take her in temporarily. At the station, Lyndon asked Danielle, "How did it go with our key witness last night?"

"Lyndon, I like her. She picks up after herself, which is a lot more than Harry ever did. She's a good listener. Not much of a talker; she knows far more about me and Harry than I do about her. What little I learned about 'her Arthur' was that they went almost all the way the night before the wedding without doing it. She doesn't smoke. She doesn't drink. And she doesn't do drugs. When I suggested she go back and at least try to explain what happened, that started a crying jag about how much she loved him and how she could never face him after what happened. It's very obvious that emotionally, she's very fragile. Sung put her through hell."

"Anything else?"

"She was up at the crack of dawn doing exercises. I took her with me to the gym. She isn't kidding when she says she's a black belt. She is deceptive because she's so slim. All she did were defensive moves, but I ended up on the mat every time. She told me she'd been thinking about law enforcement before she met her fellow. On the way over, I asked how she slept, because I'd heard her cry out. She told me that almost every day she gets another little flashback about her time with Sung. This is a classic case of a powerful date rape drug."

"What sort of cries? Did she say something?"

"Nothing intelligible. It was mostly moaning, like she was having sex."

"Hmm. Remember those three glass vials and those bubble-wrapped pills that were inventoried in Sung's suitcase? Let's get clearance through the prosecutor to have them analyzed in the lab."

"First things first. Let's ask Sung if he wants to visit with Vera because they may notify him about testing his stash."

"My, oh, my, are you a nasty one? Do it. For my next session with Vera, I want you to take the day off. Oakland PD wants us to question her about her grandmother's murder."

"I don't think she did it."

"Good, that's even more reason for you to be out of the picture."

⇒≡◉≡⇐

Vera was doubly disappointed. They made her leave the rattail file at the door before directing her to the visitors' cubicle. On the far end was a thick glass partition and behind it, the man she had come all the way from California to kill. Papa Sung stood safely on the other side of the glass with the phone receiver to his ear. He was actually grinning, and he blew her a kiss. Over the phone he said, "Vera, dear, I've been worried sick these last days that you ignored my plea for your love. You are perfection, an answer to my prayers. What took you so long?"

"I drove down."

"Why didn't you fly?"

"You son of a bitch! I've been kicked out of the family, thanks to you. The Miata is all I own. I've had nothing but trouble since that night you spiked my drink; blurred vision, nightmares, flashbacks, you name it. Papa Sung, tell me what you put in my drink at the Park Plaza."

"Your tone and words are very disrespectful. What are you talking about?"

"Don't lie to me! One minute I was sitting there waiting for you to bring Mother down, and the next minute the room was spinning around and I could hardly walk. The last thing I remember was being in the elevator with you. What did you put in my drink?"

"Please, dear Vera, you know how much I love you."

"You call that love? I've never taken one alcoholic drink or one pill in my whole life and I ended up hung over and with these flashbacks. What all did you do? Tell me!"

"Please don't let these evil people pull you under their satanic powers. If I could only hold you in my arms, I'm sure you would understand, just as I understood your reluctance to make a commitment to that newspaperman."

"Reluctance, you lowlife bastard! I've lost my Arthur. He's the only man in my whole life that I ever really loved."

"He's weak and without passion."

"He was mine! I'll never find another as good. What you refuse to understand is that more than anything in the world, I wanted to spend the rest of my life with him. I loved him, and you destroyed my chance at happiness."

"That's not true. Once this misunderstanding about these two girls is settled, we can be together again. You loved me once. Once the jury hears my side, I'll be found innocent. I never touched either of them. And of course, you will confirm that what Jenny has come up with is simply a figment of a badly deranged mind."

Vera pounded the glass as she shouted, "Are you asking me to lie? You raped me!"

"That's not true. You were alight with passion's fire."

"How could you, when I invited you to give me away? I loved you as a daughter would a father. You betrayed me! You destroyed my life! I'll always be alone!"

"The only reason you would be alone is because of your own treachery."

She slammed down the receiver and stormed out. Sung was still holding onto the phone when the guards lifted him to his feet and led him away.

Late Sunday afternoon, Vera looked up from the book she was reading to see Shelby Extrom enter the living room. Vera took in Shelby's tan slacks, which were cut to show her long, trim legs, her flat belly, and her tight buns. It was quite a contrast to Vera's own modest, high-necked white cotton blouse and full skirt. Vera thought the other girl looked like a professional model.

Shelby said, "Honey, you've hardly changed since you left for California. When Mother told me you were staying over, all I could remember about you was that you were a skinny terror who wasn't afraid of anyone. Remember that time in school when we had to fill out the forms and they asked about our race, you put down American. The teacher was pissed when you wouldn't tell them what you really were."

"Well, I am American; I was born here. Shelby, were you really doing it with my father?"

"Right up until the week before he ran off to Costa Rica. He was very good. Detective Evans said he was carrying on with you too. Is that right?"

"Hey… you aren't jealous, are you?"

Shelby laughed. "No, dear, as long as you don't go after my sugar daddy. Perky, that's my current squeeze, is real concerned that all the men I've done will come out in court. I can't afford to have something like this screw up my opportunities."

By the time he comes to trial, I'll be back in California facing my own trial, Vera thought. She asked, "Are you saying you won't testify?"

"Perky is upset. I can't afford to lose him, he's paying tuition for me. Besides, what difference does it make? There are too many men, I mean older adult men, who would be very upset if I had to raise my right hand and swear to tell the truth about them. Why should Sung go to jail while they're chasing young skirts?"

Vera's face colored and her voice rose. "He isn't just some dirty old man. He's a terrible criminal. Do you know what that pervert did to me?"

"It must have been good, because you chased after him all the way from San Francisco."

Vera struggled to keep from blowing up. She asked herself what would convince Shelby to testify. She decided to retell her story. Half an hour later, Vera concluded, "Talk with the prosecutor. The issue here isn't your promiscuity, it's his taking advantage of underage girls. The evidence to convict requires only the proof that you had sex with him.

"Wow, that's something I never thought of. Are you planning to be a lawyer?"

Shaking her head, Vera said, "No, my grandmother was ... I used to hear her talk about her cases before she threw me out. She was a public defender. Tell me, Shelby, would you wish what happened to me to happen to anyone else?"

"Of course not."

"But it will, if any one of us stays away and lets him get away with this. I can't even give you a hint as to why, but you have to tough this out. I want to be here to testify because I want him to pay for what he did to me. Please promise you won't get cold feet, no matter what happens to me."

"What could happen to you?"

"I can't say. Maybe nothing, but please make that promise. Do it for your parents, who gave all that money so he could get arrested."

"Let me talk to Perky."

"Tell him what that bastard did to me. Ask him what he would do if that were his daughter. If he says nothing, you haven't got a sugar daddy, you've got somebody you won't be able to trust around your own daughters."

⋅⊱━━⊰⋅

Early Monday afternoon, Vera struggled to keep from shaking as she took her seat in the interrogation room with Lyndon Evans and a uniformed deputy. She made a conscious effort to look her questioner in the eye when asked if she understood the Miranda warning and if she wished representation by an attorney. She said she did understand and she did not want an attorney.

Lyndon told her the Oakland police had asked him to question her about the death of her grandmother. At this point Vera began crying and said, between sobs, "I loved my grandmother." He again asked her if she wanted an attorney, and she shook her head no. Tears streamed down Vera's cheeks. "How did she die?"

"Vera, they didn't give me that information. It was on the Saturday evening of the day you were to get married, after ten-thirty p.m. and no later than eleven-fifty p.m. Where were you then?"

"I don't know. When I got home, I thought it was Friday night. Only it was really Saturday night."

"Do you remember the time?"

"No, everything was all mixed up. Last night I tried to remember what really happened. I think most of what I'd call memories are flashbacks. I don't know what's real and what's a dream about that weekend."

"What is the first thing or event you are sure happened?"

"Reading Papa Sung's note. I was still sitting in my car. My eyes were finally working well enough to read. That's the note I gave you."

"How did you drive your car if you couldn't see well?"

"I don't know. I've had nightmares about a car almost hitting me. I got there somehow. Grandmother met me in the garage before I could get out of the car. She read Sung's note and was angrier than I.ve ever seen her. She screamed at me."

"What did you do?"

"I don't know. Everything is fuzzy. She made me take my suitcase that I packed for my honeymoon. I had a terrible headache. She kept calling me names and swearing, and told me she never wanted to see me again. I know Grandmother was alive when I left."

"Did you try to talk to her, to explain?"

"She wouldn't listen."

"Weren't you angry because you had missed your own wedding?"

"I am now. But all I remember from then is being confused. Everything was fuzzy, and I hurt like hell between my legs. It even hurt to walk. It was like that for almost a week. No, I don't remember being angry before I left the house. I just remember I couldn't understand what was going on."

"You sure were angry when you got here."

"I know. I got angry the next day when it sunk in that he had really knocked me out on my wedding day. The way I hurt, I knew what Papa Sung did to me. I was ashamed. Here it was Monday morning and I was alone in a motel room when I should have been honeymooning with my Arthur. He's no longer my Arthur either."

"Did you kill your grandmother?"

"I loved Grandmother Gloria. Like I said, she was alive when I left." *I'll keep repeating that,* she thought, *just like Grandmother coached me.*

"Was she hurt or wounded?"

"No. Listen, Mr. Evans, Grandmother Gloria and Grandpa Joe were my most favorite people in the whole world. I loved them both dearly." Vera pulled her shaking hand back against her belly. "I don't have any-body to love now."

"You could. Now that you know you were drugged with something, when are you going to go back and straighten this out?"

"I don't have any money. But even so, Grandmother told me Art was out drinking and chasing girls on what would have been our wedding night. It's over. I was in bed with my father when I should have been at the church. If Grandmother wouldn't believe me, nobody would. How could I ever look any one of them in the eye after that?"

"Don't you think she would have cooled off?"

"She told me she never wanted to see me again. Grandmother made that very clear, that much I know. Now she's dead, and I can't tell her that he drugged my drink and gave me amnesia. That still doesn't change where I was when I should have been in my wedding gown. I am so ashamed. What man will ever want me after what I did?"

"So why did you follow Sung Li to Houston after what he did?"

The officers watched the tendons in her neck stand out and her eyes narrow. "He ruined my life. I haven't been the same since he gave me the drug. I had to find out what Papa Sung gave me."

"Did you think he would tell you?"

"I know how to inflict pain. If he weren't in jail, I would ask him until he told me. Knowing how I feel now, I think the safest place for him is in jail because I'd like to break him into little pieces. My biggest regret is going against Grandmother's wishes by asking Sung to give me away. Always before, I always did what Grandmother wanted me to. I'm sorry she isn't alive so I can ask her forgiveness."

Lyndon asked a few more rounds of questions, then closed the folder. "Do you own a firearm?"

"Grandmother gave me a nine-millimeter Glock. It's still at the house in California."

"What about your grandmother's gun?" asked Lyndon.

Oh my gosh, Vera thought. She asked, "Was she shot?" She struggled to maintain eye contact until Lyndon nodded.

"Grandmother always carried it."

"So you don't have it?"

She shook her head, then looking at her hands resting on the table, said "No."

"Would you object if we search your car?" asked Lyndon.

"No."

"After our Forensics goes over it, I'll transmit your statement and samples to the Oakland PD. I'm sorry I had to put you through this ordeal. By the way, Vera, Rose Bondurant, our prosecutor, asked me to thank you for the pep talk you gave Shelby on Sunday. We've been quite concerned about whether she would be a willing witness. Your presence at St. Bede's on Sunday is appreciated. Frieda Trujillo and her mother took a lot of heat; but they took heart from seeing you there and knowing your willingness to tell people why you're here. You are a courageous lady. One of the people, who wrote a very nasty letter to the editor about me, called and apologized. Thank you, I can't tell you how much I appreciate it." He shook her hand and opened the door for her.

As Vera stood up, Lyndon continued, "Danielle told me that you will be replacing those California plates with Texas plates."

"Yes, I'm starting work the day after tomorrow at Baxter and Wenderly in downtown Houston. Technically it's a temporary clerical job, but the man at the interview said they hire permanent from temps. After six months or so, I could have a shot at one of their staff positions. How long will they need my car?"

"Unless Forensics finds something surprising, they'll be done before you have to start work. By the way, the department is always looking for qualified women. Think about sitting for the civil service test. We'll give you a ride home."

"Thank you, Detective. Everyone here has been very good to me. I'm feeling better already." Vera thought, *I can't believe it. I survived. But I'm sure there will be more.*

CHAPTER 16

Detective Hackelby was curious why Alameda County Supervisor Gregory Rojas asked him for a meeting. He knew nothing of the man beyond what was in the news. Following introductions, he watched the supervisor close the door with care, as if he didn't want someone to hear. The detective noted Rojas's wide-eyed look and the bobbing of his Adam's apple before the first tense words were spoken. "Jim, this is my attorney, Janet Scott. I am aware that what I'm about to tell you could end my career, but it's a risk I'll have to take."

Attorney Scott said, "Mr. Rojas has been briefed on his rights. He asked me to be here."

"Please go on," said Hackelby.

"I understand that Dale Bleasman is considered a person of interest in the Caulfels murder and that you've been digging into ties with the Russian Mafia."

"That's what the papers printed. What do you know?"

"Do you remember the Symon Dubinski case?"

"Yes, very well. Mrs. Caulfels verbally kneecapped Bleasman. She gave the Oakland PD a black eye as well. On hindsight, it was a case that left me with a terrible taste in my mouth--too much cooked evidence. What do you know?"

"I'm in the middle of this, and I'd rather be the first to speak up than be sucked down when the ship sinks. Yuri Tsamonicoff got his balls shot off by that old woman. Alexander Tsamonicoff is his uncle. The last time we met, just before the Memorial Day weekend, he was still blowing off about what 'that feminist bitch' did to his nephew. I've always humored him. The man has been a very generous contributor to the party and to our candidates, including Dale Bleasman's exploratory committee for State Attorney General."

Jim watched his subject squirm about and eyes that spent most time staring at the floor. "Mr. Rojas, why do I have the feeling that you did something foolish? Isn't that why you brought your attorney? Please cut to the chase."

"I knew better, but I did it anyway. During the Dubinski trial, I carried a message from Alex to Dale. He urged Dale to press on with the case against that Russian kid. Then later in the trial, he asked me point-blank what could be done about her."

"Her?"

"Mrs. Caulfels."

"Who asked you?" Hackelby watched Rojas's eyes dart back and forth before he looked down.

Rojas replied, "Alexander Tsamonicoff. He was furious with Detective Tiburon Fuentes. They killed the man in broad daylight! He was just as furious with that other fellow, Ramirez."

"Ramirez was convicted of assault against Mrs. Caulfels and is safely behind bars. Stop, how do you know they hit Fuentes?"

Rojas's hands were shaking. For the first time he looked the detective in the eye. "I'm scared. Nobody has confessed to me, but you don't have to be a rocket scientist to see the connection."

"What has this got to do with the murder of Gloria Caulfels?"

"I've seen the TV reruns of Bleasman threatening her on the courthouse steps. Both of them made threats. You're obviously going to question both. So I'm in the middle, and I'm scared as hell. These Russians don't screw around, they waste people who can be a threat. Alex made it clear to me that he would even the score with Mrs. Caulfels one way or the other. Detective, I'm afraid for myself. I'm afraid for my family."

Hackelby opened a folder and pushed a composite sketch across to him. "Does this individual look familiar?"

"No, but he sure looks like one of those fat Russians."

"Are you aware, Mr. Rojas, that the investigation of the Prosecutor's Office is in the hands of state and federal agencies?"

Janet Scott said, "Detective, my client needs protection for himself and his family. He is willing to cooperate, especially if he can be spared from serving time."

"Hmm," said Hackelby. "I'm running a murder investigation, not an organized crime task force." He was thinking, *So he's scared. I don't know much about Rojas here, but from what I sense about the man, I don't think he's good for much of anything. Hey, I've got an idea.* "Let me talk to my captain," he said. "By the way, when was the last time this office was swept for bugs?"

"Bugs? You mean clandestine listening devices? Why?"

"There were some Russian-made bugs discovered at Mrs. Caulfels' house. You never can tell. Everything you've said in this office may be on its way to the same people."

Bingo! The color completely drained out of the supervisor's face, and Hackelby knew he had hit a home run. Rojas looked around the room. "Could they do that here?"

"Mr. Rojas, they can bug the Secretary of State's office in Washington, D.C. Did this Russian goon ever say or do anything that would lead you to believe he was doing this kind of thing?"

Rojas asked his attorney, "Should I tell him the rest?"

Janet Scott said, "Wasn't this the reason you asked me to be here?"

Rojas nodded. "During the Covington trial, you know, the last one Dale lost to Mrs. Caulfels, he dropped by here almost every day during noon recess. Twice while he was there, I got a call for Dale from a guy with a Russian accent. I only heard one side of the conversation, but the prosecutor just about came unglued the second time. He said to the guy, and I remember the exact words, 'What do you mean, you have nothing to report? I thought you could listen!' Then he slammed the phone down and said, 'That's what you get for nothing, nothing!'"

"What about the first time?"

"That first call was right after the trial started. He thanked the guy and said he could 'handle it.' Then he told me I should forget I heard anything."

"Mr. Rojas, since you are an elected official and you have reasonable grounds to fear for your and your family's safety, I'm going to recommend that the department give you temporary protection. I'm going to rely on the other agencies to carry the ball on this. I'm going to relay to them what you told me. When they contact you, I suggest you fully cooperate and vigorously appeal for protection."

Later the clerk told Hackelby he had a call from Harris County, Texas, "Hello, this is Detective Lyndon Evans. We interviewed your young lady as you requested. She cooperated fully, as she has done in the Sung case. She gave us free rein to search her car and her possessions. There were no firearms. The only weapon she had was a mean-looking rattail file she told us her grandmother gave her for self-defense. We will identify all the stuff we found in her car. Frankly, I didn't see anything promising in the car unless you're trying to prove she lived in it between here and California."

"What is this stuff about not remembering anything?" said Hackelby.

"Sung, the Korean fellow, who is here awaiting trial, apparently slipped her some kind of date rape drug. She displayed all the classic symptoms."

"Has she still got the hots for him?"

"Just the opposite, there's blood in her eye. She will testify against him on the charge of incest. She pumped up one of the other young women witnesses, who was wavering."

"Won't the defense challenge them for getting together to compare notes?"

"There were no notes compared. We have this bastard. Back to your case: Vera Li is adamant that her grandmother was alive when she left. Apparently the old woman was nasty as hell."

"I read that in your fax. It fits with the way Mrs. Caulfels treated everyone that day. Here it's been a full month and we aren't getting the breaks. I need to close this case. Tell me, what's your gut feeling about Vera?"

"I don't know. When she arrived here, she was an emotional basket case. And who wouldn't be after all that's happened to her? She's mellowing out. My partner feels she'd make a good officer. She's got a job and is going to her dad's old church."

"Do you think she did it?"

"Could she have done it under the influence of that drug? I don't know. We interviewed her just after she pulled in. She talked about blurred vision and amnesia. She told my partner Danielle that she had flashbacks of almost being in a wreck. In her statement, she said she had trouble reading Sung's note. If she can't see straight, how is she going to shoot straight?"

"I see what you mean. If she's going to be a witness for you, it's obvious she won't be traveling. About the near-accident, she generated three nine-one-one cell phone reports between her hotel and home. I'm not through with her. She was definitely there during the time window. I'll put off coming down there until we work our way through what we have on our plates here."

⊸⊶◉ ◉⊷⊸

Art parked in front of the Caulfels house and walked toward Detective Hackelby, who was standing on the other side of the weathered yellow crime scene tape. "Jim, why did you ask me to come up here?"

"I'd like some help," said Hackelby. "We've been over this house with a fine-tooth comb, and I can't justify keeping it sequestered any longer. Of all the people left in town, I suspect you're the one most knowledgeable about the contents just before the murder."

"I don't know. I spent evenings and a few days here. How about Eudora?"

"She's gone back to the Philippines. Here, put on these disposable gloves and booties. The criminalist may make one more sweep."

Hackelby tried two keys before he found the correct key. "This is not for publication. The front door was unlocked. The outside was wiped clean. The inside wasn't. That leads me to believe she let the killer in, and he wiped the outside on the way out."

Art followed the detective into a dark, dank-smelling house. *The place stinks of death,* he thought. *What a contrast. One of the special things about this house was the brace of ocean air, fresh from the Golden Gate, that you always smelled coming through the door. Yet there was a warmth, a good feeling once inside.*

In the family room, Hackelby pointed to the tape outlining where the body had been. "This is where she fell."

Art gasped at the bloodstains. "Look at that wall. Damn, it makes me angry to see the killer blew her head apart."

"That's pretty close to the way it was."

"I see the laptop is open. She must have been working here when the killer came in and surprised her. I wonder what she was working on."

"The battery was dead. I don't know."

They continued on to the kitchen. Art said, "This is surprising. Everything is cleaned up. It was full of dirty dishes when I left."

"Eudora was surprised too, but since she had three days off and nobody else was here to clean up, I figure the old woman rolled up her sleeves."

Art thought, *Vera did it. She took care of the kitchen on weekends.* He opened the sliding door and stepped out onto the deck. Just before closing it, he wiped a tear away from his eye.

Hackelby asked, "Something touched you, didn't it?"

"Out here is where I proposed. Right here, just two days before the wedding, she told me I was the only one she would ever let touch her. She acted hot all through the rehearsal dinner evening. The way this happened, I think it would be easier for me to accept if she were dead. It still makes no sense to me that she played me along like that."

"Women have always been a mystery to me. Let's take a look down in the basement."

Downstairs, the detective turned on the light. "This is one hell of a fancy firing range."

"Yes. Gloria was a dead shot. She could hit anything, moving or stationary."

"Did Vera shoot with her?"

"Yes. She was pretty good shooting at bull's-eyes, but missed on the other range. I was the tyro. They were the experts."

"I didn't know that. Did she use a Glock? There is a second Glock just like the one that we know was used to shoot the old lady."

"You never told me you had the murder weapon."

"I didn't say we did. Again, this is not for publication, but we aren't sure. That's because the round disintegrated in her head. So our ballistics expert hasn't been able to rule out that she was shot with her own gun. Let's look at the top floor."

"Okay … not a place I particularly want to see."

"Why is that?"

"We agreed to stay here in Vera's room temporarily after our honeymoon. I say temporarily, but Gloria visualized moving upstairs and giving us the master bedroom. It's hard to say no to a place like this when it's rent free."

Art pushed open the door to a crowded bedroom and flipped on the light. "This would have been our marriage bed. What else is left to see?"

Hackelby said, "Her bathroom."

They went into the bathroom, where Art saw the diamond ring. Pointing to it, he exclaimed, "The engagement ring! Well, that says it all. She left it behind."

"Are you sure?"

"Let me tell you, I'm sure. I'll be paying for the sucker for the next ten months."

The detective pulled a glycine bag out of his pocket and slipped the ring in with a pair of tweezers.

"What are you doing that for?"

"I'll let the lab people scan it. It might have picked up a trace of something in the setting."

Art pointed toward the bag holding the ring. "Boy, that's something I'd like back."

"I can't do that. You'll have to talk to Vera if you ever see her again."

Art thrust his hands in his pockets and left the room. Finally, as he waited for the detective to lock the door, he asked, "What have you found out about Vera?"

"She's in Houston. She has a job and goes to her dad's old church."

"I mean about that night."

"Art, as much as I'd like to give you every detail, I can't. What you can print this: is I don't have enough evidence against any person of interest to bring charges." He saw a tear swelling in the corner of Art's eye. "You still love her, don't you?"

Art shrugged his shoulders. "It's hard to get her out of my mind, but I'm working on it."

"Maybe you ought to visit Houston. See if you can bring her back."

"I don't know. I'm sure Red wouldn't spring for me to go chasing after her. And then there's the liability if I get my hands on that damned Korean."

Hackelby shook Art's hand as he said, "Art, thanks for walking through the house with me. I'll have the ring checked. As for Sung Li, he's safely behind bars facing charges. Do me a favor and ask Red to call me. I'd like the public to get another chance to ID that composite of the guy who was in Linguini's. I'd like to say more, but the most I can disclose is that he is definitely a person of interest."

"And where does that put Daphne?"

Detective Hackelby's lips smiled while the rest of his face remained sphinxlike. "Williams, I'm not going to answer that question. Just say I feel optimistic."

⇥◉◖⇤

Two days later, Art stood at the counter of the Harris County Sheriff's office. He watched the somewhat overweight uniformed officer stroll toward a desk in the back of the room, where a clean-cut, muscular blonde sat. Art took her to be in her thirties. She looked up from her work when the officer said, "There's a guy out here who has a press card from some California paper. He wants all sorts of information about the perverted Father and his daughter. Lyndon ain't here. Here's the card, it's an Arthur Williams of the *Oakland Tribune*."

Danielle Dancer studied the card, then smiled. Art watched her open a drawer, remove a pair of folders, and walk toward him. At the counter she said, "Welcome to Texas, Mr. Williams. I'm Detective Dancer, may I help you?"

"I'm doing a story on a Father Sung Li, who was arrested here. He has a connection to California."

Danielle looked down at the card, then flipped it so it landed on the counter right in front of him. "Arthur Williams, now that name has a familiar ring to it. I can't imagine any California paper sending somebody down here to cover child abusers when there are so many in California."

"The card is legit. I'm an investigative crime reporter."

She glanced into a folder, then she looked Art squarely in the eye. "Weren't you and Vera Li supposed to marry?"

Art felt the question hit him hard enough to leave him winded. "Well, ah, yes. I'm also a reporter."

"Why don't you sit down? I'll put together a press packet that ought to help you get the full story."

Art thanked her, then asked, "Where can I find Vera?"

She scribbled a number and handed it to him, then said, "Wait until about six-thirty or seven to call. She commutes into Houston." After a look at the calendar, she continued, "Wait, today is Wednesday. She'll be at St. Bede's this evening for Bible study. Let me draw you a map. By the way, I'm glad you came."

"You know an awful lot about her."

"She's been working with us to put this child molester away. She's become a friend. Vera is a very sweet girl."

Sweet girl, my ass. She is the killer, thought Art.

⊶⊷

Vera made the effort to focus on what was positive and away from the negative in the same way she practiced the *budo* arts. Today she chose to focus on feelings of pride and accomplishment about what she would share during Bible study that evening. She had just deposited her first regular paycheck since starting at Baxter and Wenderly. The church's senior warden had called to tell her that she could move into the apartment she had found. Just over a thousand dollars had been raised to cover her damage deposit and last month's rent.

When Vera was one block short of the freeway entrance, a yellow pickup truck ran the red light. For a split second the heavily chromed grill was aiming at Vera's door. Miraculously, the other driver braked hard and passed inches from her rear bumper and out of the intersection untouched. She felt thoroughly shaken as she merged into the Interstate traffic heading west toward St. Bede's. She felt the dampness on her steering wheel and blinked the stinging sweat out of her eyes. Vera thought, *Why wasn't I broadsided? Dear God, why did you spare me? I deserve to die for what I did to Grandmother.*

She drove in the direction of St. Bede's at the slow pace dictated by the rush hour traffic. The Miata's air conditioning was just holding its own against an oppressive late summer afternoon's heat. In the closed confines of her car with the windows and top up, she felt she was reliving one of those terrible days on the road while she drove alone from Oakland to Houston. Anger had driven her then, with thoughts of how she would take vengeance on her father as the root cause of her loneliness and guilt. Today, in the wake of a close call on the road, she wallowed in emptiness and the pain of loss from not marrying Art. That pain alternated with the guilt of betraying her mother with Sung and losing both Grandpa Joe and Grandmother Gloria.

She held onto the memory of talking with Grandmother in a room heavy with gun smoke to justify the belief that *Grandmother was alive when I left.* Try as she might, she could not remember pulling the trigger a second time.

She couldn't shake those disturbing memories: the Rorschach-like pattern of blood and rains on the wall; the vision, playing and replaying through her dreams, of a red dot dancing on the wall before coming to rest on the back of Grandmother's head. She struggled to repress the competing thought, *Grandmother was not alive when I left. No one else was there. I must have done it.*

Vera wheeled into the church parking lot to see a mid-sized sedan parked under her favorite tree. She was a few steps away from the parish hall when she saw Art Williams look out the window. She thought, *What's Art doing here? Could this be an answered prayer? Will he give me another chance?*

She ran those last few steps and pushed the door open. More than anything she wanted to be held. She pulled up short when she realized that wasn't going to happen. He stood with his arms folded across his chest. If his body language and a cold stare weren't enough to send the message, the frigid tones of his first words removed the last doubt. "So this is where you hang out, the good Father's old church."

Vera asked, "What are you doing here?" That wasn't what she wanted to say. The words came out more or less automatically. She took another deep breath. Despair flooded her conscience as she tried to maintain eye contact. Tears overflowed her eyes. *He hates me. I'm lost.*

Art said, "Vera, we need to talk somewhere that's private."

"Yes, yes, I can explain everything. Follow me," she nodded and walked to the library. She sat on one side of a table, he on the other. She blew her nose and wiped her eyes before speaking in a soft, girlish voice. "Please hear me out. It wasn't my fault. I never stopped loving you."

He placed his cassette recorder on the table and squeezed the start button. His tones were cold and full of anger. "Love me? I can't describe the pain, the disbelief I've endured."

"You have every reason to be angry with me."

" Never once did you call or even write. Why?"

"How could I? I'm so ashamed. Yes, I should have tried to see you before I left. I hurt so much physically and emotionally, I couldn't be anyone's wife. Please, could you start to forgive me?"

"Why did you follow Sung to Houston?"

"After what he did, you have to ask? How could I ever face all those people after I invited them to my wedding and didn't show up because of him? Look at you, you're barely able to control yourself."

She reached across the table for his hand. As he drew it back, she said, "Arthur, I loved you then. Believe me, I love you now."

Art pushed his chair back a few inches as he said, "What about Sung's offer, the one to divorce Jenny and marry you?"

"That's Sung's idea. He's crazy!"

"Can you honestly tell me that if he hadn't been arrested, you wouldn't have followed him to Costa Rica and San Elmo?"

She looked out the window. "My mind was so messed up, it's taken all this time to get things unraveled. Then I have a day like today when some guy in a pickup almost broadsides me, and you show up."

Art watched her in the silence that followed as she reached up and touched the rattail file. She looked him right in the eye, "If Detective Evans hadn't thrown Papa Sung in jail, I would have iced him and gone to prison. But there is justice, because I'll testify and he'll go to prison for a long time."

"You're going to prison too, for what you did,"

"What do you mean?"

"Vera, it's only a matter of time until they sort out all the bogus leads. They have all they need to get you, it's just that they have information overload."

"Grandmother was alive when I left." She smiled and reached further for his hand.

He drew away far enough to tilt the chair on its back legs. "Sure, and Sung and Jenny Li are your real parents. You don't remember anything. Look, there are traces of gunpowder in the setting of your engagement ring that you so thoughtfully left for me to find by the sink in what could have been our bathroom. Vera, it matches the residue found around Gloria's body."

Oh my god, he knows. Her lips trembled. Her hands withdrew to hide eyes that soon overflowed with tears. "I loved Grandmother with all my heart. I wish she were alive to know that I didn't purposely stand you up. It wasn't my fault! He drugged me."

"Look at me, Vera." Art pointed his index finger at her with his thumb pointed upward, "How on earth did you get your hands on your grandmother's Glock?"

He has to know. He's so angry, I can't stand the way his eyes bore in. Vera stood up and faced away from him. She repeated in a tone of voice that even she knew sounded false, "She was alive when I left."

"Vera, they've gone over that house with a fine-tooth comb. They know everything. Gloria always left cleaning the kitchen to someone else. Eudora was away. You cleaned it up after you blew her head off."

"No, she was alive and working on her computer."

"Who else was there with you? How did you get your hands on Gloria's Glock?"

Pleading eyes tried to find his. "She handed it to me. I didn't want to do it. I never want to touch another gun ever ..."

"Vera, how could you?"

She buried her face in her hands and pulled her legs up into almost a fetal position. "I don't know how it happened. You're right, I was the only one there." Sobs wracked her body.

He arose and walked around the table. Art put his hand on her back and gently rubbed. "Vera, I'm so sorry it had to end like this." With the other hand, he lifted the rattail file from the back of her head.

She asked, "You won't tell anyone, will you?"

"You said yes to the wrong man. I'll tell the world. It's my job. Besides, not to tell is to be an accessory. You're going back to California with me right now and turn yourself in. It's the only way to cut your losses. You'll need a good criminal lawyer. It's too bad you murdered the best one in California."

"Do you still love me?"

"What a question ... You left me standing at the church while you screwed Sung."

Vera shouted, "Stop, stop ...."

"Come on--no contact, not even a postcard. You never told me he was your adoptive father. It wasn't incest. It was your affair. You couldn't get him out of your head! You're the second woman to dump me, and you did it big."

"No! No! You're wrong, I didn't dump you! I would have been there! I love you! Papa Sung drugged me!"

Art said, "Oh sure, and Gloria was alive when you left, too! You left a hurt inside me that won't go away. After you disappeared, I realized I had asked to be part of your family. With one bullet, you've denied me the chance for your aunt and uncles to be my family. I love them all, even your volatile grandmother. In the days since her death, I hurt even worse than I did that Saturday afternoon. I'll tell you now, I did love you. We were the best of friends. I wanted it all, forgive me. I'm angry at you for denying me the chance to be part of a wonderful family that has rallied around me. Right now, the most I can say is that I need time to heal. "

She lifted her hands off the table. "We could start over. Please hold me."

"No, Vera, we made a deal. We wouldn't make love until our wedding night. And you skipped out." Vera sat tall, then half rose out of her seat, as he snapped, "Don't skip out on me again!"

"I must tell Detective Evans I'm leaving."

"No, I'll tell him when we get to California. I'm sure you'll be brought back here to testify against the son of a bitch."

"You must hate me."

For just a moment, he caught her eye as he said, "Hate you? I wish I could. It would make all this far easier. Even now, I'm sitting here feeling like a moth drawn to a flame. Why didn't you just call me from the hotel? I would have understood. We could have worked it out. You sure picked a slimy bastard to give you away."

Again putting her face in her hands, Vera said, "I did call you … but you weren't home. I am so ashamed of what he did. What was I to do? After Grandpa Joe died, Papa Sung was the only father I had left."

With little effort applied, Art lifted her up by the elbow and guided her toward the door. "Vera, you've got to cut your losses. If they issue the warrant for your arrest, you'll be a fugitive. If you surrender, you could avoid spending the rest of your life in prison. Come back to California with me right now."

"I don't have any money."

"I have a Mastercard. I'll buy you a toothbrush at the airport. That's all you're going to need for a while."

While they walked toward the car, he made reservations on his cell phone. En route, she told him again that she hadn't stopped loving him and begged again for forgiveness. Art's eyes were cold and his expression fit for a game of poker. Twice she tried to tell him about what happened that night. Both times he stopped her, repeating that he didn't want to have to testify against her.

She curled her lip as her voice turned cold. "You have another girl, don't you? You were out carousing down by the *Tribune* on what would have been our wedding night!"

"No, who told you where I was?"

"Grandmother told me just before I went into the kitchen."

"So that's why you shot her. It'll take a long time for the hurt to wear off enough for me to start looking again."

"Me too."

They rode to the rental car return and then into the airport without saying another word. On the skyway between the terminal and the plane, Art called Detective Hackelby. By the time they were on board, he had told the detective she had confessed to him and what flight they were on. He asked that the flight be met. She froze in her steps until he put his arm around her waist. *My life is over* raced through her head again and again.

With the nonstop flight almost full, they had to take aisle seats in different rows. Off and on through the flight she looked at him from behind, but he didn't return her glances. He was busy, between writing and talking on the airline's cell phone.

On arrival at Oakland, Art stood by his seat to make sure Vera followed the attendant's instructions to remain seated until the plane was empty. Each time their eyes met, she looked away. Two uniformed officers preceded Detective Hackelby on board. Art handed him a copy of the cassette as he passed by.

The jilted bridegroom listened to Vera being read her rights as he walked slowly toward the front of the plane. He waited at the front of the cabin to watch the officer handcuff her hands behind her back. He stepped through the door into the terminal to find himself almost blinded by lights and surrounded by TV cameras pointed at him. He shielded his face with his hand until after he had passed through the media formation and the crowd of onlookers. He looked back to see Vera led through the skyway door with her torso twisted in a vain attempt to hide her face. For the briefest moment, he saw her figure in silhouette as she turned her head to look at him. Their eyes met fleetingly for one last time. He thought, *So long, Vera. Maybe things do happen for the best.*

While waiting for the bus, he removed the Harris County envelope he had stored in his luggage and studied a copy of Sung's charging sheet. He noted that in addition to child rape charges, there was one for possession of a controlled substance, six pills called flunitrazepam, a drug he'd never heard of. The photocopy showed that there had been twelve in the bubble pack. The pack had Spanish writing all over it, with symbols of quarter-moons and stars. Also there was a photocopy of a box and seven sealed condoms. He read a photocopy of a handwritten page, signed by Detective Danielle Dancer. It stated there were grounds to alert federal and California authorities regarding sex crimes in their jurisdiction. The page also warned of use of the drug in violation of some law whose number didn't copy well enough to be read.

Satisfied, he returned the folder to its place as he thought, *Boy, am I bushed after a round trip to Houston in less than two days. All this will be a story for another day. Maybe, just maybe, Red will pick up both of our plane fares. After all, the* Tribune *readership is getting the full story with their morning coffee. Yessir,* he said to himself bitterly, *I brought home another front-page scoop.*

CHAPTER 17

Detective Jim Hackelby sat in a padded, ergonomically designed chair on one side of the table in the interrogation room. The walls had been painted so recently that the aroma of fresh paint was discernible. He would have liked to start Vera Li's interrogation sixteen hours ago, but it was delayed by her request for a lawyer. Every public defender in Alameda County and the surrounding Bay Area bowed out. They claimed an inability to offer a defense because of their relationship with the deceased, Gloria Caulfels. Finally Cassandra Poper, a rookie PD from San Jose, agreed. He looked across the table at the brown-haired woman with a boyish figure, who sat on a straight-back wooden chair staring at the one-way glass. Gathered beyond the glass panel was what Hackelby regarded as a team of Monday morning quarterbacks: Deputy Prosecutor Baylor Gates, his boss Dale Bleasman, and Hackelby's boss. *Poper has no business being on a case this complex,* thought Hackelby. *I'm going to be extra cautious to avoid a misstep that would get it thrown out on appeal.*

He studied Vera, whose fidgeting hands twisted the ends of her long hair that was drawn back in a ponytail. One look at her told him she would draw plenty of media attention on the strength of looks alone. The delay had given him an opportunity to listen to Art's recording. He wondered why this tired and frightened woman had confessed to a reporter after fooling the Harris County detectives.

Until he heard that tape, he felt he didn't have enough evidence to recommend going forward. Even now, given the turmoil in the Prosecutor's Office and Bleasman's tendency to overreach, he was going to have to do some serious homework to back up Vera's statements with forensics. This remorseful young woman was taking responsibility while denying pulling the trigger.

Hackelby looked back over his shoulder until the light went on that indicated the camera was recording the interrogation. Then he started going through the formalities to begin the session. "Do you wish to make a statement about how you shot Gloria Caulfels, Miss Li?" he asked. "Yes," answered Vera weakly. Public Defender Poper was still staring at the one-way glass.

He remained still in a sphinx-like pose for over a minute. At last the PD stopped admiring herself in the mirror and looked at her client. Vera remained silent, with tears running unchecked down her cheeks. Hackelby leaned forward with his elbows on the table. "Please Miss Li, go on."

Vera cleared her throat and took a large swallow of water. "On the airplane, I kept going over what I think really happened. My memory is all messed up because Papa Sung drugged me. Both my vision and my memories are blurred. I don't even know what day it was. What I've patched together are memories and dreams. I still don't remember shooting Grandmother. I must have done it because I was the only one there."

He asked, "If you don't remember killing her, why did you turn yourself in?"

"Dreams, horrible dreams. I dream of her lecturing me on how to shoot her and how to do things so I won't get caught. I see the red dot clearly on the back of her head. I can feel my finger on the trigger. "

"What red dot?"

"From the laser sight. As angry as she made me, I didn't want to shoot Grandmother. I shot one bullet into the wall. I don't remember firing a second round."

That explains the second bullet, thought Hackelby. *Now what the hell is this woman up to? She accepts responsibility but won't admit pulling the trigger. How does a date rape drug swallowed on Friday night affect your judgment Saturday night? Certainly didn't reduce the quality of a professionally executed hit.* He asked, "What was her reaction to being shot at and missed?"

"She calmed way down and we talked."

"Calmed down? Bullshit! The one time I was shot at and missed, my heart was all pumped up with adrenaline. So after you shot one past her ear, Gloria Caulfels went from ranting and raving to peaceful, just like that?" He snapped his fingers,

"Pretty close. Earlier she was talking suicide. I think she realized how close a call she had. I had shocked her enough to get her attention, like Grandpa Joe used to when he scolded her. Then he'd invite her into his arms and she'd cool right off."

"What did you talk about?"

"About what Papa Sung did to me, about Art going to a bar to pick up a girl, about food. I was hungry. She wanted to work on her laptop, so I went into the kitchen and fixed myself a sandwich. I cleaned up and took out the garbage. When I came back into the room, there she was, lying on the floor with her head blown apart. Blood and brains everywhere, on the wall, on the floor. It was awful!" Sobbing, she said, "No one else but me in the house. Why? Why? I shouldn't have done it. I miss her terribly, but that's what she wanted."

Hackelby thought, *This girl has a temper and doesn't want to admit it.* "Wait, Miss Li, you say you had brought her down from a suicidal rant. No, this wasn't suicide by rant. This was murder. She put the full court press on you like she does prosecution witnesses. Here's what I see from the evidence and your statements: The message you sent with that near-miss was that you meant business. You told her to get back on her knees. You shot her from point-blank range."

"No, no, I loved her. I don't remember shooting her. She wanted to be with Grandpa Joe."

"She was throwing you out of the house and out of the family." Hackelby pushed an open folder across the table. "Didn't she also tell you that you were cut out of her will and that she'd make sure you would be cut off from any trust income?"

Cassandra Poper looked at the folder and said, "What's this?"

"It's the transcript of attachments that Mrs. Caulfels emailed to her legal stenographer in the Oakland PD office on Saturday night. The attachments included a change to her will and a letter to the administrator of the family trust. Miss Poper, that's part of the reason you came here all the way from San Jose. The Oakland PD office bowed out because, by receiving it, they were involved in the events of that night."

The PD said, "These aren't binding. They're just drafts."

Vera grabbed the documents out of the PD's hands and scanned the pages, then pushed them back to her. "This means nothing because she gave me all the inheritance I expected when she paid my way to college. The only money she talked about was what she had spent on the wedding. I would have paid it all back if Arthur hadn't made me come back. Anyway, I won't be making any money in prison."

Let's not tread upon the bull Art fed her about gunpowder residue on the engagement ring. Hackelby asked, "When and where did you figure out you had missed your wedding? Was it when your grandmother told you?"

She looked down at the table and drew a finger through a spot made wet by her tears. She nodded and said, "Yes, in the garage just as I got home."

"Didn't that make you angry?"

"Everything was in a fog. My vision was blurred. I was thirsty and hungry. I had a terrible headache. I was suffering physically from a very violent rape I couldn't remember while trying to figure out why she was so angry. I didn't want to argue."

Hackelby mulled, *Do I need to establish at this time how she got the Glock in her hand? More important, where is it now?* After she fell silent, he asked, "What did you do with the gun?"

Vera shrugged her shoulders, "I don't know exactly. I threw it away in pieces."

"Where?"

"I don't know. It was dark."

"Why in pieces?"

"That's what Grandmother told me to do."

"You remember what she told you to do … but you don't remember doing it. Is that what you're saying?"

"I remember throwing the pieces away, I just don't remember where. It was the first time I ever drove that far on the Interstate."

"You were fleeing across state lines to keep from getting caught, isn't that correct?"

"No, I was going after Papa Sung."

"He gave you money to join him?"

"Yeah, he's stupid."

"Stupid, indeed. Had he not been arrested, would you have followed him to Costa Rica?"

"Yes."

Vera sat tall in her chair with both hands gripping the edge of the tabletop. Every muscle in her body was tense. Hackelby sensed enough of her posturing that he thought, *Look at those biceps! This woman is about to explode. She's a black belt of some kind. Maybe I shoulda cuffed her. Let's see how volatile she is.* He asked, "What would you have done when you found him?"

Vera half-lifted herself off the heavy chair as she said, "I would have made him tell me what he gave me ...."

The PD put a hand on her shoulder as she said, "Don't answer that. It has nothing to do with this case. Sit down, Vera, get control of yourself. Texas will deal with Father Li."

"Vera, Sung Li denies giving you any drug," Hackelby said. "I have his statement that you came on to him on the way to the hotel."

At this, Vera almost shouted with venom, "The pervert's a liar. I hate his guts! None of this would have happened if he hadn't drugged and raped me. I never would have gone to bed with any man but Art."

"Did you have any tests to find out what drug it was?"

"That's a stupid question. How could I have drug tests when I didn't know what was wrong with me? I've had all sorts of problems I never had before that night. Detective Dancer told me I have the classic symptoms of a date rape drugging."

"How were you going to 'ice' your father?"

The PD interjected, "Don't answer that. It has nothing to do with this case."

With the PD's warning, Hackelby knew he wasn't going to get a free ride. Yet, given the way Vera looked at him, there was no doubt in his mind she would shoot Father Sung Li if given the opportunity.

By the time he finished reading the summary of Daphne Kazor's statement, Vera had cooled down. Hackelby continued his questioning. "Let's go back to the house. Was there ever a time that evening that you had to keep your grandmother from leaving the house?"

"I don't remember. I think that once I left her kneeling and begging me to shoot her."

"Did she get as far as the front door and open it part way?"

"I'm not sure. Maybe. I remember tripping her so I could go back to get the gun before she did. Running hurt so much down there, it almost made me sick. It's all like a disjointed dream. I'm not sure it really happened."

"What did you do after you shot her?"

"After I found her shot, I took a long, hot shower. Then I did some exercises and that helped clear my head. I kept telling myself it was all a big, bad dream and I would be getting ready for my wedding. Only it was real. I didn't want Grandmother to die. I loved her."

Hackelby tried to ask clarifying questions in hopes of getting a real confession or at least find out if Vera was lying. She just folded her arms across her chest and looked at her PD. The PD told her she didn't have to answer the same question twice.

Vera said, "What more do you want? I've told you Grandmother was alive when I came home, and she asked me to shoot her. She was dead when I left. I was the only one in the house with her. I remember aiming at her. I don't remember pulling the trigger, but I must have done what she wanted me to. There is nothing more I care to say."

⟶▸▨ ▨◂⟵

Hackelby left Vera with her PD and went into the observation booth. Prosecutor Bleasman shook his hand. "That was a superb interrogation. I say she's bought herself a minimum of an easy fifteen-year ticket, if not life on murder one."

"Murder one?" said Hackelby. "I don't even see murder two here. Even if you don't buy the line about Gloria asking her to shoot, she's given a good description of the classic symptoms of a date rape drug."

Bleasman sneered. "First of all, I don't buy for one minute that the old woman nagged her to pull the trigger. I battled Gloria Caulfels too many years to believe that she would ever quit. No, there's plenty of evidence for malice as the motive here. Section 188 is clear: malice 'is implied, when no considerable provocation appears, or when the circumstances attending the killing show an abandoned and malignant heart.' Greed goes with a malignant heart."

"Mr. Prosecutor, she didn't come home that night to collect an inheritance; she was a confused survivor of a severe dose of date rape drugs."

"That's what she claims." The prosecutor went on, orally building his case. "Once homicide is proved, Section 189.5 clearly places the burden of proving mitigation, or justification, or excuse, on the defendant. Cassandra Poper can't prove Vera Li was ever under the influence of any drug. One of the imponderables I worry about is fixing time of death, due to the delay in finding the body. However, we have outside confirmation of when Vera arrived, in the form of the nine-one-one call no more than five minutes after she ran the stop sign. We also have the fortuitous coincidence that Daphne Kazor saw the front door open. Coincidentally we can pinpoint Daphne's time in the neighborhood at ten thirty-eight, thanks to the reports of law enforcement looking for Vera Li."

Hackelby thought, *He'd better hope this doesn't go to trial relying on that bitter woman. Crazy Daphne is just a bit too eager to dance on the Caulfels' graves.*

Bleasman continued, "How convenient that Vera doesn't remember what happened at the front door. That was when the old woman almost got away. Then there's the federal charge of interstate flight. I'm looking forward to Miz Poper's opening offer."

My best guess is that Bleasman will do a fair amount of blustering, thought Hackelby, *but in the end he'll settle for anything to bring this to a speedy close. After all, he was officially designated a "person of interest." All bets are off if the state's organized crime task force ties him to Tsamonicoff's operation.*

"Well, Mr. Bleasman," said Hackelby, "it's your show from here on. We seldom see eye to eye. I see strong evidence that she was severely impaired. I urge you to sleep on this."

Bleasman laughed. "I also know that this is her PD's first murder case. Cassandra Poper took two tries to pass the California bar exam. She's a plea bargainer. And the only thing I will bargain to will be a minimum sentence of fifteen years."

⊷⊶

Two days later, Vera hugged Private Investigator Win Griffith in a jail meeting room. Holding her at arm's length, he said, "Child, you certainly got yourself into a mess of trouble. Now I can't get you out, but I can give your attorney solid facts to shorten the time you'll spend in prison. With your confession, you can't avoid prison."

Win is someone Grandmother trusted. Thank God, he came here today. She swallowed and said, "Win, I know I did it, but I don't know why or how. I saw Bleasman on the TV news making me look worse than I am. Art's articles are full of Bleasman's quotes. Surely Art must know the truth, that I loved Grandmother Gloria. How could I have malice aforethought?"

"Art Williams is doing his job, which is to accurately report what the prosecutor said. This is gamesmanship. The more Bleasman blusters, it's been my experience, the less he has to hang his hat on. I'm your full-time investigator for as long as you need me. I'm sure your grandmother would approve."

Vera voiced what she had been telling herself, "She died hating me. And so does Art Williams. Do you know he lied to me?"

"When did he do that?"

"He told me there were traces of gunpowder in the setting of my engagement ring ... and there weren't."

Win chuckled, "That boy missed his calling. That's one of the oldest tricks in the book. When you live a lie, it's hard to know the truth. Is that why you wouldn't look at him during your arraignment?"

Art was the best friend I ever had. I loved him, Vera thought. After a pause she said, "What good does it do? I'm facing fifteen years, and besides, I'm ashamed of what I did to him."

"Honey, people take blame when they do something and they know they're doing it. Did you agree with Sung Li to go up to that hotel room?"

All I need to do is get behind Papa Sung just once and I'll break his miserable neck. Looking directly into Win's eyes, she said, "No!"

"Then it's settled. Give Sung the blame. Isn't that what you're doing by agreeing to testify against him?"

"I guess so, but everybody blames me. Art does. Mother does. Grandmother did. I don't ever remember her being so angry. She called me a whore. All along, she really hated me."

"Don't say that. Don't even think that. Your grandmother was the master of the adult tantrum. She had been sending us all signals, ever since your grandfather passed, that she didn't want to live without her husband. We all heard them, but ignored them. Like your grandfather Joe always said, "Fill your heart with love so there will be no room for hate."

"What I remember was that she had gotten past her rant. In spite of my shooting into the wall, she acted like she forgave me. I went into the kitchen feeling she was on my side. She sat down and started working at her laptop. Then I came back and there she was on the floor, dead. I'll never get past what I did."

"Remember her from the good times. I'm going to turn on this recorder, and I want you to tell me everything about yourself, starting when you were a little girl. I too thought Sung and Jenny were your natural parents. I can only use the truth, so don't even shade it. Give me the good and the bad. I understand that you have memory problems when it comes to the time right after he gave you the drink. We're going to work on that by carefully going over everything again and again. Most likely I'll ask you to approve the use of a hypnotist. I believe in you, Vera. Can you trust and believe in me?"

If there's a way out, Win will find it. He's all I've got on my side. Vera sniffled, then nodded and said, "Yes."

"Good, tell me about your real mother and father."

"I don't remember my father. I still have the birth certificate. I left it at the house. He was Arnold Lisovec. My mother's name was Kim. He was still in the army when I was born because I was born at the army hospital in Fort Leonard Wood, Missouri. They named me Chanetta Gi-Yung Lisovec. The Korean middle name means 'intelligent flower.' The first memory I have of my birth mother is seeing the tears running down her cheeks and hearing her cries as they took her away in handcuffs. I stayed in some foster homes. I really liked the last family. I don't remember their names, but one day they put me in the car. The mother was crying the whole way and kept saying, "It isn't fair. It isn't fair.' They took me into a big building that was some kind of prison; I remember the steel doors that slammed shut behind us, just like here. The last thing my foster mother did was to give me a slip of paper and tell me to write. I didn't know how. She gave me a big hug and told me never to forget I was an American. Then they gave me back to my birth mother. We stayed together in a sort of dormitory until the day they put us on a plane. We landed in Korea. There wasn't anything I liked about Korea. I nearly froze to death in the winter. I was hungry. I didn't understand anything."

"Did your mother introduce you to her Korean family?"

"No, she left me at night when she worked the bars. One morning she came in and started packing our things. She told me that if something happened to her, I should remember that I was born in America. She sewed a pocket inside my coat and put my birth certificate in it, and made me promise never to lose it. We were at the bus station when they arrested her and took me to the orphanage. I hated the place. The only time they talked to me in English was to tell me my mother was a whore.

"One day I saw a blonde lady and a Korean man. When I heard them speaking English, I asked them to take me back to America. So they did, and they became Papa Sung and Mother. Mother told me my name was Vera Li and said I was named after her grandmother, who was a wonderful woman. I was six years old. Not long after that, we flew to San Francisco and stayed at Grandmother Gloria's house before going to Houston. Looking back on it, those were the happiest years of my life."

The seat on the metal chair grew so uncomfortable through the rest of the day that Vera stood up and paced around the table while she continued her saga and answered Win's questions.

⊷⊷⊷◉ ◉⊶⊶

That night, Vera suffered through a disturbing series of nightmares alternating with restless wakefulness. The next day Win continued his search for answers. Being a very private person, Vera was embarrassed to tell all, but she struggled to recount the graphic flashbacks. She was sure he understood that her memories of the fateful night and the following day at the hotel remained a void, except for episodes she wanted to forget.

Vera described one flashback: "I was naked and lying on the bed. There was something exciting me. At first I didn't want it, but I couldn't move, my arms and legs were so heavy. It continued. I tried to fight the feeling, but it kept building. Then I didn't want it to stop. He was there, pounding and pounding. I had a huge orgasm. What's wrong with me? I loved my Arthur, and I only wanted him. Yet I didn't want it to stop."

"And you feel guilty about it?"

"Yes."

"Do you still love this young man?"

Vera bawled. Between sobs, she said, "I'll never love anyone else."

"I know your Grandmother Gloria was proud as punch of the way you two conducted your courtship. Sung stole a perfect wedding from you, and that can never be replaced. Just maybe--and I can't promise anything--let me see if a bridge can be built over this washout."

Win is so dear. He knows I need some touch with the outside world and Art is a safe candidate. I'm not going to let myself have any hope that somehow there will be a miracle.

CHAPTER 18

Win Griffith looked around his office at the stacks and boxes of papers that seemed to occupy the seat of every one of his cheap, worn metal office chairs. The room looked more like a recycling station, he thought, than an investigator's lair. The investigation into Gloria's murder had generated more paper than he'd seen on a number of appeals. *Oh, well,* he told himself, *the family is going to have to get used to it.*

Win seated Andy Caulfels and his sister Jenny Li on opposite sides of the table, cautioning them not to touch the papers; he had taken delivery of copies of all the papers pertaining to Gloria Caulfels' murder. Win took his place with the controls for the conference phone's sound station at his fingertips and his coffee mug close by. After he dialed up Andrew Foyle in Colorado and the other two siblings, they all exchanged greetings.

Jenny said, "Family, I've never stood up before or asked for anything. Thank you for joining in on this conference call. Please listen to what Win has to say. My Vera needs our help."

Win gave Jenny a thumbs-up sign. "I would have preferred to get you all in the same room," he said, "but this will have to do. I just spent two days with Jenny's daughter in the Alameda County lockup. I am concerned that a great injustice is about to happen."

Carole Rubin's voice was rich and full of dramatic pauses. "Injustice, indeed. She has confessed to putting my mother on her knees and ending her life with a single shot."

"Please hear me out. This young woman grieves her loss far more keenly than you think. She has accepted responsibility, but she has no recollection of pulling the trigger, nor any clear memory of the twenty-four hours leading up to it. "

"What are you up to, Mr. Griffith?" asked Ray Caulfels.

"My concern is that she not be punished for more than she should. For those of you who don't live in this area, the prosecutor, a man who was the bane of your mother's existence, has been trying this case in the press. He's smart enough to know that he can't prove murder one, but he's pushing hard for murder two. That would be a fifteen-year sentence, minimum. The public defender representing Vera has never tried a murder case. Vera is at great risk."

Andy said, "Ray, after Win told me that Vera lost that day out of her memory, I talked with the medics and our Air Force justice people. What she describes fits closely the effects of a date rape drug. I talked to Detective Jim Hackelby, and he said he has no proof she was drugged. He repeated his conclusion that such a professional killing required planning. Adding in the destruction of the murder weapon, her out-of-state flight, and her false statement in Texas, he said she's lucky they aren't pressing premeditated murder charges."

Win thought, *With comments like that, I've got my work cut out for me.*

"Sounds like she's done enough to justify a fifteen-year sentence," replied Ray.

Win said, "Please look at the whole picture. The starch in the detective's neck, I'm sure, is Prosecutor Bleasman. Hackelby is a team player. Vera had to have been driving impaired to have prompted three nine-one-one calls between the Park Plaza and home. Let me ask you: can you recall any time that Vera was anything other than the perfectly obedient daughter?"

Andy and Jenny looked from one to the other. The first head to shake was Jenny's, and the others followed with their verbal assent. Win felt he was making headway. After a pause, he asked, "How often do you remember your mother being on a tear? I mean when one of you or somebody had really upset her?"

All four of the siblings and Andrew Foyle broke into laughter. Win continued, "And typically, what happened to bring pandemonium to an end?"

Jenny said, "Dad would say or do something. Or sometimes Ma Caulfels would scold her. She always ended up in Dad's arms. It didn't mean we got away with anything, but the fireworks came to an end."

"Let's go back to that fateful Saturday. Was she on her high horse?"

Four voices muttered affirmatives. Andy said, "And you, Jenny, were adding fuel to the fire."

Win asked, "Was there anybody who was saying, 'Hey, wait a minute'?"

Jenny said, "Art was, but we convinced him that Vera was bad news."

"Wouldn't it be fair to say that each of you got out of there as quickly as possible because your mother was impossible to be around?"

In the ensuing silence, Win expected to see some sort of emotion. Jenny and Andy sat staring at the table. Frustrated, he hit the desk hard enough that a dollop of coffee splashed on the nearby papers. "And then there was Vera, coming home not knowing what day it was after unknowingly being given powerful sedatives. Her vision was blurred and her memory was loaded with events she couldn't comprehend. She had a splitting headache. She was suffering physical pain after hours of rape. She had no place else to go. What did she come home to?"

Carole said, "Knowing Mother, it had to be unpleasant. But was that reason to execute her?"

"I have some evidence to share." Win handed Jenny a piece of paper. "The city's criminalists overlooked your mother's laptop. It was protected with top-of-the-line encryption and the battery was dead. I got a copy of the hard drive and took it to my expert consultant, who identified for me the last thing she was working on. The timed backup for her word processing program was saved at 10:32 on the night in question. It is an uncompleted letter that she apparently thought better of, because she erased it at 10:49. However, we were able to read it from the backup. Jenny, would you read the letter for us?"

Jenny took the paper Win handed her and started to read silently, then abruptly set it down. She was crying. Finally Ray asked, "What did she say?"

For a moment Jenny's hands shook and she wiped tears from her eyes. She handed the letter to Andy. "I can't. Please, big brother, you do it."

Andy said, "Come on, you can do it."

Jenny scowled at him, then cleared her throat as she read out loud, *"Dear Family,*

I cannot continue on this empty road of life alone anymore. My reason for living, my reason for existing, was Joe. I can no longer bear to be separated from him. Since his death I realized that you children came here to see him, not me. I apologize to all of you for being so wrapped up in my work that I didn't have time for you. I have reaped what I have sown. It is a bitter harvest.

What was the final blow for me was being lied to by you, Vera. I had opened my heart to you as I should have to my own children. When you came to live with us, Vera, Ma Caulfels was no longer there. I had to make time to be a good mother to you. Believe me, I tried. I lavished my love. I watched you blossom into an incredibly beautiful and seemingly wonderful young woman. How proud I was of your graduating Phi Beta Kappa. I had hope for this generation, through you, that good morals weren't dead. What I couldn't overcome was the fatal attraction to the man you called your father. At least, it's fatal for me. I don't think you could have picked a more hurtful time or a dramatic act of deceit than to abandon Art and me. He will always remember that it was I who introduced you and set him on his way to a broken heart."

Jenny was bawling as she concluded,

"None of you will miss me. I certainly found that out over these past months."

Win wished he had video conferencing so the others could see Jenny's expressions and gestures. As it was, he couldn't have scripted it more convincingly. A thoroughly shaken Jenny put the paper on the table and sobbed, "It's all my fault! If I'd listened to Mother and pressed charges against Sung, none of this would have happened. "

"There's a bunch of blame to spread around," Win said. "I'm in the same boat as you. I heard her say how much she wanted to be with Joe … that life wasn't worth living anymore. I let her brood up on that hill all alone. She talked that way for so long, we didn't even notice what she was saying. I'm convinced that this unfortunate young woman walked in on a suicide. She was badgered by your mother, while she was incapacitated by those drugs, until she became the instrument to do what your mother had already resolved to do herself."

"What do you want us to do?" asked Andy.

"A number of things. The reason I asked Mr. Foyle to join us is that he controls the purse strings. I want him to find the best damned lawyer we can get to go to bat for this young woman. We're not going to pull a Gloria Caulfels and rip the guts out of the prosecution, but we're not going to stand by and let her whole life be wasted."

Andy Caulfels was the first to agree. Ray was the last.

The PI pulled out a well-worn copy of the *Oakland Tribune* and laid it out on the table. "Just after Joe died, bless his soul, Art Williams wrote a feature series on his life and this family. What I didn't know until then was that your mother was the victim of a rape herself when she was a teenager. Art's series showed how that crime changed a community and shaped the lives of all of you. What he didn't write about were the deep scars on your mother. Mr. Foyle, you grew up with Gloria. Was she always the no-holds-barred and take-no-prisoners kind of person that somehow we came to love?"

Andrew said, "Before that night she was a beautiful, oversexed girl who was madly in love with the most popular boy in her class. The woman who emerged was a bronco that only one man could handle, and he was in prison."

"There was another victim of that night," said Win, looking at the Caulfels family in front of him, "and it was your father. He was a man whose life and works followed as close to the footsteps of Jesus Christ as I have ever known. Which way do you think he would want you to go?"

Carole sniffled loudly. "Win, I don't think I've ever been as moved by anything. We need you down here writing scripts. That poor girl! If it hadn't been for Daddy and Ma, Mother would have badgered me to death. What should I do?"

"There is a young woman sitting alone in a prison cell. Give her your love. Visit her. Write her. There is a decent young man that she loves. I don't know his heart now. Let's do what we can to give them one more chance."

With their agreement, Win said, "If there are no objections, I'll call J.P. Cailey in Los Angeles. He won't come cheap because he successfully handles celebrity criminal cases. Most likely, he will settle this with a plea bargain. Given her confession, that is the best she can hope for. Remember, you can't be convicted of killing somebody in California and not serve some time."

After the call, as Win walked Jenny to her car, he said, "Those credit card bills from June answered many questions. You were right, the bar staff confirmed that the second drink Sung ordered was nonalcoholic. It was a perfect cover for a mickey. It was a very sweet fruit concoction, just like what he ordered poolside for the boys the day before. And the timing is consistent: he registered for the second room right after he ordered that drink in the bar."

"He had his nerve," said Jenny, "putting her up on the same floor as our room. And he broke our budget with that last-minute unused reservation to Houston. Then there was the children's chocolate laxative. He made them sick so he could pull this off!"

"Sung told the desk that Vera was his daughter, and they accommodated him. On the evening you arrived, there was a purchase of $81.97 at BD Enterprises. This is a place that sells all sorts of sex-related goods. Do you know what it was?"

Jenny blushed. "Mr. Griffith, you are thorough. My husband and I talked some months ago about sex toys, but he said he didn't feel comfortable ordering through the mail. I didn't wish to be seen where they were sold. I forgot about it and then, much to my surprise, he bought the thing the first night we were here."

"Then you still have it?"

"Yes, but it was missing when I got back to the room Friday night. That's why I knew what he was doing when he didn't show up. He didn't buy it for me. He bought it for her! But the next day when I came back to the room and his luggage was gone, there it was, wrapped in a hand towel. And it was a sticky mess. If it hadn't cost so much, I would have thrown it out."

I can't believe the man is so stupid. Forensics will affirm Vera's testimony, Win thought. "What does this device do?" he asked.

She colored even more and looked down. "I am so embarrassed. It was his idea."

"How about a general description?"

"It's a very special and realistic sex toy. I turned it over to my divorce lawyer, hand towel and all."

"Oh, that's right, there was a charge on the other room's bill for one hand towel. Was it washed?"

"No. I almost washed it, but Carole said it could be used to show he committed adultery. Will I have to testify about it in court?"

"Bingo! If we get a match to Vera's DNA, I'm sure you'll be called. A more immediate concern is your daughter. Vera has had recurring dreams about becoming very aroused. I would like to tell her about the sex toy. It will help her fill in another gap."

"Please let me tell her. I want her to know that I'll be proud to testify. I'm going to try to visit her as soon as I can."

"Good, Jenny. Carole said you had arranged to fly down to L.A. right after the wedding instead of returning to Costa Rica with Sung. Is that correct?"

"Yes, it has been seven years since I saw my family," Jenny said. "I wanted to take this opportunity to visit. I had to fit my time with Carole around her shooting schedule."

"Sung, in his note, threw you over for Vera. Could this be a preemptive strike on his part?"

"There was quite a bit of tension between us before Vera's invitation came," she said. "When he told me he was planning to fly up to pick up a check at St. Bede's, I insisted on going to California with the boys. I called Vera. She told me she was serious about Art before he proposed. Sung seemed pleased, said he wished to give her away."

Win leaned forward in his chair. "Bingo! Did you tell Vera about his desire to give her away?"

"Mother accused me of it, both before and after the wedding day. I don't think I did. We fought over his insistence on flying in and out of Houston so quickly. Vera called after I told her about my flying up for a visit. I said very little about Sung to her because I was trying to hide my troubles with him. After she asked him to give her away, he agreed upon the time and date at St. Bede's. He was upset when I insisted on extending the stay for the boys and me."

"Did you have grounds for a divorce?"

She wrung her hands. "Mr. Griffith, I've had numerous grounds over the years, but I chose to ignore them."

"Why?"

"It's what I apparently couldn't get across to him. Day to day, it's hard not to love him. He's a wonderful father. The boys adore him. I can't put into words the great feeling of being a part of his ministry. He brings people to the Lord. He heals people spiritually. His dalliances never diminished his loving attention to me. You don't know how hard it's been to stay here in California while he's imprisoned in Texas. People forget that priests are men who have the same weaknesses as all others do."

"Tell me about the weaknesses."

"He's always been a discreet philanderer. I've had to be very observant to even catch suspicious omissions. For instance, during our second year at San Elmo, he was sleeping with a young local girl. She was probably eighteen. I wouldn't have found out about it if the man she later married hadn't confronted Sung. Early this year, a twenty-three-year-old Belgian tourist died in a car accident in mid-morning. My husband was the last one to see her alive. I found that out through the police investigation, because they found his semen in her body."

"Ouch."

"He admitted that they had been drinking together at the hotel late the night before. It seems he used to swing by the resort hotels in the evening, looking for visitors. He called it 'trolling for souls.' I learned that he picked up others there, all of them foreign tourists."

"Jenny, can you see a connection between Vera's experience and theirs?"

"I don't particularly want to. But I don't believe he drugged them."

"Even the Belgian girl? I'm no drug expert, but since the kind used by the college kids is hard to detect after four hours, I suspect it's pretty short acting. Two or three doses, and your daughter lost a whole day. I'm reasonably sure it wasn't just one dose because two more items on the bill for that room were two orders of orange juice. The Texas lab rated the stuff he had as a designer rape drug, and a victim can't drive a car safely until well afterward. Did you know exactly what happened to the Belgian girl?" He handed her a newspaper clipping.

Jenny started to read and, hands shaking, cried out, "Oh my God, just like Vera! She failed to make a turn. Witnesses said she was driving erratically. Impairment is a side effect. Win, I can't take Sung back now. He's a murderer! The detectives need to know about this.

Win said, "I'll relay this to the law enforcement folks here and in Texas. Also Vera's attorney."

"Win, thank you for bringing us together today. You made me realize how much I've let down my daughter. I promise it won't happen again. I want to help her every way I can."

⇢⊷⊙ ⊙⊶⇠

Art and Red Magen were waiting for their panini to be grilled at the Brew House when the Channel Two news flashed a file clip of Vera as a prisoner in an orange jumpsuit. She was being led into a courtroom in chains. She made no attempt to hide from the camera, as she did the night she was arrested. She neither smiled not scowled, but remained expressionless as she looked into the camera.

The news reader's voice-over began, "After the announcements, the latest from Prosecutor Bleasman regarding the charges against Vera Li, who is facing trial for murder of her grandmother."

While the commercials droned on, Red asked, "Got any regrets about the stunt you pulled?"

"I'm still working through the anger." Art shook his head. "I might be able to understand why she did something so far out of character; but that doesn't wipe out the loss of a friend and mentor. Who should take the fall, Sung or Vera? I'm realist enough to understand that even if she beats this rap, there is no way she would ever give me the time of day."

Some minutes later, the station cut to Prosecutor Dale Bleasman standing at a podium. Red said, "What is it with that son of a bitch? Did he tell you about this?"

"No."

"This is the third or fourth press briefing with only Channel Two covering. Why does he have to try the case on the TV news when he has a defendant who's confessed?"

"I dunno … maybe the fact that she refuses to confess to pulling the trigger."

"Give me a nice short update for tomorrow," Red commanded.

Bleasman's face filled the screen. The cameraman caught him looking down at the microphone held below his chin. The reporter's voice filled the speakers. "Mr. Bleasman, what is the status of the case against

Vera Li for the murder of Gloria Caulfels?"

"This office is prepared to avoid the expense of a trial and accept a plea bargain when we are faced by a remorseful defendant who has confessed, as has Ms. Li. This was a horrific crime, with the victim's life snuffed out execution style. The evidence is so overwhelming that the People will go to trial with the sole charge of murder two. The maximum sentence on conviction is life. As I said earlier, the defense doesn't have any valid mitigating circumstances."

Art thought, *That scumsucker is attempting to overcharge. Fifteen years, poor Vera.*

The screen filled with a shot of Vera from behind, with her long hair hanging down almost to her waist. The feminine voice-over began, "In an item related to the trial of Vera Li, the Public Defender's Office has announced that the eminent Los Angeles defense attorney J.P. Cailey has agreed to represent Miss Li in place of Public Defender Cassandra Poper."

Art thought, as the screen blinked into a commercial, *Who the hell is J.P. Cailey? Why does Bleasman believe he can get away with using press conferences to paint an incomplete picture of evidence against Vera? How can he ignore the evidence from down in Texas? The more I watch Bleasman in action, the worse I feel about turning her in. I need to interview him.*

⋅⊱━◉━⊰⋅

After court adjourned for the day, Art answered the phone to hear the full-bodied voice of the county prosecutor. "Hello, Art, what can I do for you?"

"Thank you for returning my call before going home. I'm putting finishing touches on a story for tomorrow morning, and I want to make sure I heard you correctly. You answered the lady from Channel Two that you felt so strongly about the strength of your case against Vera Li that you would ask the court to limit the jury to considering only murder two."

"What alternative does Poper give me? Her client has confessed. I'm dealing with a difficult, inexperienced counsel for the defense who needs to get her around to accepting fifteen years as a fair offer. As I said, the defense doesn't have any valid mitigating circumstances."

232

"Could you be setting this case up to lose? After all, your ill feelings toward the deceased were sufficient to mark you as a person of interest."

"Williams! I can't believe you'd consider writing something like that. You're still steamed because she left you standing. Trust me, my friend, Dale Bleasman will exact the full price."

What is this "my friend" crap? He doesn't show it, thought Art, who said, "I don't hold any grudges. I feel bad for her."

"Bad? You were instrumental in convincing the murderess to surrender. There's more than enough to convict on murder two. Are you disappointed I'm not seeking the death penalty?"

"I would be outraged if you did, Mr. Prosecutor. Did you query the Harris County Sheriff's Department about what Mr. Li had in his possession?"

"Well I'm sure the Oakland police made that effort."

"Does the name flunitrazepam ring a bell with you?"

"I can't say that it does. Maybe you're not pronouncing it properly."

"It's the generic name for what the folks on the street call roofies, rophies, among other things. It's the date rape drug Rohypnol. Detective Dancer just faxed me a copy of a lab report sent to the Oakland police on the analysis of contents of vials that Sung had with him when he was arrested. It was a mixture of grain alcohol and a generic that is close to being flunitrazepam. She said there were added ingredients that are derivatives of a root with hallucinogenic properties."

"So the man had the drugs in his possession when arrested. Possession in Texas by another isn't proof that she ingested them in California," pronounced Bleasman.

Art countered, "Here is my take on this case. Sung Li is guilty by proxy of the murder of Gloria Caulfels because Vera Li unknowingly took this drug. How can you give credibility to Sung's statement that he didn't give her the date rape mickey to make your murder case? Your deputy has responded to a query by Texas authorities to put a hold on Sung Li because your office intends to charge Sung for his rape, false imprisonment, and giving this mind-altering drug to Vera Li."

"I try one case at a time, but I concede that this could present an obstacle in both cases. I'll get back to you."

"One last question--who's this J.P. Cailey from Los Angeles?"

"He calls himself the best defense counsel in the state, on the strength of bamboozling a Los Angles jury to acquit a pair of NFL backs on a on a hit-and-run. He's a greedy bastard. I've never heard of him taking a case pro bono. Please hold off a day on this article until I get all the facts."

Oh sure, I'm going to let him pull another of those stunts he pulled on Gloria's clients.

Vera felt relieved to be standing between the short, brown-haired Cassandra Poper and the tall, imposing J.P. Cailey in a nearly empty wood-paneled courtroom. She never had confidence that Ms. Poper was experienced enough to get her arms around her defense, and she felt rescued five days ago when Cailey arrived. There was a moment of disappointment when she scanned the spectator gallery to see it empty. *I'd like to see Art one more time to tell him I understand why he brought me back. I just wish I could remember pulling the trigger. It would be a lot easier to accept fifteen years. Maybe, just maybe, a different prosecutor will agree with Mr. Cailey and reduce it to manslaughter.*

Cailey rose to speak. The silver-coiffured attorney looked impressive, with a receding hairline and an expensive tailored suit to hide his slight paunch. With theatrical flair, he announced in a rich baritone, "Your Honor, Miss Vera Li has asked that I, J.P. Cailey, represent her in the case before this court. In the short time I have had to review the case and the circumstances surrounding it, I have regretfully come to the conclusion that we must ask for a change of venue."

Judge Rogerson, the same judge who'd heard the Godoniski case, folded the newspaper he'd been reading. "What specific reasons do you have, Mr. Cailey?"

Cailey held up a stack of clippings in one hand and a pair of DVDs in the other. "Your Honor, I submit as evidence newspaper articles and DVD recordings of reports and interviews to substantiate that the prosecutor obviously has a fixation on this case, in light of his frequent inflammatory and now confusing press releases. The fact that he personally was named a person of interest in this case should have been enough to recuse himself."

Bleasman retorted, "This is ridiculous, Your Honor."

Hearing his whining tones, Vera knew the prosecutor was squirming. This new attorney might not change a thing, but he gave her hope.

Behind her came the noise of movement in the spectator area. She turned to identify a familiar voice whispering, "Pssst, psst, Vera." The first turn of her head wasn't enough to see who it was. She shook her head and blew out of the corner of her mouth in a vain attempt to clear her long hair from her field of vision. She had to turn almost all the way around to catch a glimpse of Jenny and her two brothers. Vera thought, *Mother, to pay for Mr. Cailey shows me I have somebody who cares. I am so sorry for all the bad things I did to you, thank you, thank you. Damn this hair. I'm looking forward to getting it all cut off tomorrow.*

Vera's attention was brought back to the proceedings when Bleasman stood up and said, "There's no justification for a change, Your Honor. I can assign a deputy."

She whispered, "But he'll still be calling the shots."

Cailey lightly laid a hand on her shoulder and said, "Shhh, I'll take it from here." He pointed to the evidence in the box and said, "When you have signs the head of the fish is rotten, do you offer your guests the fillets? I have information that this Prosecutor's Office is under investigation by the Federal Organized Crime Task Force. The incidents they are looking into relate to the late Mrs. Caulfels. Certain illegally recorded conversations were made of the defendant. As was so ably reported in the *Oakland Tribune*, positions taken by this office conflict with the pending case against the individual whose actions precipitated the unfortunate death of Mrs. Caulfels. In the interest of justice, we ask that these cases be tried in separate jurisdictions."

The judge motioned the two attorneys to the bar. He pointed to the newspaper. "Mr. Bleasman, have you considered stepping down until this tempest has passed?" The prosecutor stared back as if he hadn't heard the question.

Cailey said, "Your Honor, it is the wish of my client to have her case fairly settled prior to the time that she must be in Harris County, Texas, to be a prosecution witness against her father. In light of the tumult in the Prosecutor's Office, again in the interest of justice, please grant this prayer."

"You're taking your chances," said the judge.

"My office called around the state. I suggest you consider Slatersville County. Its remoteness is not something I particularly relish, but they have the lightest calendar. Also, since my client won't be making bail, it's convenient that they also have a new women's wing."

"Thank you, I'll take it under advisement."

CHAPTER 19

What lifted Art's spirits most was that Gloria's children had opened their arms to him. Carole wrote touching notes on cards she sent. Twice Andy Caulfels invited him to dinner. Then, out of the blue, Jenny offered him a ride to the airport. He enjoyed the contacts because they gave him a sense of family that he had lost since his mother's downward spiral into dementia. Mixed with his appreciation were pain and guilt that wouldn't go away. If only he had called the police when Vera went missing! The one time he was in court with her, he couldn't bear to look her in the eye. Her expression was so inscrutable that he couldn't discern how she felt. Art told himself that the sooner he was on his way, the better.

As Jenny pulled away from the curb, he said, "California must agree with you. You're looking great."

"Thank you for noticing. For starters, I've lost ten pounds, stored the reverend's wife's weeds, and bought a new wardrobe. Living back at home is good. The boys have made the transition well too. They speak English all the time now."

"It's good, in its way, that you have a place … and yet, sad under the circumstances. Your mother was one of my favorite people. You don't meet many in this life who have the grit she did. She renewed my faith regularly that one person can make a difference in this world. You are all fortunate to have had her as your mother."

"Thank you, Art. When I was growing up, it was more like living on the slopes of an active volcano. I was more concerned about the hot lava and falling ash than I was with the view. Sadly, it wasn't until after she died that I had the opportunity to understand her, thanks to your research and Win's insights. Have you ever wondered why bad things happen to good people?"

"Jenny, that question hits close to home. It's one that has been in front of me since the last Saturday in June. All I know is that I hurt."

"After twenty-one years in the ministry with my husband, I've seen it all and experienced too much personally, thanks to him. He regularly advised people that the rain fell on the just and the unjust. And when people tried to blame God, he quoted Job. Before that, my father told me that what is important is to have faith. He said you can always find God in the eye of the storm, but you have to have faith to see him. You wrote that my father faced a prison term of eighty years to life at age eighteen 'with faith and calm equanimity.' It reminded me that through all the upheaval I grew up in, my father was there for me. I knew he lived his faith. As you fly across the country to look for another job, here is something to think about: There is a line in the old hymn, *Have a Firm Foundation*, 'The flame shall not hurt thee, I only design thy dross to consume and thy gold to refine.'"

"What are you getting at? The way you emphasized, 'Thy dross to consume' ... Are you trying to tell me there's something wrong with me because I'm looking for a better-paying job out of town?"

"What about the young woman who is trapped in the eye of the storm, the one who glowed at the wedding rehearsal? Art, when I read the explanation of the effects and side effects of this terrible drug in your article, I figured you had to understand what happened to my daughter."

Art looked out the side window. *Yes, I understand what happened to the woman I wanted to marry.* At the next red light, he turned his head enough to see Jenny staring at him out of the corner of his eye. He cleared his throat, then said, "Yes, I know. I've done too many stupid, bull-headed things. I took my anger out on her. I tricked her into confessing. How can she stand the sight of me? Yes, I have my regrets."

"We all have regrets," Jenny acknowledged. "I regret believing that it was a fourteen-year-old orphan girl's fault that my husband preferred her bed to mine. I regret believing she was a willing partner on that fateful night. I regret spending Saturday night with my sister Carole instead of comforting my suicidal mother. I regret the weeks I didn't follow my instincts to give a mother's love to the daughter who gave so much of herself to please everyone."

They drove another mile before Jenny broke the silence. "It came as a surprise to me, Art, that in spite of all that has happened, Vera loves you."

"You've got to be kidding."

"No, I had one last visit before they took her to Slatersville. She needs our love to heal. You may feel the easy road is to seek adventure. If you do, you may never find another who fills your heart with a love so strong. You'll have a lifetime to wonder what it could have been if you had swallowed your wounded pride and reached out to her. She needs you. Please find room in your heart to at least go up and visit her in Slatersville."

What's going on here? Should I go almost to Oregon only to be told to go to hell? Art gave her a confused look. "Jenny, I'm not running away, I'm on a leave of absence. I can't say enough good about the *Tribune*. Red has been kind enough to pay me for two columns a week and negotiate a new contract on my return. There are reasons beyond job interviews for the trip. Yes, I will use the opportunity to look around, but I'm not sure I'd even like the jobs back there. The one in New York is a researcher-analyst for network news. CNN is looking for somebody willing to work out of their London office to cover hotspots like the Balkans and the Middle East. I have trouble visualizing myself as a talking head. My last stop is Houston, to look at a reporting job at the *Chronicle*."

"Sounds to me like there won't be any California dust on your boots."

"I've fallen in love twice in my life and been burned twice. I thought the first was bad, but this really blindsided me. It'll take me some time to try the waters again."

"Art, at least you can remember what happened that Saturday. How do you think she feels? She had a day of amnesia. You were my daughter's first real love. I fear she won't have the resilience to bounce back, especially after a prison term."

"Prison? That's another thing."

Jenny took a slim brochure from her purse and handed it to Art, "Please take this brochure, 'The Art of Forgiveness.' Read it on the plane. My father wrote it for his work at San Quentin, and my husband plagiarized it. Both of you are in my prayers that you will open your heart to her and that the Lord will give her strength to bear this load."

Art read silently to himself, *Don't allow anger and bitterness to poison your life. Change your point of view from being angry and bitter. Take on a new role in forgiveness. Instead of accepting the role of remaining the victim of another's evil deeds, emerge as the one who persevered, the courageous, who has learned from his mistakes.*

He slid the brochure into his breast pocket. *That says a lot about Jenny and this family,* he mused, *that she would give me a brochure about forgiveness while urging me to forgive the one who shot and killed her mother. I wish I had a family like this. Maybe staying is the best way to deal with this pain.*

They drove in silence the rest of the way to the departure lanes. Finally Art said, "I'd be a fool to ignore approval from a potential mother-in-law. Slatersville is out in the middle of nowhere, but I'll give serious consideration to going there right after I come back from Houston." Art thought, *Consideration doesn't mean I'll do it.*

⋅→▸━▸ ◉━◂←⋅

Art used the forgiveness brochure as a bookmark throughout his travels until he finally finished the book on the nonstop from New York's Kennedy Airport to Houston's George Bush International. He found himself repeating its last words, "Forgiveness is accomplished through diligent practice," again and again. He wondered if Jenny had given Vera a copy. She was very much on his mind throughout his interview at the *Houston Chronicle*. He had scheduled his flight back with extra time to get a story on his nemesis, Father Sung Li. His first stop was at St. Bede's, where he got a polite reception but no interviews. He went from there to the Harris County Sheriff's Office.

After being left waiting in a conference room long enough to feel forgotten, the reporter turned at the sound of his name. "Mr. Arthur Williams! Well, bless my soul, if it isn't the reporter from Oakland, California, who keeps covering Harris County, Texas. Maybe you oughta move on down here."

Art was caught off guard by the detective's sarcastic greeting. He knew that in ten minutes, he could craft a response. Instead he caught the detective's dancing hazel eyes and, after a pause, blurted a response. "Hello, Detective Dancer, thank you for taking time to meet. It's surprising that you should say that. I just came from an interview with the managing editor of the *Houston Chronicle*."

"Before they offer you a job, tell them to call me. Have I got some-thin' to tell them."

"What's that?"

"If they hire you for the crime beat, I wouldn't return even one of your calls. It's no worse than you treated her. I handed you all the in-formation you needed to confirm that your young lady was a victim of this priestly pervert and you pigeonholed it!"

"I beg your pardon."

"Here it was over a month after I gave it to you, when you called me about what was in that packet. She was the victim. Why didn't you at least comfort her after all she was put through? What is it with you northern boys?"

I don't need to take Dancer's crap, thought Art. He said, "As soon as I walked through the murder scene, I knew she did it. I'm sorry, but seeing brains and blood spattered all over the wall left a strong impres-sion on me."

"Am I upset--no, let me use a word you'd understand--pissed, that you came down here and pulled a cheap trick to slip my key witness back to California?"

"Hey, wait a minute, you're the law here. You interviewed her and didn't discover a thing. At least she's where you'll be able to lay hands on her when you need her."

"Yessir, I'll have to bring her back. In this job I see an awful lot of scum and very few good people. I stick by my assessment. I'd welcome her as my backup any day of the week, even knowing she offed her grandmother. I pulled your article on the date rape drug down from the internet. It was concise and accurate: the drug erases memory and removes inhibitions. It's addictive. Deaths have been attributed to this stuff. Mr. Williams, let me fill you in on an added detail: the stuff Sung fed her wasn't the typical Mexican Valium the college boys use. The tech called Sung's concoction a designer drug for rapists. Given the amount of time she was under, the tech concluded the pervert had to have dosed her at least twice, maybe three times. She could have died."

Art thought, *I knew the stuff could be fatal. I didn't know her dosage was that extreme.*

"Add that bit of information to what you already know," Danielle asked, "Can you take the step from intellectual awareness to admitting you were wrong? She didn't willingly or even knowingly go with him. She was impaired at the time of the shooting."

"I know. Will there be any long-term aftereffects?"

"As for the drugging and rape, she was getting better every day before you tricked her into confessing. As for the time she spends inside … I don't know how she'll be after that. I'd say it depends on people like me and you."

Boy, she knows where to stick the needle, thought Art. "I still kick myself for letting them talk me into believing the worst about her. I thought I was doing the right thing, lying to get her to surrender. I'm hung up on the fact that she blew her own grandmother away."

"Don't you know the depth of shame and guilt she feels? It's one thing to slug down a bunch of booze or pills and say it wasn't your fault. It's another to wake up in a nightmare and be forced to take the blame for murdering your own granny. Send her a letter and give her a time to call collect."

"I don't know if it will do much good after the way I treated her."

"Admit it, you're afraid she'll reject you just like you rejected her. Trust me. She poured her heart out to me when she arrived. She would have spent the rest of her life with you."

Art thought, *I thought I had a keeper. All I can do now is to keep asking "What if."*

Danielle continued, "Since it's my responsibility that she be here and ready to testify, I've been in contact with her regularly. Most days we exchange girl talk. Mr. Williams, I don't know why, but you still have something going there. Humble yourself, admit you were fooled. Don't be one of those hypocrites who play the field and then spurn the girl because she isn't a virgin."

Art was taken aback. "What! I could understand getting this from family, but you caught me by surprise. Let me think about it. But so I can write off all this travel, could I ask your opinion about Sung Li? How can this man believe he has a chance of beating these charges?"

"I'll be glad to after you tell me when you'll going to visit her in Slatersville."

This woman doesn't take no for an answer. Every night I go to bed and think of Vera there all alone in that prison cell. I should take time off to visit Mother in Walla Walla as the odds are that I'll be leaving California. I could see Vera on the way north.

Art said, "You're not the only one to relay this message from Vera. I don't know why she could stand the sight of me, but I'll go. I can be in Slatersville by noon four days from now."

"Good, in four days, you're on. I'll arrange for a visit." The detective pulled a photocopy of an article from her desk and handed it to him. "In answer to your question, read this. Sung Li is a classic narcissist. If he would let you see him, you'd find him bubbling with self-confidence, convinced that he can't be convicted."

"Why not?" asked Art.

"The truth is he never learned to love anybody but himself. Only Sung Li matters. Let me give you an example. How did your young lady treat you when he was around?"

"Why are you asking about that?"

"Vera and I talked about that. Were you aware he was trying to talk her out of marrying you?"

"No, she never said a word."

"What about her actions, the way she treated you when he was around?"

"Openly affectionate. She lost her aloofness, her reserve. She took her 'born again virgin' to a new level--hotter than a firecracker in public and colder than an iceberg in private."

"Was it so open and obvious that Sung saw what was going on?"

"Yes. One time she almost blew me away. Right in front of him and everybody, she put my hands on her breasts while making a bump and grind motion against me. He gave me the dirtiest look. I thought it was a disapproving father's look."

"Here is my call. He had no intention of taking Vera with him. Without going into graphic detail, he did things to her sexually that hurt her physically to the extent that, if she'd gone to a doctor, it would have been diagnosed as an extremely violent, forceful rape. I suspect that he figured she'd be in the hotel room until Sunday morning."

"What about the plane ticket, the note, and the money?"

"Lyndon disagrees with me about the plane ticket. Maybe he was fooling himself. I say it was a master stroke. That plane reservation gave credibility to his mash note. Having her memory erased, she couldn't defend herself. If she took the bait to follow him, the relationship would be on his terms. If she went to the police, he had a defense ready that he figured would save him from extradition from Costa Rica. If we hadn't arrested him, he would have been home free by sundown Sunday."

"Why would he do such a crazy thing?"

"Vera's marriage to you hurt his feelings. She'd abandoned him for you, and she was the beautiful object of his lust. He's cut from the same cloth as these mad bombers and schoolhouse shooters. "

"Mad bombers? Isn't that a stretch?"

"It's right out of the textbook. There's ample evidence of planning, from declaring those date rape drugs as his children's allergy medicine to buying that vibrator. Just like in the textbooks, he sought revenge and did it in the most dramatic way possible."

"It was dramatic, all right. Can't the man see the consequences?"

"His sense of self-importance is so great that he has convinced himself that the jury will have to believe him and not his victims. After all, he is a man of God. He fills churches with the faithful, who lean forward in the pews hanging onto his every word. He fired his first attorney and has been threatening to represent himself. I suspect he's gambling that the girls won't testify if they have to deal with him directly."

"Well, maybe he isn't too far from wrong. I read in today's *Chronicle* that there was a neurosurgeon accused of molesting his daughter over eleven years, and the jury found him not guilty."

Danielle said, "No doubt that will give Sung Li heart, but it's like comparing oranges and apples. I read about that case. It all rested on the word of the daughter, who had a stormy relationship with her father. She wasn't a credible witness. She didn't come forward until his new wife disapproved of her live-in. In our case, though, we have three young women with outside corroboration. Rose has been preparing them for the eventuality that he may act in his own behalf. What he doesn't know is that your Miss Li's spirit and what he did to her have really motivated them. They will be there."

"How is Vera? How does she sound on the phone?"

"She's having a tough time adjusting to the new jail, but it's nothing that should keep her from testifying. I'll sleep better at night when she's safely in the Harris County jail. We never know what Sung is going to think of next. His attorney just filed a motion to dismiss on the grounds that his wife's timing of the incest charge was meant to knock him out of the box to get a favorable divorce settlement. Never mind that his daughter signed the complaint. It's more self-delusion. Frankly, I want to see him fight it to the end."

"I've looked at other cases here," said Art. "He's a first-time offender and a priest. They'll slap him with a wet noodle and declare him a sex offender."

Detective Dancer said, "Have faith, Mr. Williams, the harder and longer he fights, the greater the chance he will serve his sentences consecutively rather than concurrently. On the federal drug charges, I understand he's been trying to plead to possession and get a three-year sentence, to avoid the twenty-year enhancement under the 1996 drug law."

"I want him in California to pay for what he did to Vera and, indirectly, Gloria. What's happening at Slatersville that's so bad for Vera?"

"Save California the money. Give him to the feds. They'll pay his room and board for a full twenty years. As for your question about Slatersville: There's a young guard who was off base. It's nothing big. My sheriff called up there asking to have him back off, and I'm sure it will be taken care of. The good news is that Slatersville has a reasonable prosecutor, Ms. Tyler Guerro, unlike that clown in Alameda County. The push for murder two has been shelved, and Vera is bargaining for manslaughter. Tyler agreed up front to give Vera credit for cooperation here in any sentence agreed upon. Both sides want her sentenced before we bring her back here for Sung's trial. After Alameda, I was surprised that a California prosecutor could have the case wrapped up in time."

"It sounds like it's about all wrapped up."

"It's not all wrapped up, not for the woman that loves you. I'm counting on you to reach out to her and recommit."

Art said, "Wait, you're pushing too hard."

"Am I? Do nothing and that creep wins. Think about it. He'll know he's lost when she's called to the stand as Mrs. Arthur Williams."

"You're out for his ass."

"More than that, I'm out for her happiness. Look at me, Mr. Williams. Look me straight in the eye. I'm calling Vera tomorrow. And I'm telling her you're coming. Don't disappoint her again, y' hear?"

CHAPTER 20

Four days later, a reluctant Art sat alone in one of the visitor's booths of the Slatersville County jail. He felt a little confined in the closet-size space, with one three-by-four-foot window facing into an empty stall. The front wall around the glass was poured concrete, and the other walls were painted composition board. Every surface was bright and clean. He looked around the space to see only a telephone next to the window, a narrow shelf below it, two metal chairs, and what he surmised was a video camera in the ceiling next to a recessed fluorescent light. He imagined what it was like to be in Vera's shoes and to be locked away in a cell, no sunshine, a steady antiseptic smell, with only blank walls and a locked door to stare at.

He wondered if there would be enough to say to fill the hour allotted for his visit. He had left Danielle Dancer's office in Houston telling himself that if the tables were reversed and Vera had lied to him to get him to confess, he wouldn't give her the time of day. If there was to be a relationship, what would the time in prison do to Vera?

Initially he told himself that Danielle's idea of Vera taking the stand as "Vera Williams" at Sung Li's trial would do more to anger Sung than break his spirit. By the time he was on the road to Slatersville, Danielle called him on his cell phone to confirm that he was keeping his word. "Don't you forget now, Mr. Arthur Williams, what your sweetie tells me at some point during every call. She loves you."

In the jail parking lot, he asked himself what Gloria would have done. He decided she would have invited him to dinner again and let the chemistry work. Weren't Jenny and Danielle proxies for Gloria? He also recalled Vera's reaction to seeing him at her grandfather's funeral, and braced himself for rejection.

Then Vera appeared at the window and picked up her phone. He sat frozen for a moment. *I can't believe she's the same girl I saw drive off. She looks so vulnerable in that orange jumpsuit with a nearly bald head. What happened to her hair?*

Her hair was cut short into a buzz cut. When first she saw him, her smile was broad and familiar. By the time she was seated with the phone to her ear, the smile was gone. The eyes he remembered as sparkling were cold, almost dead black. Tears flowed down her cheeks.

There was a little venom in her voice. "I never expected to see you again. I need to know, are you here to see me or to get a scoop on how I'll finally plead?"

What is it about this woman? Should I ask why her hair is so short? No, I'm not going to spend an hour fighting with her. He replied, "No note pads, no recorder, just to see you. Both Jenny and Danielle urged me to come. I'd understand if you told me to go to hell."

"Why? It's all my fault. I should never have invited Sung to be in the wedding. I should have asked Uncle Andy or Win Griffith to give me away instead. I murdered my own grandmother, whom I loved dearly. I know you were her friend. Please forgive me."

"Both of us carry too much pain and guilt caused by Sung Li. You never would have left me standing at the altar but for him. I want to put all the cards on the table: I lied. There were no gunpowder traces on your ring. I purposely wrote things that put you in the worst light."

She straightened up in her seat and lowered the phone from her ear. Art thought, *Well, that does it. She's going to hang up.*

Vera put the receiver back to her ear and stared at him before she said, "There should have been traces. I fired two shots."

"That's not what you said in your statement. Didn't you clean the kitchen and wash your hands before you found her?"

"There was no one else in the house. I've accepted responsibility. It's over. All that's left is doing the time. As for whatever you did, I forgive you. That's what Grandfather taught me."

Art said, "Thank you. If forgiveness is what you seek for what you did, I forgive you too. If it's understanding that you were greatly wronged, you have that. But I have to ask: What did you do to get your head shaved?"

Vera lightly ran a hand across her head. "I asked for a buzz cut. There was a lady on TV in San Francisco who needed hair to make wigs for people with cancer. I sent her mine. They need it more than I do. It doesn't look good at all, does it?"

"What can I say? It goes with your orange outfit. You could be one of those women needing a wig and I wouldn't love you any less. If you're comfortable with wearing it short in a place like this, I understand."

Vera laughed. "Dear friend, you always know the right thing to say."

They both relaxed then, and the conversation wandered from happy memories of their courtship and rehearsal dinner to Houston and St. Bede's, on to J.P. Cailey, Win Griffith, and the Harris County detectives. To his question about how she was being treated, she replied that she didn't want to waste time talking about it. Later he asked if the situation that precipitated the sheriff-to-sheriff phone call had been resolved.

He saw her posture stiffen and her grip on the phone tighten. "Yes, there are times I get angry. I struggle to keep my temper."

"Is there something more you want to tell me?"

She looked up at the camera fixture in the ceiling. "It's mine to deal with."

"You need help. A known withdrawal symptom of Sung's concoction is to become agitated or hyper. Sure, you have a bit of a temper, but one of the things I love about you is how controlled you are. Inscrutable, but controlled."

"I wish I were. At the end of every meeting, J.P. warns me to keep my cool and be a model prisoner. So far I've been able to rely on concentrating on aikido's 'one point'--keeping my center of gravity--but I don't know how long I can last."

"If you feel like you're having problems, ask for help."

"Ask for help controlling my temper? Get real! That's a sure way to hang another year or two on to protect the peaceful law-abiding citizens from my admitted lack of control."

Art had barely touched on his trip to New York and Texas when a tall young muscular guard appeared behind Vera. The tag on his shirt read BILLMAN.

This guy is huge, like a football lineman, Art thought.

She said, "We have five minutes for good-byes."

"Before I go, could I ask you a question?"

"What question? The last one I answered put me in jail."

"Well, this is one where your answer may put me at your side. Here it is. Going back to the end of the rehearsal at the church, what was in your mind? What did you plan to do the next day?"

Vera's eyes overflowed and she lowered her head as Art followed up, "Please look at me, Vera."

Slowly she raised her head and wiped away the tears. Her voice was small, with a near-childlike quality. "I wanted to marry you. I wanted to spend the rest of my life with you. I loved only you."

"Is there enough love left in your heart now to marry me?"

Vera stood up and pressed her hand against the glass. "When they told me you were here, I relived being handcuffed and dragged past the TV news crowd. I saw you standing there. You looked so triumphant, like some big game hunter. The stories you wrote made me look awful. If I hadn't promised Danielle, I'm not sure I would have come to the phone today."

"I'm sorry I caused you pain."

"Then I saw you and remembered how happy you made me. How could I have willingly done all this to my very best friend? The reality is that I'm what they call damaged goods. There aren't enough days in a lifetime full of regret to atone for what I did to Grandmother. I've had time to think, and I realize I'm where I belong."

"I can't get you out of my head. I don't want to desert you." After he said those words, Art thought, *Boy, I've done it now. I've committed myself to her and staying in the Bay Area.*

She sank into the chair, letting her hand slide down the glass. "Grandmother told me after you proposed that I was hitching my wagon to a star. You're not going to stay in Oakland. What's the use?"

"Don't jump to conclusions. I haven't accepted any offers. Have faith, J.P. will bargain it down to involuntary manslaughter. We'll be together before you know it. From what Jenny told me, with the suicide note that Win's man found on her laptop, plus all of your aunts and uncles making statements on your behalf, your version has credibility. Harris County has asked for clemency in light of your cooperation there. This prosecutor is more interested in serving justice than playing political games. She has accepted your expert's findings on the psychological effects of the drug Sung used on you."

"We won't be together soon, and you know it. Darling, I read the law over and over. What I did fits voluntary manslaughter to a T. I'm looking at a minimum of three years, maybe as much as eleven. They'll probably add a year for using the gun. Could you really mark time for twelve years?"

Art said, "Let's cross bridges as we come to them. If you have the heart to recommit now, so do I. If not, I need to know: Is there any spark left to rekindle your love for me? Or should I go?"

Vera asked, "Can I reach out to you now and not cause more hurt for the two of us? What hope can I have if you're on the other side of the world?"

"That fear of causing you more hurt kept me away from hearing your message. I fought facing reality. Jenny tried, but it was Detective Dancer who opened my eyes. My darling, I believe you! You were kidnaped. Sung wanted to make sure we didn't marry. I had to do some growing up to get past all that."

"This is too sudden a change. What sort of a future do we have sitting with a window between us?"

"Just a minute! Do you think I can just forget this last year and abandon my best friend? The one correct action that both of us should take is to face this together as man and wife. I've read up on the law and regulations too. The courts can authorize conjugal overnight visits."

"Big deal, forty-three hours after a year!"

"It's more than I have to look forward to today. Vera, as your husband I have standing as a victim in this mess. If you will have me, I'll find an attorney who will petition for more visits as part of your sentence."

Vera laughed, "Art, you're dreaming! No judge is going to sentence me to have sex with you, be serious."

"Why not? No court would ever find it cruel and unusual. I *am* serious. The court will control your life, including conjugal visits. I want you to be my wife in every way."

"This is more than I can handle. It's too much too soon. Let me get used to you being in my life again." She placed the phone on the hook and stood up, still smiling at him. Then she picked up the receiver again and waited for him to put the phone back to his ear before concluding, "Art, darling, please bear with me. I'm going through hell inside. A big part of me wants to say yes right now, but I'm afraid. Let me talk to J.P. tomorrow and give you a real answer at your next visit. Like I told you in Houston, I do still love you. Please don't abandon me."

Art smiled broadly and touched the glass opposite her hand. "That's what I needed to hear. Just remember, I love you too."

Art was in mid-sentence when Billman took the receiver out of her hand and put it on the hook with one hand. The other, he inserted between her collar and neck. He lifted her to her feet and backward much in the same way a parent would a stubborn child. Vera's face instantly colored. Art mouthed "I love you" as Billman turned her and she stepped out of sight.

Art slammed the receiver on the hook. "What in blazes are you doing to her? This is uncalled for." He looked at his watch and noted they had spent sixty-four minutes together. He thought, *So that's how she's treated. Billman, you picked the wrong guy's girl to treat like a piece of crap.*

⋆⫘◉ ◉⫘⋆

Art turned north with memories and visions of Vera fresh in his head. By the time he reached Walla Walla and his mother's side, he knew that, come what may, he and Vera were bound for life. He announced his decision to marry Vera to his uncomprehending mother as his "epiphany." The next morning she had just short of an hour of lucidity before slipping back into her dream world, and Art spent most of that hour talking about Vera. He stayed on another three days until he had to depart for Portland and an interview for a job writing news copy for KOIN.com, the internet version of the local CBS affiliate.

Just before the interview, he dialed the robocall to set up a time to visit his fiancé. It told him that Vera Li wasn't available. He was so upset that his interview that afternoon was a disaster. His next call to Slatersville took him to an answering machine that directed him to call again between eight and four-thirty. Neither Jenny nor Detective Dancer answered the phone. Art hopped into his car, turned south on I-5, and tore off on a nail-biter of a trip that brought him to Slatersville before breakfast.

Just after eight in the morning, he went to the jail seeking time, however short, to again make his case and hopefully hear Vera's commitment. Instead he was turned away by a smirking Officer Billman, who politely informed Art that the sheriff had ordered Vera transferred to Valley State Prison for Women at Chowchilla as a "Level 4 Offender."

Art was incredulous. He knew enough about the system to know that Level 4 is reserved for the most dangerous offenders. Art's request to speak to the sheriff put him in front of the undersheriff, who called Vera "a serious troublemaker with an incorrigible attitude." Art asked if the incident that she was being punished for involved Officer Billman. The undersheriff's eyes widened; Art could tell he'd struck a nerve. "Mr. Williams, I am not free to discuss details of the incident until the prosecutor finishes her review."

A call to Detective Danielle Dancer ended the mystery. Danielle was upset because Vera had been put in isolation at Chowchilla, with all privileges withdrawn. No visits were allowed. During the one call permitted since her transfer, she had told Danielle she wished to marry Art. Other than that, the detective knew only that Vera had been in a fight with a guard on the day after his visit. She was optimistic, however, that Vera would be allowed contact in a day or two.

Art talked to a frantic Jenny, who knew nothing about the transfer. She told him about a call from J.P. Cailey's Los Angeles office. His secretary had relayed that Prosecutor Tyler Guerro had agreed to Art attending a joint meeting at Chowchilla the next day, with Vera in attendance.

The next morning Art followed directions to the oak-paneled conference room of a local attorney that Cailey used as his office in Slatersville. Art's first words after greeting the impeccably dressed counselor were, "J.P., what the hell is going on with Vera?"

As he motioned for Art to sit, Cailey said, "She has a temper, and it got her into more trouble."

Art recalled the Vera he knew. Those accomplishments in what she called the *budo* arts gave her a self-confidence that he found intriguing. Yes, she could get angry, but he never saw her emotions spill over into violence. She was more than capable of defending herself from attack. He asked, "What happened to make them transfer her?"

"A fight in the jail's common room. It involved Vera, three prisoners, and a guard."

"Was the guard that big fellow, Dennis Billman? He seemed to be gloating when he told me she'd been transferred," asked Art.

"Art, you are very perceptive. She complained to me about her treatment on arrival. Billman handcuffed her hands behind her back prior to giving her a cavity search. He claimed that she resisted. With this fight and the way she manhandled him, there are credibility issues."

"This is outrageous!" snapped Art. "After what her father put her through, how could this be allowed to happen?"

"My apologies. I had no idea there would be trouble of this sort."

"Trouble, J.P! This Slatersville is one hell of a place you've chosen. No wonder Detective Dancer was upset. Did you know there was a sheriff-to-sheriff phone call protesting this transfer?"

Cailey said, "Win told me about that after his visit to Texas. Dancer works in a large urban department that doesn't tolerate hanky-panky. She was outraged that her key witness, a rape victim, was treated improperly."

"Why don't they let female guards do the screenings?"

"California law does require a female deputy to perform a cavity search, but this is a small county and no female officer was on duty. Of course Billman denied doing anything wrong. With his word against hers, the officer wins almost every time."

Art said, "So Vera was labeled a troublemaker. What did you do about that?"

Cailey gritted his teeth. "I make a practice of letting the sheriff run his own jail. So I choose to keep a low profile, especially when there is client misconduct. I had a talk with both the sheriff and the deputy in charge of the jail. They promised that Vera would not be singled out in any way. Billman was on duty during my visit. Had I known what he had done, I would have reacted far differently to the way he treated her."

Art recalled the very end of their visit when Billman had been rough with Vera. Now he understood the angry look on her face during the time the corrections officer was pulling her out of the booth backward.

Cailey asked, "Please explain. How did he treat her?"

"He horse-collared her," replied Art, "We had overstayed the limit, so I took this to be his response although we could not have been over by more than four minutes. I could see that Vera was angered by being manhandled, but she didn't resist. I didn't like it, but I didn't feel it was worth making a complaint."

"As for what you saw, Art, put it down in writing and give it to me. I will add it to the evidence Win Griffith has been gathering by snooping around the community. Slatersville is a small community, and now the sheriff feels his back is against the wall." The lawyer paused to look at his watch before he continued, "I had hoped Win would be back in time to join us. He's meeting a local girl who was recently booked into the jail."

Art was impatient. "What's the connection with the fight and with sending Vera to a state pen before she has been tried? And why is Vera a threat to anyone?"

"Calm down. State law permits it. I was in court in Los Angeles, so I didn't find out until she called from Chowchilla. I had a hell of time getting her to calm down. They put her in the Class Three section in isolation. The classes are 1, 2, 3, with three being the most restrictive. This really complicates my life and raises the costs tremendously because of the distance between here and Chowchilla."

"How is she now?"

"When she arrived in Chowchilla, she was hard to handle. I had difficulty communicating and understanding her. Even with the meds they gave her, it took me about ten minutes of talking on the phone to get her to see that fighting for principles could result in winning a very small skirmish but losing four to fifteen years of her life. What frustrates me is that I'm afraid the many hours of bargaining have gone down the drain. I hope the prospect of a longer sentence won't change your mind."

"It won't." Art thought, *Like grandmother, like granddaughter. Well, I made the commitment. I have to keep my word.*

Cailey said, "The reason our lady prosecutor, Tyler Guerro, invited you is to satisfy the Texas authorities about briefing the two of you on the issues relating to marrying her prior to her testifying down there."

"Good, I was on cloud nine after my visit with Vera. She said she was going to talk with you about our getting married."

"She did. She's willing. I see no reason you can't. Marriage to a partner behind bars is trying, so you're going to have to learn to adjust."

"I haven't heard from her lips how she feels."

"You'll have that opportunity. My major goal today is to find out just what's left of the agreement I thought we'd hammered out. An integral part was a twenty-four-hour stay between sentencing and reporting. Unless you want to, I see no need for you to have your own counsel. I'll guide you through the process and negotiate the best terms I can for conjugal visits."

Art's smile was brave as he rubbed his hands together. "What does it look like now?" Cailey explained that Prosecutor Guerro was shifting from involuntary manslaughter to voluntary manslaughter, with an additional year for use of a firearm. "I expect her to recommend a mid-range sentence," he said, "provided Vera pleads guilty on all charges resulting from her fight, with the sentences to run concurrently. This could mean as much as seven years."

"This is a far cry more than the two to four years you were talking about earlier. What was Vera's reaction?"

Cailey said, "We've only talked on the phone. I'm hoping for her to agree. She is adamant that she was the victim throughout and wants to stand trial if there are charges. What I couldn't get through to her is the high probability of acquittal on the assault charge here and conviction on murder two on the other."

"This is a serious setback," said Art. "Just what did she do to this Billman? The man towers over her and probably outweighs her by seventy-five to a hundred pounds." *What have I let myself get talked into?* he thought. *The best I can do to prove I love her is to show support and yet be a diplomat to convince her to take the offer that demands the shortest sentence.*

Cailey said, "My reason for coming all the way back up here was to persuade the sheriff to allow her back as a first step toward compromise. It's a hard sell. What I heard from the jail superintendent was that Vera more than lived up to the reputation that preceded her. She came here billed as a professional-level hit woman facing murder two, who probably ought to be facing murder one. She looks and acts the part. She challenged their authority, forcing them to treat her with kid gloves."

"Vera looks like a professional killer? I don't believe that."

"She's aloof. They see her with that buzz cut, her athletic build, and watch her spend her days doing martial arts warm-ups and breathing exercises. She appears to be a caged tiger. Now they've discovered first-hand what 'black belt' means. She disarmed Billman not once, but twice, and in the process roughed him up a little."

"I've seen her work out at the dojo. It's always been defensive," Art said. "Yes, she has tremendous reflexes. I don't think it's that she moves so quickly, as it is that she reads her opponent's mind. But they have to do something to her first."

"Come on, if it was all defensive, why was she disarming a guard? I have a copy of the surveillance tape showing the incident. I think you'll be able to see why they reacted as they did. Let me turn on the VCR."

Just then the door opened behind them and Win entered. "Good news! Billman doesn't do many body searches, so I only have yesterday's lead. The woman admitted she was so stoned she hardly remembers much, but she pretty much confirmed there was some fingering. Of course she's been through it enough times to pretty much accept whatever happens. She felt that what he does during the strip search is his way of grooming them for more. If there's no complaint, he goes further later. I talked to two more women on the phone who described Billman as a classic screw. He puts them down and demeans them verbally. All three said he never crossed the line in a place covered by the camera system."

"Where does he cross the line?" Cailey asked.

"His favorite gambit is having them clean storage areas, followed by a pat-down for contraband. He's a fondler. Trouble is, I didn't see enough to prove much beyond his being careless." Win saw that the VCR was starting to run. "Anyway, what are we seeing here?"

Cailey said, "Well done, Win. Your good news is good enough to document a little bit of real abuse. It's not as strong as I would like, but we have a pattern, meaning that Vera wasn't blowing smoke. You saw this video before. It's the fight."

The screen came to life with a view of a room filled with women in orange tank suits amid a near-white-noise rumble of voices and activities. Vera was facing away from the camera, doing martial arts warm-up exercises. Art recognized an exercise where she rotated around a circle, moving almost like a ballet dancer. Every half-circle, she halted, thrust her hands out, and exhaled.

At her side were three overweight Black women talking with one another. The one closest to Vera kept staring at her. After a couple of minutes, she rose and shouted, "You gotta stop all this movin' and noisy exhalin'. I don't like it."

The woman, who was taller than Vera, rhythmically opened and closed her fists. Vera continued her exercise for another turn, then stopped facing the woman with her back to the camera. Art marveled at his fiancée's courage to stand her ground against such odds. She began shaking her arms loose while the big woman swore at her. As soon as the big woman took a boxer's stance, Art knew what would come next. Just as he had seen her move at the dojo, Vera sidestepped the blow and dragged her attacker in a circle with her arm. The woman stumbled and fell face first in front of the other two. Voices rose to a bedlam. The two on the side charged the slim Eurasian, but Vera miraculously wove her way between the equivalent of charging bulls. She dragged the lead woman into the path of the other, causing both to fall. The one who had started it all screamed foulmouthed threats. She had risen enough to regain her feet, but not enough to be fully upright. Vera swung a foot upward in a sweeping arc. It struck her opponent in the jaw and snapped the woman's head back. By the time the big woman hit the floor, the second and third were scuttling away like crabs. Vera stood with arms at her side, facing away from the camera.

A khaki streak flew from beneath the camera. Half turning, Vera checked the swing of a billy club with a blow to the wrist and tripped the guard, all in one fluid move. The guard, whom Art recognized as Billman, landed on his knees. Even on his knees, he was almost as tall as Vera. She reached out and handed him his club, then with the other hand helped him to his feet. She gestured toward the three Blacks and, her voice barely discernable above the din, said, "These are the ones who started it, Officer Billman, sir. Sic 'em."

Billman looked back over his shoulder, his face an angry red mask.

He rotated the long end of the nightstick toward Vera. Stepping backward and driving it forward as if it were a sword, he aimed the end toward her belly. She nimbly turned to the side, almost as if it were choreographed. Her hand caught his wrist, and again the club dropped to the floor as she spun him in a circle. This time she kicked the nightstick away while the huge man stumbled and fought to keep his feet. Twisting his wrist, she raised his arm up, forcing him to his tiptoes. The noise in the room dropped enough so Vera's voice could be clearly picked out, "Don't you ever try to sucker punch me again! Officer Billman, you're supposed to protect me from people who try to beat me up. Do your job!"

As she was twisting the guard's arm, he screamed, "Don't talk to me about sucker punches!" The surprise registering on Billman's face turned to pain when she turned him around in a complete circle and more or less threw him back in the direction of the camera.

A voice off camera shouted, "Everyone! On your knees, place your hands on your heads!"

There was the sound of flesh hitting flesh and mumbled profanity mixed with the order. Vera was among the first to be on her knees facing the camera. She placed her hands on top of her head before the order was repeated by others off camera. Two guards with clubs at the ready surrounded her, then Billman came into view. Red faced, he forcefully closed an open manacle around Vera's wrist, then jerked her arm behind her back, lifting her almost to her feet, and cuffed the other hand before pushing her back to her knees. She shouted, "Owww, oh, my God! You had no reason to use that billy. It was three against one. They attacked me. You attacked me. I don't deserve this, you bastard!"

He cuffed her ankles and, reaching through an armpit, pressed his hand against her breast as he lifted her to her feet. Vera's eyes were narrow and full of dark fire. As he pointed toward the camera, Billman snapped, "Call me a bastard! That's disrespect to an officer, Li. You're going to the hole. It's all on tape. You tried to escape." Then the screen went blank.

Counselor Cailey said, "Of course Vera didn't try to escape, but let's face it, inmates don't disarm guards."

Win said, "I didn't see it that way. Her actions were pure reflex. Billman is a loose cannon. She handed him the billy and helped him to his feet. The way he jerked her around by the arm could have caused unnecessary injury. He needs to find a new line of work. That last thrust also could have caused her serious injury. That's a no-no, especially in light of Vera's complaint. What happened to the one who started it all?"

"All of them were transferred to Chowchilla," answered Cailey. "Lorrila Rae Green, the one she kicked in the chops, is a thirty-two-year-old crack addict and dealer. On conviction she faces life without parole as a three-time loser."

"It looks almost like a setup," guessed Art.

Cailey shook his head. "No, I talked to Lorrila Rae's counsel on the phone. She's uptight about facing life and watching Vera slip through with what she feels is a slap on the wrist. Getting back to the point, before all this happened, Prosecutor Guerro conceded enough that I could almost taste involuntary manslaughter. She wasn't talking at all about Vera's actions after the shooting. She took into account the analysis of the residuals from the empty bottles found on Sung Li when he was arrested in Houston. She was comparing Vera to the victims in the two date rape drug cases she prosecuted."

Art asked, "Did she have anything good to say about Vera?"

"She went as far as to volunteer that, up to the instant she fired that pistol, Vera Li was the kind of young woman she would wish her own daughter would grow up to be. Tyler also speculated that if Sung hadn't overdosed her, she probably would have come around enough to wake up by noon and not miss her wedding."

Art spit out, "Or she might have been able to call for help."

Win said, "She did call you, Art, just before she left the hotel Saturday night. The phone company has a record of it. Too bad you weren't home."

"I don't believe it. She could have left a message."

"No, she couldn't," said Win. "She was just coming out from under Sung's drug's spell."

Cailey waved his arms. "Enough beating a dead horse! Let's strategize what to do to turn this around."

Art said, "I worry for her. How much punishment can she absorb before they break her?"

"We all do," said Cailey. "She told me at the end of my last call that she prefers a cell alone in Chowchilla to Slatersville with Officer Billman. Your offer to marry her before she goes to prison is what gives her hope."

"I'm afraid they'll find some way to block it. Are you sure they'll let me sit in during your session with her?"

"It's arranged." Win pointed at the darkened screen. "I think we can make lemonade out of this. First of all, I've watched her for years. Like you said, aikido is a defensive art. Billman's actions were out of line from the start. Why didn't he do like the other guard did and order everyone down? Maybe a threat of playing the civil liability card would be a good counter. I understand the reason they built the women's wing in the first place had something to do with a lawsuit the county lost."

Art said, "If what she did at Slatersville is going to be considered in her sentencing, we need an expert in aikido to demonstrate how each move was defensive. I'll contact the *sensei* at her dojo. If there is a trial, the jury needs to have an understanding of her abilities."

Art recalled the times he had watched her at practices and meets. He thought she displayed the same complete self-control in that county jail as she did in a dojo. He was sure that she didn't even break a sweat. *This is the real Vera Li. She's no threat to society. She has control when she isn't doped up.*

"I won't risk going the route of seeking a jury verdict of diminished capacity as long as the alternative is murder," said Cailey. "The videotape of her confession is too melodramatic and damning. I must negotiate the best plea I can for her."

Win asked, "Any changes on old man Sung?"

"His Harris County trial date is still set," said Cailey. "No more delays allowed. Both the Harris County prosecutor and the U.S. attorney are champing at the bit to get Vera back down there. Rose Bondurant is worrying that without her in town, the other two main complaining witnesses will back out. Before this fight happened, Tyler and I agreed she'd be sentenced before his trial date, so she isn't left turning in the wind."

"What happens if those two women won't testify?" asked Art.

"Sung could make out like a bandit. Under Texas law, believe it or not, the depraved priest could draw more time for diddling the girls at church than for two years of the same thing with his adopted daughter. If he's convicted on all counts, Vera will do him the most harm during the penalty phase."

Art injected, "Danielle Dancer thinks the federal charges are the ones that will do the most damage. I checked it out. He could be facing twenty years for possession."

"Those are maximums, Art," said Win. "Mark my words, federal sentencing guidelines will net him a significantly shorter sentence. As soon as I get back to Alameda County, I'll go over again everything I gathered, plus the evidence from Harris County. The feds will need it all to convict him."

Cailey looked at his watch. "Please, we need to get on the road to Chowchilla if we're going to be there in time for our conference with Vera and the prosecutor."

CHAPTER 21

In Chowchilla, they all crowded into a little conference room. J.P. Cailey made the introductions. "You've met Mr. Griffith, Tyler. Art Williams, this is Tyler Guerro, chief criminal deputy prosecutor for Slatersville County."

Ms. Guerro smiled as she extended her right hand. "So you are serious about marrying Miss Li?"

Art's first impression of the big-boned prosecutor was the firm grip of her handshake and striking blue eyes hidden behind fashionable wire frame glasses. He felt that her plump look of middle-aged motherhood, with patterned dress and a knit sweater, was a form of camouflage in the presence of Counselor Cailey in his all-star wardrobe.

Art replied, "Yes, I am. It took some time and some gentle persuasion to realize that it was events beyond our control that ruined our wedding day and placed Vera in the eye of a storm."

"That was eloquent. I can understand why you chose her to begin with. She has many fine qualities. I hope you're aware that beneath her veneer of youthful beauty lies a ferocious temper and a serious contempt for authority."

Art looked her directly in the eye. "Inscrutable, but controlled. She's no threat to society."

The prosecutor rolled her eyes. "No threat? I thought they were filming a female Bruce Lee film right there in the Slatersville lockup. The County Corrections officers have made it clear they regard her as a threat. She was a principal in a free-for-all. She attacked and disarmed a guard, not once, but twice."

Art didn't respond to her comment; he knew that anything he said about what went on in the women's common area would provoke an argument. He thought that before all this started, Vera never would have been a life partner he could take for granted. The wild card in this game he was playing was just how she'd emerge from this crisis. He told himself that if he turned his back on his best friend, she might never again take a chance on love or forgive herself for what her perverted father had done.

On his way to his seat at a metal table with a Formica top, Art paused to study the only decoration in the spartan conference room. It was a large aerial photograph of the prison, labeled "Valley State Prison for Women at Chowchilla."

Behind him, Cailey asked, "Tyler, have you ever met a prisoner in this room?"

"No, I thought you were the one with the pull."

Over the next few minutes, the relationship between Cailey and Ms. Guerro changed from cordiality to verbal fisticuffs. Ms. Guerro focused on the fight and all that Vera had done to cover her tracks, upping the ante in years served and finally saying she would ask for eleven years. Cailey emphasized the family's support, Vera's acceptance of responsibility, and her good character.

Art didn't understand the significance of the prosecutor's admission that she had no say in the decision to transfer the four inmates to Chowchilla. The officer who made the decision was a female deputy sheriff who was reassigned to the jail while Billman was being treated at the hospital. Neither Cailey nor Ms. Guerro had seen Vera since her transfer.

All turned their heads when they heard the door open. A female guard held the door for Vera. She wore blue denim trousers and a light blue shirt with a chain locked around her waist. *Wow*, thought Art. *This tells me they don't know how to handle someone who can move as fast as she does and kick with such force.*

Vera shuffled through the door, hobbled by the chain on her ankles. Her left wrist was cuffed to the chain around her waist. Her right arm was in a cloth sling held in place with Velcro straps. A manila folder stuck out of the top of the sling. Her short, dark hair was brushed back. When she saw Art, her face lighted up in as beautiful a smile as he had ever seen.

Art stood up and opened his arms wide; but the guard stepped in front of him, turned, and pointed toward the empty chair next to Art's. They watched the guard release Vera's left wrist from the manacle and close it around the leg of a chair.

What a contrast, thought Art. *The tall, beautiful, graceful woman dressed to the nines, with a head of thick rich brunette hair, versus this plain, pale, shorn creature in shapeless prison garb.* As soon as the guard turned her back to leave, Art put a hand on each side of Vera's head, kissed her lightly on the lips, and whispered, "What happened to your arm?"

"My right shoulder was separated when Billman jerked me up."

"That must have hurt. Are you okay?"

She responded by holding out her left arm. "My wrists and ankles are chewed up a little, and I can still feel a bruised rib from being kicked. All that is nothing. I've had worse from a tae kwon do tournament. Sorry about the smell. I don't get a shower until tonight."

He reached out and grabbed her free hand. "I love you. Don't worry about the small stuff. Can we set the date as soon as possible?"

Her eyes immediately overflowed and tears rushed down her cheeks. "Lover, you don't give up, do you? I'd do it tomorrow except I've managed to get into more trouble. I've lost all my privileges." She raised one leg to show the steel cuffs hobbling her ankles. "I have to wear these anytime I'm outside my cell. There could be more charges."

"Mrs. Guerro," said Art, "is there any way you can intercede so I can visit with her?"

The prosecutor stiffened. "Mr. Williams, you'd better get used to this; this is just the first of many problems you're going to have to deal with. It will take some time for her to learn to take responsibility for her actions."

Cailey held up his right hand. "Tyler, wait a minute. I can't believe that what happened in Slatersville would affect the terms of our agreement. This incident, like the one Detective Dancer brought to your attention, involved the same County Corrections officer. It is his retaliation, his misconduct, not my client's, that must be at issue."

Vera leaned forward in her chair. "Mrs. Guerro, after what I went through in your jail, I'd rather be in Chowchilla, thank you. There was a time, while I was being brought here gagged and bound, that I felt the weight of injustice and physical pain so great that I simply didn't have the strength to go on alone. I surrendered myself to the Lord and prayed for His help. The first guard who looked at me during the strip search spotted the dislocated shoulder. They are treating me fairly. I've been getting good medical care and counseling. But enough about me … Didn't they bring me out to talk about the plea agreement and my Arthur?"

Ms. Guerro replied, "Thank you, Miss Li, for reminding us."

Art turned toward the prosecutor. "Since I have standing as a victim, I would like to ask that special consideration be given to making our marriage and conjugal relations a part of this plea agreement."

Ms. Guerro smiled. "Mr. Williams, if I were in your shoes, I'd call myself a victim too. However, California law doesn't give you that status any more than the spouse or lover of any other criminal."

"Williams is the victim of the same crime that precipitated the death of Gloria Caulfels," Cailey said. "Sung Li's criminal acts denied him the opportunity to marry on their chosen day. You can't deny that. He isn't asking for monetary compensation, just an accommodation to secure his future with his prospective wife, Vera."

Art held up Vera's arm. "I need your help, Mrs. Guerro. Please convince the judge that it's in the best interest of justice for him to let me have time as a husband with the woman I promised myself to for life. The statute specifically gives judges the power to grant conjugal visits."

"Wasn't it you who convinced Vera to return to California to face charges?"

Art's voice rose. "Yes, and I'd be a fool to think that you're just going to let her go without serving time. I'm standing by her because she has the guts to take responsibility for what she did, even though she was impaired."

The prosecutor tapped her pencil on the table. "Did you put this Detective Danielle Dancer up to lobbying in your behalf?"

Vera shook her head, and Art said, "No."

"I don't know who this woman thinks she is, calling me on the phone. She's running a regular letter writing campaign. I got letters from her, the family, and other people in Texas, all arguing that Sung will be denied the fruits of his crime, and the interests of justice will be served, if your marriage is permitted before she's brought to Texas to testify."

She pointed to a lavender envelope. "There's even a letter from that soap opera star, Carolyn Connolly."

"Carolyn is Vera's aunt and Gloria's daughter," said Win.

Ms. Guerro made a note on a lined pad. "There are other issues here that impinge on how my office reacts. Our weekly paper, the *Sentinel*, will be publishing a photo of her kicking Lorrila Rae Green in the face. Lorrila Rae is Black. I'm sure this is the kind of sensational photo that will hit the news wires."

Vera squeezed Art's hand. "How can this be?"

"The paper requested a copy of the tape just after it was released to your counsel. It was the sheriff's decision to release it."

Vera leaned toward the prosecutor and snarled, "Why the hell don't they print frames of all three of them attacking me at once? Or that perverted son of a bitch trying to sucker punch me with his billy?"

"Miss Li, get control of yourself!" snapped the prosecutor.

Boy, does she have a hair trigger. Art made calming motions with his open hand. "Vera is correct. There is no balance here. Vera couldn't retreat, and her reactions to avoid injury are being held against her."

"Art has a point," Cailey said. "Miss Li's successful self-defense is being used to deny him contact. It compounds the injustice when Miss Li was essentially kidnaped from the steps of the church. Could you give some consideration to a postponement of, say, twenty-four hours?"

Ms. Guerro studied Vera for a time, then said, "Story or no story, the whole county knows about the fight and that it involved disarming a guard twice. I can't recommend letting her loose in town when she has to wear restraints inside a state prison."

Cailey argued, "I'm at a loss to comprehend the grounds for this classification. If she were in the jail's general population without misconduct between the guilty plea and the sentencing, wouldn't your conclusion be different?"

"The County Corrections staff feels uncomfortable with her running around loose."

Art found it hard to believe that Vera's skills in aikido were that big a threat. He wondered what he could do to convince the prosecutor. Then he had an idea. "Mrs. Guerro, when do you expect Officer Billman to be fit for duty?"

"Beyond the time in the emergency room, there is no restriction on him beyond light duty for a sore arm."

"Would it be fair to say that his only long-term injury is to his ego?"

"Maybe, but then there's prisoner Green, who is wearing a neck brace. There were torn uniforms." Ms. Guerro pointed at the prisoner. "Miss Li, your little outburst today reminded me how extremely abusive and disrespectful you were in the hours immediately after that incident."

The lawyer answered, "Come on, Tyler, you and I were making more noise before she arrived. You'd be ticked on learning about what looks like a planted story. The only one to suffer serious injury was my client. Billman did it while she wasn't resisting in any way. Neither you nor I knew until today that Vera suffered a serious injury at his hands. Please keep the involuntary manslaughter option on the table."

The prosecutor pressed the buttons that released the snaps on her briefcase. Every eye in the room watched her lift out a worn manila folder. Art glanced over at Vera and back at Ms. Guerro, thinking, *What I saw here today was a show. Hell, she had her mind made up before we met. I don't think J.P. has pulled it off.*

Ms. Guerro thumbed through her stack of papers and extracted one. She looked at Vera, shook her head, and cleared her throat. She spoke in a reader's monotone, "Counselor, Miss Li, I concede that the evidence to sustain a second-degree murder charge is questionable. The people can't forget that Gloria Caulfels, a longtime and prominent member of the California criminal defense bar, lies buried with a bullet hole in the back of her head. The California Code requires a year's enhancement for use of a firearm in a felony. Your actions at the crime scene greatly complicated and delayed solving the crime. You destroyed evidence. You fled the state. You lied to investigators. Your subsequent conduct shows that you have an overflowing reservoir of anger. Our best offer is five years for voluntary manslaughter, plus one year for use of a firearm."

Vera lightly tapped her fingers on the tabletop as she spoke in a soft, sweet voice. Art thought she almost sounded like her grandmother Gloria. "Mrs. Guerro, I suppose I should be happy with five years. It is better than eleven ..."

"I'm not done. We acknowledge the tragic congruence of not just your diminished capacity, but that of Mrs. Caulfels also, as matters in extenuation. We will ask that not less than one full calendar year be served in state prison, with no reductions. The remainder is to be suspended on condition you complete an anger management program, plus you fully cooperate in the case in Texas against your father Sung Li. The feelings and sensibilities of the victims need always to be factored into sentencing. Without the cooperation and intervention of Mrs. Caulfels' children, there would be a longer sentence and no suspension."

Ms. Guerro slipped the sheet back into the folder and nodded at Art. "Mr. Williams, I suggest you contact the judge directly regarding his willingness to perform a marriage ceremony, along with your plea for conjugal time together. I won't oppose reasonable access."

J.P. Cailey looked at Vera as he said, "Tyler, correct me if I'm wrong. Vera, Mrs. Guerro is offering you your time spent in custody since arrest, plus one year in prison from the sentencing date. That will include the time you spend testifying at Sung Li's trial. I urge you to accept it." The prosecutor gave a thumbs-up signal.

Vera smiled at the prosecutor. "Thank you, Mrs. Guerro, Mr. Cailey led me to believe the bargain would reduce the charge to involuntary manslaughter. Was this change influenced by my success in countering the attacks on me in the women's common area?"

"Attacks on you? You twice disarmed a guard. You continued to fight even after you were in restraints. You were verbally abusive. I can drop the suspension."

"Please, Mrs. Guerro, please hear me out. I sat with my grandmother many times while she reviewed a case before trial. It wasn't until I was locked away in solitary here that I reviewed mine. Please bear with me while I ask a few questions. If you didn't have my confession, what evidence could you give a jury to convince them beyond a reasonable doubt that I was the one who ended my grandmother's life?"

The prosecutor looked surprised. Cailey raised his hand. "Vera, what are you doing?"

"Mr. Cailey, you've done a superb job, but after hearing Mrs. Guerro's comments, I need to make some points." Vera gestured with her free hand as she spoke. "The only clear conclusion from the ballistics test was that it was a nine-millimeter Glock. There was no clear match with Grandmother's gun. You don't have any real forensic evidence to affirm my admission, not even a trace of gunpowder residue on my engagement ring. You said I lied to investigators. How can I lie when I can't remember what I did? I don't know how many times and how many ways I've been asked if I remember shooting her. I don't. I've been hypnotized, and it's very clear in my mind that she was alive when I left the room. Yet I accepted responsibility for her death."

The prosecutor rubbed her chin. "Is this a retraction? Why did you confess?"

Vera shook her head and pointed at Art. "Because he lied to me. I believed I was alone in the house with her."

"You're playing with fire, Miss Li."

Vera looked at her fiancé out of the corner of her eye. "Maybe. I can't satisfy myself that I didn't murder Grandmother. I still have nightmares about the red dot on the back of her head. I remember being angry, but I also remember feeling relieved that Grandmother was calming down."

Ms. Guerro held up the sheet with the offer. "Where are you going with this?"

"Justice for my grandmother, justice for me. What if I wasn't alone? Daphne Kazor said she was parked across our driveway and she saw the front door open."

"So?"

"That's impossible if she was doing what she did every other time, sitting in her car. Daphne always approached from the south and pulled up just onto our property, blocking two lanes into the garage. She'd roll the window down to make sure we saw her, then sit there until the light over the driveway went out. Now the problem with her story is that the front door is on the north side of the garage. You can't see the door from where she stopped."

Ms. Guerro began typing on her laptop. "That is speculation and makes no difference to the case."

Win's eyes widened as he drew in a breath. "Is this Crazy Daphne, the woman subject to the restraining order?"

"Yes, the same one. She's not telling the truth. She mentioned the tapes in the security system. That's plural, 'tapes.' But if she'd never been in the house, how did she know there was more than one, or that we even had a taping system? I do remember Grandmother removing all three tapes and putting them on the table next to the laptop. I don't remember taking them with me. I don't remember throwing them from the car, like I remember tossing everything else."

Ms. Guerro leaned forward. "What's your game, Miss Li? Are you trying to evade responsibility here too?"

"No, ma'am. Grandmother said there are two things that convince a PA to deal: a satisfaction that the plea fits what's just, or a weak case. What I'm trying to establish is that I do take responsibility for my actions. If I'd kept the gun when I left the room, maybe Grandmother would be alive today. But I draw the line when you try to blame me for what happened in that dayroom. I was attacked by three women, all bigger and heavier than I was. I had to fight for my very life. Billman should face charges of attempted murder. He would have scrambled my brains or murdered me if his second strike had connected with my solar plexus."

"I don't see it your way, Miss Li," said the prosecutor. "I have bent over backwards regarding the effects of date rape drugs. There has to come a point where the responsibility is yours and you claim it."

Art was frustrated that this woman prosecutor, who acted as if she had walked a mile in Vera's shoes when it came to drugs and rape, was so oblivious to misconduct on the part of the Slatersville jail staff. He feared for Vera, thinking about a scholarly article he had read on abuse of inmates in California prisons. The latest "casualty" was the head of California Corrections, who was replaced because of incidents of brutality. The author's good news was that the new director promised changes. The article noted that the legislature showed the conscience of the state when it amended the law to add "tricing" (tying up), but left unchanged that it was only a misdemeanor to inflict a cruel or unusual punishment in jails and reformatories.

Through most of the meeting, Art had noticed that Vera kept touching or turning the folder in her arm sling, often enough to make it a distraction. At last she lifted the folder and laid it on the table. "Mr. Cailey, I don't want to be a lamb sacrificed so Dennis Billman can play out his sick fantasies on other woman prisoners."

Tyler Guerro focused on Vera while she pointed at the folder. "Specifically, what does this have to do with your case?"

Cailey scanned the top page. "I believe my client is seeking a break to confer."

Twenty minutes later, Cailey laid the folder on the table as if he had taken it off a hot stove. "What my client is presenting is a file that the new director requires to be prepared whenever an inmate complains of abuse. This is Valley State's response to complaints of abuse of women serving time. It covers all of Vera's complaints since she was logged into Slatersville. The original has been forwarded to the state attorney general. "

"Talk about a thoroughly whipped dead horse! Is this more about the strip search?" Tyler Guerro waved her hand in direction of the folder. "Enough is enough."

Cailey took in a deep breath. "Enough is certainly enough. Billman separated her shoulder. However, that's not all that happened at Slatersville. This report contains an incident I was unaware of. It happened when she was escorted back after her visit with Art Williams, and it set the stage for the incident that sent my client to Chowchilla. Are you willing to hear Miss Li out on this subject?"

Art joined the others as they watched Tyler Guerro flip through the pages after Cailey handed her the folder. The prosecutor didn't broadcast her feelings with many gestures, but the few she made, along with a nearly whispered, "Damn you, Billman," said it all.

When Ms. Guerro was done, she took off her glasses and laid them on the folder. She looked at Cailey. "Major portions of this report are going to boil down to a 'he said, she said,' but there is no doubt that pictures don't lie. The way Miss Li and Miss Green were triced up and gagged for transport clearly violates the law."

Vera said, "I'm glad you agree that the hog-tying and gagging were wrong. Are you saying I lied when I told on him? Officer Billman gets a sick satisfaction from feeling us up after he's cuffed us. He threatened to tell Art I'm a lesbian."

Ms. Guerro put her eyeglasses back on and scanned the folder's contents. "I need enough evidence to convict. Dennis Billman may get his jollies by making inmates endure his slow pat-downs, but without witnesses or surveillance, the odds are he will walk."

Vera said, "How about the way he uses a billy?"

Win, who had just written three names on a piece of paper, pushed it across the table. "Mrs. PA, I'm going to give these names to whoever is investigating Vera's case."

The prosecutor looked at the names. "What is the significance of these names--other than they are young and use drugs?"

Win said, "I've interviewed them. All three were fondled in some corner of the jail by Dennis Billman. This guy is a shift supervisor! You have more lawsuits waiting to be filed."

Art felt like a spectator as he shifted gaze from one speaker to the next. His reporter's instincts made him want to write down every sentence; but overriding this instinct was the understanding that negotiations were Cailey's business. Art was welcome as long as he kept his mouth shut. Yes, his concerns were on the table, but he didn't feel he'd heard much of a commitment from the prosecutor. What made the wait tolerable was Vera's presence and being able to hold her hand.

Ms. Guerro looked at her laptop screen. "We have this conference room until four-thirty. I need to talk with my boss because he gave me little flexibility in bargaining your sentence. I propose we break for lunch now and bring back Miss Li to our four o'clock for a wrap-up. J.P., I understand you are seeking involuntary manslaughter with no firearms enhancement. Mr. Williams, you're asking for a twenty-four-hour stay plus conjugal time."

Vera squeezed Art's hand. "Yes, Mrs. Guerro, please grant us just one night of happiness."

⋅⊱⋅⊰⋅

Four o'clock found the same people at the conference table except for Win Griffith. Art would have held Vera's hand except that the guard who escorted her remained standing right behind her chair. Art felt hopeful, for the first time, that Vera's time in prison would be manageable.

The prosecutor glanced in the prisoner's direction, then focused on her laptop screen. "Miss Li, yours was a well-written statement. If fate hadn't placed you there on that night, I believe you would have done well at law. With regard to Dennis Billman, he has been suspended pending a full investigation. The same applies to both the driver and the guard who transported you to Chowchilla."

Cailey asked, "What about my client's disciplinary infractions precipitated by Billman?"

"They'll be reviewed during the investigation. The most I've wrung out of the sheriff and my boss is an agreement to restore Miss Li's good time provided there are no more infractions.

Miss Li, per your counsel's request, you will be taken back to Slatersville the day before your next court appearance and will remain there until sentencing. The corrections staff are unanimous in holding you as a level four. They don't want to be near you without restraints."

Vera said, "I expected it. Now what about my sentence and Arthur's request?" Art gave her a thumbs-up.

Ms. Guerro said, "My office has no objection to the marriage. You'll have to talk to Judge Silverman about details. As for the twenty-four-hour stay, again, the judge makes the call. Now for the bad news. You should have jumped at my offer. My original instructions were that you were to either agree to acknowledge your role in precipitating a riot, or serve five years."

"I precipitated a riot?" shouted Vera. "They attacked me!"

"You were asked to stop those exercises, and you refused to do it. My boss felt I had given away the store. He's adamant that the sentence should be five years with no suspension."

Art bounced to his feet. In spite of hearing it once before, he still felt like he'd been kicked in the stomach. "Five years! What brought this around?"

"There was a whole bunch of charges relating to Miss Li's actions after the murder that were ignored. We have copies of letters that were sent to the judge from the public defense bar from around the state."

Vera was crying. She reached out for her fiancé with her free hand. "Please Arthur, don't desert me. I have to do the time."

The guard guided Vera's arm to the steel band that he closed around her wrist. "On your feet, Li. It's time to get back in the line."

Art lifted Vera to her feet. "I'll be there for you as your husband. Sung Li won't win. You and I will. Pray for Win to find an answer when he gets back to the Bay Area."

"If anyone can smoke out the truth, it's Win. He's our last hope. Thank you for being here. I love you."

275

CHAPTER 22

Late in the evening, Win Griffith pulled across the opposing lane of the quiet residential street and onto the broad apron of the driveway to the Caulfels house. Just as the front bumper crossed the curb, two bright lights over the garage doors blazed the apron into noontime brightness, extinguishing his night vision. He pushed the button that rolled down the driver's window. Looking ahead, he thought, *Vera's right. There is no way to see the front door from here.*

He backed out into the street and rolled slowly forward. It wasn't until he was even with the corner of the garage that he could see the front door in the shadows. And then the lights went off over the garage. He backed the car slowly at an angle until the lights turned back on. His left wheels were less than a foot in from the curb. The twisted limbs of an oversize bonsai tree partly obstructed the front door. He eased the car into a parking place across the driveway so its front end was even with the north edge of the driveway. The front entry wasn't visible.

The PI turned off the ignition and turned on the dome light. He read Daphne's statement, then muttered, "There is no way she could have stopped on this driveway coming from the south to actuate the lights, and see the front door open. Either she parked right out front, or she was out of the car. Wait, there may be a third alternative. Let's see."

He punched the familiar numbers on his cell phone. "Li residence," came the answer.

"Jenny, Winston Griffith. I just got back into town from Chowchilla and I'm sitting in your driveway. Please turn on your front porch light, then open the front door and call out to me in a conversational voice."

"What's this all about?" answered Jenny. "How is Vera?"

"I'll give you a full report when I get inside. Please do me this favor."

He sat and watched the corner of the garage until he heard, "Mr.

Griffith, Win, do you hear me?"

"Yes, I do. Is the porch light on?"

"Yes," Jenny shouted.

Daphne lied. The tough part will be to nail her before the sentencing, Win thought. He asked, "Are you expecting anyone to use the garage tonight?"

"No."

Win locked the car and went inside. Jenny greeted him with a carafe of coffee and a plate of sweet rolls. "Thanks to the kindness of friends at San Elmo, here is a cup of the finest coffee in the world. Please tell me about my daughter."

He sniffed the cup as if savoring wine, then took a bite from the roll that added a cinnamon flavor to the ambience. Afterward, Win answered her questions about the plea bargain and Vera's sentence.

Jenny responded, "What a disappointment to have a one-year offer changed to five. That must have frustrated Mr. Cailey. Yes, five years is a chunk of one's life, but it's much less than fifteen or twenty. Now tell me what this mysterious method of coming to the door is about."

"I don't think Vera shot your mother."

"What!" Jenny's eyebrows arched, then she smiled broadly before both eyes teared up. "Praise the Lord. This is more than an answered prayer. How could the offer go from one year to five in light of this new evidence?"

Win took the time to review the give and take of the day's revelations and negotiations, along with the impact that the publicity about the fight in the women's dayroom had on the county's elected officials. He reviewed the points Vera made about never remembering pulling the trigger, as well as the lack of forensic evidence. Win concluded, "I'm going to devote my full attention to finding out if Daphne has a rational explanation for the inconsistencies in her statement."

"What's going to happen to Vera now?"

"If she listens to J.P., she will plead guilty--unless I can get enough evidence to pin this on someone else."

"If you don't think she did it, how could this be?"

"She confessed. Being so impaired that you can't remember is a two-edged sword. It could have been worse. Vera had a seven-year apprenticeship with the master plea bargainer. There were times when I felt as if Gloria's spirit filled your daughter, even to that sweet voice. I don't think I've ever seen Gloria play a hole card as masterfully as Vera did with the mistreatment in the jail."

"Mistreatment, what mistreatment?"

Win told her about Dennis Billman, Vera's separated shoulder, and the actions against Billman and other jailers. He concluded, "I left with the feeling that the prosecution's case has been thoroughly shaken. J.P. could still pull it off."

The PI answered Jenny's questions about Art. He concluded by saying, "Plan to be there for the sentencing because Art and Vera will be getting married."

Jenny wiped away her tears. "The news that my daughter could be innocent is an answered prayer! Mr. Griffith, you and J.P. Cailey have worked a miracle."

"The miracle will be when the judge buys off on the evidence that lets Vera off the hook. The reason I drove straight through was to get started right away. With your forbearance, there is one more thing I'd like to check out. Jenny, I need to know how well the basement is insulated for sound. I've never been upstairs when the gun range was in use."

"Well, you don't have to worry about that, I won't even keep a gun in my house! If Mother had listened to me, this never would have happened."

"Vera told me how you feel about guns. The reason I ask is that Vera said that when she went downstairs, your mother was alive. She ran the compactor and put garbage in the compost pile. Forensic evidence confirmed that, because they found residual amounts of the garbage where she said she spilled it. Since you don't have a gun, I'm going to fire one shot into the range. I'll leave my recorder on up here. Also I want you to listen for it and remember how loud it was."

"Isn't this the sort of thing the police are supposed to do?"

"As far as they're concerned, this case is closed and the killer is just about to be sentenced. I need clear and convincing evidence that a mistake has been made. Given the switch on the offers, J.P. can buy a little time to do more bargaining. If negotiations fail, this could drag on for years until the case is tried.

Five days later, Win motioned Trevor Howe into booth of a San Francisco Market Street bar. Here was a man who could fill one-and-a-half airline coach seats. His hands were big and calloused, with nails cut almost to the quick. He folded his fingers around Win's like the coils of a hungry boa constrictor as they shook hands. After the greeting, he leaned forward. "What is it you wanted to talk to me for, anyway?"

Win pushed a calling card across the table. "I'm a private detective hired by the family of Gloria Caulfels. She was found murdered in her home on the last Saturday of June."

"What the hell does this have to do with me? Besides, I heard that one of her kids fragged her." Trevor flipped the business card onto the table.

"Yes, her granddaughter is pleading guilty. Since the young woman was mentally incapacitated, they asked me to check out a few details about that day. I understand you were in Covington at Linguini's for dinner with Daphne Kazor on that last Saturday night of June."

"Yeah, that's right."

"Where did you go after dinner?"

"Rode the BART from Walnut Creek to the city. It was a long, hot day and I was tired."

"Was this just a dinner date?"

Trevor gave him a sideways glance. "No, it was a day in the country. A friend has a farm outside Bethany next to the slough. I took her there to do a little target practice."

"Daphne didn't strike me as somebody who would plink tin cans with a twenty-two."

"Hardly, she has a Glock, nine-millimeter. I got it for her last year, and I've been teaching her how to use it."

"A Glock, those are mighty fine weapons. What model?"

"Model 19."

"Now that's interesting. Why did she choose that one?"

"She told me she researched on the internet, and she wanted a quality piece."

"Why did she ask you?"

"She didn't want to be seen coming out of some gun store."

"Is that the reason she gave you?"

"Look, she's been active in Democratic politics and didn't want any publicity. You know, her being a teacher and not being able to afford to move out of a deteriorating neighborhood. People don't understand. It's a dangerous world out there."

"You're right. An armed citizen doesn't have to wait for the cops to save her bacon. You and Daphne must be good friends. Where did you meet her?"

"We've worked together on the North Bay Labor Council since the ninety-two election."

"So you've had a little something going?"

Trevor smiled for the first time, showing a bridge with pale white teeth between his yellowed natural ones. "No, I do little things to keep her happy and in contact. When it comes to election years, that woman can turn out enough teachers at the drop of a hat to man a whole phone bank. She'll walk a picket line. In a lot of ways, I feel sorry for her. She's had a tough life, thanks to that Caulfels bunch."

"Good for you. What sort of little things do you do for her?"

"I've taken her up to Santa Rosa a few times for dinner, and I bought her some ammunition last spring."

"Did she ever show you where the Caulfels family lived?"

"Yeah, a couple of times. She pulled up in their driveway and told me the whole story, from seeing the woman right after she murdered her dad, to the way they were hounded out of town. Talk about paranoid people. The Caulfels house has security cameras and spotlights."

"So you pulled into the driveway?"

"No, across it. You don't think Daphne was involved, do you?"

"I don't know. By the way, do you know what kind of security system they have?"

"One that turns on bright lights outside and has a camera. Beyond that, I don't know. Why the questions?"

"They asked me to check out where she was and who she was with. Why didn't you go up there with her that night?"

"Because I'd heard it all before. Look, I was tired."

"By the way, how many times have you been shooting with her since last June?"

"Lemme think. Last August, I thought we were going to … but instead we spent the afternoon going over political stuff. We met with some activists, and I took them to dinner in Covington. To tell the truth, she seems to be losing interest in shooting. It's too bad; you don't run into many liberal women these days that like to shoot."

"Since Gloria died, has she said anything about the Caulfels family?"

The muscular union man eyed the detective and shrugged his shoulders. "Nothing that would indicate she had anything to do with it. Although she did say the world is a better place without old Gloria … and how fitting it was that the old bitch was wasted with her own gun. I saw in the *Chronicle* that the granddaughter who did it was involved in a riot with some crackheads up in Slatersville. She must be bad news."

"Where did you hear that it was her own gun?"

"Daphne told me. It was in the papers, wasn't it?"

The PI pushed his card back in front of Trevor. "I suggest you keep this. By the way, did you know Daphne Kazor has had a series of restraining orders filed against her?"

"So?"

"Didn't you know she's not supposed to have access to firearms?

"Oh, crap."

Win left the meeting satisfied that Trevor wasn't involved, but also satisfied that the political activist had implicated Daphne.

◦►═◉ ◉═◄◦

Vera Li shuffled down the steps of Slatersville County Jail to the waiting van, with the newly hired female guard at her heels. She wished she could shade her eyes with one of the hands locked to the chain around her waist; or at least wear sunglasses in the sunshine so bright it hurt her eyes. Just short of the van, the guard halted her prisoner and moved past her to put the step down so her hobbled charge could climb aboard on her own. The guard couldn't get the door open. She stood facing the door until the driver came back. Then there was more delay while the driver corrected the new guard for leaving her prisoner standing behind her unattended.

Vera stood curling her toes inside the prison-issue sandals. She imagined she was barefoot and could feel between her toes the droplets of early morning dew on freshly mown grass. A butterfly with beautifully colored wings fluttered around her. Some say butterflies are attracted to bright colors like the orange jumpsuit Vera wore. Or maybe it was the scented soap she had bought at the jail. She held her arm at a right angle, and the beautiful insect landed on it.

Look at the colors, iridescent blue and yellow. That's an Emperor Butterfly. Grandmother used to call me that. Dear Lord, have I been in the hole that long? I've lost a whole season of my life rotting in that cell. That's the way it's going to be. Life will stand still for the next four or five years.

The butterfly lifted off when the guard roughly spun her prisoner around until she faced the step. Vera turned her head in a vain attempt to watch it flutter away. *Thank you, Grandmother, for sending me the Emperor.*

The chastened guard snapped, "Don't play games with me or you'll never get out of the hole."

Vera had spent the last three months in solitary with but one hour and thirty minutes a day allowed outside her cell, except for physical therapy during the first six weeks. The only other interruptions to the enforced solitude were letters, visits, and phone calls from her attorney and Detective Dancer. She timed them to coincide with Vera's "air time." The Harris County detective's almost daily calls evolved into girl talk and a belief in Vera's innocence.

Of all the freedoms taken from her, she resented most that every step outside the cell was a shuffle forced on her by the hobble. It wasn't lost on her that she could end her level four status by agreeing to the terms of the plea agreement. Counselor Cailey, in turn, gave her pep talks about his Fabian tactics, the moves deemed necessary to delay acceptance of the plea agreement, to stall for time to gather enough evidence to convince the judge that Daphne was the murderer.

Tyler Guerro used every occasion to indoctrinate Vera about the comparison between isolation as a level four versus level two. All Vera had to do was agree, said the prosecutor, and she would be moved into an open dormitory.

Just after Cailey relayed encouraging news from Win, she was again whipsawed when Ms. Guerro said, "All has been for naught. Take the plea agreement with its five-year sentence now or face trial on each and every violation, including second-degree murder."

Cailey advised, "Take the offer. You'll have an opportunity to marry Art and testify as his wife at Sung's trial. It's nigh on impossible to take back a confession. It'll take more time to get ready for trial with near-certainty of a far longer sentence."

Now that she couldn't do anything to change it, Vera remembered to ask the last question Grandmother had on her checklist. "Will this restore my good time?"

Ms. Guerro nodded and smiled. "Of course, you don't miss a detail."

Vera signed the plea agreement. She was returned to Slatersville that afternoon.

All the way back, Vera was a whirlpool of mixed emotions. Disappointment because there wasn't evidence to prove Daphne was the murderess. Satisfaction that she would see Art. Hope that he would keep his word to marry her. Knowledge that she would spend a minimum time being indoctrinated in "Group U," the reception center for inmates under processing, before assignment to living in an open dormitory with visiting privileges. She could then meet with Caulfels family members who had flooded her with letters.

Beyond the single meeting with Art early in her time at Chowchilla, today would be the first time they were allowed to see one another. She knew she had to show a brave face to him. She didn't want him to feel guilty about turning her in.

Vera was guided down an elegant marble-sided hall, a product of another time when gold was the backbone of the local economy. She turned the corner to see Judge Silverman, a nice looking white-haired man who was shorter than she was. He was talking with a man she had never seen before. This judge would be the one who would pronounce the words that would take away at least another three-and-a-half years of her life. Her thoughts were interrupted by the judge's instructions. "Guard, put the prisoner in my office with her fiancé. I'll be there in a minute. Stand by to escort her back to the jail." Judge Silverman returned to his conversation.

Vera saw Art as soon as she turned to enter the door. He rose from his chair and was running toward her with his arms wide open. She almost tripped as she forced herself to take the short steps the hobble demanded. In an instant she stood with her body pressed as close as she could, with her head resting on her fiancé's shoulder. Art's arms were wrapped around her while her hands were cuffed to her sides by a chain locked around her waist. She inhaled deeply, savoring his male aroma.

Vera's voice had a breathless quality. "Darling, just feeling your arms around me again gives me strength. I've missed you terribly."

"We're going to be okay. I love you."

The guard grumbled, "Come on, break it up."

The judge noisily cleared his throat and bumped the door. Vera wanted to be held, but Art let her go just as the guard grabbed Vera's waist chain and pulled her backward. She held onto his belt long enough to pull him a step closer.

The guard said, "Li, this is a violation."

The judge said, "Oh, cool it. He was the one with his arms wrapped around her. She's helpless in those chains. Guard, stand by outside the door. I'll call you when I'm ready for the prisoner to return to the jail."

That brief exchange reminded her of the obvious dislike she had felt from just about every jailer. Not only had Billman and the two deputies who took her to Chowchilla been fired, they all were facing criminal charges. They were particularly teed off about Art's articles about mistreatment of women in California jails and prisons.

The judge pointed to two chairs placed side by side in front of his desk as he strode across the room. "Please be seated."

After offering Art coffee from a decanter, the judge poured himself a cup. "I'd offer you a cup, Miss Li, except I don't know how you'd drink it, given your restraints."

Art held his cup out in her direction. "Honey, would you like some of mine?"

Sitting tall and forward in her chair, she twisted her left arm out to the side so he could see her manacled wrist. "It's all right. These come with the territory."

Art reached out and held her hand. "Your Honor, I'm having a difficult time understanding why my fiancé must be held in isolation and chained up like this whenever she is outside her cell after this Billman fellow has been fired for misconduct."

She squeezed his hand and shook her head. "Art, please don't talk about the case. My lawyer has to be here for that. You and I are here to talk about our marriage."

Judge Silverman smiled and nodded approval. "Thank you, Miss Li, for keeping us on track. As I promised at the pre-sentencing hearing, I need to meet with both of you without counsel. The most pleasant side of a judge's job is to perform marriages. It's not often I have mixed criminal sentencing with matrimony. After all the lobbying by Harris County, Texas, I wonder if this marriage was your wish or theirs. I take the duty to bring couples together in marriage seriously, especially under this kind of circumstance."

Vera thought, *I don't know where I'd be without Danielle. She's been a candle in the darkness, always there for me to talk to. It would have been nice to talk to Art every day too.*

Judge Silverman looked directly at Art. "Mr. Williams, eight days from today I will accept the terms of the agreement reached with the state and Miss Li. I will require her to spend five years in prison. She will be marked for life as a murderous felon for the tragic and senseless execution of her grandmother. Now that I've said that, Mr. Williams, why do you want to marry this woman?"

Art looked directly into Vera's dark eyes. "I love her."

"Be more specific."

Art rambled as he told about a courtship that wasn't storybook perfect. He began with her overreaction to his editor's embellishment of Art's article with a nude photo of Gloria as a 1955 Playmate of the Month. He alluded to other conflicts as he summarized, "We had our fallings out, but we weathered what I thought then were our rough times. I know now that they were only basic training for the challenges we must endure."

He blamed himself for her predicament. "You speak of her as a murderess. I trust her to become a good wife. The Vera I know is not a violent woman. What I focus on is the woman I chose before all this began. Vera had an innocence and a trust. She doesn't smoke, drink, or use drugs. She isn't promiscuous. Ours wasn't a love affair, it was a courtship. I asked her to marry me for all the right reasons--having made a best friend, appreciating all she is, and accepting her warts, including now her criminal record."

"So you think you can pick up where you left off?" asked Judge Silverman.

"No, Judge. The best words I've found to describe love were from Vera's grandfather. He wrote 'Love isn't what you think. Love is what you do. Love is showing faith and making a commitment when it's not the easy thing to do.' For me, love must include understanding and coping with the demons unleashed by her father."

"Very well thought out. And you, Miss Li?"

Vera looked at Art and tried to smile. Racing through her head were all the warnings from Cailey and Win not to say anything about the case, her sentence, the charges against her, or her treatment in the jail and the prison. She pushed to the back of her mind those overpowering thoughts that she had shared with Danielle. More than anything, she wanted this man. She kept thinking about seeing the butterfly fly away. *Please don't let that be Art. I love him.*

Tears erupted from both of Vera's eyes. "This man sitting beside me is the only true friend I have in the whole world. Go back to the night Art and I met. We stayed up half the night talking to each other and never kissed. I knew then that I had found someone special, but I was afraid. I pushed him away. Grandmother Gloria kept me from going back into my shell. More than once she saved my happiness. My dear Arthur again and again has found room in his heart to forgive me. Your Honor, I know how precious the life of the one you love is. I miss Grandmother terribly. I will grieve forever the terrible thing I did. Please give me a second opportunity to commit myself to my Arthur. I will love him to the day I die."

"What assurance can you give your young man that when you are ultimately granted your freedom, you'll bring strength and stability to your relationship?"

She stared at the judge for a time, then looked toward Art while even more tears flowed. Vera could only think of the butterfly flying away while she was being dragged along in bondage. She twisted in her seat, making the chains clatter. Vera felt that she understood why the Lord had sent that butterfly. Her voice was clear. "I'm like the Emperor butterfly. Yes, I am the Emperor butterfly. As painful and humiliating as prison must be, I have to struggle and fight on my own to emerge from this cocoon of my own making. With that struggle, I will build my strength to meet life's future tests like an Emperor prepares for its migration. The most important thing I can do for my children is to make sure they will never be abandoned. I need strength to be a good example to them."

"Interesting. Emperor butterfly? Where did you learn that?"

"In a biology course at Mills College. The chrysalis we cut out of the cocoon died, but the ones that fought their way free, lived."

While Art wiped the tears from her cheeks, the judge rattled papers and made notes on a lined pad. These were the loudest sounds in his chambers

Judge Silverman said, "I was surprised to hear you say that this man is the only friend you have in the world. I can't think of a case I've heard where the family of the victim so openly and voluntarily came forward in support of the defendant. I sensed considerable feelings of guilt on their part that they didn't recognize or act on Mrs. Caulfels' fall into depression. Without their statements on her state of mind, you would be facing a far different outcome."

After Judge Silverman had lectured on many aspects of marriage that Vera regarded as academic for the time being, he closed his notebook and leaned forward in his high-backed office chair. "I believe I can count on one hand the couples I have taken through my prenuptial counseling who gave more thoughtful answers. I'm saddened by the other duty I must perform prior to your nuptials."

Art said, "Please allow us to complete what you will begin with our vows."

"After Miss Li is sentenced, I will recess the court for fifteen minutes. During that recess, I will perform the service. Mr. Williams' request for a twenty-four-hour stay will be part of the agreement." The judge turned to face Vera. "You will be released into your husband's custody for twenty-four hours, at the end of which time you must report to the Central California Women's Facility at Chowchilla to complete your sentence. I understand that Harris County will pick you up shortly after your arrival for transport to Texas."

◦─▸▦◦ ◦▨◂─◦

Like every other time he had called Vera since she was returned to

Slatersville, Win Griffith dialed the jail and waited by the phone while they chained her up and brought her out. He was anxious to find out if the pre-marriage counseling with the judge had happened on schedule. It had.

Win felt sick inside while she recounted that her Arthur had, for the briefest moment, held her in his arms and the judge granted an un-heard-of twenty-four-hour stay of her sentence so they could have a "honeymoon." All he could think of was that his own honeymoon had been eight days, and eight days hadn't been enough.

There was now a mountain of evidence pointing to Daphne Kazor. *If only people would open their eyes right now*, thought Win. *With the delays in the appeals process, tomorrow will be too late. Vera will have served her time before it's decided.*

Win knew he shouldn't allow emotional attachments to grow, but she was like a daughter to him. Unlike other cases, he was choking up while he gave her the news that there was ample evidence to point to Daphne Kazor, but no one would act until the forensic evidence was in.

As for taking the fall for Daphne, Vera said, "Win, in my heart I can't believe I would ever want to harm Grandmother. But the only way I can face what I must endure is to step up and take responsibility."

He wished his own children had such strength of character. Vera said something he didn't understand, about her being an Emperor butterfly, before she hung up.

Win didn't want to admit that it was impossible to free the accused after she had confessed. He was convinced that from an evidentiary standpoint, everything Vera said had panned out. His problem was to overcome what he called bureaucratic inertia. On the plus side, Detective Jim Hackelby had been won over after a single two-hour interrogation of Daphne.

The place where the wheels had come off was dealing with the Prosecutor's Office in the wake of Dale Bleasman's arrest on federal charges. Although the Board of Supervisors had appointed an interim prosecutor, Win felt the office had the mobility and conscience of an amoeba. Never mind that yet another injustice was about to happen. They didn't want to admit the tapes as evidence until some coded symbol was verified by the National Crime Laboratory, whose backlog extended out almost a year. The state crime lab had performed all the tests during Gloria's original murder investigation. The evidence included two unidentified hairs that could be Daphne's, but the re-test was at the end of their queue.

What irked him most was Vera's attorney's attitude that a plea bargain was the best Vera should hope for. His choice for change of venue to Slatersville had proved to be a disaster. Besides the obvious harm from sexual abuse, she had been held in isolation even after her return from Chowchilla. Cailey felt the prosecutor was using punitive isolation as a stick and the prospect of minimum security after acceptance of her plea as a carrot, but he did nothing to stop it. For whatever reason, he sought approval for Vera to begin new prisoner classification at Chowchilla while she was awaiting trial. It was denied.

Win had had one small victory the week before. His note to the school board got results. Daphne had been placed on administrative leave pending resolution of firearms charges relating to her possession while subject to a restraining order. Jim Hackelby had lamented that this one solid charge against Daphne was hung up in the Napa County Prosecutor's backlog. Napa County was where she lived.

Then there was the phone call he waited to return until after dinner the next day. The caller ID spelled out GODONISKI. Win recognized Alya's Russian accent. "My friend Tatty Tsamonicoff and I saw TV news story about the granddaughter going to prison for senseless murder of Gloria Caulfels. Tatty has proof granddaughter didn't do it."

"Who? What?" exclaimed Win.

"Tatty is daughter of Alexander Tsamonicoff. She said her father had bug in that room. No one found it because it's hidden in television recorder."

Win realized that whatever the Russian Mafia collected was tainted. If the prosecution didn't get it thrown out for being collected illegally, they would challenge its authenticity. Yet it was too good to pass by.

⟶⊷◉⊶⟵

Win sat in his office in the late afternoon with Detective Jim Hackelby, who was slouched in a chair with his feet on the front side of Win's desk. Deputy Prosecuting Attorney Baylor Gates stormed into the office. The door bounced off boxes of paper stacked behind it.

Gates said, "Look, Mr. Griffith, I don't appreciate having to tell my wife I'll be late for dinner to get a tour of your storage unit of an office."

Win looked about his office and admitted to himself that it was worse than usual. Yes, he had let Vera's predicament monopolize his time. He opened a white envelope and let a tape cassette slide onto the small cleared space around his telephone.

Detective Hackelby stood and greeted Gates. "Thank you for coming, Counselor. Time is working against Miss Li. I need your support to make Ms. Kazor an offer. I have information that changes the whole case."

"You damn well better have."

"The Caulfels murder room was bugged," said Win, holding up a tape cassette. "Listen, you can hear it go down."

"But is it admissible?"

"We'll discuss tactics with you afterwards. Listen, the first voice is Gloria Caulfels."

VOICE 1: "Who are you calling?"

VOICE 2: "Art."

VOICE 1: "I'm terribly sorry. You'll only get his answering machine. He's out. Andy told me that he left him at a bar down by the *Tribune*. He was talking with a girl he met there."

There was a pause, with background sounds continuing. The recorder clicked off. Win said, "My best guess is that this is a voice-activated system that stored conversations for burst transmission."

VOICE 1: "After you fix yourself something to eat, please clean up the mess I made."

While the tape continued to roll, Win said, "The second voice is Vera Li. Since you have dinner waiting, let me spare you twenty-three minutes of female chatter amid background noise." He skipped the tape forward.

VOICE 2: "Grandmother, I'm taking the trash out."

VOICE 1: "Okay, dear."

After a little over a minute:

VOICE 3: "Don't even think about going for your Glock. Get up and stand over there. One false move and you'll die slow and painful. "

VOICE 1: "Daffy Daphne, what the hell are you going to do, shoot me?"

VOICE 3: "Damn right! I heard your confession. You murdered my father. Face the wall. Get down on your knees. Don't you ever call me Daffy again."

VOICE 1: "Murdered? No, I removed a piece of human shit from the world."

VOICE 3: "How dare you? You're rotten! How you got away with murder, I don't understand."

VOICE 1: "I'm on my knees. Do it now! Don't dawdle and let my niece see you. Put the muzzle against the back of my head and fire just once. People hearing one gunshot will listen for more. Most will think it's a backfire."

VOICE 3: "What's with you anyway?"

VOICE 1: "Shoot me and feel good about it. Take Vera's innocent life and it'll eat your conscience. Don't forget the three tapes from the surveillance system there. Record over them so nobody knows. Stop shaking, you crazy bitch, Daffy, Daffy, Daf..."

One pistol shot.

VOICE 3: "I told you to stop callin' me names. Holy shit! I gotta git."

Footsteps followed by silence.

"Oh, my God, where did you get this?" Gates asked.

"There's more, listen." Hackelby put an index finger to his lips.

VOICE 2: "Grandmother! Grandmother! Oh, my God!"

After a pause:

VOICE 2: "Dear God, there's no one else here but me. I must have. Why? How? I don't remember shooting her!"

VOICE 2, farther away from the microphone: "I aimed but I talked to her afterward. She was okay. That red dot, I must have done it."

VOICE 2, almost shouting, after a click: "Dear Lord, help me. I stood up Art today and now I've murdered my own grandmother! Why! Why?"

Win watched Baylor Gates throughout. Gates wet his lips, and his eyes darted back and forth. Win had seen that look on Gloria many times when she had an airtight answer to a question that would totally destroy a witness's credibility or upend the prosecution. It was her job to get that witness to tell the truth in spite of the inadmissibility of that piece of evidence. Win felt he didn't have enough time for Gates to figure this one out on his own.

Gates asked, "Where on earth did you get this tape?"

"Let's say it was from a Russian friend, who saw the news clip that Vera is being sentenced next Tuesday. You must remember the bugs they planted at Gloria's. They cost Dale Bleasman his job."

"There's no way to prove its authenticity between now and next Tuesday."

Win said, "Yes, there is. Let Daphne do it."

"Why would she do that?"

Win detected a loss of patience in the tone of Gates's voice. He would have to lead this prosecutor by the hand. "You are going to offer her a deal she can't refuse. Say voluntary manslaughter and a low range for time served if she confesses before Vera is sentenced. Or promise hellfire and purgatory if she waits until the lab results tie her to the murder."

"I can't get an offer approved before Wednesday at the earliest. Our interim insists on a collective decision process. Presentations are made to the vetting committee with a turnaround of two days to a month."

Win rolled his eyes and shook his head. "Mr. Gates, you have expressed an ambition to run for prosecutor. Give the people a reason to vote for you. Go to your boss. Make your case to avoid injustice. If he insists on his procedure, then ask for the sentencing to be delayed. Vera has suffered enough for three lifetimes."

"What if he says no?"

"Roll the dice. Threaten to go public."

CHAPTER 23

Art Williams sat across the desk from Red Magen, watching his boss with one eye and reading the letter from management with the other. He felt his pulse pound in his temples. By the time he read it to himself for the fifth time, he could almost quote the operative sentence, "Should you not be at the Oakland Federal District Court and submit copy on the arraignment of certain public officials, you will be terminated."

"Tuesday's arraignment! You son of a bitch, be honest and simply say, 'You're fired!' I have a fifteen-minute window following her sentencing Tuesday to marry Vera, and the next twenty-four hours for a honeymoon. There's no way I'll stand her up."

Art stared at Red, who averted his eyes and kept sticking his tongue just to his lips, then slightly biting the tip. The editor's voice was a blend of false harmonics. "I can't meet my deadlines indefinitely with interns and shifting people around."

"The last time I asked to come back full time, you said the security consultant advised against it."

"That was then."

"Red, this is one hell of a wedding present. I won't comply. I haven't seen my love since the meeting at Chowchilla. The first opportunity will be Sunday for a half-hour visit. I must deliver her to Chowchilla not later than one p.m. Wednesday. I follow her down to testify during the penalty phase. I have agreed to appointments with both Harris County and the federal prosecutors in Houston."

"They ought to be trying him here. That's where Sung committed the crime."

"He was found with the drug in his possession in Texas. There's another thing. I can visit her in jail there, but the rules for new inmates don't allow it here."

"Boy, if ever I have seen a place where love is so blind. Why would any rational woman marry a man after that railroad job you pulled on her? As for you, you're rolling the dice after all the stuff she's been through."

"Red, we both made mistakes. With love, there is forgiveness. I'm thankful she gave me the opportunity to learn from mine."

"You came back all pumped up about Daphne. What happened?

"Win says she's guilty, but Vera confessed. He hasn't produced enough evidence to exonerate her. Wednesday will begin at least four, if not five, years of trials and tribulations for us."

The editor shrugged his shoulders and looked Art in the eye as he answered, "Between you, me, and the gatepost, I hate to lose you. I don't often get a reporter who has the energy and abilities you have, but you're not writing in Oakland if you're down in Houston. The man upstairs is damned unhappy. Do you know where we picked up the story about Daphne Kazor's connection to the Caulfels murder? Off the wire, from the *Houston Chronicle*! The publisher called them up and they let it slip that you have some agent negotiating with them for a job."

"I didn't feed them the story. They've been after me since my interview last summer. My only contact was through my agent because I don't want to be shorted on screenplays and books. They just sweetened it with very generous terms."

Red shook his head. "Come on, you were there at Chowchilla. It's in the article!"

'Yes, I knew that Vera spotted Daphne's lies. Beyond that, Win has kept me in the dark. I suspect the source was Detective Dancer. She calls Vera almost every day."

Art thought, *Red has been a fantastic man to work for. Let's not burn any bridges. Maybe they'll reconsider after Vera's sentenced.* The young reporter stood and extended his right hand. "If this decision came down from above, I understand. You've been a good mentor and I've learned a lot here." They shook hands and Art left.

⇥⊙ ⊙⊱

Vera's head was spinning ever since Sunday when she was allowed a whole hour of visitation, a half-hour with Jenny and another half with

Art. Those precious minutes with Art had been the high point of her life since that fateful evening she drove off with her adopted father. Art would fly to Houston on the same flight with her.

She detected something bothering Art during the last minutes before the guard took her back to her lonely cell. Then Monday, they took her to visit Art without what they referred to as "full jewelry," manacles on her wrists and ankles. The words he used to explain that he was no longer with the *Oakland Tribune* resonated in her ears. "Given the choice between a paycheck or one night with you, I chose you."

Vera felt loved and reassured that he was committed to marrying her. She concentrated on the single night when she would be valued as his wife and not on what she expected to lie ahead for the next four or five years.

Tuesday morning, the guard awoke Vera when she entered her cell holding a folded newspaper in her hand. "Li, you are one lucky perp. I overheard the PA Guerro talking to the undersheriff. Your sentencing will be postponed. She's asking for your plea agreement to be vacated."

Vera felt faint until she looked at the picture of an older woman and the article under the headline, SHE CONFESSED, DIDN'T SHE? She recognized the face she had seen on the monitor at her grandmother's house so many times. Vera read aloud, "Was it Vera Li or Daphne? Daphne Kazor of Napa confessed to the murder of Gloria Caulfels, eminent public defender, on the last Saturday in June, after overhearing Caulfels confess to the murder of her father in Colorado in 1946. Detective Hackelby said that the evidence from the Caulfels residence found in Kazor's home confirms Ms. Kazor's statement. Coincidently, Vera Li, Caulfels' granddaughter, awaits sentencing for the same murder. She pled guilty under an Alford plea, accepting responsibility because she believed she was alone with the victim and lacked proof to overcome the prosecution's case."

Thoughts of a reprise of her last wedding day flooded Vera's mind. After all, she was going to be taken back to Texas late Wednesday night to testify against Papa Sung. Would the judge still marry them before she was taken away?

The mental fog lifted with a phone call from Art. Everything was falling into place. Art's acceptance of the position in Houston wouldn't separate them. Then there was St. Bede's. She could be with the people who had stood by her. She could be married before God, in church, in her wedding gown. They could go there and have a fresh start!

J.P. Cailey called. His voice sounded upbeat and confident as he gave her a briefing on Daphne's acceptance of a four-year term for voluntary manslaughter, plus a fifth added for firearms enhancement. He concluded by warning Vera, "You're not out of the woods yet. Guerro could throw the book at you for what you did to screw up the investigation. Gates told me he would be happy charging you for enough to sentence you to time served."

"I was totally mixed up from that drug."

"Tyler Guerro said she will be reviewing everything you did after the murder. Prosecutors don't like to agree to set free the people they've convicted. She's going to make a recommendation that could be close to what she took off the table. My advice is to accept anything offered that gets you out without serving more time. Remember, whether the judge hands you a get-out-of-jail-free card will be up to him."

She feared getting her hopes up for the effort needed to overcome the disappointment.

Vera returned from her shower to find Harris County Detective Danielle Dancer standing outside her cell door. The detective gave her a welcoming hug. She told Vera she was there to escort her to Harris County. They'd leave immediately after her sentencing hearing on Thursday.

"No, no, why can't I have just one night with my Arthur before I have to report?"

Danielle said, "Vera, darling, you won't have one night with your man--you'll have a lifetime of them. Art will be in the next seat on our red-eye flight to Houston Thursday night. We'll help you heal, whether you choose to settle in California or in Texas."

All of the bargaining between the prosecutor and J.P. Cailey had been done in fifteen minutes late Wednesday morning.

Much to Vera's surprise, she was brought out for visits with her family and Art. Her mother, surrounded by her aunts and uncles, lovingly greeted Vera during these short visits. She no longer felt like an abandoned orphan.

The last visitor was Uncle Andy Caulfels, who came alone. Of all the family members, Vera hardly knew him. He was the uncle who seemed bigger than life, the fighter pilot, veteran of the Gulf War. His infrequent visits with her grandmother and grandfather had been short during his leave periods.

After the greetings, Andy said, "You look good in that white suit Aunt Carole gave you."

"Thanks, I'm all ready to go except for the bracelets." Vera thought about the beautiful wedding dress Grandmother had bought for her. She would wear it at the church wedding. Danielle had suggested St. Bede's. Right now, what was important was that she wanted to be called to testify as Mrs. Arthur Williams.

Andy asked, "Have you gotten everything packed up and ready to go, including my father's Bible?"

"Yes, it was a great comfort to me, especially looking for Grandmother's coded messages to Grandfather when he was in prison at Canon City. I'll always miss them both." Her voice broke and Vera was fighting back tears.

"Do you remember my father's special prayer?"

She sat tall and smiled. "How could I ever forget that? He said it so many times. 'Thank you, Lord, for giving us this day in freedom with no bars on the windows and no locks to keep us in. Guide us that we may find the way to all the good works that you have prepared for us to walk in.'"

"I've talked with my brother and sisters. After the judge ties the knot, with your approval, we'd like to gather the family around in a circle with you and Art and send you off with this prayer. It'll have to hold you until you have the real ceremony at St. Bede's."

"I would like that. I've gotten all sorts of letters from people there, but I'd rather do it where we live."

"Hasn't he told you? The *Tribune* let him go and Art took the offer at the *Chronicle*."

She thought, *Houston! Why didn't he tell me?*

As if Andy had read her mind, he said, "Art was devastated when he found out his replacement came to work Monday. I'm sorry I stole the opportunity for him to give you the news. There's going to be plenty of time to talk after all this is over. We feel you suffered a great injustice from the day my sister's husband laid hands on you. We want to explore things we can do to make it right for you."

Moments later a deputy entered the room, swinging a pair of handcuffs from his index finger. "It's time to go, Miss Li." After closing the manacles around her wrists, he said, "The sheriff said to use these handcuffs so you won't muss that nice wedding dress."

Alone in the caged back of the sheriff's SUV, she felt detached. She thought about what Uncle Andy had said, then about the many prayers she had said. The pieces of her life were coming together. She felt that the invisible hand that swept away Art's job had recognized that she dreaded the thought of ever going back into Grandmother's house again. It had touched her aunts and uncles so that they agreed to pay for Win's efforts to set her free. Most important, Daphne Kazor had been moved to confess in time to save her from prison. *Yes, if there is one thing I gained from all this, I've learned the power of prayer.*

Then the deputy opened the SUV door. Vera was surprised by the media attention. All the ruckus and distraction caused by scrambling TV broadcasters and swarming freelance paparazzi added to the feeling of excitement welling up inside her.

At last she stood between her attorney and the prosecutor in a well-populated courtroom. Time and again she raised her manacled wrists to wipe tears from her eyes. Three or four times, she turned to reassure herself that Art was in the first row behind her.

Judge Silverman gaveled his court to order. "Mrs. Guerro, I understand that you have some startling information from Alameda County."

"Yes, Your Honor. Alameda County Prosecuting Attorney Gates informed me that they have a confession from Daphne Kazor, corroborated with sufficient supporting evidence to void Miss Li's Alford plea. After examining it and Miss Li's statement, I cannot in good conscience continue to assent to the plea agreement before you. I have met with Mr. Cailey and we have agreed to substitute the misdemeanor of reckless endangerment. We agree to a sentence equal to the time Miss Li has served while awaiting trial."

Amid loud sniffles, Vera's clear and loud reply to the question was,

"Yes, Your Honor, I plead guilty to the charge of reckless endangerment."

Before she could unfold the paper on which she had written a statement the night before, the prosecutor formally agreed to the terms of the plea agreement before the judge, and he struck the bench with his gavel. He declared Vera Li guilty of reckless endangerment with a sentence equal to time served.

As he adjusted his robe and cleaned his eyeglasses, Judge Silverman asked, "Is Detective Danielle Dancer from Texas in the courtroom?"

Danielle arose from her seat in the back of the visitor's gallery. The big-boned blonde drawled, "Yes, Your Honor."

"I'm Jewish, so I hope you'll forgive me." The judge smiled. "Detective, you are as close to a yenta as I have ever met. Yes, I should have sentenced this woman two days ago. I didn't. As you can see, this short delay averted a miscarriage of justice. I understand you have a properly executed court order to escort the defendant immediately to Texas to give testimony at the trial of her adopted father, Sung Li."

"Yes, Your Honor, I do."

"Miss Li will shortly be discharged from custody in this jurisdiction. She will be ready to accompany you after we finish the marriage ceremony you have been lobbying for."

Judge Silverman's smile was warm as he concluded his sentencing. "Miss Li, you are a remarkable young woman. As I read through the documents on this case, the words you used to describe yourself, 'The Emperor Butterfly,' came to mind repeatedly. You have indeed gnawed your way through your chrysalis. Spread your wings, you are free. Bailiff, unshackle the bride."

The End

Principal characters:

1. Gloria Knight Caulfels - Matriarch of Caulfels Family - Public Defender.
2. Winston "Win" Griffith, - Private Investigator funded by Caulfels family trust.
3. Arthur Willliams, Art (Protagonist) - Newly hired Oakland Tribune Reporter & love interest of Gloria's niece, Vera Li.
4. Vera Li (Protagonist) - Plays down she was adopted by Gloria's daughter Jenny and Father Sung Li. She was born in U.S. to American soldier father and a Korean mother.

Other

5. Joseph "Grandpa Joe" Caulfels, Phd - Patriarch - Successful Inventor & investor - Retired University of California professor - Dies en route hospital.

Chapter 1's 3 muggers:

1. Oleg - dead.
2. Yuri Tsamonicoff - castrated
3. Officer Martin "Marteen" Ramirez, Undercover Narc - wounded.
4. Detective Lieutenant Tiburon "Tibbie" Fuentes - Head of Undercover Unit - murdered
5. Officer Larry MacBrogan - Oakland Police Officer
6. Peter Godoniski - Russian immigrant, auto mechanic, introduced as PD Defendant & Gloria's client.
7. Alya Fuentes - wife of Tiburon Fuentes, key witness in Godonski trial.
8. Symon Dubinski - Godoniski accused of his murder.
9. Red Magan - Metro Editor Oakland Tribune, Art's boss.

Gloria's children

10. Major Andy Caulfels - Oldest child.
11. Carole Caulfels aka stage name, Carolyn Connolly.
12. Ray Caulfels - Surgeon practicing in Flagstaff, AZ.
13. Jenny Li - Youngest, married Sung Li at 17

Other California characters

14. Jesse Sollair - long time friend of Caulfels' family.
15. Gregory "Greg" Rojas - Alameda Board of Supervisors.
16. Alexander Tsamonicoff - Russian mob boss. Uncle of Yuri Tsamonicoff, who was shot by Gloria.
17. Dale Bleasman, Alameda County Prosecutor.
18. Baylor Gates - Deputy Prosecutor
19. Shane Joyce & Mitch Brown - Criminalists
20. Dolph Rogerson - Presiding Judge
21. James Hackelby - Oakland Detective
22. Clyde Lacwurth - Convict/witness
23. Peter Louis Duparre – Perjured Witness
24. Eudora - Caulfels'- Family housekeeper

Colorado characters

25. Daphne Kazor - Daughter of slain Colorado Deputy John Diamond, School teacher, Bay area labor activist.
26. Andrew Foyle - Director of Knight

Family Trust
27. Philip Sydney - Current Sheriff Goodwin County, CO
28. Ray Tudbury - Colorado Congressman, former Goodwin County Prosecutor.
29. Larry Shyflinski - Former Sheriff, Goodwin County
30. Calvin Bohl - Goodwin County rancher, friend of Caulfels' Family.
31. Jenny Vaughan - Gloria's College roommate.

More California characters
32. Leonard Demmartino - Head Covington Community and Development Department.
33. Elizabeth Holtzmann - City Councilwoman, Wheel horse of Bay area environmental group, POZUD, Protectors of Zoological Underdogs.
34. Van Boh Tranh -Owner of demolished building.
35. Yun Pei - Korean TV technician.
36. Amy Pankery - Gloria's bridesmaid.
37. Jason Omertsu - Vera's high school classmate.

Texas characters
38. Lyndon Evans - Harris County Detective Lieutenant
39. Danielle Dancer - Detective Sergeant, Evans' Partner.
40.Rose Bondurant - Prosecutor assigned to Sung Li's case.
41. Frieda Trujillo - Claimed sexual abuse by Father Sung Li.
42. Coruda Trujillo - mother of Frieda.
43. Shelby Extrom - -Fifteen year old vamp put make on Sung and he tumbled.
44. Extroms - Parents of Shelby Extrom

45. Perky Handblin - Older man, currently Shelby's lover.

Returned to California
46. Cassandra Poper - Public Defender.
47. J.P. Cailey - Criminal Defense Attorney from Los Angeles.
48. Dennis Billman - Jail Guard
49. Tyler Guerro - Deputy Prosecutor
50. Lorilla Rae Green - Awaiting trial on drug charges
51.Trevor Howe - Labor organizer - Bay area
52.Tatty Tsamonicoff- Daughter of Alexander Tsamonicoff
53. Judge Silverman - Slatersville County